COTTAGE IN THE MIST

COTTAGE IN THE MIST

DEE DAVIS

Published by Pocito Press
Print Edition, copyright 2016 by Dee Davis Oberwetter

Cover design: Frauke Spanuth, Croco Design

ISBN: 0997183411
ISBN 13: 9780997183412

http://www.deedavis.com

ALSO BY DEE DAVIS:

Random Heroes Collection:
Dark Of The Night
Dancing In The Dark
Midnight Rain
Just Breathe
After Twilight

Liars Game Series:
Lethal Intent (novella)
Eye Of The Storm
Chain Reaction
Still of the Night (novella)

Last Chance Series:
Endgame
Enigma
Exposure
Escape (novella)

A-Tac Series:
Dark Deceptions
Dangerous Desires
Desperate Deeds
Daring (Novella)
Deep Disclosure
Deadly Dance
Double Danger
Dire Distraction

Matchmaker Chronicles
A Match Made on Madison
Set Up In SoHo

Time After Time Series
Everything In Its Time
Cottage in the Mist
The Promise
Wild Highland Rose

Devil May Care Series
Hell Fire (novella)
Hell's Fury (novella)

Every book requires a tribe! Julie Kenner and Sherri Erwin, don't know how I'd face the day without you both in my life. Lexie and Robert Oberwetter, you are the lights of my life and the reason I'm not a total and complete mess. Kim Whalen, you keep me fixed on true north. And special thanks to Kasi Alexander and Melody Brislin for careful reading and an awful lot of work!

CHAPTER 1

🔺

"ONCE THE PROPERTIES are sold and the possessions liquidated, there should be a small amount left. But certainly nothing like you've been accustomed to, I'm afraid." Mr. Banderson's expression held both a note of finality and pity as he looked across the desk. "I know this isn't what you were expecting."

Lily Chastain fought against the urge to throw up. What she'd been expecting was that her father and mother would come home from their latest trip, brimming with tales of adventure. That the two of them would grow old together. That they'd share the joy of her marriage and be there for her children when the time came. That everything would be as perfect as she'd dreamed it would be.

But none of that was going to come true now. She reached for Justin's hand, needing reassurance, but he'd risen from his chair, his face contorted with anger. "What do you mean there's nothing left? Lily's parents were worth a fortune. Everyone knows that."

She twisted the sparkling engagement ring on her finger, her stomach taking a polar plunge. She'd always known that Justin cared about the fact that she'd come from good breeding, but she'd never thought that it had been about money.

"It'll be okay," she whispered, finding it odd to be comforting him. But it didn't matter; as far as he was concerned she might as well have not been in the room.

"What the hell happened?" he asked the lawyer, grinding out the words.

"I'm afraid I don't know. Thomas never really confided in me. I just handled contracts and so forth when he needed me to." Mr. Banderson paused, his attention shifting to Lily. "I'm so sorry, Lily. I swear to you, I had no idea. Your father always invested in property. I'm guessing when the bubble burst, he got hit hard."

Lily nodded, still trying to make sense of everything Mr. Banderson was telling her. One week ago, she'd received the news that her parents' sailboat had capsized during a freak storm in the Aegean Sea. There'd been no survivors.

"I don't care about the money," she said. "It's nothing. I just want my parents back." Tears filled her eyes, and again she turned to reach for Justin. But instead, he stepped back, shaking his head.

"I'm sorry, Lil. Really I am. But I can't do this. Not now."

"But Justin, I…" She sucked in a ragged breath, searching for something of the man she'd loved in the stranger standing before her.

"Look, I've been fighting to get ahead my whole life. And I'm certainly not ready to be saddled with your parents' debt."

Lily swallowed, the panic rising in her chest. "But you heard Mr. Banderson. Once everything is sold, the debts should be covered."

"Even if that's so, there won't be anything left."

She struggled to breathe, to keep herself calm. She'd been so sure that Justin hadn't been like the others, but apparently she'd been wrong. "So you're saying that you were only marrying me for my money?"

He at least had the decency to flinch, but the resolve in his eyes didn't lessen. "I'm saying that circumstances have changed. Of course

I care about you. But not enough to bind myself into all of this." He waved at the desk and the papers Mr. Banderson had been consulting.

"I see." Lily clenched her fists, trying to maintain a calm she didn't feel. How had everything gone so wrong so quickly? With shaking fingers, she slid the ring off her finger. "Then I guess I won't be needing this."

She held it out to him, praying that somehow this horrible nightmare would end. That none of it would turn out to be real. But Justin took the ring with a small shrug, then turned and strode from the office.

For a moment, she stood frozen, staring at the chair he'd just vacated, emotion threatening to swamp her. How could she have been so blind?

"Lily, I know this is awful, but..." Mr. Banderson trailed off, sounding as if he wished he could follow Justin. People were like that. Quick to the party, but running from disaster. And that's what her life was now. A disaster. No money. No parents. No fiancé.

She shook her head, holding up a hand, pleased to see that it wasn't shaking. "Don't. I can't handle any more sympathy. I appreciate your giving me the truth. And I'll probably want to talk to you later about how to best handle everything. But for now I think I just need to get out of here."

He nodded, his expression now flooded with relief. "Are you sure you don't want me to call someone?"

"And just who would that be, Mr. Banderson?" Lily felt the tears again. "Thank you. I'll do fine on my own." She forced a smile and then walked out of the office and through the foyer into the hallway, her whole body shaking as she slid down to the floor.

What in hell was she going to do now?

"I wasn't sure you'd be up for a visit," Valerie Robinson said as she walked into Lily's parents' living room and took a seat on the sofa.

"You're not a visitor." Lily shook her head, trying for a smile. "You're family. Mother would haunt me if I treated you any differently." The words hurt, but she forced herself to hold on to the tremulous smile. There was nothing to be gained in losing it now. "Anyway, I'm glad you're here."

"I came as soon as I heard the news." Word traveled quickly in a small town like Greenwich. Her parents' deaths and the news of their insolvency had made all the papers. Even the *New York Times*. Watching the mighty fall was a blood sport in their circle. Particularly when the story involved tragedy and, if one counted Justin's defection, betrayal.

"It's been kind of a nightmare around here. I thought things were bad enough with the funeral. But now, the phone rings constantly. And it's either the press or creditors. The sharks are circling."

"Oh, darling, I'm so sorry you're having to go through this." Valerie was her mother's oldest friend. They'd known each other forever, and as such Valerie had always been a part of Lily's life too.

"I just keep praying that I'm going to wake up." Lily shivered, wrapping her arms around herself as the shrill ring from the phone splintered the calm façade of the room.

"Just try to ignore it." Valerie waved at the phone and took a sip of tea. "Have you talked to Justin?"

"No." She rubbed her ring finger with her thumb, the pain still raw. "Not a word. I just can't believe I was stupid enough to have fallen for him."

"He loved you, Lily. Everyone knew that. It was plain on his face when he looked at you."

"Yeah, or maybe he was just high-fiving himself over all that money."

"Oh, darling." Valerie's face twisted with concern, and Lily felt her fragile hold on decorum slipping. "Sometimes men just don't deal well with change."

"Don't make excuses for him, Val. He was just like the others, only he was better at making me believe he was different. But in the wake of everything that's happened, it almost seems inconsequential. You know?"

"I just want what's best for you."

"Truth is, I'm not sure I know what that is any more." Lily threaded her fingers together, her stomach twisting with the enormity of what she'd lost. "Ten days ago, I had two loving parents, a devoted fiancé and pretty much no worries about anything more pressing than whether to serve chicken or fish at the reception. And now...now I..." She trailed off, choking on her tears.

"Lily, I wish I could make it go away. But I can't. And I know if your mother were here, she'd want you to go on. To find a new and better life."

"Easier said than done. Dad didn't exactly leave things neat and tidy. There's property to be sold, and I've got to arrange an auction for their belongings." She tipped back her head, rubbing her temples. "Mr. Banderson tells me I have to sell everything."

"Surely they understand that this is your home."

"That's just it. It isn't mine. I was only living here until the wedding."

"What about your apartment in the city?"

"Technically it belongs to Dad. He never put it in my name. Basically, except the money in my bank account, and my clothes and personal things, everything is fair game. At my apartment, here—and in the other houses."

"And you had no idea there were problems?"

"No. There was nothing. I've been over it and over it, and there just wasn't any sign. Dad was happy to be retired. And he and Mother were having the time of their lives. There wasn't anything to indicate that there was this kind of debt. Did my mother say anything to you?"

Valerie shook her head. "It's like you said. They were happy. At least you can hold on to the fact that they loved each other very much."

"And that they were together when they died. I've thought about that a lot. And as much as I wish that one of them at least was here with me now, I know the truth of it is that they'd never have wanted to be apart. So now they're together forever."

"And you're left with the mess."

Lily nodded, grateful that Valerie wasn't sugarcoating the truth. "But I'll deal. I always do." She'd been the third wheel in her parents' relationship her whole life. Which meant that although she had always known she was loved, she'd also learned, as an only child, to be self-sufficient from an early age. "The hardest part, really, is dealing with all the people. If it isn't the press or the creditors, it's all of the others, friends and acquaintances, hovering, trying to fix everything. Or bringing food. There must be ten baskets from Zabars in the kitchen."

"People don't know what to do, darling," Valerie said. "They're just trying to help."

"I know. But sometimes it just makes it harder. Like I have to comfort *them*. And I don't know how much more of it I can take."

"Well, then maybe I shouldn't feel guilty for not bringing muffins."

"Actually it would have been a nice change from bagels." Lily laughed, the sound surprising her. "Oh, God, Val, what would I do without you?"

"Hopefully, you won't be finding out anytime soon. But just because I didn't bring food doesn't mean I didn't bring something." She held out a small white box.

Lily slipped off the top, her breath catching in her throat as she looked down at the narrow silver band nestled against the cotton inside. "Daddy's ring."

"I hope I did the right thing. I know how much it meant to your father. And it's been in your mother's family for years. She always talked about how it created happy endings as it was passed from one generation to the next. So I thought it should be with you. I asked the funeral director to give it to me."

"Oh, Valerie, it's perfect," Lily said, unclasping the silver chain she was wearing. She strung the ring with its intricate silver knots onto it, refastening it around her neck, the weight of the cool metal comforting in some deep, intrinsic way. "I should have thought of it myself."

"You weren't up to making those kinds of decisions." Val reached over to squeeze Lily's hand.

"Well, I'm glad you were." Her hand tightened around the ring. "It's like having a small part of them here with me."

"You'll always carry them in your heart. Just as they carried you. But it is nice to have something to hold on to. And that ring is as much as symbol of their love as you are. They loved you very much, you know."

"I do. And I'm really glad to have the ring. Much better than muffins." The phone started ringing again and Lily flinched. "It never stops."

"Actually," Valerie said with a hesitant smile, "I think I have a plan for that, too."

"You've cancelled the phone subscription?"

"That definitely would be a solution, but this will be even better. At least I hope so." Valerie reached into her bag and produced a white envelope, handing it to Lily.

Lily opened the envelope and quickly scanned the contents. "A plane ticket? To Scotland?" If nothing else, Valerie had caught her completely by surprise.

"I know it seems insane. But I've got a friend who runs an inn in the north of Scotland. And she's offered to let you stay there for a bit. They're in the middle of changing owners, so the inn is temporarily closed. Don't you see? It gets you away from all of this." She waved her hand at the room, as though it held the source of all Lily's problems. But then in many ways, maybe it did.

"I can't accept this," Lily protested.

"It's nothing. Just a plane ticket. The rest is taken care of. Agnes is delighted you're coming. And the new owners are lovely as well."

"But I can't leave, Valerie. I have to take care of things. What kind of daughter would I be if I just left?"

"Your mom and dad are gone, Lily. They don't expect anything of you. The only thing they'd want is for you to be happy. Mr. Banderson can handle everything here. It's what he does, for goodness sake. And God knows he's been paid well enough to do it. If you need to sign anything it can be messengered to you. And besides, you know how slowly this sort of thing moves."

Lily opened her mouth to protest, but Valerie waved her quiet.

"You need to get away from here. Distance will do a world of good. And in Scotland no one is going to give a whit if your father lost his money. And there won't be anything to remind you of Justin or the debt—just peace, quiet and maybe a little solace."

"It does sound enticing, but I can't just walk away."

"Of course you can. I'll be here. I'll be sure that things are taken care of. That everything is moving forward. I can handle the press. And I can certainly handle the predators." She crossed her arms, her eyes shooting sparks. "Marisa was my best friend. And I loved Thomas like a brother. I'll not let anyone make them seem any less than the wonderful people they were."

"I can't think of anyone better. But I still think I should stay." And she knew that she should. That she had to meet her responsibilities. But the idea of escaping, if only for a little while, was so very tempting. And Scotland. It had called to her from the very first time she'd visited. A fishing trip with her parents. It had been one of her favorite vacations.

"Lily, take the ticket. I'll deal with the fallout. I can handle it." As if to prove the point, the phone rang again, and Valerie answered, her clipped voice putting a quick end to the attempted conversation on the other side. "See? I'm good at it." She smiled, her gaze locking with Lily's. "Darling, go to Scotland. Let your heart heal."

Lily closed her hand around her father's wedding ring, the cool metal giving her strength. "All right, then. I'll go."

CHAPTER 2

SCOTLAND – 1468

THERE WAS DANGER. He could feel it all around him. Fire raced up the wooden steps that led up to the door leading into the tower. And he could see more flames thrusting out of the windows, black smoke spiraling into the windswept sky. He ran up the steps, but was stopped by one of the tower's guards.

The man raised his claymore, his eyes narrowed as the deadly blade began its descent. Bram pivoted and then swung his own weapon, confused as to where he was and why he was fighting. The man fell, only to be replaced by another. Bram called to him, some part of him recognizing a face that still seemed a stranger, but this man, too, seemed intent only on stopping him.

His mind argued that nothing made sense, even as his heart screamed that he must get inside. If he did not, then that which was most precious to him would be lost. He knew this as surely as he drew breath.

With a twist and a parry he drew the man off, and then made quick work of him, dashing through the opening of the tower, down the hallway and into the great hall. A place meant for comfort, it offered only danger now. It too was full of flame, and lined with enemies.

Again the thought brought him up short. But there was no time to try and understand. Fear pushed him forward. He surged into the fray, moving toward the stairway at the far end of the room. It gave access to the chambers above and it was there he knew he would find her.

His brain recoiled. Find who? But his heart urged him forward, and he fought his way to the bottom of the steps, then ran up them, taking them two at a time, knowing the other swordsmen were fast on his heels.

At the top, he froze for a moment, the thick smoke disorienting him. The fire was much worse here. Pushing forward, he breathed through the heavy wool of his plaid, keeping his sword at the ready. The first chamber was empty. As was the solar and the chamber beyond it. But then from down the narrow hallway he heard a cry.

Heart thundering in his ears, he ran through the flames and smoke. A timber fell, glancing off of his shoulder, and he hardly felt it, the need to find her overriding everything else.

He called for her, his voice swallowed by the raging fire. Another timber fell, and a wall collapsed. He jumped across a gaping hole in the floor, landing hard, but still moving. The doorway ahead was edged in flames, the smoke and fire roiling like some kind of evil spirit.

Ignoring the danger, he sprinted forward, bursting through the opening, again calling her name.

And then, through the shimmering heat, he saw her, tied to the bedpost, her long hair unbound, her green eyes wide with fear.

A shadow moved behind her. Rage threatened to engulf Bram. "God's blood, what have you done?"

"Naught but what you deserve," came the answer. Other shadows moved. He was surrounded.

"Go back," the woman screamed.

But he pushed onward, stumbling as still more of the burning tower fell. "I'll no' leave you." His words were whipped away by the inferno surrounding them. But he knew that she had heard him. The men from the shadows rushed him, but still he pushed forward, his entire being focused on her.

There were only a few feet separating the two of them now. There was bruising on her face and a trickle of blood at the corner of her beautiful mouth, and he swore there would be hell to pay.

But first, he had to free her.

He reached out a hand, but as he did so the floor in front of him collapsed, crashing to the ground below. One moment he was looking into her eyes and the next, she was gone.

"Wake up, lad," a voice called urgently.

Bram shook his head, his mind still filled with smoke and fire. *The rubble threatening to bury him. He had to reach her...*

"Bram, I beg you. Wake now, for they're coming. And they'll no' spare you."

Someone was pulling him back, the images fading, the dream dissipating into the night. Bram struggled from sleep, his heart still pounding. "I'm awake. What in God's name has gotten into you?" He stared up into the ruddy face of his friend Robby Corley.

Robby, the Macgillivray horse master, wasn't a man easily frightened, but there was fear present now, and Bram's brain cleared in an instant.

"The tower has been o'er run. They're coming to kill you," Robby said.

"That canna be." Bram shook his head, wondering if he'd woken from one nightmare into another. "Where are my father's guard?"

"They're either dead or they have thrown their lot in with the invaders."

"And my father?"

His friend's eyes cut to the floor. "He's dead."

Pain ripped through Bram, his hands clenching with the enormity of what Robby was saying. "Dead."

"Aye." His friend nodded with finality. "And so will you be if you dinna go now."

Seamus Macgillivray had not suffered fools lightly, and he'd not be pleased if his only son were to let grief overcome his duty to the clan. With a grimace, Bram rose from the bed and wrapped himself in his plaid, still struggling to understand what was happening. "You're telling me that no one at Dunbrae remains loyal to my father—" He paused, the hard truth sinking in. "—Or to me."

"Nay, there are a few left." Robby lifted his chin, his brown eyes steady. "Me for one. But that is no' enough. Come now. We must go."

Bram grabbed his sporran and his claymore, following Robby to the door.

"We'll take the front stairs. They'll no' expect us there."

"But surely there will be guards," Bram protested, even as he knew it was the right move. In battle, surprise was everything.

"Aye," Frazier Macbean, his father's captain, agreed as he rounded the corner. The three men stood for a moment, Frazier eyeing the younger men's arms. "I havna' a weapon," he said. "I barely got out of my chamber alive."

Robby drew his dirk and tossed it to the man. "'Tis all I have, but 'tis better than naught."

The older man deftly caught the knife and the three of them ran along the corridor. They could hear the clanking of footsteps on the back stairs behind them. Rounding a corner, they pulled to a stop as Bram took a look out onto the landing. Below, the great room was empty, but he could hear the sounds of men moving in the corridor that led to the kitchens.

Silently, they made their way down the stairs and through the great room, pausing in the hallway outside the door.

"There'll be men outside, surely," Robby whispered. "Take my clothes. And I'll wear yours." He was already pulling off his plaid and the course linen shirt that he wore.

Frazier nudged Bram. "Hurry, lad. The boy is right, ye've a better chance o' makin' it out of here if yer dressed as a common man."

Robby Corley was anything but common. But as the horse master, he wore only a muddy brown plaid and his shirt. Bram pulled his own plaid free and slipped out of his fine linen, quickly donning Robby's clothing. "I'll wear your clothes but you canna wear mine. To be seen in them would mean certain death."

His friend held his gaze for a moment, jutting his chin out in stubborn defiance.

"I need you alive, Robby. At the moment, I've got more enemies than friends, and I'll no' lose another this night."

"So be it." Robby shrugged, pushing the plaid behind a barrel, clad now only in the linen shirt and his trews. "But you stay behind me. I'll no' have your blood on my hands either."

Bram allowed himself a smile. "Agreed. We all survive this night."

Moving low, they made their way along the shadowed walls of the tower's courtyard. The main gate was well guarded. And the only chance they had to escape was through a small gate in the back wall. Bram prayed that the key was where his father had always kept it.

As they rounded the final corner, a great commotion sounded on the steps in the front of the tower.

"They've discovered you're gone," Robby said, pushing Bram forward, even as he raised his claymore. "Go now. We'll stay here and deal with anyone who tries to follow."

Frazier nodded his agreement.

"No." Bram shook his head. "If they think you helped me escape, they'll kill you both for sure."

"Mayhap, but I swore an oath to serve and protect the laird of Dunbrae, and from where I'm standing that man is you." Robby's tone brooked no argument.

"But I'll need you," Bram said, his gaze locking with his friend's then cutting to the other man. "Both of you. God's blood, if I'm going to fight this, I'll need all the men I can get."

"Then we'll convince them we're on their side." Frazier swung his fist, connecting with Robby's chin, showing surprising strength for one so old.

"Now, what did you go and do that for?" Robby asked, whirling angrily on the man, his claymore raised.

"So they'll believe I took your clothes." Bram laid a hand on his friend's arm. "You'll make sure Frazier comes to no harm?"

"I'll do what I can." Robby shrugged, rubbing his chin, his gaze still angry. "Now go. Or it'll have all been for naught."

Bram took one last look at the two men and the tower behind them. "I'll be back," he promised. "And we'll avenge my father's death together."

The two men nodded, their expressions fierce, and, fighting a surge of emotion, Bram sprinted into the shadows, the noise behind him growing louder. Slipping behind the small stand of bushes that grew in front of the gate, he prayed that the invaders wouldn't know of its existence.

For a moment he grappled with the pain of losing his father, his mind turning to the men he was certain were behind all of this.

Comyns.

He could think of no other enemy strong enough for an assault on the scale of this one. But even if he was right, someone still had to have betrayed them. Someone on the inside. He fought a wave of anger, pulling a loose stone out of the wall and reaching behind it for the iron key that opened the gate.

His fingers hit cold metal and in a few moments more he'd unlocked the gate and pushed it open, slipping outside into the relative safety of the moonless night. His fist tightened on his claymore, his heart screaming for him to stay and fight. To avenge his father, here and now.

What else was there for him to do?

And somewhere deep in his mind, even as he moved back toward the tower, his rage building, a soft voice soothed him, the memory of a face floating through his mind.

"Live," she whispered. "You must live."

"You must be Bram Macgillivray," Katherine St. Claire said as she moved into the chamber off of the great room where he'd been taken to wait.

Iain Mackintosh's wife was more beautiful even than the stories he'd heard, tall and regal with a heavy plait of golden hair coiled at the nape of her neck. Her smile was warm and welcoming, and for the first time in days, Bram felt himself relax.

"I thank you for agreeing to meet with me." He stood and gave a terse bow, uncertain of the protocol. With his mother dead, there'd been no one to teach him the finer arts at Dunbrae.

"And why wouldn't I? You're my husband's cousin, which makes you my family too." She motioned for him to take a seat and then sat across from him, her chin resting on her hands as she studied him. "I'm only sorry that it's me here to greet you and not Iain, for I suspect he's who you've really come to see."

There was something melodic about her cadence. Different from the voices he heard daily in the Highlands. There were rumors that she'd come from a strange land. And people who even thought she was something more than human. But Iain loved her. And so, for that matter, did Bram's other cousin, Ranald Macqueen. And since the two men were the closest Bram had come to having siblings, he trusted their judgment.

"I went to *Tur nan Clach*, but they told me that Ranald and Ailis were here." Ailis Davidson was Ranald's wife. Although he'd served as Iain's captain for a brief time, Ranald had inherited his wife's holding when they'd married.

"And so they were," Katherine replied. "But Iain was called to Moy and Ranald and Ailis decided to accompany him." Moy was home to the Chief of Clan Chattan, Iain's uncle Duncan.

"But you stayed here?"

"I've just had a baby." Her smile grew wider. "And at the moment, neither Anna nor I are up to that kind of a journey."

"Tis sorry I am then to have intruded." Bram made to rise. "If they're no' here, then I should take my leave."

"Nonsense," Katherine said, waving him back into his seat. "Iain would kill me if I let you go."

Again, her wording seemed a bit strange, but he was too grateful for the welcome to worry over it much.

"So tell me what's happened," she said, her expression growing pensive. "We've heard about the troubles at Dunbrae. So I'm assuming that you're here to seek Iain's help."

"Aye." He nodded. "How much do you know?"

"Very little." She shrugged apologetically. "We're isolated here and so news is often garbled. Fergus told me this morning that there was some kind of coup."

He shook his head, not understanding her words.

"Sorry." She shook her head with a smile. "An uprising. He said there'd been bloodshed."

"My father," Bram said, the pain still twisting in his gut. "The intruders killed him."

"While you were at Dunbrae."

Katherine St. Claire was more than a pretty face. Bram should have known that Iain would never have fallen in love with a fool. "Aye, and they tried to murder me in my bed."

"But you managed to escape."

"With the help of my friend Robby and my father's man Frazier. If no' for them, I wouldna be here now."

"Do you know who it was who did this?" Katherine asked.

"Nay. No' for certain. But if I had to wager I'd say it was Alec Comyn. There's no love lost between my father and his. And the bad blood between the clans goes back longer than I can remember. The Comyns and the Macgillivrays are sworn enemies."

"But I thought a peace had been brokered."

Bram nodded. His great uncle was the head of the Macgillivray clan, and he had held it with an iron fist, but the old man was beginning to soften with age. "There was an agreement. But clearly the Comyns have no' honored it."

"And you think they're still looking for you?"

"Aye. As long as I live, I'm the rightful heir. And Alec knows I'll fight for what is mine. But if I'm dead…"

"Won't your great uncle have something to say about that?" she asked. "Shouldn't you have gone to him?"

"My great uncle turned his back on my father years ago. I canna expect him to help me now."

"Well, then you were right to come here," she said, resolve strengthening her voice. "Ranald and Iain both think of you as their brother. They'll be only too willing to aid you in regaining what you have lost."

Bram nodded, thinking of his cousins. He was related to Ranald through his father and Iain through his mother. And because of that, when he'd been sent to foster at Moy, Ranald and Iain, only a couple of years older, had taken him under their wing. They'd been like brothers, dispensing equal parts of advice and mischief.

"Aye," he said, pulling from his thoughts to focus on Katherine, "but they're no' here. And I canna put you and your bairn in danger."

"I have quite a company of men at my disposal. Iain never leaves me without protection."

Bram nodded, remembering that Katherine had been kidnapped not long ago. "I'd expect nothing less, but..."

Katherine raised a hand to cut him off. "And if that's not enough security for you, I've also got fifteen of Ranald's men here as well. They came with Ailis and Ranald, but weren't needed in Moy. So they're here waiting to escort their laird and his lady home as soon as they return. Anyway, as you can see, we have more than enough men to guarantee your safety. So I'll not hear another word about your leaving."

Bram nodded, surprised at the relief that flooded through him. When he'd set out to find Ranald and Iain, he'd not considered the possibility that neither man would be at home.

"They'll be back before you know it," Katherine said, reaching out to cover his hand with hers. "And in the meantime, I'll be glad of the company."

"But if my enemies were to come here, looking for me, then it would be dangerous for you. Even if ultimately your men held the day, there would still be a battle. I canna put you in that kind of danger."

Katherine considered his words, then nodded resolutely. "Very well, then we won't house you here. But I'll still see you safely under my watch. There's a cottage just across the river. It belonged to a crofter, but he died recently. So the place is empty. And it's tucked away in a stand of trees. No one would ever think to look for you there. I'll have Fergus assign men to keep watch. Then when Iain and Ranald come home, the three of you can figure out how to get your holding back."

She rose and he followed suit.

"But before you go," she said, "let's get a hot meal in you. And I'll have Flora put together a basket of food to take with you—along with anything else you might need." She glanced at his threadbare clothing. "Like maybe a clean shirt and a plaid. If you dress as a Mackintosh, you'll be that much less likely to be discovered."

Bram nodded, grateful for her foresight. There was something comforting in handing oneself over to a woman. For a moment, his mind filled again with the memory of haunted green eyes, but he shook his head. There was no time now for dreams.

Instead, he'd fill his belly and then hunker down to wait for Iain and Ranald. Katherine had the right of it. He'd survived the horror at Dunbrae for one reason only—for the chance to avenge his father and take back that which was rightfully his.

CHAPTER 3

✦

DUNCREAG, SCOTLAND — PRESENT DAY

"SON OF A..." Lilly slammed on the brakes, swallowing the rest of the curse as she jerked the wheel to the right, the rental car shuddering as she struggled for control. Directly ahead, a startled sheep emerged from the mist, its mouth open in bawling protest as both machine and animal came to an abrupt halt.

For a moment the animal stood frozen, its gaze locked with Lily's and then, with a final chastising bleat, it was gone, the mist closing behind it like a tremulous gray curtain shimmering in the fog lights' beams.

With a sharp release of breath, Lily forced herself to let go of her death grip on the steering wheel. Her heart pounded against her ribs, and she wondered, not for the first time, what in the world had possessed her to think she was capable of driving on her own through the wilds of the Scottish Highlands.

It was hard enough trying to remember that right was left and left was right on the steep curving roads without also having to deal with a startled ovine with a death wish. And to make it even worse, the mist had thickened to the point where nothing much was visible beyond the short swath of light cut by the headlights.

The day had been blustery when she'd left Inverness, but the inn-keeper there had assured her that she'd make the castle long before sundown. The term was obviously a euphemistic one because there had been no sign of anything remotely resembling sunlight all day. The only hint she had that evening was turning to night was the deepening shadows amidst the swirling mist.

And there was no sign at all that she was nearing her destination. For all she knew she'd turned onto the wrong road.

Still, it could be worse.

She could be here with Justin.

With a sigh, she laid her head on the steering wheel. How was she going to manage without her parents? It seemed on the surface a simple question when one considered the fact that they'd more or less left her alone most of her life. But that didn't mean they hadn't loved her. And when they had all been together it has always been wonderful.

But now they were gone again.

Forever.

And she was driving alone in the middle of a Highland maelstrom.

She smiled at the exaggeration. So maybe it was only a little fog.

With a fortifying breath, she pressed her foot to the accelerator. Upward and onward and all that. Literally in this case, as the curving road wound its way up through the narrow valley.

On her immediate left, Lily could just make out the mountains' craggy rocks jutting from between clumps of gorse and broom. On her right, she could see nothing but the swirling fog, but she knew that it cloaked a steep dropoff and was grateful for the protective strip of asphalt in between.

She'd been right to listen to Valerie. Staying at home would have been a mistake. Watching people paw over her parents' belongings.

She'd taken what she'd wanted and stored it in Val's garage. And the rest...well, maybe she'd wind up better off without it.

They were only things, after all. She touched her ring finger, surprised not to find the heavy weight of her engagement ring. Old habits seemed impervious to the truth of the matter.

She was better off without Justin. Even if she was all alone.

In the middle of nowhere.

She blew out a breath and slowed the car, staring out of the windshield. What if she'd made a wrong turn? What if she was truly lost? What if she managed somehow to drive herself right off the edge of a cliff?

The practical side of her nature insisted that as long as she stayed to the left she'd be all right, and that the road had to lead somewhere eventually. Eventually being the operative word, of course. Then there was the fanciful side of her personality—the side that Justin had always discouraged. It was fully capable of imagining all kinds of less than optimal outcomes to her desperate attempt to escape the pain of her current situation and the inevitable rush of well-meaning pity that followed in its wake.

Determination, fueled by anger, spurred Lily onward. There was nothing to be gained in wallowing. Better to seize the day—at least what was left of it. Things could actually be a lot worse. After all, she'd managed to miss the sheep.

As if to squelch her budding optimism, the gray clouds rumbled and a spatter of rain hit the windshield.

"Clearly this just isn't my day." Lily sighed, flipping on the windshield wipers as the skies opened in earnest and the rain pelted down on the little rental car. In all honesty, it wasn't her week or month or year either.

And last night hadn't helped at all. She'd hardly had any sleep, and when she had slept, her mind had surrendered to strange dreams. The floating face of a man with ice-blue eyes and jet black hair. There had been danger, too. A fire. Angry men. Swords.

She shook her head, clearing her mind of the memory. She'd woken covered in sweat, her heart pounding. But what had startled her the most was the fact that the fear hadn't been for herself. It had been for the man. The stranger with the crystalline eyes.

Scotland had obviously taken its hold. Now she was dreaming of men in kilts.

She smiled, thinking that perhaps Justin hadn't hurt her as badly as she'd imagined. Or maybe in truth it was her pride more than her heart. It was hard to know really. The enormous weight of her parents' death obliterated pretty much everything else.

But even as she had the thought, she knew that more than anything her parents would want her to move on. To love them and to mourn them, but above all else to continue to live.

The word echoed in her mind, and for a moment she almost felt as if she'd spoken it out loud. Meant it as an entreaty to someone else. Again her brain flashed the image of the man from her dream.

Nightmare really. Some weird amalgamation of the events of the past few weeks.

The mind had a way of playing tricks.

She shuddered, pushing aside her rambling thoughts, instead peering out into the storm, looking for a sign, something to tell her she was on the right road. The dark and the mist had closed around her, making visibility of more than a few feet impossible. On the sides of the road, she could barely make out the shadows of the trees, gyrating in the wind.

A darkened outline of a hedgerow on the right indicated that at least she'd made it past the cliffs in one piece. She glanced at her purse, wishing again that she'd thought to update her cell plan for coverage in Scotland. But the trip had been too rushed, and besides, who would she have called anyway?

In truth, she doubted this remote valley ran to cell coverage at all. The inn that Valerie's friend ran was actually a castle, or tower as the Scottish called them. It had been built sometime in the early fifteenth century. A fortress that rested at the top of a rise just over the River Findhorn. Assuming she was on the correct road, the river ought to be off to her left somewhere, following the line of the road.

Eventually, according to the instructions she'd downloaded from their website, she should be crossing the river, and once on the other side, she'd begin the climb up to Duncreag.

The rain spattered against the windshield, the wind howling as it buffeted the little car. Lily tightened her hands on the steering wheel as she frowned out into the downpour, trying to see a light or some other sign of humanity.

Sadly, there was no sign of civilization save for the ancient hedgerow and the rutted road. But there had been sheep. So surely that meant human inhabitants as well. Inhabitants from her century preferably. Still, she couldn't shake the feeling that this valley had changed little since the tower had first been built. That there were secrets here.

The last thought seemed to pop up out of nowhere, and she shook her head at her addled musings. Clearly the rain and the mist were getting to her. She pushed the pedal down, and the car groaned but obligingly increased speed.

Just a little bit farther. She had to be close now. The road ahead shone in the pale wash from the headlights, and she concentrated on staying to the left. Not that she'd passed a car all day. Not since she'd turned off of the main highway. She was well and truly alone out here.

A shiver traced its way down her spine, and she swallowed, forcing a smile. She turned the dial on the radio, but there was nothing but static. She reached to push a button to try and find another station, but before her hand touched the panel, the road ahead suddenly turned to the left.

Jerking the wheel, she felt the little car swerve, but the tires gained traction and the car moved safely through the turn. But before she could congratulate herself, she looked out to see the river suddenly rising before her. Swollen over its banks, it had either washed away the bridge, or swallowed it.

Lily slammed on the breaks, but this time the little car refused to cooperate. The wheels spun and the car shimmied sharply to the left, the rushing river looming through the windshield.

Wouldn't it be ironic if she'd run away from her parents' death only to careen into her own?

Calm rationality pushed through her hysteria, and Lily turned the wheel to the right, away from the river, as hard as she could. The car was sluggish, but it responded, whipping away from the road and the river, roaring through the brush and slamming into something hard.

Lily jerked forward, her head colliding with the steering wheel. And then there was nothing but the sound of the rain as it pattered against the roof.

Someone was banging a pot or a pan and the sound was driving her crazy. Lily forced her eyes open, trying to remember where she was.

For a moment fear crested, and then she remembered. The car. The river. The rain.

She pushed her hair out of her eyes, surprised to find something sticky. She pulled her fingers away, and recognized blood. Her blood. Clearly she'd hit her head. Feeling gingerly along her scalp line, she found a gash. Surrounding it was a growing knot, but despite the amount of blood, she didn't think it was life threatening.

She rolled her shoulders and checked her arms and legs. Nothing broken. Except the car. Though the motor had died, the windshield wipers were still going strong. And the "pot" she'd heard was a tree branch banging against the roof of the car in the wind from the storm. The trunk of said tree was planted, literally, directly in front of her, the front end of the car crumpled against it.

She tried the key, but the motor coughed and died. Without the headlights, the night had closed completely around her, the mist swirling past the side windows like a living creature.

She tried the ignition again, but there was nothing, the car's engine apparently too damaged to start. Which left her feeling grateful on the one hand—it had been a close call with the river—and terrified on the other. She was out in the middle of nowhere, without any means of communication, and the river was blocking all access to Duncreag.

Great.

She blew out a breath and considered her options.

She wasn't exactly dressed for a rainstorm. Her peasant blouse and long cotton skirt were holiday frivolity. A mistake for early spring in the Highlands. Jeans and boots would have suited her better.

Her suitcase was in the trunk. And while she didn't exactly have hiking gear, she did have warmer clothing. But she'd get soaked trying to get them. The sane option would be to stay in the car until morning.

They'd been expecting her. So someone was bound to come looking. Except of course that they couldn't cross the river.

The wind shook the tree, and the branch beat harder against the roof.

Lily fought to contain a shiver of fear. There was nothing out there but a little wind and an aggravated tree. But even with that thought, the idea of staying in the car had lost its appeal.

She bit her lip, trying to figure out what her best of course of action might be, as she leaned forward to peer out of the windshield. She could see the hood of the car and the battered tree, and then just beyond that what looked to be a second, smaller tree. The mist looked ghostly as it twined among the leaves.

Fine mess she'd landed herself in.

She tried the ignition again just for the hell of it. But, as before, it refused to even turn over. The cold had become penetrating and her head was pounding. Instinct pushed her to curl up and sleep. Just forget about all of this until morning.

But the knot on her head reminded her that there could be a concussion and sleep wasn't the answer. At least not while she was on her own. Tears threatened, but as she angrily brushed them away, something beyond the two trees caught her attention.

She stared for a moment, waiting to see if it was a trick of the mist. But no, she blinked once, then again and it was still there. A small light, beckoning through the storm.

There were people here.

People who could help.

She tried to open the door, but it was jammed somehow, so after loosening her seatbelt, she slid across the front seat and opened the passenger door. The rain whipped into the car, soaking her to the skin.

Grimacing, she pushed open the door and got out, holding on to the car to keep her balance in the wind.

With a quick fortifying breath, she struck out for the light, stumbling in the mud and brush as she made her way. The rain battered her skin, the wind whipping her hair across her eyes. The air was icy cold, the storm only making it worse. Her clothes were soaked through in an instant. And each step took more and more effort, the light stubbornly staying just out of reach.

Thunder crashed, and a bolt of lightning illuminated the sky for an instant. With a sigh of relief she recognized the outline of a stone cottage. Its windows flickered from the firelight within, a thin trail of smoke winding up from the chimney.

Just a few steps more. Water ran in rivulets down her neck and back, her long hair a sodden mess. Her skirt trailed behind her, dragging in the mud, and she again cursed the foolishness of her stylish summer outfit.

This was the Highlands.

Lightning flashed. She stumbled up the front steps and with the last of her energy pounded on the door. But no one answered. She knocked again, as the storm continued to buffet her. Finally, in desperation, she tried the handle, and the door opened into the warmth within.

For a moment, she hesitated on the threshold. But the thunder rolled again, the rain beating upon her shoulders. This was no time for niceties. She was soaked to the skin and her head was throbbing.

She stepped inside, the wind slamming the door behind her.

She called out. But there was no answer. Shaking from the cold and wet, she moved across the room toward the fireplace and the warmth of the fire burning cheerfully there. She held out her hands, her fingers trembling, struggling to stay upright, to stay focused on the fire. But her body had begun to shudder and her teeth were chattering. She was so damn cold.

"And where in God's name did you come from?"

She heard the voice and turned toward the sound. The man in the doorway was tall, rugged and devastatingly handsome. And oddly, he was familiar somehow. The dark hair. The icy blue eyes. She knew him, didn't she?

"I asked you a question, lass." His gaze raked down her body, taking in the wet clothes and sodden shoes.

She shook her head, trying to clear her thoughts. "The river," she managed, her voice less than a whisper. "There was an accident." She took a step toward him, but stumbled. Warm hands closed around her upper arms. Her eyes slid shut as she reveled in the blessed heat from his touch.

"Ach, you're freezing." His voice caressed her ear as his hands slid up and down her arms. "Are there more of you out there then? Should I go to them?"

She was so cold her teeth were chattering, but she struggled to find her voice. "No." She shook her head so hard her bones rattled, her mind tumbling, past and present all mixed together as one. "There's no one. Not anymore. They're all gone." She paused, looking up into the crystalline blue of his eyes, her fingers gripping his shirt. "Promise... promise you won't leave me, too."

"I promise," he said, his gaze clear and steady, his hands warm against her skin as he stroked her arms. "I'm no' going to leave you. I just need to get you warm."

She nodded, the gesture almost lost as a series of shudders wracked through her body. The room started to whirl.

"Come on then, lass, stay with me," he urged, his eyes filled with concern, his grip tightening on her arms. "Tell me your name."

She opened her mouth to answer his question, but words wouldn't come. And to be honest, she couldn't remember what he'd asked her anyway, and then everything started to go dark. Like slipping into the velvety softness of a blanket.

Her name, she remembered as she struggled to hold onto consciousness. That's what he'd asked her.

"Lily," she whispered as the darkness swallowed her whole.

CHAPTER 4

✦

BRAM CAUGHT THE lass as she fell, wondering where in God's name she had come from. He had no doubt that his enemies would stoop to any level to catch him off guard, even sending a woman to do their dirty work.

But this woman, Lily, was soaked to the bone and a knot high on her forehead was already purpling from what looked to be a pretty substantial blow. He felt along her hairline and located a deep cut. That accounted for the bleeding. But it seemed to have stopped and for the moment he had bigger problems.

She was shaking violently, her body almost spasming as her muscles contracted. He'd seen this before. Exposure to this kind of cold, wearing nothing but what looked to be her shift, was dangerous. He could only suppose what kinds of hell she'd been through to arrive at the cottage in such a condition. An accident, she'd said.

She was wearing next to nothing and her slippers, though made of fine leather, were hardly adequate for traveling in the rough terrain that surrounded Duncreag, especially in the midst of a storm like this one. 'Twas possible she lived or worked at the tower. But her hands were soft and her skin unmarred. And the silver bracelet she wore on her arm had been made by the finest of craftsmen.

Nay, despite her state of undress, this was not a peasant. This was a lady. And not one from around here, if he were to have to place a wager on it. He touched the base of her throat with one finger, satisfied to feel the rush of her blood. She lived, but if he didn't get her dry and warm, there was still a chance her condition could turn for the worst. He'd seen people die from exposure in a storm like this.

As if to echo his concern, she moaned and another shudder ripped through her. It was important to get her warm as quickly as possible. He glanced around the cottage. While it was well enough equipped, it was not built for warmth and even with the fire burning, the small room was still cold.

The best way to warm a body quickly was contact with another body. And although he was not the kind of man to lie with a woman without her willing participation, he could see no other course of action.

He walked over to the pallet that served as a bed. A plump mattress sat on a wooden frame covered by a sheet of linen beneath a blanket made from animal fur. Between that and his own body heat, he should be able to help her regain her own. Trying not to think about the softness of her skin or the sweet slope of her breasts, he peeled off the wet clothing, stopping with the odd underthings she wore, slips of colored silk that barely covered her not inconsiderable assets.

He felt his body awakening and forced himself to ignore the growing urgency. This was a woman in trouble, not a barmaid wanting nothing more than a roll in the hay with the laird-to-be.

He swallowed a laugh, the irony of his thoughts not lost on him. Whatever this woman had been through, he could at least in part relate. Less than a fortnight ago he had been the young master. Today he was a hunted man without a clan.

Lily moaned again, but didn't open her eyes. Her breathing was quick and shallow now, as if the cold were pulling it from her body. Bram carefully laid her on the bed. Her lips trembled as her body reacted to the loss of his heat. Quickly he stripped off his garments and climbed onto the bed, and after covering them both with the fur, he pulled her close against his body, her back curled against his chest.

He rested his chin against her hair, the smell of spring flowers teasing him with familiarity. It was almost as if he'd held her like this many times before.

Perhaps he, too, had been addled by the storm.

He smiled and pulled her closer, willing the warmth of his body into hers. He was fairly certain that the bump on her head wasn't dangerous, but unlike his mother, he had none of the healing ways about him.

Lily sighed and nestled into his warmth. And again he was struck by the familiarity of their intimacy. It was almost as if they fit somehow. Two halves of a whole.

He was a bloody romantic fool. She was a lost soul who needed his warmth, nothing more. And he was a man with no room for a woman in his life. Still, he pulled her closer, wrapping his arms and legs around her to provide a cocoon of warmth. And even as he sought to give her comfort, she gave it back to him in the soft inhale and exhale of her breathing and the way her fingers curled around his.

For the first time in more days than he cared to remember, he felt at peace—or at least temporarily assuaged. Maybe there was magic afoot tonight, in the wildness of the storm or simply the sweet allure of the woman in his bed. Or maybe he had gone quite mad and this was only a dream. Either way, tomorrow's sun would banish the mists and whatever fantasy the night might have held.

But for now, in this moment, he wanted nothing more than to hold on.

Lily drifted to consciousness slowly, her first thought that she couldn't remember the last time she felt so safe and secure. She curled her toes, letting the warmth of the bed seep through her. The fire had died down, the room deep in shadows. Outside she could still hear the rain lashing against the roof and windows. With a sigh, she dug deeper into the warmth, simply luxuriating in the comfort, but then memory returned like a sledgehammer.

The car. The cottage. *The man.*

She struggled to sit up, but strong arms pulled her close as he whispered soft, soothing words. The action was rote; the man was still sleeping and despite the absurdity of the situation, she felt herself relaxing, her body savoring the feel of his skin against hers. There was nothing here to be afraid of. She knew that as clearly as she knew her own name.

The rational part of her brain questioned her sanity, but her heart felt like it was home. She could feel it in the strength of his arms around her and the hot whisper of his breath against her cheek.

And yet he was a stranger.

A stranger who had saved her life.

Or at least gotten her warm again.

Her head still ached, but she was no longer wet and cold. She reached down to cover his hand with hers, and in so doing brushed across her bare breast. She was naked. He shifted against her.

So was he.

A hot blush rushed to her face, but she didn't pull away. There was something so wonderfully decadent in the fact that she was lying here with a stranger. A man who'd stolen her breath when she'd first seen him.

Or maybe that had been the cold, some rational corner of her brain insisted. But she pushed the thought away. Life was for living.

If she'd learned nothing else in the wake of her parents' deaths and Justin's defection, it was that the things you loved most could disappear in an instant.

And she wasn't going to lose this moment. Even if it was only fantasy. Because lying here next to this stranger, she felt as if everything was right with the world. As if having him with her was more important somehow than breathing.

Of course none of that made any sense at all. It had to be her brain compensating for the pain. She smiled. If this was compensation, she'd hit the mother lode. She lay for a moment, just relishing the cadence of his breathing and hers. The soft inhale and exhale of breath. Life at its most basic.

In and out, in and out.

And then suddenly she found herself wondering what would happen if she were to roll over. To press herself against him. To open herself to his kisses. To relish the touch of his hands on her body. To feel him moving deep inside her.

The thought was both enticing and insane. God, she wanted him. More than she'd ever wanted a man before. And again the enormity of what she was considering hit her hard. She wasn't the kind of woman to take risks. To throw herself at a stranger.

But then again, look where playing the girl next door had gotten her.

Again she smiled, the wind outside still whipping beneath the eves of the house. Maybe this *was* just a fantasy. And if that were true, then she'd be damned if she'd wake without knowing at least what he tasted like. There was nothing to be gained in virtue. She was already lying skin to skin with the man.

And besides, she still couldn't shake the certainty that she had done this before. With this man. There was nothing here to be afraid of. No risk. No danger at all. He belonged to her.

The thought startled her, and yet she didn't reject it. Instead, she rolled over.

His face was deep in shadow, but she could still make out the strong line of his jaw. This wasn't a man to trifle with, even in sleep. The thought was fleeting but she knew it to be the truth. And still she wasn't afraid. Slowly, half fearing that he'd disappear, she reached out her hand, brushing her fingers across his cheek.

His eyes opened, and his gaze collided with hers.

She waited, holding her breath, her heart pounding even as her body tightened in anticipation. For what seemed an eternity he looked into her eyes, and then with a groan, he pulled her close, his lips closing over hers, his mouth hungry, demanding.

She opened her mouth, their tongues dueling, her body trembling with the contact. He deepened the kiss, and she drank him in, his taste seeming almost familiar.

"Lily." He whispered her name and she pressed against him, desperately needing to feel his heat.

His lips stroked hers, taking and giving, stirring the fire inside her. The little voice in her head called for her to stop. But God help her, she didn't want to. All she wanted was him. Lightning split the sky, the crescendo of thunder chasing behind it. Where before the storm had threatened her, now, its fury fed her senses. His strong hands cupped her breasts as he kissed her, thumbs circling, desire mixing with pleasure until she could hardly breathe.

"Lily," he whispered again. "Are you sure, then?"

"Yes," she answered, her voice hoarse with desire.

His lips trailed along the line of her neck, shivers of pure passion rocking through her. She pressed against him, wanting to feel closer—to feel a part of him. His lips moved lower, tracing the swell of her breast. She arched upwards, needing more, and he obliged, pulling her nipple into his mouth, the resulting pressure almost her undoing.

She ground her hips against him, offering herself, and he slid his hand lower, his fingers hot as they moved against her skin. While teasing her nipple with his lips and teeth, he slid a finger inside her, the friction setting off shivers of pleasure. She fought for breath even as she pressed closer—wanting more.

His finger moved, in and out, stroking teasing. And then his thumb pressed against her secret spot and she moaned as pleasure surged through her.

"Tell me what you want," he whispered, his breath hot against her breasts, his finger moving in and out, each succeeding stroke deeper, stronger. "Tell me."

"You," she whispered. "Dear God, I want you."

The thunder drowned out her moans as his mouth and his fingers danced across her skin, sensations ratcheting tighter and tighter until she felt herself shatter, pleasure racking through her in shuddering waves.

"Please," she rasped. "Please. More."

Again the thunder bellowed, the cottage shaking, the intensity mimicking her body's release. Lightning flashed, flickering against his face as he pulled her close, his touch gentle and soothing—almost worshipful. As she trembled against him, he caressed her with murmured words and soft kisses.

For a moment, they stayed like that, his arms around her, their legs entwined, hearts beating almost as one. Then she felt her body awaking, felt desire begin to blossom again. She tipped back her head, offering herself. And he greedily accepted the invitation, exploring every inch of her, leaving nothing untouched.

Trembling with the sheer power of the feelings he evoked, she rolled on top of him, indulging her need to taste him. She'd never felt so reckless and yet so sure of herself. The sounds of the storm played out like a symphony, a soundtrack accompanying the splendor of their lovemaking. She ran her hands along the rugged planes of his body, reveling in the hardened muscles. She traced the line of a scar, then followed her touch with kisses.

And then he straddled her, pinning her with his weight. Catching her gaze, he waited, poised above her, his glittering eyes promising everything. With a sharp intake of breath, she wrapped her legs around him, and with one swift move he buried himself inside her. The pleasure was exquisite, and she pushed against him, taking him even deeper.

There was passion reflected in the depths of his eyes, passion and triumph—and something else, something so tender it almost took her breath away. She lost herself then, in the icy blue depth of his eyes.

"Are you ready, lass?" he whispered, the touch of his breath against her ear almost as sensual as his sinewy movements inside her.

"Yes," she sighed, pressing against him, wanting only to pull him deeper still. "Oh, please. Yes."

His arms circled around her, anchoring her to him as he thrust, their bodies fusing together as he began to move, slowly, almost languorously at first. The movement both tormented and delighted. With a moan, she slammed upward, driving him home, and the fury erupted, the storm reaching crescendo. Still, moving inside her, he slipped a hand between her legs, one finger stroking her core.

She gasped, arching up to drive him deeper, tightening around him, wanting to give him as much as he was giving her. They moved together faster and faster, pumping and thrusting, locked together in their own special dance. With a crash, thunder filled the room, the reverberation echoing off the walls. For a moment they teetered at the edge of the cliff. And then with one last powerful thrust they fell.

His arms tightened around her as white hot pleasure raced through her, her body shaking with the intensity, sensation overriding all rational thought. There was only the two of them together. And even though she knew it was an illusion, she held fast to the dream. There'd be time enough for reality tomorrow.

CHAPTER 5

BRAM LAY IN the stillness listening to Lily breathe. The worst of the storm had passed now, the light patter of rain against the thatched roof the only sign it had been there at all.

That and the woman in his bed.

He knew he should not have taken advantage of her. She could not be thinking clearly after all that had happened. And yet when she had turned to him, he could not stop himself. Holding her had been like holding something precious. Something that he could never replace. And he'd only wanted more. And so when she had offered, he had accepted, meaning only to steal a kiss. To feel her lips beneath his. But one kiss had not been enough and now—well, now he felt as hungry as before. As if there could never be enough.

Not with her. Not with Lily.

She stirred beside him, her eyes fluttering open.

"You are awake," he said, stating a blinding glimpse of the obvious, but then she had a way of stealing his words.

She nodded and ducked her head, clearly embarrassed.

"Dinna turn from me, Lily. There is no shame here." And as he said the words he knew that they were true. This was his woman. He knew it in his heart and in his soul. She belonged to him. And he to her.

"I'm not ashamed," she said, offering a small smile. "Just feeling a little odd. As if I've woken in your arms a million times before. It's silly, I know..."

"But 'tis the truth," he whispered. "I feel it, too."

She lifted her face, her eyes meeting his. "Then this isn't a dream?"

"If it is, then I hope never to waken." He pulled her close against him, feeling the steady beat of her heart.

They lay like that for moments or hours—time didn't seem to matter. But then she stirred again, rolling away to prop herself on one elbow. "It isn't fair. You know my name but I don't know yours."

He smiled into the darkness. "Bram Macgillivray," he replied with a flourish of his hand. "At your service, my lady."

Her laughter rang through the room. "Actually, I'm the one indebted to you." Her expression sobered. "I've a feeling you saved my life."

"Well, you owe me naught. I am just glad you've recovered. 'Tis a nasty bruise you have on your forehead. What happened to you out there?"

She shivered at the memory and he reached for her hand. "I wasn't paying attention, I guess. The storm had turned fierce. Then the river rose out of nowhere and I lost control and hit a tree and slammed my head on the wheel. But I saw the light and made my way to the cottage. And you were here and..." She trailed off, clearly remembering exactly how that had all ended up.

"And I got you warm again," he finished for her. "So where were you going?" He'd not ask why she'd been alone. If there was a story to tell, she'd do it in her own time. He'd not press her now.

"I was on my way to the castle when the storm hit and the river washed out."

"The castle?" He frowned.

"Duncreag," she replied, her pronunciation awkward. "I think you call it a tower."

"You know Katherine and Iain, then?" The idea appealed. If she knew his cousin then she could not have been sent by his enemies. He hated himself for even having the thought. Her plight had been real, that much he was certain of. And what had passed between them this night was real as well. He pushed his traitorous thoughts aside.

"If you mean the new laird and his wife——" she said, thankfully unaware of the turn of his thoughts, "——then no. I don't actually know them. My aunt—well, actually she's my mother's best friend—she's the one who knows them. Or at least some of the people that live there. She arranged for me to come. She thought that maybe the Highlands would be good for me."

"And how is that turning out for you?" he quipped with a smile, his worries forgotten as his body responded to the memory of their lovemaking.

"I'd have to say that despite a soggy start, really well, so far." Again she laughed, the joyous sound doing wonders for his tortured heart.

"And what was it that you needed to get away from?" he asked, realizing suddenly that if someone had hurt her, he'd hunt them down to the ends of the earth.

She chewed on her lip, clearly considering how much to tell him, but then she blew out a sigh. "My mother and father were killed in an accident a few weeks ago."

This was a pain he knew only too well.

"There were complications," she continued. "More than I could deal with actually. So Valerie, my mom's friend, suggested I come here."

"'Tis as good a place as any, I suppose. You're no' from the Highlands, I take it?"

"No." She shook her head. "Connecticut."

'Twas an odd word. "I dinna know it," he said.

"It's only a little state and it's very far from here." She lay back, and as she did so the silver necklace she wore slipped over her shoulder. He caught it between his fingers.

His heart twisted. 'Twas a wedding ring.

"Is this yours?" he asked, his voice so low that he feared she had not heard the question. He held his breath, waiting, praying that it wasn't true.

"No." She shook her head, her gaze locking with his. "Of course not." There was a multitude of meaning behind her denial, but for the moment he simply accepted the words for what they were, relief washing through him like the western tide. "The ring belonged to my father." She reached out to take it from him, her thumb caressing the silver band gently. "My mother gave it to him when they were married. I thought if I wore it, I'd feel closer to them somehow."

"Your father would be honored."

"I hope so." Her voice was sad and a little wistful.

"I lost my father, too," he said before he had time to think about it. He only wanted to help. To make her feel better somehow.

"I'm sorry." She reached up to touch his face. "I wouldn't wish that kind of pain on anyone. Was it recently?"

"Aye." He nodded, staring at the ceiling. "'Tis been no more than a se'nnight." He'd actually lost track of time, between running and hiding.

She frowned. "A week. Oh, Bram, I'm so sorry." She reached for him, her voice filled with sympathy. "What happened?"

Bram swallowed, the bitterness rising in his chest. "He was murdered."

"Oh my God. How awful." Her fingers twined with his. "I don't know what to say. Do you know who did it?"

"No' for sure, but I have an idea." The words felt ripped from his chest.

"Someone you knew then?"

"The son of an old enemy of my father's. But he would have had to have help. Which means my father was betrayed."

"Which makes it all the worse. It must be tearing you apart." She pushed close, as if somehow she could wipe the agony away with merely her physical presence. And he blessed her for it, pulling her tighter against him.

"I have no' had the time to really think it all through yet. It happened so fast. I barely got out of there alive."

"You were there?" Her eyes widened, her fingers tightening on his arm.

"Aye. And they were coming for me next."

"But you escaped."

"For the moment, yes. But they know that as long as I live, I'll seek vengeance."

"And so this enemy wants you dead?" She frowned, a tiny line forming between her eyes. "Surely the authorities can do something."

"Mayhap. I dinna know. That's why I came to Duncreag. I need Iain's help."

"Then surely he'll give it to you."

"That he will. It's just a matter of whether it will be enough. But I dinna want you to worry. And I need you to know that whatever happens, being here with you has helped me to forget—at least for a little while."

She nodded. "Me, too. I mean, you've helped me too. It's almost as if we were meant to find each other. As crazy as that sounds."

Despite the gravity of the conversation, he laughed. "Well, if you are a wee bit daft then I must be as well."

For a moment he simply let his mind drift, relishing the feel of her lying next to him, and then he bent his head, first kissing her eyes and then the line of her nose and the curve of her brow. Then finally kissing her lips, the sweet intoxication almost more than he could bear. She opened her mouth and he traced the line of her teeth with his tongue, her taste at once familiar and exotic.

He wondered if he could ever truly get enough of her. Or if he would forever be doomed to wanting more. He smiled against her mouth, realizing there were far worse fates.

There was magic in the bright green of her eyes and Bram marveled at the emotions rocketing through him. Emotions that *she* inspired. There was desire, certainly, more than he had ever known, but there was so much more than that. There was a kind of fierce possessiveness, a protective urge as old as time itself. Something he had never felt before.

And even more surprising, there was a gentle tenderness, the need to cherish and revere, the power of his need almost unmanning. And finally, there was a selflessness as foreign to him as breathing under water. He knew in that instant that he would give anything, do anything, if it would make her happy.

She smiled up at him, her eyes like a spring meadow. And with a groan, he captured her mouth with his, his tongue and lips communicating all that he was feeling. It was a take no prisoners kiss, both of them taking and giving.

Then he shifted, kissing her cheeks and eyes, the soft curve of her ear and the gentle slope of her neck. He trailed kisses along the cleft between her breasts, then he pulled one swollen peak into his mouth, his tongue flicking over the taut nipple until she cried out, the sound filling him with pleasure.

Sucking harder, he caressed the other breast, unable to get enough of her, secretly willing the night to last forever. Her fingers twined in his hair, urging him onward, her body like a fine bow, primed and waiting. Waiting for *him*. He smiled at his own rhetoric, wondering when he had become a bard.

Slowly he inched downward, his tongue tasting first the soft skin of her belly and then, lower still, trailing soft kisses along her inner thighs, his tongue stroking her skin, his desire demanding he take more, that he taste all of her, that he make her once and forever his.

Shifting slightly, he pushed her legs apart and bent to kiss her, lapping at her delicate softness, drinking in her sweetness. Her hands tightened in his hair, her body arching joyfully upward, meeting him, wanting him.

Using his tongue and his fingers, he drove her closer and closer to the edge, feeding on the soft sounds of her passion. And then her body tensed, arching up off the bed.

"Bram," she cried.

Needing her now more than life itself, he slid upward again, covering her mouth with his as her hand closed around him. Fire raged through him and he thrust his tongue into her mouth, the moist, hot feel almost his undoing.

God's blood, he wanted this woman. Wanted her with a fury unlike anything he had felt before.

Her hand slid up and down, stroking, squeezing, caressing, the pain sweet, his need burgeoning into white-hot desire. With a groan, he rolled onto his back, taking her with him. With a crooked grin, she sat up, straddling him. And then slowly lifted and slid down again, taking him deep inside her.

He sucked in a breath, wondering if there could be anything better than the feel of her hot and wet against his taut skin, only to lose the thought as she began to move, her hands on his shoulders, her long, wild hair falling like a screen around them.

Grasping her hips, he helped her set the pace, slow and easy, each upward motion almost separating them. She licked her lips, her eyes glazing over with passion.

"Now, Bram."

Her words bit into him, as much an aphrodisiac as her movements. He increased the pace, driving deeper, harder, with each stroke. She threw back her head, her body glistening from the exertion.

Lost in the moment, she rode him for all she was worth, her eyes closed, her face beautiful in her abandonment. He stroked her breasts, his hands cupping and fondling as together they climbed higher and higher. In, out, in, out, harder and faster, until there was nothing but the motion, the friction, and the incredible union of their bodies— their souls.

Finally, standing at the edge of the precipice, he dropped his hands back to her hips, timing their movements for one last powerful thrust. She cried his name as she tightened around him, and he felt the spasm of her release, the ecstasy driving him higher, taking him over the edge until there was nothing but heat, and light—and Lily.

Lily yawned and snuggled closer into the warmth of the bed, lost for a moment in the magical seconds between sleep and the conscious world, a place where everything was possible and nothing bad could ever happen. But, as always, it slipped away as her mind became fully awake, reality slamming home with painful finality.

Her parents were dead.

Her life would never be the same again. And now, now she was truly alone.

But then another thought pushed its way front and center.

Bram.

She'd spent the night making love with Bram.

On the surface it was insane. But in the cold, pale light of morning, she felt no sense of regret. Last night had been magnificent. And no matter what happened next, she wasn't sorry.

Sucking in a deep breath, she opened her eyes and rolled over, but Bram wasn't there. The bed was empty. Her heart constricting, she sat up, pushing her hair out of her face. Everything else was as she remembered. The fireplace. The bed. The only thing missing was the man.

The gray dawn through the cottage windows proved that the storm had passed, although there was still no sign of the sun. She could see coals glowing in the fireplace, and her clothes had been spread across a chair to dry. So it hadn't been a dream. The cottage was real. And that meant that Bram was real, too.

And he'd left her there.

Except that even as she had the thought, she rejected it. Bram wouldn't just leave her on her own. No matter how he felt with the morning's light, he wouldn't just walk away. Would he?

With a shiver, Lily pulled the fur closer around her, running through the things they had said. The things they had done. Her cheeks burned as a blush stole across her face, and she shook her head, trying not to let her thoughts grow maudlin.

Last night had been amazing. Never in her life had she considered that lovemaking could be like that. So powerful, so explosive, yet at the same time so gentle, almost worshipful. With Bram she'd been fearless. Willing to trust him in a way she'd never dared trust anyone else.

But there had been no promises. No words of love. She and Bram had both admitted feeling a strange connection. As if they'd known each other for more than just a few hours. But even as she had the thought, she realized how foolish it sounded. How was it possible to establish that kind of intimate connection with someone in so short a time?

Her fingers closed around her ring, and she remembered her mother telling her once that she'd known Lily's father was the man for her the first time she'd set eyes on him. And that she'd never doubted that first impression. She'd known, even then, that they would spend the rest of their lives together.

So maybe this was her moment. Her man.

Except that said man was currently missing.

The cynic inside her whispered that he was long gone. Taking what he wanted and then heading for the door. But her heart wasn't as certain. Their lovemaking had been too powerful for it to have been all an act.

Something beyond the physical had passed between them. Something that bound them together in a way she had no words to explain. Which meant that he was coming back.

Feeling decidedly more positive, Lily threw off the covers and quickly crossed the room to pull on her clothes. Her skirt and blouse were thankfully dry, although stained with mud and grass. She doubted they'd ever come completely clean. One of her shoes lay by the edge of the bed, but even after kneeling to look at the floor underneath, she couldn't find the other one. And impatience was beginning to gnaw at her stomach.

She needed to find Bram. To prove to herself that he felt the same as she did about last night. And the simplest course of action seemed to be to go outside and look for him.

To heck with the shoe.

And so, clutching the one she had found, she strode barefoot across the room and threw open the door. The mist still swirled across the clearing, but it had been relegated to the ground now, and was already beginning to dissipate. The air was crisp and fresh. Cleaned by the rain.

There was nothing left to show the fierceness of the storm but a few puddles and a broken branch or two on the neighboring trees. She supposed she ought to go and check on the rental car. But only after she'd found Bram. She hadn't seen his car last night, but she presumed there must be one. Maybe he'd gone to get help. Or maybe he'd gone for breakfast.

Or maybe he'd just gone, the little voice in her head insisted.

"Bram?" she called, her voice sounding hesitant. Why couldn't she just sing it out? If she believed he was here, then why was she suddenly so afraid? *Because Justin left you*, the little voice goaded.

"But this is different," she whispered fiercely. This was Bram.

Again she felt as if the words held more meaning than just the things that had happened between them last night. Even now, she couldn't shake the feeling that somehow they had always known each other.

"Bram?" she called again, this time with more conviction.

From somewhere within the trees that surrounded the cottage she heard a noise. An answer. With a smile she walked across the clearing, stepping into the shadow of the trees, just as the sun burst out from behind the clouds.

For a moment everything was quiet, and then the hairs on her neck stood on end. Turning slowly back toward the cottage, she found herself holding her breath without understanding why.

For a moment the clearing before her looked the same, and she started to turn away, to call for Bram again. But then her mind made sense of the reason she'd felt so uneasy, and she turned again to face the clearing.

The *empty* clearing.

Where only moments ago there had stood a stone cottage, there was nothing but vines and weeds accentuated by a tumble of stone where once, at least in her mind's eye, there had been a chimney.

CHAPTER 6

"ACH, YOU PUIR wee lamb, I canna believe you were out there in that storm." Agnes Abernathy dabbed the cut on Lily's head one last time and then firmly affixed a bandage. On the surface, Agnes had the buttoned-up sensibility of a wise old woman, but the sparkle in her eyes gave her an impish quality that hinted at a much younger soul. "That should hold you for now. The cut isn't deep. But the knock on your head was pretty severe."

Lily winced at the pronouncement. Severe enough to have made her imagine the cottage in the mist.

And the man who'd changed her forever.

Grief did strange things, but she wasn't a person normally given to fantasy. And yet this morning she'd woken in her car with Jamie Abernathy, Agnes's husband, pounding on the window, worried no doubt that her injuries had been far worse than they actually were.

She hadn't bothered to tell him that she hadn't spent the night in the car. That she hadn't been out in the storm much at all. How could she possibly explain the light in the woods? The shelter of the cottage. The warmth of the fire. The heat of the man.

There was no cottage. Or at least there hadn't been one in a very long time. She'd seen the ruins with her own two eyes. Touched the tumble of stones with her own two hands.

There was no cottage.

And so there could have been no man.

She'd made it all up. Out of desperation or panic or God knows what. And now...now she was sitting in Mrs. Abernathy's cozy parlor at Duncreag trying to pretend that nothing had happened. That everything was normal.

"Are you sure you dinna want me to call the doctor?"

Lily pulled her thoughts away from last night, shaking her head. "No, really. I'm fine. Just a little banged up. It could have been a lot worse." In truth she wasn't sure how, but she wasn't ready to discuss it. Especially with a woman she hardly knew. No matter how lovely she might seem.

"Aye, I suppose it could. That river can be nasty. Especially with the kind of rain we had last night. I'm grateful that you and your wee car weren't washed away."

"You and me both," Lily sighed.

"'Tis no' much of a welcome we've given you, I'm afraid. But that doesn't mean we're not delighted you're here. Valerie was really worried."

"I'm grateful that you called to let her know I was okay. My cell isn't working up here. I forgot to arrange for European coverage when I left."

"Well, it wouldn't have done you any good." Mrs. Abernathy shrugged. "Between the hills and the valleys there is no' much coverage even if you've got a Scottish phone. Can I get you anything else to eat?"

The woman had been fussing over Lily since her husband had brought her home.

Home. Now there was a thought. The tower was imposing. Magnificent in its own way, but it was hard to think of it as anyone's home. Even though the inside had been remodeled to turn it into an inn, the bones were still clearly medieval.

Something chased across her spine and she shivered.

"How about some more tea?" Mrs. Abernathy urged, her keen eyes taking in Lily's discomfort.

Lily nodded, holding out her cup, grateful to be taken care of.

Mrs. Abernathy poured the tea and then sat back, her gaze assessing. "I canna help but feel that there's more to the story than what you've told us."

"If there is, then I don't remember it," Lily answered. "I'm afraid everything went a bit hazy after I hit my head." Actually it had gone the way of Alice down the rabbit hole, but she wasn't about to admit that. "So how do you know Valerie?" she asked, trying to shift the conversation away from the talk of last night.

Mrs. Abernathy held her gaze for a moment more, and then smiled. "Actually I met her through your mother."

"You knew my mother?" Lily wondered why Valerie hadn't mentioned the fact. But then decided that if she'd known, she might not have wanted to come. Ghosts of the past and all that.

"Aye. And your father, too," Mrs. Abernathy was saying. "They stayed here once, a long time ago. Just after they were married. Long before you were born." She sat back, taking a sip of her tea. "They were lovely people, your parents."

"Yes, they were. I'm glad you had the chance to know them. But then where does Valerie come into it?" She frowned, trying to put it all together.

"Well, actually she came to stay not long after that. On your mother's recommendation. It was just after her first divorce." Valerie had been married three times. None of them keepers, as she was fond of saying. "I think she needed a friend, and frankly, so did I. Anyway, we bonded over red wine and old American movies."

"And you've kept in touch all these years."

"Aye. She's been here a few more times. And I met her in New York one fall. My grand adventure, Jamie calls it." Mrs. Abernathy smiled, her eyes softening with the memory. "I canna tell you how sorry I was to hear about your parents. But I was glad when you decided to come here. Duncreag is a magical place. You can feel it in the air. If there's anywhere that can soothe your soul, it's here."

"And are Katherine and Iain in residence?" Lily asked, wondering idly what a Scottish laird would look like.

"I beg your pardon?" Mrs. Abernathy asked, her brows drawing together as she frowned.

"Valerie said that the new laird was moving in. Something about an inheritance?"

"Well," Mrs. Abernathy said, tilting her head to one side quizzically, "that much is surely true. But the new laird's name is Jeffrey. Jeffrey St. Claire. 'Tis him and his wife Elaine who've come to live here."

Lily frowned. "I'm sorry. Clearly I've gotten the names wrong. I must have misunderstood." She mentally chided herself for the mistake. Katherine and Iain were the names that Bram had given her. And Bram wasn't real. Which meant, of course, that his Katherine and Iain never existed either.

Again Mrs. Abernathy seemed to be searching her face and Lily struggled not to blurt it all out. It would be so nice to confide in someone. But she was fairly certain that even in the Highlands, a woman spouting tales of disappearing cottages and dark, rugged strangers would result in a call to the nearest psych ward.

"Ach, well, that's easy enough to do." Mrs. Abernathy smiled, but there was still something Lily couldn't quite put a name to reflected in her eyes. "Especially after all that you've been through. Jeffrey and Elaine have gone out for the day. They should be back later this evening."

"Are you certain that I won't be intruding? I mean, Val said they'd only just arrived. They might not want a stranger in their home. Is there another inn somewhere close by?" She actually hated the idea of leaving, but she equally hated the idea of imposing where she wasn't wanted.

"They were delighted to know you were coming. After all, they're only a wee bit older than you. And I expect they'll be happy to have someone their own age about. Mr. Abernathy and I aren't exactly spring chickens."

Lily was fairly certain Agnes Abernathy could keep up with the springiest of spring chickens. "Well, I'll look forward to meeting them, then. And I am happy to be here."

And surprisingly, she realized, she spoke the truth. Despite everything, she was glad she'd come. Glad that she'd wrecked her car. Because if she hadn't, she'd never have found the cottage. And even if it had been a figment of her imagination, she had no regrets.

Bram Macgillivray was more than worth losing a little bit of her sanity. And the memory of their night together—real or imagined—was something she'd always cherish.

Smothering a yawn, Lily pulled her attention back to her hostess. "I'm sorry. I guess I'm a bit more tired than I realized."

"And me going on like a chatterbox," Mrs. Abernathy said. "Let me show you to your room. What you need is a good sleep. Everything will be clearer in the morning. You'll see."

Lily was too tired to ask how Mrs. Abernathy knew there were things that needed to be cleared up. As she followed the older woman up the stairs to her room, she had the crazy thought that maybe Mrs. Abernathy already knew about the cottage.

About Bram.

Although that was hardly possible.

Still, this was the Highlands. And as Mrs. Abernathy had said— there was magic in the air.

"Is she here?" Bram asked, striding into the small room where Katherine was hanging dried herbs.

"Is who here?" Katherine asked as she tied a piece of twine around a bunch of dried leaves. Rosemary, if he was smelling right. His mother had kept a room much like this one, ready with the herbs and poultices she needed to heal various ailments.

"Lily." Bram tried but failed to keep the impatience from his voice. "She said she was coming to see you. And when I couldn't find her this morning, I'd hoped to find her here."

Katherine frowned. "I'm not acquainted with anyone by that name. And as far as I know, no one has arrived today. I think with all the concern over your situation, Fergus would have told me if they had."

Bram dropped into a chair, his heart constricting. "Then where can she be?"

"Where can who be?" Iain Mackintosh's voice filled the room as he entered, Ranald Macqueen following on his heels. Iain was a giant of a man with inky black hair and intelligent eyes. There was little he missed. And nothing he couldn't handle. Especially when he was with

Ranald. The two men had been best friends since they were just wee boys and Bram counted their kinship among his most cherished.

"Bram seems to have lost someone important," Katherine said, crossing over to her husband.

The joy reflected on both of their faces made Bram's heart twist even more. Before last night he would have admired their commitment. Maybe even been envious of their obvious devotion. But it now...now he had some inkling of how powerful their love really was. And how rare.

"I'm so glad you're back." She rose on tiptoe to kiss him, her arms sliding around his neck.

"I was only gone a few days." Iain's laughter filled the room. "But I missed you as well."

Ranald cleared his throat. "Not that I dinna appreciate the fact that the two of you canna stand being parted, but I think we have more pressing matters to deal with."

"Aye," Iain said, his arm still around his wife. "We came as soon as we got Katherine's message."

"Is Ailis not with you?" Katherine asked.

"Nay," Ranald said. "She's with my mother. She's no' been well, and Ailis wanted to stay until she's feeling better."

Bram's Aunt Ealasaid had always been a favorite and he hated to hear that she was unwell. "Is it something to worry about?" he asked.

"Nay." Ranald shook his head. "She's only caught a wee chill. But Ailis insisted on staying."

"Well then, your mother is a lucky woman. She'll be in good hands with Ailis." Katherine smiled.

"That she will," Ranald agreed. "But of course it means you'll have to suffer my presence here. I canna imagine going back to *Tur nan Clach* without her." It was no secret that Ranald wasn't as fond of his wife's holding as he was of the lady herself.

"So tell me, then," Iain said, his gaze moving to Bram, "who is this woman you have managed to lose?"

"I dinna know much about her, really. Her name is Lily," Bram said, leaning forward on a sigh. "And I found her by my fire last night. She got caught in the storm. Soaked to the skin, she was. With a knot on her head the size of a bannock. I took her in. And I took care of her."

Ranald covered his mouth with his hand and smothered a laugh.

Bram shot him a quelling look, and at least his cousin had the good sense to look chagrinned. "'Twas no' like that. She was hurt and she needed my help."

Actually Ranald was right, but he wasn't about to admit it. God's truth, he'd taken advantage of Lily, there was no getting around it. Which might explain why she'd run away. But he'd be damned if he'd let her go so easily.

"So when you woke this morning she was gone?" Iain asked, obviously sensing the note of desperation in Bram's voice.

"Nay. She was there. Sleeping. So I went to get more wood for the fire. And then I heard her call for me. Or at least I thought I did. But when I got back to the cottage, she was gone."

"Poof," Ranald said, snapping his fingers. "Like a fairy."

"That's no' funny," Bram snapped. "Something could have happened to her."

"I know, lad. I'm no' making sport of your plight. 'Tis just that the three of us have had some experience with the fairies." He shot a smile at Katherine, who blushed as Iain grinned.

"Well, if you're saying that I'm imagining her, I can prove otherwise." Bram reached into his sporran, removing a piece of folded leather. "I have her slipper. She left it in the cottage." He held it out and Iain took it.

"'Tis very fine." He frowned, staring at something on the inside of the sole. "There's something written here. To-ry Burch," he read, then looked down at his wife. "Do these words mean something to you?"

Katherine took the slipper from her husband as if needing to see the words for herself. Then with a quiet nod, she sat down, the color draining from her face. "It's a name. A woman who designs shoes."

Ranald and Bram moved closer, the four of them staring down at the leather slipper in Katherine's hand. Bram's stomach was churning. Something in Katherine's face made Ranald's talk of fairies seem suddenly less offhand.

"And this woman," Iain said, his gaze moving to his wife's, "this designer——" He stumbled a bit over the word. "——is she from your world?"

"Yes." Katherine nodded, handing the slipper back to Iain. "She is."

"Which means, cousin o' mine," Ranald said, this time his voice somber, "that your Lily is no' of our world either. Which goes a long way to explaining why she simply seems to have disappeared."

CHAPTER 7

✦

"SO YOU'RE TELING me that Katherine—your wife—is no' from our time." Bram drew in a deep breath and released it. Just saying the words out loud seemed ludicrous.

"Aye." Iain shrugged. They'd moved from Katherine's keeping room to the great hall and were sitting on the benches by the fire. Iain's arm was around Katherine. "We dinna know the how or the why of it, but 'tis the truth."

"Ach, come now, man," Ranald said. "You know the why of it." He turned this attention to Bram. "Their love binds them together. It was the strength of it that pulled Katherine through to our time."

Bram's head was reeling. Their tale was as fanciful as any he'd ever heard, and yet, looking at the two of them, he knew it had to be true. Some of it he'd even heard himself. He'd known that her appearance had seemingly come out of nowhere, and that some of the people who'd met her doubted the story of her coming from France.

But no one dared force the issue. Not with Iain.

And Katherine was well loved by the Mackintoshes. Not much chance of anyone taking issue with her supposed history when she had all of Clan Chattan behind her. And besides, those who'd met her had nothing but good to say. She was a strong woman, a perfect match for Iain.

And here he was again thinking about love and marriage as if it were important to him. Two days ago he'd have laughed at the notion. But now...

"So did this Lily say anything that made you think she dinna belong here?" Ranald was asking.

They hadn't done that much talking. But he wasn't about to share that, not even with his cousins. "There were words that were a bit odd. She told me she wasna from the Highlands, but somewhere far away. Conn-ec-ti-cut, I think she called it."

"It's a state," Katherine said. "In America. And you wouldn't have heard of it. It won't exist for another two hundred years or so."

"Were you from Connecticut, too, then?" he asked, still trying to wrap his mind around the enormity of what they were saying.

"No." She shook her head. "At least not anymore. I was living in New York. But it's nearby."

"But York is in England," Bram said, his tone suspicious.

"Seems in this new world, they're keen on using old names." Iain shrugged again, as if it was nothing at all to be talking about a future that was yet to exist. But then again he'd no doubt had practice.

"Anyway," Ranald inserted, bringing them back to topic, "the point is that if your Lily is from the future, she's most likely been pulled back there again. Just like Katherine was the first time she met Iain."

"And how long was it before you were together again?" Bram asked, not certain that he wanted to hear the answer.

"Eight years," Katherine and Iain said almost in unison. The two of them smiled at each other, but Bram grimaced.

"Bloody hell. How did you stand it then?" Bram fought against frustration.

"They didn't," Ranald offered with a wry grimace. "At least not easily. Iain refused to consider any other woman even though he feared she'd only been a figment of his imagination."

"And my brother, Jeff," Katherine offered, "always called Iain my fantasy man. He was convinced I'd made him up."

"Jeff was the one who came here to find you?" Bram asked, remembering the story they'd told.

"Yes." Katherine's eyes grew misty, and Iain squeezed her hand. "We were really close."

"But now, you're here," Bram said. "And nothing is going to pull you away again?"

"No." Again the two of them answered as one.

"How can you be sure?" he asked.

"Because they share one heart," Ranald answered for them.

"We had to overcome a great many obstacles to be together. But we never doubted our love," Katherine said.

"And when did you know for sure?" Bram thought again of Lily and the powerful connection they'd shared. "That you were meant to be together?"

"From the first moment he touched me," Katherine said. "I never forgot. Even with all the time we were apart." She twined her fingers through Iain's. "And here we are. Just like any other old married couple."

Ranald snorted.

"I'd watch who you're mocking," Iain said. "I seem to remember a certain silver-haired lass bowling you over with merely a smile."

"I'll no' argue with that," Ranald acquiesced. "I make no' secret o' the fact that I adore my wife. But she happens to hail from our very own century—which doesn't make as interesting a tale."

"So you think that Lily will come back to me?" Bram asked, hating the pleading note in his voice. "For I have the notion that she's taken my heart with her back to this Connecticut."

"I canna say anything for certain," Iain said, "except that the heart is a powerful thing. And what it wants canna be easily put aside. Even when separated by the boundaries of time."

Bram nodded, feeling a stirring of hope and fear.

"Perhaps 'tis best that she's no' here now," Ranald said. "With your father dead, and your enemies hunting you, she'd surely be in danger."

Again Katherine and Iain exchanged a look.

"You're thinking of Alisdair," Ranald said.

"Aye." Iain nodded. "May the bastard rot in hell."

"But we survived," Katherine said, her fingers tightening around Iain's. "And so shall you, Bram. And with luck you'll find your Lily as well." She stood up. "I'll leave you now. I know you have important things to discuss."

The men stood.

"You're a lucky man, Iain," Bram said as he watched her walk away.

"Ach, don't I know it." They sat again, and Iain leaned forward. "But Katherine's right. We need to talk. What happened at Dunbrae?"

Bram told them everything that had transpired. About his father's death. The Comyns. And the idea of a traitor in their midst.

"What have you heard?" Bram asked, after finishing his tale.

"You're no' going to like it," Ranald said, his grim expression foreboding.

"Tell me."

"They're saying you were the traitor." Iain's expression was inscrutable, and Bram felt anger rising. "That you were the one who killed your father."

"They lie," Bram rose to his feet, reaching for his dirk.

Ranald held out a hand in supplication. "Of course they do. The question being who exactly *they* are."

"It has to be the Comyns," Bram insisted. "They're our closest enemy. And Alec Comyn would gain much by taking our holding."

"Dunbrae wasn't taken, Bram," Iain said. "If it was Comyn, it wasn't because he wanted the tower."

"Then why the attack?" Bram asked.

"I dinna know." Ranald shrugged. "But revenge seems the most likely explanation. Had your father done something to anger the man?"

"Not that he told me. But I'd only just arrived, and there had no' been much time for talking. If he dinna take the tower, then are my father's men in charge again?" His thoughts turned to Frazier and Robby.

"Nay." Iain's eyes were filled with regret. "There were no survivors."

Rage threatened to overcome him, and Bram's fingers closed around the dirk, the faces of his friends running through his mind. "I swear on my life, Alec Comyn will die for this."

"You know I'll stand with you," Iain said. "But you must also know that Comyn is denying his involvement. And for the moment, your great uncle has chosen to believe him."

"Because he values peace over his own kin." His words echoed his earlier conversation with Katherine. But it was the truth.

"You know as well as I do that there was no love lost between your father and the Macgillivray chief." Iain's tone was firm but there was a note of sympathy as well. "And though the holding 'tis a bonny one, 'tis of no strategic significance to the clan."

"Well, surely he canna hold with the notion that I killed my father. We were no' at odds. And besides, as I said, I'd only just returned to Dunbrae."

"True enough. But you wouldn't be the first son to grow restless playing second fiddle." Ranald wasn't trying to goad him, but Bram reacted anyway, his tone harsher than he'd intended.

"But 'tis no' true." He drew a breath and forced himself to calm. Nothing was gained in losing control. He was among family. Family he could trust. Iain and Ranald would help him. Of that he was most certain. "If I had killed my father, why then would I have run? The tower was taken. I surely would have stayed to celebrate the victory." The words choked him, but it was still a point well made.

"I agree." Iain nodded. "There is much to the story that doesn't ring true."

"But Ian Ciar believes the lies."

"Your great uncle hears what he wants to hear." Ranald shrugged.

"Right now, emotions are holding sway," Iain said. "Anger and fear are ruling the day."

"And so now I am hunted not only by my enemies but by my kin as well?"

"We heard nothing that would indicate that the Macgillivray is taking action against you," Iain was quick to assure.

"But we heard nothing to the contrary either," Ranald added. "And in light of the accusations against you, Malcolm petitioned your great uncle for Dunbrae."

"Which he, no doubt, granted." Bram blew out a frustrated breath. There was a long history of anger between Bram's uncle Malcolm and his father. And their uncle, Ian Ciar, had always favored Malcolm.

"Aye. He did," Iain said, anger sparking in his eyes.

"Then my great uncle believes I'm a traitor." Bram fisted his hands. "And what of Moy? Does your uncle think I am a killer?"

Iain sighed, his expression apologetic. "My uncle has more important matters to deal with. He's been called to Stirling to meet with the king. There's talk of a marriage between James and Margaret of Denmark. James is seeking support from the chieftains."

"Support he's no' likely to get," Ranald mumbled.

"So I'm on my own, then," Bram said, not surprised. Great men were interested only in the things that made them greater. And his father's holding was but a small one on the far edge of both the Macgillivray and Chattan lands. And, as Iain had said, the remote mountain valley was of little strategic use.

"Nay, you're no' alone," Iain said, his tone commanding. "You've got the two of us and the men under our command."

He kissed her neck and then the hollow between her breasts. Lily sucked in a breath, his touch sending shards of electricity arcing through her. Slowly, so very slowly, his lips caressed her skin, moving up the soft slope of her breast to pull the nipple into his mouth.

Her body contracted as he tugged, desire threatening to tear her apart. "You're real," she whispered, her heart singing with the realization. Bram was real. She arched upward, wanting more. Wanting him...

But suddenly the room faded and he was gone. Instead she stood high on a rocky precipice looking down into a narrow gorge. The wind whipped through her hair, its frigid breath leaving her uneasy. Across the way in the distance she could see Duncreag, the stone walls white in the pale moonlight, mere extensions of the rock surrounding them. From this vantage point it was easy to imagine its former grandeur.

The gorge below was narrow, carved by an ancient river perhaps. The path, such that it was, veered upward sharply toward the fortress, a series of switchbacks climbing up the mountain, carefully designed so that travel would be truly safe only with the cover of night. It was barely wide enough for a single horse to pass.

An odd way to think of it, but even before she could complete the thought she saw them. Riders. A dozen or more. Unease turned to fear. Somehow she knew, even without being told, that these were not friends, their intent anything but benign.

Her mind flashed back to Bram. He'd said that his enemies would come after him. And somehow in her heart she was certain that these were those men. Some still sane part of her mind knew that she was dreaming. That this was simply an extension of her fantasy. But somewhere deep in her soul she was equally certain that the danger was real. She had to get to Bram to warn him.

She looked beyond the gorge, out across the valley, a ribbon of silver marking the path of the river. But there was no light where the cottage should be. Nothing to indicate that he was there. Perhaps he had gone to Duncreag. Her gaze moved back to the tower. In this light it looked invincible.

But no one knew there was danger.

She tried to take a step, realizing only then that she was nothing more than a spirit. A wisp of nothing. She was here and yet she wasn't. Her heart cried out. She needed to find him. To warn him. Real or fantasy, she needed him to live. To survive. If only so they could find each other in their dreams.

The men below continued on, winding their way higher, their movements cloaked by the darkness and the sound of the wind as it whistled through the gorge. Above her, the tower was dark, stark against the sky. It was late, the inhabitants most likely sleeping in their beds. Which meant that Bram would be caught unaware.

She screamed, but if she had a voice, the wind whipped it away. Was this a punishment then? Another death to carry in her heart? How had he come to mean so much to her in so little time?

Clearly she was insane. The smack on her head must have caused real damage because here she was standing on an imaginary cliff, in some imaginary time, frightened for a man that had probably never even existed.

Below her a horse whinnied, and something clicked shut.

69

The sound was incongruous with the scene below her. And the gorge began to fade...

Lily jerked awake, her heart pounding. A tiny stream of moonlight shone from a thin opening between the drapes covering the mullioned window. Duncreag. She was safe. In her room. Relief warred with disappointment.

There were no invaders. It had been only a dream.

All of it, the little voice in her mind insisted.

She ran a finger across her bottom lip, remembering his touch, and shivered, suddenly cold. Then she heard a footstep and turned toward the dark part of the room. The shadows were deep. But she was certain she was not alone. Something had awoken her.

She blinked, trying to focus, but suddenly everything shimmered, as if a mist had descended, the room growing hazy. Then as quickly as it had come, it was gone and her vision cleared. She frowned into the darkness. The room was the same, and yet it wasn't. The window was deeper. Arched. And the bed was larger. More primitive.

And then he stepped into the sliver of moonlight.

Bram.

"Lily?" he asked, his eyes widening with surprise. "How did you get in here?"

She shook her head, unable to find words. But she held out her hands, and he was across the room in two strides, pulling her into his arms as he sank down onto the bed. "I thought I'd never see you again. When I came back this morning, you were gone. I was half out of my mind. I feared my enemies had found you."

He pushed her hair back from her face, his gaze locking with hers.

"I woke up and you weren't there," she whispered. "So I got dressed and came to find you. But before I could, the cottage disappeared." Her eyes pricked with tears and the memory. "It was gone, Bram. Nothing left but a pile of stones. I thought I'd gone crazy."

"Nay, you're no' daft, we're just part of something beyond our ability to ken. Somehow your world and mine have intersected."

"I don't understand..."

"Neither do I, *mo ghràidh*." He kissed her then, the fear in her stomach changing to something more primitive. Imaginary or no, she wanted this man. And if that meant a life lived in half worlds, then so be it.

The kiss deepened as he demanded more, and she opened her mouth, surrendering herself to him, knowing that at any moment the dream—if indeed that's what this was—might end.

His hands skimmed across the soft cotton of her nightgown, and she pressed herself closer, reveling in the feel of his lips as they moved against hers. He pushed her back onto the bed, straddling her, the hunger in his eyes stoking the passion raging within her.

"God's blood, I've never wanted a woman the way that I want you. 'Tis as if I've known you forever and still I canna get enough. Have you bewitched me, then?"

She smiled, her lips trembling with emotion. "Whatever is happening, it's happening to us both," she said, reaching for him.

The wind whipped against the window, the howling reminding her of her dream—if this could be counted as reality. Suddenly she was frightened again, and Bram must have seen it in her eyes. He moved to pull her into his lap, concern overriding his hunger.

"What is it, lass? What troubles you?"

She swallowed a bubble of hysteria. That was the sixty-four thousand dollar question. But she knew the most pressing thing was to warn him of what she'd seen. Even if she couldn't explain how she'd actually been able to see it.

She sucked in a deep breath. In for the penny, in for the pound. "There are men in the gorge. Here. Below Duncreag."

"How do you know that?"

"I saw them from the top of the ridge. They were on horseback. At least a dozen. They were using the darkness as cover. Oh, God, Bram, I think they're coming for you."

"But how could you possibly have seen them?"

"I don't know. One minute I was dreaming that you and I were..." She stopped, ducking her head, hot color staining her face, but then she shook her head, pressing on. "...together, then you just faded away and I was standing on the cliff. Only I wasn't really there. It was like I was floating or something. I could see, but I couldn't do anything."

"And that's when you saw the men?" He was listening now, his mind clearly moving to the threat at hand.

"Yes. They were going slowly. And silently. They were dressed oddly, too. In kilts with blankets or something." For a moment she stopped, taking in his attire. A roughly woven linen shirt and a kilt that wrapped around his waist and twisted up over his shoulder. "They were dressed like you."

"The same colors?" he asked, his gaze probing.

"I couldn't see. They were too deep in the shadows. But the pattern was different from yours. Bigger maybe. If that makes sense."

"Aye. I'm afraid it does. Can you tell me exactly where you were?"

"I can't say for positive. I haven't really seen much of Duncreag yet. But the gorge was to the left of the tower. I could see it high on the opposite ridge to my right. There was a large outcropping of rock. Almost like a ledge. Do you know it?"

"Aye, that I do. 'Tis the entrance to the tower. Iain has men at the gate, but they'll no' be expecting intruders at this hour."

The fear she'd felt while standing on the ridge rose again. "They're on their way now. I can feel it. You have to go. You need to warn Iain."

"But I canna leave you."

She could see the flash of worry cross his face. "I'll be fine."

"What if I lose you again?" Pain crested in his eyes. How in the world had they come to this place so quickly?

"You can't lose me," she whispered, reaching up to caress his face. "I'll always be right here." She touched his chest and he covered her hand with his. "Now go."

He sat for a moment, still holding her hand as it lay against his chest, indecision warring. And then as if something else had taken control, the room started to shimmer again.

"Lily." Bram reached for her, but she could barely feel his touch.

"Go," she urged again. "Please. Protect yourself."

"I willna let you go," he whispered fiercely, even as he started to fade from her sight. "I promise you that."

As if in defiance of the words, the room flickered once and he was gone.

Lily closed her eyes and slowly opened them again. The moonlight still cut a swath across the floor and she recognized her suitcase in the corner. There was no longer a sense of danger, but she still felt a chill work its way up her spine.

Whatever door between worlds had opened, it had closed tightly again.

And be it real or fantasy, she was certain that her heart lay on the other side.

CHAPTER 8

✦

"YOU'RE SURE THAT Lilly was right?" Iain asked as they held their horses at the top of the gorge.

"Aye. She was certain. And afraid for us. If nothing else convinces me, that would."

"Then we advance." Iain waved his men on, and Bram marveled at how much faith Iain had in his word. It had only been hours before when he'd woken his cousin to tell him of Lily's warning. And all credit to Iain, he'd not questioned the demand, instead acting immediately, without doubt.

The night was dark save for the waning moon and the twinkle of stars in the sky. The wind moved restlessly through the canyon and Bram sat his mount, waiting.

Below, the valley was quiet. But silence was deceptive, and as they waited, beyond the dark, they heard the whinny of a horse. Lily had been right.

Bram looked to Iain, waiting his command. Behind him, he felt the restless energy of Iain's men.

"Wait for it," Ranald whispered, and somehow the night came to life.

"Now," Iain cried, and the horses leapt forward.

Bram had been in battle before but not in such close quarters and never when the stakes were so high. The screams, both horses and men, echoed off the walls of the gorge.

He brought his claymore down against the weapon of an enemy, the contact ringing through his arm, pain singing through his brain. The man fell, but another threatened just beyond, and again Bram swung his weapon—two-handed, the blade cutting deep into the man's gut.

With a surge of superhuman strength, he pulled the claymore free and pivoted to take on the next man, ducking to avoid the blow. Beyond the shadows he could see Iain and Ranald fighting, their blades flashing in the moonlight. These men were fighting for him. And whatever happened this night, the consequences fell on him.

The moon slipped beneath a cloud.

Ranald let loose a bloodthirsty cry and Iain's men surged forward, having the advantage of knowing the gorge, even in the dark. Bram allowed himself to be led forward, still using his claymore to fend off attack.

Ahead, the canyon narrowed even more, gnarled branches arching overhead, intertwining like bony fingers. Behind him, Bram heard something clatter and he turned in anticipation, but his horse shied with the movement, rearing up and braying in fright.

He clung to the reins, fighting for control, and for a moment, he thought he'd managed to maintain his seat. But then he was flying, landing hard against the rocky floor of the gorge. His horse reared again, the hooves coming perilously close to his head. How ironic it would be to die here under the feet of his own steed.

Still dizzy from the fall, Bram gathered his wits and rolled from beneath the horse, pushing to his feet, scrambling to maintain hold on his sword. From out of the shadows, a man's face loomed as he leaned low over his horse's shoulder. His feral gaze cut into Bram's as he raised his claymore, ready for the kill.

But Bram was faster, swinging his blade in an arc over his head.

Their swords met once and Bram swung again. Around him, he could hear the sounds of others battling, but he forced his focus onto the man in front of him. His enemy's claymore sliced through the air again. But Bram pivoted, the blow glancing off of his sword. And then a second man surged out of the dark, this one on foot, dirk in one hand, claymore in the other. Bram backed away as he tried to figure out which man to attack first. The one on the horse or the one on foot.

They both looked equally lethal. And though he had no doubt he could take one, he was not as certain of taking them both.

The man on foot charged, and the decision was taken from his hands. Bram swung the claymore, satisfied when it made contact, but the blow was only a glancing one.

His assailant swung his sword, plunging the knife forward at the same time. Bram countered with his own weapon, the impact sending both of them backwards. Seeing that his friend had failed, the horseman lunged forward. But Bram managed to catch his arm with the tip of his blade. Blood spurted through the horseman's shirt, and he cried out in rage.

Bram twisted to avoid the man's claymore and thrust his sword upward, satisfied as he felt contact. The man fell from his horse, sightless eyes looking up into the night sky. But before Bram had the chance to feel relief, the second man rushed forward again, leading with his claymore.

He swung hard, and though Bram deflected the blow, the impact sent his claymore flying. Seeing that, for the moment at least, he had the upper hand, the man raised his dirk, closing in for the kill. Bram scrambled for his sword as the man swung the knife, but then Ranald was there, and his blade sank deep.

The man fell next to his friend and Bram grabbed his claymore, turning first to the right and then to the left, searching for another threat as Ranald wheeled his horse around, doing the same. But the fight was over, the Mackintosh men winning the day.

"You saved my life," Bram said to Ranald as he gathered his horse's reins and pulled himself back into the saddle again.

"Aye, that I did. But you'd have done the same for me." Ranald grinned, pumping a fist in the air. "Looks like we've sent the bastards straight to hell."

After the whooping of success settled, Iain pulled his mount close to Bram's. "We're blessed that your woman warned us." He reined in his horse. "I have no doubt that we would have prevailed, but with her warning we suffered no loss of life. And you're still in one piece."

"Which is of little importance to anyone but me, at the end of the day." Bram grimaced, gingerly rolling his injured shoulder.

"And mayhap your Lily," Iain said, his smile guarded.

"I canna complain that we have routed our enemy," Ranald said, reining in his horse, "but we've also managed to kill them all. Which means we canna question them to find out who the traitor might be. Did you recognize any of the riders?"

"Nay." Bram shook his head. "But they wear the Comyn colors."

"That they do," Iain said, "but none have the look of a Comyn. They're known for their wild black hair."

"But not all of them share that trait," Bram protested. "And the plaids dinna lie."

"We canna know for certain," Iain said. "'Tis possible they're Comyns but we've had firsthand experience with men wearing colors that were no' their own."

"I canna disagree, cousin," Ranald said, "but despite the fact that they dinna have the look of the Comyns, we canna dismiss this." He opened his hand, a silver brooch glimmering in the pale light.

"God's blood." The words came out before Bram could stop them. "My father's crest."

Silence stretched across the gorge.

"In truth, I suppose some part of me wanted to believe that this wasna happening. That the events at Dunbrae were somehow limited to a location, a moment in time. That no one was truly after me."

"I'm afraid you've no' the luxury of allowing yourself that fantasy," Ranald said. "Whatever happened at Dunbrae, the ramifications have spread. If for no other reason than because you live."

"Then I have brought danger to your door," Bram said, his stomach churning.

"We're cousins, are we not?" Ranald asked, his tone carrying his disbelief. "Nay, more like brothers. So, unless I'm no' understanding, your enemy is mine."

"Aye, 'tis true," Iain agreed, and Bram felt a weakness he was loathe to admit. These were his brothers as truly as they had been born to him. He did them disservice to have doubted.

"So what happens now?" Bram asked, not sure what the next step should be, but knowing that if he were going to survive, he needed to take a stand.

~

Lily shivered as she stared out at the dark mountains surrounding Duncreag. Unable to sleep after her encounter with Bram, she'd followed the staircases up until she'd emerged onto the rooftop of the tower. Surrounded by crenelated edges and holes cut through the stone that must have been for dropping God knows what on an attacking enemy, the floor was made of hewn stone. Despite the precipitous drop below, the view was quite stunning.

Stars twinkled in the sky. And a few lights winked in the distant fields and mountains. Signs that she was not alone. At least not in a literal sense. Still, she couldn't shake the feeling that she'd lost something more precious than even her parents. Although just entertaining the thought seemed sacrilegious. She was choosing a fantasy over the people she claimed to have loved most.

Her fingers closed on the cool silver of the wedding ring. Her parents would have wanted her to be happy. Of that she was certain. They wouldn't have wanted her to drown in her grief. Or to let it drive her crazy.

She smiled at the thought, knowing somewhere deep in her heart that there was an explanation. Maybe not a logical one. But at least something real. She glanced down at the ragged cliff edges below, her mind trailing back to the vision, or whatever the hell it had been, of men climbing the narrow fissure, primed for attack.

There were no sounds carrying on the breeze, save for the whispering trees. No horses, no battle cries. No stronghold gate. Bram had mentioned that Iain kept men on guard.

But there was no gate. At least not here. Not now.

And no Iain either.

She tilted back her head, letting the cool night air soothe her. Maybe she'd been wrong to come. Maybe she was too fragile. Maybe Mrs. Abernathy was right and she should see a doctor.

Behind her a loose stone rattled, and she spun around, heart pounding, praying that it was Bram.

But instead a woman emerged.

"I'm sorry," she said, holding up a hand in apology. "I didn't know anyone was up here." Her voice was deep, with just the slightest hint of a brogue.

"No." Lily shook her head. "I'm the one that should apologize. I don't even know if guests are allowed up here."

The woman smiled, her eyes crinkling at the corners with the movement of her lips. She was tall and curvy, her hair winking copper in the light from the doorway. In full light of day she was probably a beauty. But now, here in the moonlight, her expression was open and friendly. "You must be Lily." She crossed the parapet and held out her hand. "I'm Elaine Macqueen. Or rather Elaine St. Claire. I'm still getting used to that part." Her smile widened.

"Congratulations," Lily said, taking the other woman's hand. Her grip was strong and sure. "Mrs. Abernathy said that you were only recently married."

"Aye. And now with the honeymoon behind me, I'm a married lady." Together they walked back to the edge of the rooftop, both of them looking out into the night.

"And the owner of Duncreag," Lily said, her gaze sweeping the darkened panorama. "That must feel amazing."

"Actually it's a bit overwhelming," Elaine admitted. "Which explains the midnight sojourn. Jeff doesn't worry as much as I do. He sees the magnificence and ignores all the things that cry out for fixing."

"I'd imagine a place like this isn't easy to maintain."

"No. And it's even more overwhelming to think about paying for it." Elaine sighed.

"Then why do it? I mean, you only just found out that your husband inherited, right? So you don't have to keep the place."

"Ah, but we do. It's a family thing. And honestly, I can't imagine being anywhere else. So we'll manage. It's not as if we're totally destitute. I just worry about the details. Part and parcel of being an attorney, I guess."

"Right. Mrs. Abernathy mentioned that, too. But will you be able to practice here?" Mrs. Abernathy had explained earlier that Jeff and Elaine were both Americans.

"Actually, it is possible. I have dual citizenship. My father was originally from Inverness." Which explained the hint of an accent. "I was born here before we moved to the States. So I still have my passport. All I'd have to do is pass the equivalent of the bar here. But for now, I think I'll just be concentrating on Duncreag."

"But doesn't Mrs. Abernathy do that?" The question was out before Lily could stop herself. It really wasn't her business but it did seem that Agnes Abernathy and her Jamie loved the place dearly.

"Of course." Elaine smiled again. "I can't imagine life here without her. Or Jamie either for that matter. They still handle the day-to-day things. And of course the hotel. But I'll be dealing with restoration issues. And believe me, there are more than enough to keep me occupied."

As if to echo the sentiment, a loose stone fell from the battlement onto the rocks below.

"Still, it's stunning, isn't it?" Lily said, her gaze moving back to the surrounding mountains.

"It is." Elaine nodded. "And even more so when you think of all the people who've stood here before us. Same tower. Same magnificent view." She shivered, wrapping her arms around her waist.

"Are you cold?" Lily queried.

"No. Only thinking about a friend I've lost. Being up here reminds me of her. She wasn't fond of heights. But she loved it here."

"She's dead, then?" Lily sighed.

"Yes, I suppose she is. Although I still have trouble thinking about it that way. I miss her every day."

It was an odd answer surely, but Lily understood the sentiment. "I know what you mean. I miss my parents, too."

"Oh God, I'd forgotten." Elaine reached for Lily's hands. "I'm so sorry. Mrs. Abernathy told me your parents were lovely people. I shouldn't have been talking about my own losses."

"Nonsense," Lily said, squeezing her fingers, feeling like she'd found a new friend. "It was nice to share with someone. Grief is a funny thing. It isn't quantifiable. And people who haven't suffered through it have no idea how to comfort those who have. So it's nice to know you truly understand. Although of course I wish you didn't have to."

They turned and looked out into the valley again, stars winking overhead.

"Was that the original gate?" Lily asked, pointing to the shadowed tumble of stone and the half arch that marked what she assumed had been the entrance to the tower in past times.

"Yes." Elaine nodded. "Just beside the road. Although of course that didn't exist at all when Duncreag was a fortress. In those days, I'm told, there was a pathway that wound up from the river to the tower through that crevice there." She pointed. "You can just make it out in the moonlight."

It was Lily's turn to shiver. "And it was narrow. Only wide enough for horsemen to pass one in front of the other."

"Yes." Elaine tilted her head, her gaze on Lily now. "But how did you know that?"

"I must have read it somewhere." She shrugged, her mind's eye bringing forth a vision of riders making their way stealthily up the steep canyon. "But there were guards, surely. At the gate."

"Aye. But Duncreag was part of the federation that was Clan Chattan and so it wasn't threatened often. I expect the guards were only perfunctory unless there was an imminent threat." Elaine paused, seeming to consider her words. "Mrs. Abernathy said that you mentioned Iain and Katherine."

Lily blinked in surprise. "I, ah, don't know where I heard the names. Maybe I read about them?"

"Maybe." Elaine nodded. "But you'd have to be quite the scholar. I know they're not mentioned in any of the brochures."

"Still," Lily said, scrambling for something to appease her new friend—something besides the truth, "I obviously heard of them somewhere or I wouldn't have mistaken them for you and Jeff. But honestly, I don't know where. The innkeeper in Inverness was very talkative. Maybe he's the one who mentioned them?"

Or maybe her imaginary lover had told her. But that didn't seem the kind of information that would cement a new friendship.

Elaine studied her for a moment longer and then smiled. "Would you like to meet them? Katherine and Iain, I mean?"

Lily's heart started to pound. If they were indeed real, then that meant that Bram...

"Follow me," Elaine said, cutting into her tumbling thoughts. "I'll show you."

CHAPTER 9

ELAINE LED HER to a large parlor on the second floor.

The room was sunny, faded tapestries decorating two walls, a huge stone fireplace centered on the third. Like the rest of the main tower, the room, though comfortable, echoed with traces of its past.

"This would have been the ladies' solar in medieval times," Elaine said, reading her mind. "Sometimes I fancy I can see them here. Laughing and talking. Sewing their tapestries." Again there was an edge of sadness in her voice.

"You're thinking of your friend again." Lily crossed the room to lay a comforting hand on Elaine's arm.

"I suppose I am. She was a bit dotty about all things medieval." She smiled at the thought, her face brightening. "She was a scholar. Specializing in medieval British history. So this place was like walking into the past. A bit of a miracle, I suppose. Anyway, we're not here to relive the past...or at least not the recent past."

She motioned toward the wall behind Lily, and she turned to see that it was lined with paintings. Some of them were enormous. Stern faces peered out from the gilded frames—captured there in pigment upon canvas for all time.

Lily shivered.

"They're over here." Elaine gestured. "It's actually one of the oldest paintings we have on display."

It was smaller than some of the others. And more rustically paint-ed. As if the artist hadn't quite the skill of some of the later works. Still, it captured the images nicely—a man and a woman, arms linked, her hand resting on the crook of his elbow. She was smiling up at him, blue eyes shining and even through the darkened paint, Lily could feel her joy.

A painted sun lit her golden hair, and the man's eyes feasted upon her beauty. He was large and fierce, even in repose. And the shirt he wore reminded her of Bram's. Coarse yellowed linen. His plaid was similar as well, although she thought the pattern was dif-ferent. Still, he wore it in much the same way, twisted about his waist and thrown across his shoulder, his dark hair blowing in an invisible breeze.

"They're beautiful," Lily whispered, her breath catching in her throat.

"Yes, they are." Elaine's voice had grown soft. "And so very happy. You can actually feel it, I think. Katherine loved Iain very much. And to hear it told, he loved her as well."

Again an odd turn of phrase, but Lily was distracted by the emo-tion captured on their faces. Elaine was right; the love radiated from the painting. For a moment, Lily allowed herself simply to bask in the beauty. And then the enormity of it hit her. This was Katherine and Iain. And this was the oldest painting in the tower.

"You said the painting was old." Lily choked out the words, her gaze still locked on the couple.

"Yes." Elaine nodded, watching her now. "It dates back to the late fifteenth century. A rare portrait for the times."

"The fifteenth century," Lily mouthed, her head spinning now as Bram's voice echoed in her ears.

"Iain has men at the gate." Present tense. But it couldn't be.

Again she heard his voice. "*Your world and mine have intersected.*" But that was insane. Completely and totally insane.

"Elaine, was there another Iain?" She forced out the words, closing her eyes, her stomach churning as a cold sweat washed across her skin.

"I'm sure there must have been, somewhere along the line," Elaine said. "But not another laird. Iain was the first and only."

Lily stumbled forward, fighting the dizziness that threatened to consume her. Elaine's arm slid around her shoulders, helping her to stay steady. "And were there Macgillivrays?" she asked. "Could one of them have been friends with Iain and Katherine, do you think?"

If Elaine thought the question odd, she gave no clue to it. "Aye, more than friends. Family of a sort. I don't know the history as well as Mrs. Abernathy, but I do recollect some of it and there was a man called Brian or Bran or something like that. He was Iain's cousin and also a cousin of my ancestor Ranald."

"Oh God..." Lily said, her voice trailing off as blackness threatened.

"Here now." Elaine's arm tightened as she led Lily to a sofa, helping her down. "You look as if you've seen a ghost."

Lily laughed, the sound bordering on hysteria.

"Is everything all right?" a deep voice queried as a man walked into the room. His blond hair was tousled, no doubt from sleep, but his eyes widened in alarm as he took in the two of them. "I woke up and you were gone."

"I couldn't sleep and I didn't want to wake you, darling," Elaine said, looking up at her husband. "But then I ran into Lily and I'm afraid I've upset her."

"No." Lily shook her head, trying to regain focus, but it felt as if she were clawing her way through molasses. "Not you." It was so much more.

"Then perhaps your head," Elaine said, kneeling beside her to push back the hair covering the bandage. "Mrs. Abernathy said it was a nasty bump."

Jeff knelt on her other side, reaching for her wrist to check her pulse. "You're freezing cold," he said, his blue eyes filled with concern. "Were you out on the roof?"

She nodded, closing her eyes as Elaine pressed gentle fingers against her wound.

"But she was fine." Elaine sounded so apologetic that Lily wanted to assure her that everything was okay. But then again it wasn't. Not really.

"Her pulse is strong," Jeff said. "But maybe we should call a doctor."

"No." Her voice was sharp and thready and sounded as if it were coming from far away. "It's not my head. Or at least I don't think it is." She forced her eyes open and found herself staring into Jeff's worried face. And for a moment she was transported back to the painting.

The golden hair. The bright blue eyes. The shape of the mouth and cheekbones.

"Oh, God," she whispered, her head threatening to explode. "You look just like her. You look like Katherine."

Jeff frowned, still holding her hand. "Well, of course I do. She's my sis..." He stopped mid-word, a look of regret chasing across his handsome face.

"Your sister," Lily finished for him. Not sure if she was elated or terrified. Probably both. But at least she wasn't alone. If Katherine was really Jeff's sister, then she wasn't insane. And more importantly, Bram wasn't a figment of her imagination. He was real. Or he had been—five hundred odd years ago.

"So you're certain this is your father's crest?" Iain asked, looking down at the silver brooch in Bram's hand.

It was finely wrought, the figure of a fierce mountain cat, muscles bunched for attack, one paw raised. Tiny green stones glittered in its eyes. A circle of metal surrounded it. And the Macgillivray motto was carved into the banner. *Na bean do'n chat.* Touch not this cat.

"Aye." Bram nodded, his finger tightening on the pin. "My mother had it made for him. See there at the bottom." He pointed just beneath the cat. "The initials intertwined. S and A. Seamus and Aileen. 'Tis most certainly my father's."

"And there's no chance he gave it to another?" Ranald asked. Though the hour was late, they were sitting at the broad table in Iain's working chamber, talking through the events of the last few hours. Trying to make some sense of it all.

"'Tis no' possible," Bram replied. "I saw it on him the day before the attack. He always wore it to secure his plaid. From the day my mother gave it to him."

Aileen Mackintosh Macgillivray had died just before Bram's tenth summer. A fever had rushed through the holding with the swiftness of a forest fire. Taking this person and leaving that, with no mercy at all. Seamus and Bram had survived. Aileen had not. But though Seamus's mind and body were sound, his heart had gone with his wife, buried in a grave behind the tower walls.

Bram had only faint memories of her. Black hair and blue eyes, and a wonderful laugh that had once filled Dunbrae with joy. That joy had vanished with her death. And Seamus had had nothing left to give his only son.

"It was the only thing that mattered to him," Bram said, his voice colored with bitterness. "He would have had it with him in his chamber the night he was murdered. Of that much I am certain."

"Then there can be no doubt it was brought as a message for you." Iain leaned back, crossing his arms over his massive chest. "Proof of your father's death."

"At the hand of the Comyns." Bram slammed his hand on the table, the brooch dancing against the wood, the cat momentarily seeming to spring to life.

"Tell me why you are so certain 'tis the Comyns behind all of this?" Iain asked. "I know there is no love lost between the Mackintoshes and the Comyns. Their treachery at Rait willna e're be forgotten. But that was almost forty summers ago. And the Macgillivrays were no' part of it. So was there something particular between your father and Robert Comyn?"

"Nay. At least no' anything in recent years. There was no love lost between the two of them. They skirmished when they were young men. Posturing for their respective chiefs mostly. But as my father grew older he wasna interested in the past. Or in fighting. Robert also appeared no' to have a taste for battle as he aged and so the raiding and battles stopped. And there was no real interest on the part of their chiefs. As you've stated before, Dunbrae is of only minor consequence in the grand scheme of things. As was *Tigh an Droma*."

"Robert Comyn's holding," Ranald added for clarification.

Iain nodded. "But Robert died recently, did he no'? And his son Alec took over?"

"Aye. Alec and I are of an age. And like me, he was fostered out early on." Again, Bram felt a surge of loss, remembering. His father had sent him to foster first at Dunmaglass only months after his mother had died and then at Moy. In all those years, he'd only been allowed the occasional visit home. Until several months ago, when his father had sent for him, wanting at long last to acknowledge his heir.

He blew out a breath, gathering his thoughts. "My father never mentioned a specific problem with Alec to me. But that does no' mean that Alec hadn't an interest in my father's lands."

"But he didn't take them. Which suggests some other motive. Perhaps something happened between the two of them. You said your father called you back to Dunbrae," Iain said. "Perhaps that's why?"

"Nay." Bram shook his head. "My father called me home because he wasna well and knew that it was time for me to take over as laird. There was no talk of Alec or his holding."

"If there was no quarrel with *Tigh an Droma*," Iain posited, "then why would the Comyns attack? According to my uncle, Alec Comyn denies it."

"I dinna doubt that Alec would lie. And in truth there doesna have to be a reason except that we are Macgillivrays and they are Comyns," Bram said with a shrug.

But Iain frowned. "There must be something more. Something I'm missing?"

"A blood feud," Ranald said, leaning forward, he and Bram exchanging glances. "A very old blood feud."

"But you said your father didn't care about the past."

"Aye, but I do. For all practical purposes, I was raised at Dunmaglass, you ken. And there the memory stretches back much farther. Back to the atrocities that were committed against the Macgillivrays at the hands of the Comyns. I learnt the story when I was but a wee boy, but I carry it here"——He pounded his chest—"in my heart."

"And you think that Alec does as well?"

"I dinna know. But if he knew that I was coming back to take over, perhaps he worried that I wouldna be as forgiving as my father. Were it not for the Comyns, our clan wouldna have fallen so far."

"But just as my people do, yours belong to Clan Chattan," Iain said. "There is nothing more powerful."

"Aye, but unlike the Mackintoshes, the Macgillivrays are nothing more than a sept. An afterthought. Once we were among the greatest clans in all of the Highlands. Until a woman brought us to our knees and destroyed us."

"I dinna ken." Iain shook his head, still frowning.

"'Tis an old tale." Ranald shrugged. "I heard the story as a child as well. Perhaps because the Macqueens and the Macgillivrays have so long been associated."

"It was when David was king. When the clans were above all," Bram began. "And the Macgillivrays were second to none and fierce rivals of the Comyns. The two clans dinna mix except in battle. But as is the way with such things, my kinsman Graeme fell in love with a Comyn woman. Tyra was her name. A real beauty, so the story goes. They met in secret, each time with him falling more in love and her wrapping him around her little finger, until she gave him the news that she was with child."

He paused, his mind recalling the story he'd heard so very many times.

"Graeme was o'erjoyed with the idea of becoming a father. And immediately asked for her hand. Tyra agreed, and Graeme went home to prepare the way with his father. Eventually, after much argument, Graeme's father, Naill, agreed to the marriage, for there was no turning his son's devotion aside. And the Macgillivrays issued an invitation to the Comyns. A meeting to seal the betrothal."

"I think I remember this story after all," Iain said, eyes narrowed in thought. "I'd just forgotten the clans that were involved in it. The Comyns, the girl and her family, came to the Macgillivray holding."

"Aye, and the Comyns, because of Graeme's love for Tyra, were welcomed into the Macgillivrays' tower. They all gathered in the great hall to break bread and celebrate the union of the clans. Only there was to be no union. The entire affair had been a ploy. A way to gain access into an enemy's stronghold." Bram paused, feeling the betrayal as if it were his own. "The Comyns attacked. And the unsuspecting Macgillivrays were slaughtered. Graeme was among the first to die. In some tellings it was Tyra herself who did it. Naill managed to escape, but not before watching his son and most of his clansmen die.

"Naill, it is said, went mad from grief, and without a laird, the clan foundered, split into septs and were thrown to the wind. And all of it because of Comyn treachery."

"Still, it was a long time ago," Ranald cautioned.

"Aye, but the hatred is still there. It was drilled into me at Dunmaglass. Comyns are and always will be the enemy. There can be no peace. And if Alec heard much the same, then perhaps as I said, he came back to *Tigh an Droma* with the intention of removing the threat Dunbrae posed."

"That's a lot of supposition," Iain said. "But a blood feud is no' something to take lightly. And just because your fathers dinna actively engage in it, doesna mean that Alec wouldn't take an opportunity when it was given to him."

"You're talking about the traitor."

"Aye. That I am. Did your father have enemies among his clansmen?"

"'Tis possible. But I know that at least some of his men were loyal." He thought of Frazier and Robby, his heart aching at the thought that his friend and the older man were dead. "In truth, my father wasn't an easy man to love," Bram said.

"Maybe not——" Ranald reached over to touch the silver pin, lying on the table. "——but Auntie Aileen loved him more than anything. I remember my mother talking about it after she died. Worrying that Seamus would no' recover."

"She was right," Bram sighed. "He was never the same."

"But he loved you," Katherine said, appearing in the doorway, the candlelight making her hair glisten gold.

"I dinna think he loved any but my mother," Bram said, watching as she crossed the room to sit by Iain. There was empathy in her eyes. And kindness.

"Sometimes, a man gets lost in a woman. So much so that he can't see anything else." Katherine shrugged, laying her small hand on top of Iain's. "But that doesn't mean that he doesn't care. Only that he can't find the way to show it."

There was right in what she said. Bram was certain of it. His father had cared for him in his own way. But still he mourned what could have been. And what, now, could never be.

"The danger has passed. You should be sleeping." Iain's tone was brusque, but his eyes lingered on the soft curves of his wife's face.

"I couldn't. Not when I knew you were down here, worrying. Besides, it's almost morning." She nodded toward the window, where the first pink fingers of dawn were splitting the sky.

Another woman, older but with an equally concerned expression, walked into the room carrying a large tray.

"I asked Flora to bring you something to eat. I know it isn't much." She smiled as the older woman set the tray of meat pies and ale on the table and retreated. "But we wanted to do something." She rose and started to leave, but Iain held onto her hand.

"Dinna go. I have need of you here."

Bram watched as she sat again, her fingers still entwined with his. This was what he longed for. Someone to share his life with. Someone to love. Lily's face sprang unbidden into his mind. Her wide green eyes and soft dark hair. But as soon as he had the thought he pushed it away. Their love was an impossibility. Separated by centuries.

He looked again at Iain and Katherine, and shook his head. God's honest truth was that even if she were here, he had nothing to offer her.

Nothing at all.

CHAPTER 10

"I'M STILL HAVING trouble getting my head around all of this," Lily told the assembled company, her mind still reeling. But at least she was feeling more stable. They'd moved down to the great room to sit at one of tables in the breakfast area. And at the insistence of Elaine, Mrs. Abernathy had joined the three of them, bringing with her the requisite pot of tea and a basket full of warm pastries.

The story they'd shared was even more amazing than her own. And despite the fact that the whole idea was almost beyond comprehension, it felt really good to know that she wasn't alone in all of this anymore.

"Drink your tea," Mrs. Abernathy scolded with a wave of the hand. "You've had quite a shock."

"I'm not sure that tea is really going to help." Lily shot Mrs. Abernathy a rueful smile and lifted her lips to the cup in an effort to soothe the older woman.

"I could pull out the scotch," Jeff offered. "After all, we are in Scotland."

"Already put a nip in the pot." Mrs. Abernathy beamed just as the warmth started to spread through Lily's chest.

"Nice country, this." She took another swallow and then sat back, her gaze moving amongst her new friends. She'd never really had what she'd call great friends growing up. Too much moving. Too much money. Neither circumstance breeding intimacy. At least *honest* intimacy.

Of course this wasn't all that different. Nothing like a little time travel to force a feeling of closeness. But with Mrs. Abernathy hovering and the look of concern on both Jeff's and Elaine's faces, Lily was forced to accept the very real possibility that these people actually cared, despite the outrageousness of the situation or the fact that she'd only just met them.

Sometimes it happened like that, she supposed, her mind turning first to her mother and father and then to Bram. There wasn't a doubt in her mind about her feelings for him. She just had no idea what she was supposed to do with them. Follow Katherine's lead? Go to him? But how? And would he even want her? Maybe she'd mistaken his feelings. But the moment she had the thought she knew she hadn't.

Perhaps it was the comparison to Justin. He'd never made her feel like that. Never. In truth, he'd filled a void. An empty place in her life. But now, having been with Bram, she realized Justin had just been a placeholder. She shivered at the thought of how close she'd come to settling.

"Penny for them?" Elaine quipped, cutting into Lily's tumbling thoughts.

"It's going to sound ridiculous."

"More than the fact that my sister is alive and well in the fifteenth century?" Jeff asked, his lips quirking up at the corners.

"Well, maybe. No. Oh God, I don't know, really." Lily frowned. "I was thinking that maybe it was lucky that Justin dumped me."

"It's never easy to be jilted," Mrs. Abernathy said. "But sometimes it is for the best. Everything in its time, I always say."

Jeff and Elaine exchanged glances with a smile, then returned their attention to Lily.

"Well, the difficult part of all that is that my parents had to die for it to happen. And despite how things have turned out, despite finding Bram, if that's indeed what I've done, I'd give anything if I could have them back again. And it breaks my heart to think that I could only find my happiness as a result of them losing theirs."

"Ah, my puir wee lamb, therein lies the joy of being a parent. Although Jamie and I were no' blessed, I've seen it first hand over and over. The love a parent has for a child has no limits. And if indeed death were the requirement for their child's everlasting happiness, then there would be no hesitation. Not that I'm saying that's what happened here, Lily," Mrs. Abernathy reassured. "I'm just saying that's how much they loved you."

Lily nodded. "It just seems so disloyal somehow. I've lost them forever. And yet here I am discussing the man who makes me…well… happy. And a man, I might add, that doesn't even live in my century." She shivered suddenly, the enormity of it hitting her full force. "Oh my God, Bram is dead. If he lived in the fifteenth century, then no matter what happened or *when* it happened, he's dead." Her gaze locked with Elaine's. "That's why you were so sad on the rooftop. You were thinking of Katherine. Of the fact that she's…"

"It's not as easy as all that," Jeff said, his expression turning serious. "In a linear world, what you're saying would be true. But if time isn't linear, if it's more like a parallel universe, then no, neither of them is dead. They're just living their lives on another plane. Which doesn't really make complete sense, but you get the idea."

"And the important thing to remember is that nothing is cast in stone," Elaine said. "We managed to change the future with Katherine and Iain."

"But didn't that change the fabric of time or some such?" Lily asked, still not really convinced that any of it was possible, but needing it to be so.

"It did," Jeff admitted. "Slightly. Nothing that threw things completely out of whack though."

"Speak for yourself, Jeffrey," Mrs. Abernathy said, a note of teasing in her voice. "Jamie and I lost possession of Duncreag in the process of all those changes."

Lily's eyes widened, and Jeff ducked his head in embarrassment.

"Now, now, don't worry, either of you." Mrs. Abernathy reached over to pat their hands. "I was teasing. My ancestors turned out not to be very nice people. At least Alisdair wasn't." She let out a satisfied sigh. "Things happened the way they were supposed to. And I've no regrets as to where it all ended up. Jamie and I have still got our home and more importantly, now we have a family. And I canna think of anything more important than that."

"Well, we agree on the last bit, Mrs. Abernathy," Jeff said. "You are part of our lives, now and always."

The older woman beamed. "So, more tea." She reached for the pot to fill the cups. "And try a bannock. My cook makes them just the way they were meant to be."

"She's not kidding," Jeff said as he scarfed one down. "They're awesome."

Lily reached into the basket for one of the little cakes. "So you're saying it's okay to change things?"

"No," Elaine said. "Not randomly." She looked over to her husband and he nodded. "What we believe is that time for Katherine and Iain was stuck in a loop. The wrong loop. And it was important for that loop to straighten out. To play as it was meant to play, if you will. Jeff's going back did that very thing. With a substantial shove from Katherine and Mrs. Abernathy."

"And a lot of love from you," Jeff added, his eyes reflecting the depth of his feelings for his wife.

"Well, there is that." She smiled and leaned over to give him a kiss.

"It's all very confusing," Lily admitted. "But basically, you're saying that what happened, even though it changed things, was what was truly meant to be."

"Yes." Mrs. Abernathy folded her arms over her argyle sweater with a nod. "And we're also telling you that none of it could have been accomplished without love. Romantic love certainly. Like Katherine and Iain's, and Elaine and Jeffrey's. But also love between siblings. Love between parent and child. And love between friends." Her warm gaze encompassed them all now. "There's magic here at Duncreag. But only those with love in their hearts can find it."

"So what I feel for Bram," Lily posited, turning the idea over in her mind, "you're agreeing that it's love? Even if I was only really with him the one time?"

"I canna tell you how you feel, lamb." Mrs. Abernathy shrugged. "I just know that if you found him it was for a reason. And it's up to us to figure out what that reason might be."

"Which means we need to understand what's happening in Bram's time. Mrs. Abernathy, what do you know about him?" Jeff asked.

"Not a lot, I'll admit. But I do recognize the name." She turned her attention to Lily. "I've always had a keen interest in the past. And especially Duncreag and the people who've come and gone over the years." She spoke as if they were talking about last month or last year instead of over five hundred years ago. But then if time really wasn't linear, then in a way, it wasn't any different.

Mrs. Abernathy scrunched her nose in thought. "His father was the second son of the brother of the Macgillivray chief at the time. He had a small holding, called Dunbrae, to the northeast of here. Seamus, his name was. He married a Mackintosh, so there was kinship with

Iain as well as with Elaine's Ranald. Bram was their only child. Aileen died early on when Bram was quite young. He fostered at Dunmaglass, the Macgillivray seat. And then went on to Moy, which is where he probably would have met Iain and Ranald if he hadn't already. He would only have been a few years younger." She spread her hands with a shrug. "And I'm afraid that's where my knowledge ends."

"You said the Macqueens are your family?" Lily asked Elaine.

"Yes." Her friend nodded. "But they are also Mrs. Abernathy's as well. So although it's quite distant, we're actually related. And since she grew up near the Macqueen seat, she's had access to all the historical documentation."

"But there's nothing after the time at Moy?" Lily asked. "No documentation at all?"

"Not on the Mackintosh side of things, but there wouldn't have been, really. Once Aileen was gone, the family tie would have been considerably weakened. Although Bram's relationship could have continued with Iain. And as for the Macqueens, the truth is their records from that time period aren't nearly as extensive as the Mackintoshes." She shrugged. "Head of Clan Chattan and all that."

"But at least we know that there was a family connection through both the Macqueens and the Mackintoshes, which explains why Bram was going to Iain for help."

"Help with what?" Jeff asked.

Lily had told them the gist of what had happened. The car wreck, the cottage, and the fact that she'd seen him again here at Duncreag. But she hadn't gone into the details.

"His father." She paused, searching for the name Mrs. Abernathy had used. "Seamus. He was murdered."

"By whom?" Elaine asked, her gaze narrowed in contemplation.

"I don't know." Lily shook her head. "He didn't say. Only that it was an old enemy. And that he'd had help. Someone on the inside. A traitor."

"Did Bram say when?" Jeff, too, had leaned forward, abandoning half a bannock on his plate.

Lily laughed, the sound strained. "As in a year? No. Wait," she said, sucking in a fortifying breath. "He said a week. It had been a week. And Bram was there. He must have meant Dunbrae." She looked up, trying to order her tumbling thoughts. "He said that the man was trying to kill him, too. But Bram escaped." Again a bubble of hysteria rose in her throat, and she felt Elaine's hand close around hers. "Oh God, I asked him if he'd gone to the authorities. He must have thought I was crazy."

"No," Mrs. Abernathy said. "He'd have thought you meant the Macgillivray chief."

"What did he say?" Jeff questioned, urging her on.

"That he was going to Iain. That's why the horsemen were there. They'd come for him."

"Where? At the cottage?"

"No." Lily forced herself to focus on the present. "I'm sorry it's all rather terrifying in context. But anyway, I told you that I saw him a second time. That he was there and then sort of faded away."

They all nodded and Lily clung to Elaine's hand like a lifeline.

"Well, I didn't tell you everything. Before he came. I was dreaming of him." Despite the serious nature of the conversation she felt herself blush. "And then I wasn't. I was standing on the edge of the cliff that rings Duncreag and I could see down into the valley below—"

"That's how you knew where the path was that led to the old entrance," Elaine said. "You'd seen it."

Lily nodded. "And there were horsemen. A lot of them, I think. It was dark. Late, I'm certain. And I just knew in my heart they were there for Bram. And then it all faded away again, and I was awake—at least I think I was—in my room. Only then it sort of shifted. I can't say how exactly, except that the windows were different—"

"The trappings of our century gone," Jeff finished for her.

She nodded. "And then Bram stepped from the shadows. It was just so good to see him. He'd disappeared and I thought I was insane. But then I remembered the men. And I warned him. And almost as soon as I'd gotten the words out, he started to fade." She stopped, tears filling her eyes. "And then he was gone. Oh, God, what if they got to him? What if he's dead?"

"No way," Jeff said, with a decisive shake of his head. "Iain's Duncreag was a fortress. No way would a handful of men have managed to get in, no matter who they were. Especially with forewarning. And you gave them that. My guess is that Iain and his men met the challenge head on. And prevailed."

There was comfort in the thought. But it wasn't enough. "But we can't know that for sure," she said, putting her fears into words.

"No, the only way to do that is to go back," Elaine said.

"But who's to say that I can?" Lily asked, not even bothering to verify what they all already knew. "Even with Katherine it took time. Eight years, right? And she really never had any control of it."

"True," Jeff agreed, "but I seem to have. I mean, I went after my sister when it was important. And brought her back when that was necessary as well. Not that she appreciated the last."

Elaine put a hand on his shoulder. "You had no choice. She'd have died if you'd left her there. And anyway, it all worked out in the end."

"That it did," Mrs. Abernathy agreed. "But you don't know where Bram is. And to date, at least, you've only been able to find him when there was a need. First, for him to care for you after the accident and second, for you to let him know about the intruders. And although you have a need now to know that he's all right, it's not specific enough. What we need is more information."

"But you already said that his branch of the clan was a small one," Jeff broke in. "So there isn't much written about Dunbrae or about him."

"But if there is anything," Elaine continued. "It would be at Dunmaglass, right?"

"There might be something there," Mrs. Abernathy admitted. "But the Macgillivray seat has no' been there for a couple hundred years. Better, I'm thinking, to go straight to the source."

"Dunbrae?" Lily's heart started to pound. "It still exists?"

"Aye. Not in its entirety, mind you. But there are walls still standing. And if you can put stones together again here," she said, clearly referring to the cottage, "then perhaps there's something you could learn there."

CHAPTER 11

"I DINNA KNOW if this is still accurate," Bram said, looking down at the crude map he'd drawn on the piece of parchment. The three men were in the great room, the drawing spread upon the massive table on the dais. "I've no' been to *Tigh an Droma* except the once. And I was just a wee lad at the time."

"So we're going in blind," Ranald groused.

"We can send men ahead to get the lay of the land," Iain assured him. "Besides, I'll wager the two of us have ridden into far worse."

"I canna remember when." Ranald still seemed less than convinced. "We have no idea how many men Alec Comyn has nor where they might be waiting for us."

"So then dinna come," Bram snapped, feeling irritation rise. "I'll handle it in my own way."

"Nay." Ranald shook his head, his eyes reflecting regret. "I dinna mean to imply we wouldna go with you. I only wish the odds were slightly more in our favor. Or that we could trust the memories of a wee boy."

Bram sighed, his frustration vanishing as quickly as it had come. "'Tis sorry I am that I canna remember more. I dinna like the idea of riding into the unknown any more than you do. But I canna sit by and let my father's death go unavenged."

"I understand your need," Iain said, a shadow crossing his face. Iain had lost his father to treachery not much more than a year ago now. "And you know that we'll stand by you. But Ranald makes a good point. We canna go into this without a better understanding of our enemy."

"And how do we do that?" Ranald queried. "We canna contact Moy or Dunmaglass. We dare not let anyone know that Bram is here. Or that we're riding with him. Not when there's even the smallest doubt that he might have been the traitor."

"I told you——" Bram began, the heat of anger shooting through him again.

"You canna ignore the facts, Bram," Iain said, cutting him off. "And Ranald is right. Whatever we do, we must do on our own. 'Tis too great a risk otherwise."

Bram nodded, dropping down onto a bench, wondering how the hell it had all come to this. If only his father had called for him sooner. Or if Bram had insisted on coming home. But there was nothing gained in wondering *what if.*

"Alec Comyn is no' a man to ignore the possibility of retaliation," Ranald said, pulling Bram from his thoughts. "Even if he is denying that he attacked Dunbrae, he'll no' be sitting idle on the chance of your coming."

"Well, if this map is accurate," Iain responded, "then our best shot is going to be to come at him from the hills to the west."

"You're right, 'tis the most logical choice," Ranald mused.

"And the one the Comyn will least expect," Bram added. "He'll assume we'll come from the south. From Dunbrae. At least from this point"——He tapped the map——"it gives us the possibility of surprise."

A commotion off to the right pulled Bram's attention away from the drawing. Iain's captain, Fergus, strode into the great hall, two more of Iain's men beside him, a fourth man hunkered between them, anger turning his face a deep red.

"What's this then?" Iain asked, his hand moving to his dagger.

"We found him outside on the path coming up to the gate," Fergus called as they crossed the chamber. "Figured him for one of the bastards that snuck into the canyon last night."

"I'm no' Comyn," the man in the middle spat, lifting his head. And Bram raised a hand, recognizing the voice—the age-weathered face.

"'Tis my father's man," he assured them, then rushed across the floor to meet Frazier, the two embracing as the others watched. "I feared you were dead."

"Nay, lad, 'tis no' easy to take down a Macbean," Fergus said, his smile fading as a shadow crossed his face. "Although there were no' many survivors."

"Robby?" Bram asked as the two of them crossed back over to Iain and Ranald by the dais, Iain's man Fergus following behind them.

The old warrior shook his head. "Dead. After you were safe, we turned back to fight the bastards."

"Do you ken who it was?" Iain asked, as Ranald offered the old man a tankard of ale.

"Aye." He nodded. "'Twas Comyns. I recognized their colors. Besides, there's no mistaking the look of them. Those eyes and all that hair."

Bram and Ranald exchanged a look.

"You were Seamus Macgillivray's captain?" Iain asked.

"Aye, that I was. For more than thirty years." The older man shrugged. "But time has a way of making a man weak." He shrugged. "Seamus and I faced that together. His goal was to step down. Leave the holding to his son." Frazier's eyes cut to Bram, his expression grim.

"Why did I hear nothing of this?" Bram asked, grief rocking through him with the power of a lance. "He said naught to me."

"Ye were no' ready, lad," the old man answered.

Bram fisted his hands, but Frazier waved him quiet. "I dinna mean you were weak. Only that you had to want it. Being laird is a right, but it is also a privilege. One earned. And yer father needed to know that you were ready to handle it."

"I was born ready." Bram pushed away from the table. "But my father could never see that."

"In his own way, he loved you, lad," Frazier said. "He just had no way o' showing it. And you were gone more often than not."

"Because he sent me away."

"Isn't that always the way of it with men?" Katherine queried as she swept into the room, a fresh pitcher of ale in her hands. "Pushing each other about, talking around everything but what's important. It's a wonder any of you ever get anything done at all." She stopped, eyeing the newcomer.

"Bram's father's man, Frazier," Iain said by way of introduction. "He's managed to escape the carnage at Dunbrae."

Bram watched as Katherine studied the man and then her husband. "And you believe him?"

Frazier ruffled, clearly unaccustomed to being found wanting by a woman. But then if Frazier knew half of the truths of this household he would no doubt be running for sanctuary. The thought brought a smile.

"What are ye laughing about, boy?" Frazier snapped.

"Nothing." He lifted a hand, swallowing his mirth. "Nothing at all." He turned his attention back to Katherine. "I swear on my life, this man is a friend. He helped me to escape Alec and his men—at great risk to himself, I might add." And to others. Bram shuddered, his thoughts turning to Robby.

"Well, then," she said, setting the pitcher on the table. "Any friend of Bram's is more than welcome here. I'll see that Flora sends some food. I'd imagine it's been a while since you've eaten." She bent to kiss her husband, her golden hair swinging forward like a curtain. And then with a smile, she was gone.

"Hell of a woman, that," Frazier mumbled.

"Aye, that she is." Iain's smile was warm, but there was still a sliver of doubt present. Bram recognized the caution for what it was. Iain hadn't survived all that he had endured without keeping a clear head. And despite the fact that Bram trusted Frazier, he understood the need to tread carefully. "So tell us, how did you manage to get away?"

"And more importantly," Ranald added, his gaze narrowed as he studied the older man, "how did you manage to track Bram here?"

Flora bustled into the room with a platter of meat and cheese, her ruddy face filled with curiosity as she put the trencher in front of Frazier. "Lady Katherine said that you were hungry."

Bram swallowed another smile. Clearly Flora and her mistress were of an accord when it came to Frazier. Neither inclined to completely trust this newest addition to the household. With a last shake of her head, she turned and waltzed from the room.

"Women," Frazier mumbled, stabbing a piece of cheese. After following it up with a swig of ale, he sat back, eyeing the assembled company. "I wasna planning to follow you. I'd thought to fight to the death. To stay and avenge Seamus. But 'twas no' possible. We were far outnumbered. And they'd no plans to spare anyone.

"After we saw you away, young Robby and I headed back for the tower. The battle had already turned. So many men lost. But we fought on. Determined to take as many Comyns with us as we could. We'd fought our way back into the great room. And were close to surrounded. There were only about four of us left that I could see. Robby, me, Angus Macfarland and his son."

Bram blew out an angry sigh. Hamish had been not more than a boy.

"I thought for a moment we might prevail. Not overall, mind ye, but at least there in the great room. We had them down in number. But more arrived. Eight, I don't know, maybe ten. We continued to fight hard, but we were sorely outnumbered. Young Hamish fell first. And then his father." Frazier looked down at his hands. "And then they took Robby. Not before he'd kilt four of them, mind ye. But I knew he was dead before he hit the floor." The older man's gaze locked on Bram. "I know he was yer friend, lad. I only wish that I could have saved him."

Bram nodded, swallowing his pain. "I am certain you did what you could."

"If you were surrounded, as you say," Ranald asked, his voice deceptively mild, "how is it you managed to escape?"

"I got lucky. There was a loud noise of some kind." He stopped, his hands clenched as he remembered. "I've no idea what it was. But as the men reacted, I took my chance." He paused again, this time regret coloring his face. "I made a run for it. I'm no' proud of the fact. But in my heart—" He pounded a fist to his chest, his gaze meeting Bram's. "—I knew that yer father would expect me to protect you above all else. And there was no way I could do that if I were dead." He sighed. "So I slipped away through the same gate as you." His grizzled eyebrows rose as he shot a look across the table at Bram. "I canna say it sits well to have run, but were I given the chance to do it over, I'd have done the same."

Iain sat forward, his mind clearly turning over the weight of Frazier's story. "And so you followed him here? Bram, I mean?"

"Nay." Frazier shook his head. "Too much time had passed. And there had been no time for plans to rendezvous." He looked to Bram, who nodded in agreement. "But I knew he wouldna go to Dunmaglass. Yer father never had any use for his uncle or his brothers. And I dinna think you'd see it differently."

"I do not," Bram said in agreement. "But——"

Frazier waved him quiet. "'Twas no' a great leap to see that you'd come here. You've idolized yer cousins since you were a wee lad. Even now you talk of little else but the adventures the three of you have shared."

"Aye, but he always liked me more than Iain," Ranald said with an affable laugh.

"I dinna like either o' you much at the moment," Bram groused. "And Frazier exaggerates."

"Ach, well, that doesna follow so well with my recollections of you always being underfoot where e'er Iain and I were to be found." Ranald laughed, and Bram relaxed. He might still be youngest, but he was far from a lad. And there were bigger concerns afoot than his relationship with his cousins.

"Ranald's right. We've always been close. So why not assume I'd go to Ranald's holding?"

Frazier dipped his head, his bushy-eyed gaze shooting toward Ranald. "Without meaning offense, Iain has the backing of Moy and I knew it would be the wiser move. Besides, 'twas no' trick to learn that the two of you were only just returning from there. And Duncreag is far closer than *Tur nan Clach*."

"I suppose it is," Ranald grumbled. "But let it be known the wrath of the Macqueens is every bit as fearsome as that of the Mackintoshes." Despite the teasing tone of his voice, there was a feral glint in Ranald's eye.

"No one is claiming otherwise," Iain assured his cousin. "And I agree that coming here was a logical move. But since you obviously had your ear to the ground, Frazier, why did you not go back when you learned that Malcolm had been given Dunbrae?"

"Loyalty," the old man said simply. "They were saying that Bram was a traitor and I knew for certain that it was a lie. Better, I thought, to find Bram and help him first. Besides, as I say, there was no love lost between the brothers. My allegiance has always been with Seamus. Because o' that, I canna know for certain that Malcolm would have welcomed me."

Iain nodded, his expression inscrutable. "Well, then I'd say you made the right decision. And now that you've found Bram, what would you have him do?"

There was no hesitation. The old man pushed to his feet, anger and grief cresting in his eyes. "Avenge his father's death—and the others. Seamus canna rest until the Comyns have paid."

"Then we are agreed," Bram said, nodding toward the map on the table. "And to that end we're already making plans. But apparently so are they. Last night, we were attacked."

The man drew a sharp breath, his brows drawing together. "Comyns?"

"Aye, looks as though. The colors were true," Iain said, quickly filling the older man in on the details of the attack. "But considering what you've told us about the fighting, I canna see how they got here so fast."

"Can you no' ask them?" Frazier frowned, his eyes narrowing.

Iain's smile held a hard glint of steel as he casually shrugged. "There were no survivors."

"Just as well," the man said, clenching his fist, a nerve in his weathered jaw twitching. "For what they've done, they deserve to go straight to hell."

"I canna argue with that," Ranald agreed. "But it might have proved useful to have had a prisoner to question."

"It is what it is." Bram shrugged, impatience rising as his fingers closed around the pin on his plaid.

Frazier's gaze followed the movement. "Seamus's crest." He frowned, his hand automatically closing on his dagger. "How came you by it, then? Yer father ne're went anywhere without it."

"The men who attacked Duncreag left it behind," Bram said, swallowing bitter bile. "We found it in the aftermath. A message, I'm guessing."

"Aye." Frazier nodded, his face still flushed with anger as his eyes fell to the parchment on the table. "Proof that the bastards killed yer father. And that if you dinna stop them first, they'll find a way to kill you, too."

"Which is why we have to concentrate on our next move," Bram said, his fingers still touching the cool metal of the crest. "You have the right of it, Frazier. Whatever path we choose, my father must be avenged."

"Well, you canna come in this way and expect to meet with success." He pointed to the west on the map, the place they'd marked for their approach. "There's an outpost here. And Alec will certainly have made sure that it is fully manned."

"But they'll be expecting us to attack from Dunbrae."

"Mayhap. And they'll no doubt be watching that way as well. But they know that you're no' there. And that you've no support from that quarter. Yer uncle is no' interested in retribution. Or in you. So they'll be watching for other places as well."

"But the rest of the valley is guarded by mountains. Best I remember, there's no way through at all," Bram argued.

"Aye." Frazier smiled, his eyes narrowing in triumph. "So it would seem. But, ye forget, yer father and I grew up in these mountains. 'Tis my feeling we should come in here." He pointed to an area in the northeast.

"But——" Bram began in protest.

"You think it looks impassible, I know. But, that's where yer wrong, lad." Frazier tapped a weathered finger on the map. "There's a passage of sorts here. A narrow twist of a path following alongside a burn. Seamus and I used it when we were no older than you, Bram. For reiving, ye ken. It'll be the perfect approach. They'll ne'er see it coming."

CHAPTER 12

✛

IT WAS AN impossibly normal day, which on the face of it was ridiculous. Maybe it was the company or maybe it was the beauty of the surrounding fields and mountains, but whatever the reason, for the first time since she'd learned of her parents' deaths, Lily felt as if life might actually go on.

Which immediately made her feel guilty.

She'd lost everything. Her family. Her home. Her fiancé. Or at least the idea of him. And yet, here in Scotland she'd *found* something as well. *Hope*. Although, truth be told, it was fleeting at best, impossibly insane at worst.

Lily sighed, closing her eyes against the enormity of it all.

"I know it doesn't feel like it now," Elaine said, lifting a hand from the steering wheel to cover Lily's, "but things have a way of working out."

"Aye, that they do." Mrs. Abernathy nodded sagely from the back seat as they barreled along in Elaine's tiny car.

They'd spent the morning combing through the records in Dunmaglass. First at the vicarage and then at the little museum that passed as an historical society. Unfortunately, they'd come away with little to show for it. A notation of Bram's birth, and a record of his service as a page as a small boy. There was also a record of his father's death, but no details, and nothing at all of Dunbrae. It was as if the place had never existed.

Lily tipped her head back with a sigh.

"'Twas a long time ago," Mrs. Abernathy said, accurately guessing her turn of thought. "'Tis no' surprising that there is nothing more. Events recorded centered around the heads of the clans. The smaller lairdships were no' often documented well. And when the clans lost power and scattered, what records that existed were often abandoned or lost. 'Tis lucky we found anything at all."

"And at least we did manage to confirm that Bram existed," Elaine soothed.

"Yeah. Over five hundred years ago." What remained of Lily's spontaneous burst of happiness evaporated. She knew she sounded defensive, which was inexcusable when she considered that her new friends were driving across the Highlands on her behalf. But it seemed like such a lost cause. She was chasing a man long dead.

How was that any better than accepting Justin when in her heart she'd known he wasn't the one? She'd settled because she'd wanted so much to find what her parents had had. To be loved exclusively. Above all else. What a laugh. Justin hadn't loved *her*. He'd loved her money. She'd just been too blind to see. Hungry for attention. Desperate for love.

And wasn't that what she was doing now? Pretending that what had happened with Bram was something more than it was? She laughed, the sound harsh in the quiet of the car.

"Sometimes you just have to believe," Mrs. Abernathy said, again reading her mind. "Have a little faith."

"Easy to say when you have Mr. Abernathy. I don't seem to be quite as adept at making good choices." Lily's fingers closed on the cool silver of the ring her mother had given her father, her heart swelling with guilt and grief.

"Justin was a fool," Elaine said.

"Maybe. But even if that's true, I was as big of one. I believed he loved me."

"Sometimes the heart sees only what it wants to see." As usual, Mrs. Abernathy hit the nail on the head.

"So what's to say I'm not doing the same now? Chasing a dream. Even more so than with Justin? At least he's alive and breathing in my own time."

"I don't think love has boundaries." Elaine shrugged. "You can't discount what's happened to you because of the past. Maybe all of it had to happen in order for any of it to be possible." She smiled.

"You mean that each event led to the other? I can certainly see my parents' death and the subsequent discovery of their poverty sparking Justin's defection, but how does any of that feed into my traveling through time?"

"Maybe your heart had to be open to the idea. Or maybe you just needed to come here, and the tragedies at home set the wheels in motion."

"But that would mean…" She trailed off. This was territory they'd already covered. And no amount of guilt was going to bring her parents back.

"They'd have wanted you to be happy," Mrs. Abernathy reminded her.

Lily sighed. "I know. And I'm sorry. You've both been so kind. And here I am complaining."

"Not at all," Elaine said. "You're confused. Your emotions are raw and you've been through hell. I'd be shocked if you weren't a little bit on edge. And when you add to the mix the fact that you've fallen for a man who lives in another time, well, I'd say it's enough to make anyone a little cranky."

"And don't forget, we've been through this before," Mrs. Abernathy added.

"With Katherine." Again Lily felt embarrassed. They'd both lost someone dear to them. Even if, in some other timeframe, Katherine was indeed alive and well. And loved. The last words echoed through her mind.

"Look, I know we implied that Katherine never doubted." Elaine glanced in her direction, then focused again on the road in front of them. "And on the whole, that's true. She never really wavered. But that doesn't mean there weren't moments. Eight years is a long time to wait for someone who might not even have been real."

"But she did wait."

"Yes, but not passively. At least not at the end. She fought for what she wanted. What she believed in her heart was right. And it was worth it in the end. All the hell that they went through. It was worth it."

"So you're saying I have to fight? But fight for what?"

"I don't know. For Bram, maybe. Or for the idea of him. And I'm saying that it's all right to have doubts. Just don't let them take over what you know in your heart is true." She touched her chest to underscore the words. "We all have doubts, you know. I never believed for a minute that Jeff and I would find our way together. We were too locked into the way things had always been. But it was Katherine leaving that pulled us together. That made us see how much we really cared about each other."

"Sometimes the answers are right in front of us." Mrs. Abernathy nodded. "But we have to open our eyes to see them."

"Well, I can't really argue with any of that, I suppose. So I guess we'll just have to keep looking."

"Never give up." Mrs. Abernathy nodded. "That's always been my motto."

They drove on in comfortable silence. Lily leaned back against the worn leather seat staring out the car window. There was a rough majesty about the Scottish countryside, broom and gorse mixing together across the rocky foothills of the mountains in a wild mix of yellow blooms, green undergrowth, and the milky gray of lichen-spattered chunks of stone jutting up through the coarse vegetation.

They were heading for Dunbrae. Or what was left of it. She shivered, not certain if it was with anticipation or worry. Both probably. Odds were she'd learn nothing new. But it was important somehow to see the tower for herself. To see Bram's home. To reach for him there across the years.

Elaine and Mrs. Abernathy were right. She simply had to trust herself—trust her heart. Maybe she was chasing moonbeams. But then again maybe she wasn't. And if the latter were true—if, like Katherine St. Claire, she'd somehow managed to cross the boundaries of time, and if the reason was because her soul was somehow linked with Bram's—then she had to believe. Had to have faith.

Her hand closed around the wedding ring. It had most definitely traveled through the years, as Val had said, from one happy ending to another—blessing those who loved with their whole hearts.

It was her ring now.

Her journey. Hers and Bram's.

In truth, she had no choice but to believe.

The track leading to the ruins of Dunbrae was almost invisible. In fact, despite the vicar's helpful map, they'd passed the turn-off twice.

It was only on the third try that Lily spied the faint markings between two ancient rowan trees, their narrow green leaves cradling creamy white blossoms.

"I see it," she cried. "Or at least I think I do. There. Between the trees." She pointed at the shadow of a rutted road running between a rock wall and an open field.

Behind the wall, the meadow was dotted with sheep. On the open side, the terrain was wilder, overgrown, and to Lily's mind somehow wrong. Her inner eye was quick to create cottages and outbuildings. Smoke in chimneys, livestock in pens. And everywhere people.

For a moment her heart swelled, joy singing through her veins as if at long last she'd come home. And then it was all gone. Nothing more than a figment of imagination or the wisp of a memory. Discomfited, Lily shifted on the seat as Elaine steered the little car down the half-hidden lane.

"Are you all right?" Mrs. Abernathy asked from the back, her eyes, as always, seeing everything.

"As much as I can be, I suppose," Lily replied, turning to smile at the older woman. "For a moment I let myself get carried away. I thought I saw a village."

"There would have been one here," Mrs. Abernathy assured them. "There was always such around a tower. People who depended on the laird for safety when danger came calling. In peaceful times they'd have built their wee stone cottages, and their lives would have sprawled out across fields such as these."

"But there's nothing here now." Lily shook her head, turning back to the overgrown meadow, watching as it was obscured from view by a small forest.

"Aye, but you see with more than just your eyes."

"You mean I'm crazy." Lily couldn't help herself. The words spilled out of her, even as her mind sought to recapture the image of the village.

"She means you have the sight," Elaine said matter-of-factly. "And if I'd a pound for every time I wished for the same as a child, I'd be a rich woman today, and Duncreag would have the new roofing it's so badly needing." She reached out to pat Lily's hand. "Almost there."

They drove slowly, the road now shrouded in the trees, their ancient branches dropping overhead to form a canopy of dappled green. The track, what there was of it, rose sharply now, climbing up the side of the mountain, sharp protrusions of rock visible beneath the gnarled trunks of the trees.

Then suddenly they rounded a bend and broke free, the sunlight almost blinding after the gloom. Elaine pulled the car to a stop and Lily blinked, waiting for her eyes to adjust.

And then there it was. Dunbrae. Bram's home.

Or what was left of it.

What had clearly been a tower once was now not much more than a great pile of stone. Perhaps two stories remained, most of that dilapidated and clearly unstable. The center was filled with rubble from what had most likely been upper stories. Broom grew amidst the fallen stone. And a rhododendron's waxy leaves and purple flowers hid what had once been stairs.

For a moment the world seemed to shift, the tower taking on clean lines and powerful proportions, a crisp banner waving from the parapet. Huge wooden doors at the top of the stairs marked the entrance. And inside, Lily knew there would be a welcoming fire. She could almost smell the smoke.

Again her heart swelled with joy. She reached for the car door handle, but before she could wrench it open, the image faded, the jumble of stone heartbreaking in its neglect. She pulled herself from the car, oblivious to her friends, and walked across the grass to the fallen tower. In the sunlight the fallen stones glittered silver and when she reached out to lay her hand across one, it was warm to the touch.

Like a living thing.

She shook her head, wondering when she'd become so fanciful. *Probably when she'd slept with a man dead five hundred years*, a little voice whispered. She shivered. Eyes closed, she listened for the heartbeat of the place, her mind searching again for images. Memories. But there was nothing except the whistling wind and a soul-deep feeling of loss.

She shifted, opening her eyes, and reached to touch another stone, this one long and thin, like a threshold or a window sill. It was also warm to the touch, worn smooth by time. And she smiled, a vivid feeling of peace descending. An image flashed. An intricately carved table. Wooden trenchers and jeweled goblets. A massive stone fireplace, the flames flickering and bright. Above the mantel, a crest of some kind. Weapons fanned in a semi-circle above it.

She'd known this place. Known it intimately. She'd lived here. Slept here. Loved here. She was as certain of the fact as she was of breathing. And yet it was impossible.

"Are you seeing anything?" Elaine asked, the words jerking Lily from her reverie.

"The great room, I think." She blinked at the tower rubble. "I only saw it for a second. Like the village below. But it was beautiful. And as familiar to me as my house in Greenwich. But that's impossible. There clearly hasn't been a working tower here for a very long time. And even if there were, I've never been here before in my life."

"This life at least," Mrs. Abernathy said, hands on hips as she surveyed the ruin. "It almost looks to me as if there were two towers here. See?" She pointed to the place where Lily was standing. "That seems to be the main ruin. Or at least the one in the best shape. But over here——" She walked across the fallen stones to another lower mound, this one almost completely covered with broom. "——there's clearly another building. Or at least there was one."

"An outbuilding of some kind?" Elaine suggested, as she and Lily made their way over to Mrs. Abernathy.

"No telling. At least not without a little help." She smiled, turning her attention to Lily.

"It's not like I can just call it up," Lily protested. Although even as she spoke the words, she leaned down to touch the pile of debris.

This time it was as if a hand had jerked her into the dark. One minute she was standing amidst the ruins of Dunbrae and the next she was surrounded by blackness.

She sucked in a breath, turning her head, straining into the dark. The smell of smoke was thick here. But where before, with the image of the great room, it had brought pleasure, here it was oppressive. Frightening even. Her eyes watered, and somewhere below her she could hear the clanking of metal against metal.

A candle flamed in the darkness.

"He comes." The voice was low, grating. A shiver ran up her spine.

She turned toward the light and the sound, but nothing was visible except the flame, and the shadowy shape of a hand and an arm.

"Who?" she asked, the words a whisper. "Who comes?"

The clanking sounds drew closer. Swords, her mind whispered. Someone was fighting. She looked down, recognizing plank flooring. Between the gaps she could see flames flickering below. She jerked her head up, recognizing now that flames also wreathed the doorway and licked at the floorboards and walls.

As if on cue, a figure burst through the doorway, calling her name.

"Bram," Lily cried, trying to run to him, but as before, in her dream of the men in the pass below Duncreag, she couldn't move. It was as if she were bound in place.

"God's blood, what have you done?" Bram bellowed, his pain and anger carrying across the space between them.

Lily jerked as if she'd been hit, but then saw that his gaze was on someone else, someone beyond her.

"Naught but what you deserve," the voice replied as, still cloaked in shadow, he took a step closer to Lily.

Bram's eyes narrowed, and he lunged forward as a second and third shadow detached themselves from the dark. It was a trap.

"Go back," she screamed, knowing he couldn't possibly hear her.

His head jerked, his shoulders tightening with rage. "I'll no' leave you."

The men circled him now, their swords glinting as the flames continued to spread. The entire room was ablaze, the acrid smell filling her lungs, choking her.

For a single moment, Bram hesitated, his eyes entreating, his words lost in the cacophony of swords as the men advanced.

She opened her mouth to scream another warning, but it was too late; the men were upon him. She struggled, fighting against bonds, real or imagined. And then suddenly the room exploded in flames, the floor beneath her collapsing.

One minute Bram was there...and then he was gone. For a moment, the flames seemed to engulf her and then everything was a soft velvet black.

"Lily." The voice was insistent. But she fought against it. She couldn't give in. She needed to get back. To find Bram. "Lily, please, wake up."

It was the note of concern that made her open her eyes. That and the hopeless feeling that whatever had occurred, it had happened long ago, and nothing she could do would make it change.

"Oh, thank God." Elaine's worried face swam into view. "I thought we'd lost you."

"Here, have some of this," Mrs. Abernathy said as Elaine helped Lily to sit up. Lily took the offered cup and sipped the hot tea, almost sputtering as she swallowed. The brew was liberally laced with whisky. Mrs. Abernathy screwed the lid back on the thermos. "A little fortification." She shrugged, her eyes narrowed with worry. "It'll do you good."

Lily shook her head, the last vestiges of her lethargy wearing off. The clearing was exactly as she'd left it. Tumbles of stone and overgrown masonry. The remnants, no doubt, of that long-ago fire. Her heart clenched with the agony of the memory.

Bram.

"Did you see him, then?" Elaine asked. "Bram."

Lily hadn't realized she'd spoken the name out loud. Her eyes met her friend's worried gaze. "Yes. He was here. Or rather, I was there. I don't know." She shook her head in confusion and then, sucking in a deep breath, took another sip of tea, letting the heat of the whisky warm her. "Everything was burning."

"What was burning?" Mrs. Abernathy asked. "The tower?" She shot a gaze over the rubble, eyes sharpening.

"I think so." Lily ran a hand through her hair, still shaking off the vestiges of what she'd seen. "It was too dark to see anything for certain. Except for Bram. They had him cornered. There were so many of them."

"Were you there?" Elaine frowned. "I mean, could Bram—could anybody—see you?"

"I don't know." She shook her head, trying to remember. "I don't think so. It was like before on the ridge. I couldn't move. Couldn't make a sound. I was just stuck there—watching." Except that for a moment, in the end, it had almost seemed as if…she shook her head. If he'd seen her, he'd have reacted more strongly than he had. "No. I don't think I was really there. Not in a corporeal sense, anyway." She shivered, taking another sip of her tea.

"Maybe it was a flashback," Elaine suggested.

"Now, that's stating the obvious," Mrs. Abernathy said, lifting her eyebrows.

"I mean, maybe it has already happened. Both in this time and in the past. Didn't you say that Bram's tower"—Elaine waved a hand, the gesture encompassing the rubble—"was attacked? Maybe that's what you saw."

"But it was so awful." Lily pulled in a trembling breath. "They had him surrounded."

"Yes, but then he escaped." Mrs. Abernathy slid a comforting arm around her. "And found you. Elaine's right. It must have been the attack Bram spoke of. Did you see enough to know who was behind it?"

Lily shook her head. "As I said, it was too dark to see any faces. I heard a voice. But it was hardly more than a whisper. And he didn't say anything much at all. Just that Bram was coming." She closed her eyes as the anguish of her vision swam through her head again.

"Well, whoever it was, I doubt we'll find more answers here," Elaine said.

As if to test the theory, Lily reached out and touched a fallen stone. It was cool to the touch, a crust of lichen covering one side. She stroked it as though urging something more, but there was nothing except the wind in the trees and the chattering of crows.

"Aye," Mrs. Abernathy agreed, her eyes moving from Lily to the sky. "And it'll be dark soon. We'd best head back."

Lily nodded and pushed to her feet, letting her gaze wash across the ruins of Dunbrae. There had been happiness here. She recognized it deep in her heart. But there'd also been pain. Bram's pain. She shuddered as she again saw the flames rising, saw the floor beneath her collapsing. If her friends were right, Bram had escaped. He'd lived.

But if they were wrong...dear God, if they were wrong, then she had to reach him before it was too late.

CHAPTER 13

✦

"EVERYTHING IS SET," Ranald said, striding across the great hall's flagged floor to where Bram, Katherine and Iain were sitting in front of the massive stone fireplace. "The rest of my men have arrived, and Fergus is seeing to their well-being. After a good night's rest, they'll be ready to ride with us in the morning."

"Always glad to have an increase in numbers," Iain said, lifting a tankard of ale. "And your lot more than most."

"I canna complain." Ranald dropped down onto a bench across from Katherine and Iain, who were seated in intricately carved chairs.

Katherine immediately filled another tankard and passed it to him. Bram, sitting adjacent on another bench facing the fire, allowed himself a moment of complacency. It was good to be among family, no matter how dire the circumstances.

"I've managed to cut out the worst of them." Ranald sighed. "And the rest are loyal to me and mine."

"I'll wager serving under you is a vast improvement o'er having Davidson as laird." Iain's jaw tightened as his hatred of Alisdair Davidson washed across his face. Not that Bram blamed him. After all, the bastard had almost killed Katherine. "If naught else then they're finding out what it means to be treated fairly."

Ranald nodded, his eyes narrowing. "I canna abide a man who doesna respect the worth of those about him. And when I think what could have happened to Ailis. From her brother no less."

Ranald's big hands closed into fists and Katherine laid a gentle hand on his arm in an effort to soothe. "But it didn't happen, Ranald. You and Iain were there to save her." She shifted her gaze to her husband. "To save me. Anyway, it's all past history now. No need to relive it. It's more important to concentrate on the here and now."

"Our plans to ride on the Comyns." Bram set his tankard beside him on the bench, pulling his thoughts firmly back to the present. "There are no' enough words to convey my gratitude——" he started, only to be cut off with a wave of Iain's hand.

"You'd do the same for us."

"Aye, that I would."

"And you'll have your own man as well," Katherine observed, her gaze assessing.

"I understand you dinna know him. But I swear he's a man who can be trusted. He served my father long and well."

"I remember him from our visiting once when I was a lad," Ranald mused. "He seemed as big as a bear. And as fierce as one, too. But he could be kind." His cousin smiled. "As I'm sure you can imagine, and as Iain no doubt knows, I was a bit of a handful in those days."

Katherine harrumphed as she swallowed her laughter. "Those days?"

Ranald shrugged. "Let's just agree that I was worse. Anyway, I'd taken it into my head to walk the upper parapet."

"On the roof of Dunbrae?" Bram couldn't help the surprise. Built to withstand the vicious attacks of an earlier century, the ledge of the crenelated walls was narrow and dangerous.

"The very one," Ranald agreed. "Anyway, I'd set about doing just that, when I managed to lose my balance. I fell, and quite frankly saw my very short life passing before my eyes. Fortunately, Frazier was there—standing watch, so he said. And he hauled me back over the edge to safety."

"Standing watch over *you*, most likely," Iain quipped, his eyes crinkled with amusement. "I guess we all owe him a debt."

"Speak for yourself," Bram mumbled. "I was never even allowed to go up there on my own. Now I understand why."

They sat in comfortable silence for a moment, the fire crackling merrily in the grate. Bram's thoughts turned to the tower. His home. Or what was left of it. Anger rolled through him, hot and heavy. Thanks to Alec Comyn, Bram no longer had a home to call his own.

Instantly his mind filled with the memory of soft skin and curly black hair, his body tightening as he remembered the smell and taste of her.

Lily.

"Are you going to tell her you're going?" Katherine asked, her voice soft, her grey eyes knowing.

"How can I?" Bram asked, shaking away from his rioting thoughts. "She is no' even here in this place."

"Perhaps not at Duncreag. But you know where you're most likely to find her." There was challenge in Katherine's voice. One he couldn't ignore. Still he fought against the idea. Now was not the time for distraction.

"What if this is your only chance?" she urged.

"Leave him be, *mo chridhe*," Iain said. "He's right. A man canna go into battle when his mind is on his woman."

Again Katherine swallowed a smile. "I believe, my love, that it is precisely because of said women that most men head into battle in the first place." She'd shifted the challenge from Bram to Iain, and based on Iain's grin, the challenge had been accepted.

They rose of one accord, but as they walked away, Katherine shot a knowing look over her shoulder. "Don't throw away what fate has given you. For that, most definitely, is a pathway to regret."

Ranald drained his tankard, watching the two of them depart. "I wish I could tell you she's wrong," his cousin said. "But when you find the woman you want, there's naught to do but claim her. And hope to hell that she claims you in return. That much I'm certain of."

"But Iain's right. Now is no' the time for me to be making promises. I canna ask her to place herself in the middle of the hellish mess that has become my life. 'Tis far better that we win the day and then I make my claim." For the latter at least he was certain of. No matter the distance that separated them, Lily was his. For now and for always. No matter what century.

"I canna disagree." Ranald shrugged. "Until you've finished this, the woman is safer in her own time. But is there a reason why you canna at least go to the lass and say goodbye?"

"You make it sound as if I've but to walk o'er to her holding and knock on the door. 'Tis a bit more complicated than that."

"Is it?" Ranald's eyebrows shot up in question. "Last I heard, when there was a need, the two of you seemed to find each other well enough. First at the cottage, and then here at Duncreag."

"So what? I go to bed and just wait?" He hated the petulance in his voice. But it all seemed so bloody impossible. Both the harsh reality of his situation and the admittedly passionate fantasy.

"Were I a betting man, I'd say that Katherine has the right of it and you're far more likely to find your fairy woman at the cottage. And because I am no' a foolish man, I suggest you take a couple o' men to stand watch beyond the clearing."

Bram frowned. "You think there are Comyns still about?"

"Nay. I think if there were others nearby they've gone. But 'tis never wise to take a chance."

"Then maybe it's best I don't go to her." The idea of going had been building inside him from the moment Katherine had first mentioned it, gathering momentum as the need for Lily quickened inside him, urging him onward.

"I'm no' telling you not to go. I'm just cautioning you to have a care. When have you ever balked at a little risk?" Ranald smiled, pushing to his feet. "And dinna pretend you ne'er walked the parapet at Dunbrae. Ban or no'."

Bram grinned at his cousin, moving to stand. "I suppose I'll be off then."

"I'd expect no less. We'll see you here at first light."

Bram sobered, the enormity of what they were undertaking hitting him full force. Perhaps he did deserve a send-off. A night of unbridled passion. A night only one woman could possibly give him.

Lily.

He strode across the great room, praying with his entire being that she'd still want him. That she'd be there.

***

"Come to me, mo ghràidh. Come to me."

Lily's heart pounded as she was yanked from sleep.

Her gaze swept across the room, searching for some sign that he had found her again. But the room was empty and, based on the hissing radiator, very much an occupant of the current century.

Frustrated, she swung her legs to the edge of the bed. Outside, the shadows of night shifted beyond the window. She pushed a hand through her unruly hair, mentally trying to recapture the sound of his voice. She'd been so sure that she'd heard him. His entreaty had pulled her from sleep as effectively as if he'd reached out and touched her.

She shivered, remembering the feel of his fingers against her skin. Then closed her eyes at the memory of his lips, his hands, his lean hard body. The power of his touch stroking, caressing, driving her higher and then higher still. The strength of their joining, him thrusting deeper— filling her, stretching her—driving her on to immeasurable pleasure.

"Come to me."

Her eyes flickered open, his voice washing over her like a physical touch. Her body had tightened with need, her breasts swollen, her nipples taut, heat pooling between her thighs. She swallowed, desire making her throat dry. Never had she wanted anything—anyone—more.

Tears of frustration filled her eyes as she reached toward the emptiness of her room. This, then, was madness. All the talk of Highland magic aside, this wasn't normal. To want someone she'd just met more than life itself was crazy enough. But add to that the idea that her lover didn't even exist in this time and surely that meant that she was certifiable.

Or if not, then forever lost.

"Lily, come to me."

The words echoed in her head and she willed him to appear, staring into the shadows in the far reaches of the room. He'd come to her here once. Or at least she'd believed he'd been here. Surely if he was a part of her imagination she could conjure him at will. And if he were real?

Well, then she needed to find her way back.

There was nothing for her here anymore. No reason to stay. Perhaps Mrs. Abernathy and Elaine had been right. Maybe everything that had happened had led here, to this place. This man. Maybe it was all about having faith. Trusting her heart over her mind. Believing in the magic. Or at least accepting the possibility.

Pushing to her feet, she walked to the window and looked out across Duncreag's courtyard to the river and the valley floor beyond. The wind howled through the trees, the sound eerie as it swirled around the stone tower.

Turning back to the room, she closed her eyes, again willing him to appear. To find her. To come to her. But the room remained empty. She sighed, her heart twisting. She was chasing a ghost. A man long dead and buried. And yet, a man, impossible as it seemed, who now held her heart.

She'd been right the first time—she'd lost her mind.

Not that it was surprising. Less than a week ago, her life had been upended in the most catastrophic of ways. And now she stood in a medieval Scottish castle letting the magic of the Highlands color her perception of everything.

She wrapped her arms around her waist, turning back to the window. Her gaze automatically moved to the distant fields, where she knew the ruins of the cottage lay. The countryside was dark, the fallen stones lost to the night.

Deserted. Destroyed.

She sucked in a breath and closed her eyes, emotion threatening to overwhelm her. Desolation, a loss as great as that of her parents, threatened to consume her. It had to be real. He had to be real.

Fighting tears, she opened her eyes, her gaze moving again through the darkness, settling on a tiny pinprick of light that hadn't been there before.

The cottage.

Bram.

"Come to me."

CHAPTER 14

✤

"I COMMAND YOU to come to me." Bram fisted a hand and brought it down on the mantle in angry frustration. How many times did he have to say it? The fire burned brightly, filling the cottage's single room with flickering shadows. He'd done everything but get down on his knees, but despite all entreaties, he was still alone.

He tried to tell himself that it was for the best. That she'd be safer in her time, at least until he'd ridden against Alec Comyn. But the thought brought no respite. His need for Lily only burned stronger. With only one full night between them, the damned woman had somehow become more important to him than breath.

It wasn't as if he had no experience of women. He'd lain with more than his fair share, but none of them had mattered beyond the short time he'd spent with each of them. The encounters had simply been a matter of finding mutual pleasure. This was something more. Much, much more.

Perhaps they *were* enchanted.

Bram shook his head at the notion. He'd never been one to fall for that sort of nonsense. He believed in what he could see. What he could touch. And yet, he'd done more than touch Lily. He'd held her, kissed her, loved her until they'd been shattered by the glory of it all. He might not believe in magic and time travel. But he believed in her.

"Please," he pleaded on a whisper, his eyes locked on the flickering flames, his heart tight with longing. "Come to me."

The fire popped and hissed as the door behind him swung open. Spinning on his heels, he reached for the claymore leaning against the hearth.

"Lily." Her name came out on a groan as the sword clattered to the floor. Heart pounding, he took a step toward her.

Her dark hair spilled over her shoulders, curling in wild abandon, moonlight gilding it with silver. Her slippers were faded gold, her gossamer gown the palest of green. He let his eyes caress the curve of her hips, the taut plane of her belly, moving up to the smooth skin of her neck and the slope of her shoulders. Then let them drop again to settle on the sweet swell of her breasts as they rose and fell beneath her garment. His mouth ran dry, his body tightening in anticipation.

Then he lifted his gaze to hers, their eyes locking as they communicated without need for words. For a moment, they stood caught in the magic, and then with a little cry, she launched herself at him and his arms closed around her, reveling in the feel of her as he pulled her tightly against him. He breathed deeply, her scent surrounding him. Fresh and earthy. Like a warm summer day.

For a moment he simply held her, marveling in the fact that she was real. That she was here in the cottage with him. He could feel the rise and fall of her breasts, his own breathing matching hers. And then she pushed back, reaching to run the back of her hand over his cheek as if reassuring herself that he was indeed real.

"I thought I'd lost you." She swallowed, her eyes searching his face. "The men in the pass—"

"Were vanquished," he finished for her. "Thanks to you. To your warning."

She sucked in a breath, nodding, her eyes still locked on his. "But after you disappeared, I went to Dunbrae. I wanted to find you. I...I touched the fallen stones and the tower appeared. Only it was burning and there were men fighting everywhere. I was alone amongst them. And then you were there, but before I could reach you, you were gone. I thought...Oh, Bram, I was so afraid."

"Ach, *mo ghràidh*, there was no need," he soothed as he smoothed back her hair. "'Twas naught but a vision. I escaped the blackguards in the pass and at Dunbrae. And I'm here now with you." He cupped her face in his hands. "That's all that matters."

She nodded, her eyes glistening with unshed tears, the corners of her mouth lifting with a tremulous smile. He brushed the moisture away with his thumb. And then, with a low groan, bent his head and slanted his mouth over hers. Their lips brushed lightly, almost reverently, as if afraid that in touching one the other might disappear.

But the gentle touch only heightened Bram's need, a simple kiss no longer enough. He pulled her closer, his mouth firming as his lips pressed harder against hers. Tasting. Teasing. With a sigh, she opened to him, and he plunged his tongue into the moist heat of her mouth, deepening the kiss.

Firelight flickered around them and he drew her farther into the warmth of the room, his hands sliding down to the small of her back. She arched against him, mewling softly as she lifted her arms to twine her fingers through his hair, her breasts pressing against his chest.

Heat seared through him, desire so potent he feared it would engulf them both. And yet, even as the thought occurred, he pushed it aside. This was what he wanted. He needed her more than he'd ever needed anybody. Wanted her with a passion that was almost beyond ken. It was as if she'd reached inside him and touched his core. Set free that part of him that was most basic—most primitive.

He let his mind go as he lost himself in her kiss. Their tongues danced together, parrying and thrusting in a prelude to things to come. She tasted of something dusky and sweet. And he pressed for more. Drinking deeply. Wishing there were a way to take her inside of him. To hold her safely there.

Desperate now to feel her skin beneath his fingers, he reached behind her to undo the buttons that held her gown closed. Her skin beneath was silky and smooth, and she shivered beneath his touch. He smiled, pleased with her reaction, his mouth caressing the corners of her lips, and then kissing a line across the satin of her cheek to the soft whorl of her ear. He dipped his tongue inside and smiled as she tensed beneath his ministrations, her rising desire evident in the stuttered inhale of breath as he sucked gently on her earlobe, his breath caressing her.

Then with impatient hands, he pushed the bodice off her shoulders, baring her to the waist, delighted to find no further obstruction to his goal. With an open-mouthed kiss to the tender hollow at the base of her neck, he slid his hands up to cup her breasts. Her nipples were tight little buds. Pink against her alabaster skin. Ripe for the tasting. As if privy to his thoughts, she moaned and arched her back, eyes closed as she offered herself to him.

His body hardened as his passion rose to match hers. And he shifted, laying her back across his arm, his mouth taking one of her nipples. Biting lightly, he sucked her breast deeper into his mouth, tongue swirling around the crest as he suckled.

Her fingers laced into his hair again as he continued to taste her. Torment her. Then he shifted his attentions to the other breast, the other nipple, biting and sucking, pulling and teasing until she writhed beneath him, calling his name.

His groin literally throbbing with need, he swung her into his arms, still raining hot kisses along the swell of her breasts. In two strides, he'd reached the bed, laying her down on the pallet, his breath catching as the firelight danced across her skin.

With a slow smile, she rose on her knees. Then with graceful finesse, she pushed the gown over her hips, the fine material sliding down her thighs to pool on the bed around her. Moving slightly, she picked it up and tossed it to the floor, clad now only in a wisp of white lace that slid over her hips and between her thighs.

When she reached for the lace, he shook his head. "Nay, *mo ghràidh*, let me."

He reached down and slid a finger between the lace and her skin, then slowly inched the wee band down until it barely covered the soft dark curls at the apex of her thighs. She was already wet and ready. And she swallowed a moan when his fingers brushed across her mons, teasing the opening as he pushed her back onto the bed and slid the lacy undergarment from her legs.

Kneeling then on the floor at the edge of the pallet, he pushed her thighs wide and bent his head, blowing softly against the curls before slipping a finger inside to stroke her. In and out. In and out. Deeper, then deeper still as he added a second finger, his fist moving as he pushed inside her, stroking, possessing, pushing her closer and closer to the edge.

Crying out, she bucked up off the bed, but he held her with his hands as he exchanged fingers for lips and tongue. Licking and sucking, tasting her essence—feeling her body tighten with her need. Finding the tiny nub of her desire, he closed his lips around it and suckled, her strangled moan sending his own pulses pounding. Licking and laving, he circled and flicked. And then slid his tongue lower and thrust it deep. Once and then again. And yet again. Until she screamed his name and fell from the precipice.

He slid onto the bed and pulled her into his arms, holding her tightly as she shuddered, the climax still holding her in its thrall. Finally, when he felt her breathing ease, he pulled away.

"Not yet, please—"

"Easy now. I'm no' going anywhere." He smiled down at her, his body heavy and aching, the time for giving almost past. Quickly, he shed his garments and then returned to her side, pulling her into his arms. Skin to skin. Breast to chest.

He covered her mouth with his, the kiss languid and slow. His hand slid between her legs again, and he delighted in the warm wet heat that greeted him. "So then are you ready for me?" His voice was low, almost a growl, as he rolled to his back, pulling her on top of him.

Straddling his hips, she smiled down at him, her green eyes flecked with amber fire, her black hair a wavy curtain as she leaned forward to kiss him again. His hands closed around her breasts and he kneaded as they drank from each other, their tongues delving deep.

Then with a toss of her head, she sat back, lifting her hips and settling herself over the tip of his erection, the suction of her wet heat enveloping him as she slowly slid down. His hands still on her breasts, he waited until he was buried inside her, then slowly began to rock as she slid upwards again, setting the rhythm for their ride.

Despite his burning need to possess her, he allowed the torture of her slow, sensuous movements simply because he was spellbound by the beauty of the passion reflected in her face. Passion for him. For their joining.

She slid down again, taking him deeper as she moved her legs wider. Then suddenly he sat up, taking her breast in his mouth, tugging her nipple as she tightened her sheath around him. Sensation stretched, both of them captured, and then he grabbed her hips and the dance began in earnest.

In and out. Up and down. Her head thrown back in abandon, she arched her back. A goddess on fire. His body tensed as they rode higher and higher. Her hands tightened on his shoulders, her nails biting into his skin. She rode him harder and harder as he thrust inside her. Deeper and deeper until they were bonded together, not just physically but somehow intrinsically. Body to body. Soul to soul.

The excruciating joy ratcheted higher still and Lily tensed, then called his name as her body contracted around him, stroking and caressing, urging him to follow. Still holding her hips, he plunged up as she moved down. One last thrust and his mind exploded into sensation and light, his seed spilling deep inside her.

As unlikely as it might seem, they belonged together. Here between worlds. And now that he held her again, he never wanted to let her go.

~

Lily lay in the flickering firelight listening to the steady beat of Bram's heart. Her cheek nestled on his heavily muscled chest, she sighed and wiggled closer, grateful when his arms tightened around her. They were lying there, boneless, the power of their climaxes still an almost tangible thing.

He smelled of wood smoke and leather. And something uniquely Bram. The essence sent her emotions tumbling, her body tightening with desire all over again. It made absolutely no sense. But this man, this Highlander, had touched her in a way that no one else had ever done. It was as if he'd touched that part of her she'd always kept hidden away. The one that feared being hurt. Feared taking a risk.

And yet here she was. Surrounded by his warmth. Lying on a bed that hadn't existed in her world for hundreds of years. It was insane. It was miraculous. And she never wanted it to end.

"Are you comfortable?" His deep voice rumbled up through his chest, and she nodded, still content just to feel him breathe.

"I am. More than I think I've ever been. If you can believe that."

"Aye, 'tis the same with me." He smoothed back her hair and she tipped her head so that she could see the stark planes of his face. It would be so easy to let herself get lost in the cool blue of his eyes. It made her think of the waters of the Mediterranean Sea. Clear and deep and full of promise.

"So," she began, "not that I'm complaining, but I thought you'd be at Duncreag. With Iain and Katherine." The names came out almost a whisper, as somehow in saying them out loud she'd break whatever spell bound them.

"I wanted to be with you. And the cottage seemed the obvious place. But you know them both? You ken who they are?"

She nodded, lacing her fingers with his. "Katherine is like me. She traveled through time."

"For Iain." Bram nodded. "The two of them belong together."

As do we. She wanted to say it but again she found she was afraid. "I've met her brother. Jeff. He's the new laird at Duncreag."

"And that's where you've been staying?"

"Yes. Valerie is friends with Mrs. Abernathy. She and her husband look after Duncreag. They've been helping me—all of them—as I've been trying to make sense of things."

"Sometimes there is no sense to be had. You just have to take it all on faith."

"So says Mrs. Abernathy. Would that it were that easy." She smiled up at him. "But it's all been a lot to deal with. You. Me. The gap between your world and mine."

"Ach, but despite the incongruity, we fit together, you and I." He ran a hand over the curve of her breast and across the taut skin of her belly. Desire flashed, heated and strong.

"We do. At least when we're together."

"You said you'd been to Dunbrae." His brows knitted together, his hand still idly stroking her skin.

"I was trying to find you. Or at least some proof that you didn't just exist in my head."

"And were you successful in that?"

"Yes. I mean yes and no. It was all a really long time ago."

"In a manner of speaking." His smile was slow and a bit crooked. Her heart hitched and her breath caught. He reached out to tuck a strand of hair behind her ear, then his expression sobered. "And my father's holding?"

She paused, chewing on her bottom lip, her gaze locking with his. Then on a sigh, she shook her head. "There's nothing much left. Only stones and overgrown rubble."

He was still for a moment, and then he nodded. Accepting her words as truth. "As you say, there are many years between the two of us. I canna expect that any legacy of mine would survive forever."

"Were there two towers when you were there?" she asked, still watching him.

He frowned. "Nay, only the one."

"Well, there were the remains of two. One older than the other. It was the older one that gave me the vision. The one of you in danger and the tower burning."

"That would be the bastards who attacked my father. And tried to kill me."

"They're the ones behind everything? Your father's death? The men at Iain's tower? You said it was the son of your father's enemy."

"Aye, Alec Comyn. He and his father have always hated me and mine."

"And you're sure what I saw was the past?" She swallowed a rising bubble of hysteria at the absurdity of the question.

"*My* past. Yes. And I was most certainly in danger. But I escaped. And as I said, we killed the men in the pass as well."

"All of them?"

"It couldna be avoided. I would have preferred one or more of them had lived so that we could question them. But 'twas no' possible."

"But you recognized some of them?" She rolled a little bit away, so that she could see him more clearly in the flickering light.

"No' specifically. But they were wearing Comyn colors. And if that isn't damning enough, one of my clansmen escaped and found his way to Iain's. Frazier swears they were Comyns as well. And he'd know better than I."

"Frazier?"

"My father's captain. He's a good man. I trust him with my life. So yes, I'm certain it was the Comyns."

"Were there others? Who escaped, I mean?"

Bram's blue eyes clouded with pain. "Nay. There were no survivors. My oldest friend almost made it. He fought alongside Frazier, but, in the end, the Comyns killed Robby too."

"I'm so sorry," she whispered, knowing words were inadequate. "I know what it's like to lose all your family."

"Aye, and what it means to make a new one," he said, his gaze meeting hers as one finger traced the line of her lower lip.

She swallowed, worry tearing at her heart. "Now that you know about Alec Comyn," she asked, "what will you do?"

"I'll destroy him. After all that he did, he canna go unpunished."

"How? How will you punish him?" She wasn't certain she wanted to hear the answer and yet she knew that she needed to know.

"Iain, Ranald and I are riding for Alec's tower tomorrow."

"Ranald Macqueen? Your cousin?"

"Aye." He smiled, the gesture warming her to her toes. "You were able to glean that much, I see."

"It wasn't hard really. Elaine is related to Ranald. And Jeff was here once. He met Ranald then. Thinks of him as a friend, actually."

"Ah yes, Katherine told me about Jeff. About how he helped Iain save her."

"They were very close, I gather. He misses her terribly."

"I think the same is true for her."

"It can't be easy. Living in one time with memories of another."

"To hear Iain and Katherine tell it, nothing would do but for them to be together. And having seen them so, I canna say I see the wrong in it."

And having shared what she had with Bram, Lily couldn't either. But she was still afraid to put voice to the thought.

He reached out to cup her chin in his hand. "Some things, Lily, are just meant to be."

"Like us?" she whispered, holding his gaze.

"Mayhap. I canna say what fate has in store for us. But were I to have my way, I'd keep you with me forever."

A shudder of potent pleasure washed through her. "Then don't go. Stay here, with me."

Regret flashed in his eyes. "You know I canna. I have to take back what is mine."

"Even at the risk of losing what we've found?"

He nodded. "Even so."

"But why? Why is it so important to make him pay?"

"Because, thanks to Alec Comyn's treachery, my uncle has been given my holding. The lands that should now belong to me have been taken away, my name tarnished with lies. There are some among my kin who believe I killed my father. I canna let that go unanswered. I have to prove my innocence and bring the real culprit to bare."

She covered his hand with hers, fighting against her fear. "Then take me with you when you go."

"A battle isn't a place for a lass, *mo ghràidh*."

"And that's what it's going to be—a battle?"

"Aye. I see no way around it. Nor do Iain and Ranald. The only way now is to stand against Alec. And I canna fight if I'm worrying about you."

"But if you leave me, then I'll have to go back. Or forward or whatever. I can't stay here unless you're with me. And I can't bear the idea of losing you again." Put into words, it sounded so needy. But she couldn't help herself. She'd lost so much already. She couldn't stand the thought of losing him too.

"Lily, you know that I'd take you if I could, but..."

"Please, Bram." She was begging now. "Please don't go. Don't put yourself in that kind of danger."

His features tightened, his expression harsh. "I have no choice. It has to be done. And it has to be me. If you care for me at all you'll no' ask me to stay."

"Fine." She crossed her arms, anger making her brave. "Then I'm coming with you. I'll stay out of the way. But I won't leave you."

His face softened, his eyes reflecting an emotion she was afraid to put a name to. "Ach, if only it were that easy, *mo ghràidh*. I dinna know what it's like in your time. But in mine a woman is to be cherished and protected at all costs. Nothing is more important than that. And as you've found your way into my heart, I willna risk your safety for my own selfish pleasure."

"It isn't your choice. It's mine. If you value me at all, then you'll value my right to make my own decisions. To know my own mind." She glared at him, daring him to argue. "I won't be left behind. Unless you can look me in the eyes and tell me you don't want me, I'm coming with you. It's as simple as that."

Silence stretched between them as she watched him digest her words. One hand clenched into a fist and then slowly, slowly he relaxed his fingers and reached out again to run the back of his hand along her cheek.

"So you agree?"

"Aye. I'll grant that you have the right to make your own decisions. But I dinna have to like them."

She smiled, willing to take the win any way she could get it. "I won't get in the way. I promise."

She lay beside him, her heart pounding, partly because she'd triumphed, and partly because that triumph would be short-lived if they both wound up dead. His wasn't an easy time. Men were brutal. She'd sensed as much in her visions. And she knew that Bram was right; a battle wasn't the place for a woman. Especially one with modern sensibilities. But what choice did she have?

She couldn't leave him. No matter what the cost, she needed to be here with him.

Assuming fate would allow it.

There was nothing to say she wouldn't be ripped from his arms again. It had happened before. Panic reared its head and she fought to breathe slowly.

"I need you," she whispered.

"As I need you." He pulled her closer, her back nestled against his chest, his hands settling around her breasts. Deftly he stroked and circled her nipples, his touch rekindling the fire deep inside her, pushing away her fear with passion.

She started to turn but he held her firmly, one hand splayed across her belly, the other moving down from her breasts to the hot, wet juncture between her thighs. His breath teased her ear and neck, sending shivers of need racing through her as he plunged first one finger and then a second deep inside her. Stroking, caressing, pushing deeper and then deeper still. She choked on a sob, wanting him inside her more than she wanted to breathe.

"Please, Bram," she begged, her voice rough with desire. "Take me. Take me now."

With a low growl, he pushed one of her legs upward, replacing his fingers with the head of his erection. She squirmed against him, trying to move closer. But he held her firmly in place. Then, with a single thrust, he was inside her. Deeper than before. His balls pressed against her bottom.

For a moment, he held her like that. Joined. Two parts of a whole. And then he pulled back almost to the tip. She swallowed and shifted restlessly against him.

"Patience, *mo ghràidh*."

He inched back just a little more and then thrust deeply again, this time with more power. His other hand closed around one of her breasts, his breath still hot in her ear. He rolled her nipple between his thumb and forefinger. Slowly he rocked back and forth, the motion sending exquisite shards of pleasure rocketing through her.

She arched her back, pushing her bottom more firmly against him, taking him deeper, the sensation almost beyond bearing, pleasure so great it was almost pain. Then slowly he withdrew again, and she whimpered with need.

His fingers tightened on her nipple, tugging as he surged into her again, and she fractured, her entire body convulsing with the power of her climax. She spasmed around him, breath stuttering, heart pounding. His arms tightened around her, holding her safe as she spiraled out of control. Her mind blanked as the power of their passion overrode every other sense.

He held her for a moment, then gently rolled her over until he was propped above her, his hips nestled between her legs, his body braced on his elbows. Their gazes collided and she struggled for breath. Then with a slow, sure smile, he lifted and surged into her again. Her body responded in an instant, desire building again as he began to ride.

She wrapped her legs around him, and his mouth found hers. The kiss was searing. A take no prisoners possession. Each of them claiming the other with lips and tongues and always the driving rhythm of him moving deep inside her.

Opening wider, she took him deeper, meeting him thrust for thrust. Her muscles tightened around him. Holding him. Caressing him. Taking and giving. Their fated dance beyond all time.

This was what she had been born for. This moment. This man. And nothing was going to keep them apart.

He murmured her name, and then his lips claimed hers again, their bodies moving together. The magic tension built again, stretching tighter and tighter as they continued to move together. Then suddenly the world exploded into shards of light.

He swallowed her cry, his hands linking with both of hers. And there was nothing in the world but the two of them, joined together as surely it was meant to be.

CHAPTER 15

"BRAM?" THE CRY tore through him. "Where are you?"

He turned from the fireplace as Lily pushed to a sitting position, her ebony hair curling wildly around her head, her sleep-heavy eyes holding traces of fear. His heart twisted.

"I'm here, *mo ghràidh*. I'm only stoking the fire." Placing the poker back by the hearth, he crossed the room to slip into bed beside her, pulling her soft, warm body against his, his lips moving in her hair. Within his embrace he could feel her trembling. "Dinna fash yourself," he soothed. "Everything is all right."

"I'm sorry." She tilted her head so that her emerald gaze met his. "It's just that I woke and you were gone. Like before. And I..."

"I know," he whispered, stroking her hair. He fought the urge to assure her that it would never happen again. That they'd never be parted. But he wasn't a lying man. The future—their future—was clouded. "I'm here now," he murmured, leaning down to brush his lips against hers.

He'd meant to offer comfort. To hold her until she fell asleep, but the spark between them ignited, his senses exploding as he deepened the kiss. Never had he felt so engulfed by passion. He'd always been the possessor, never the possessed. The idea should have alarmed him, but somehow it only made him want her more. Maybe he'd had it right the first time. He was bewitched, body and soul.

With a groan, he rolled her beneath him, pinning her body with his, his hips resting between her thighs. Their gazes locked and held, her glittering green eyes dark with desire.

Again he bent his head, this time to trace the line of her jaw with open-mouthed kisses, letting his lips trail lower to caress the curve of her neck and the valley between her breasts. She whimpered and arched her back. And he took what she offered, circling one nipple with his tongue and then the other, teasing them both until he felt them pebble hard beneath his touch.

Where their lovemaking before had been ruled by raw hunger and need, this time, although desire still pressed, Bram was determined to take it slow. To make time for exploration. For slow, sensual loving. Using his hands and mouth, he explored every part of her, rejoicing in the soft tangle of her hair, the velvety whorls of her ears and the supple, smooth curves of her shoulders.

He kissed her fingers, her toes, the hollows behind her knees. He tasted her lips, her breasts, and finally her soft molten core. His hands worshiped her, his lips reverent. She belonged to him. And he to her. It was as simple as that. Or perhaps as complicated.

But now wasn't the time for thinking.

Bram pushed her thighs wide and thrust his tongue deep, feeling her shudder and clench around him. She cried out as satisfaction burned through him, his need to please her almost overriding his own desire.

Sliding up again, he took possession of her mouth, his kiss growing more insistent. She yielded to him, her tongue dancing with his, her taste intoxicating. He wound his fingers through her hair as her hands stroked his shoulders, his back, his hips. And then her fingers slipped between them, circling his erection—her touch almost unmanning him.

She squeezed and stroked, caressing and enticing. Inch by inch, his carefully fought control slipped away until he stood on the brink, his body heavy with his need. "Enough," he whispered, reaching down to remove her hand.

She frowned in question, but he smiled, pushing her thighs apart as he settled himself between them. Then, arching his hips, he entered her with a single, powerful thrust, burying himself to the hilt, her tight, wet heat threatening to finish what her hand had begun.

Resisting the urge to move, he held her passion-filled gaze, drinking in her strength, her beauty. "No matter what happens—know always that you are mine." He hadn't meant to say the words; they'd come unbidden. And now they stretched between them, filling the silence.

"And you're mine," she whispered as she pulled him down into a kiss, her body shifting to take him deeper. And he was lost on a sea of passion and emotion beyond anything he'd ever kenned.

There was nothing but the two of them and the power of their bodies moving together, each stroke taking them higher and then higher still, until he wasn't sure where he ended and she began.

And he knew in that moment that he'd do anything to protect her—even if it meant letting her go.

—⁓—

Bram shivered in the cold as the first pink fingers of dawn reached up from the horizon. Lily lay sleeping in the bed, one hand clutching the bedcovers, the other folded beneath her cheek. Her dark curls splayed out across the pillow. Her ring lay against her bare breast, the cool silver almost encircling her nipple.

He clenched his fist, fighting the desire to abandon all honor. To climb back into the bed. To take her again. To lose himself in her sweet heat. But to do so would be to deny his heritage. To dishonor his father and his clan.

Dawn was upon them. And his duty lay above all else. Even his love. *His love.* The words echoed through his mind. He tested them, considered them, and then accepted them as truth. He loved Lily. Had loved her almost from the first moment she'd collapsed at his hearth. And yet he had to walk away.

His world wasn't safe for her. Not with the threat from the Comyns. And worse from his own clan. Until he'd proven his innocence and avenged his father, there was no place in his life for her. He couldn't be sure he'd be able to keep her safe. And that suddenly was more important even than having her with him.

Still his heart twisted, his stomach clenching. Their coming together had been a gift. And now he was risking losing it forever.

He secured his plaid, and still watching her sleep, reached for his father's brooch, the mountain cat's eyes glittering up at him. Closing his hand around it, he bent to retrieve Lily's gown from the floor and then carefully pinned the brooch to the bodice. If he could not stay, then at least he'd leave her a part of him.

Clenching a fist, he laid the gown across the end of the bed, then secured his claymore and strode for the door, turning for one last look, praying that fate would be kind. That once the fighting was over, they would find each other again. But even more so, he prayed that if his boon were to be granted and they were indeed reunited, that Lily would find it in her heart to forgive him.

"The bloody bastard left me. He told me I belonged to him and then he walked away without looking back." Lily paced in front of the stone fireplace in the great hall at Duncreag, her voice echoing across the room.

Mrs. Abernathy, Elaine and Jeff all watched her with trepidation. She knew she was losing it, and had it been any other situation, she'd have laughed at her own dramatics. But in truth, there was nothing to laugh at. Bram Macgillivray had left her. Just like everyone else in her life. She'd believed in him, let herself hope again. And now...now he'd left her and shattered her heart all over again.

"I'm such a stupid fool. How could I have believed him? I thought he cared about me. I thought he...he..." She trailed off, unable to say the words.

"Ach, now you don't know what he was thinking," Mrs. Abernathy soothed. "Maybe he didn't mean to leave you. That's what happened before, right? Neither of you could control it."

She shook her head, clenching her fists. "Yes, but this time we knew better. We knew that we couldn't be parted. I even told him I'd go with him. That I'd fight the damn Comyns if that's what it took. Be a part of his stupid battle. But it didn't matter. He left me anyway. For Iain and Ranald and honor. Believe me, he knew what would happen if he left. But that didn't stop him, did it?"

"Maybe he had good reason," Jeff offered.

"Like what?" She eyed him with suspicion. One man was very much like another after all. And, at the moment, she wasn't inclined to trust any of them.

"Well, you mentioned a battle. I assume it has something to do with Bram's father's death?"

"Yes." She nodded, anger still propelling her to pace. "He blames a man called Alec Comyn. Bram's and Alec's fathers were enemies, I think."

"Would make sense." Mrs. Abernathy nodded, her lips pursed as she considered the notion. "There's never been any love lost between the Comyns and the Macgillivrays."

"Yes and to make it worse, apparently Bram's family—some of them anyway—believe that he is the one who killed his family. So they gave what's left of Dunbrae to his uncle."

"That can't have gone over well," Jeff said with a frown. "But why would they think it was him?"

"Apparently, in order for Alec Comyn's men to have taken Dunbrae they would have had to have inside help. And someone is putting it about that Bram was the traitor."

"Which makes his loss that much greater," Mrs. Abernathy mused. "Poor lad."

"I'll grant you that," Lily said, her heart squeezing as she thought of the pain in Bram's voice. "But that doesn't mean I forgive him for what he's done."

"Did Bram believe the Comyns were behind the attack at Duncreag as well?" Jeff asked, still clearly focused on Bram's situation.

"Yes," she admitted on a sigh. "He says they wore the right colors. Although everyone was killed, so they couldn't confirm it. But a man from Dunbrae—" She stopped before the fire, trying to remember. "—Frazier. Seamus's captain, I believe. He confirmed it."

"He's there?" Jeff questioned. "At Duncreag?"

"Well, if Bram is to be believed, they're all gone now," she grimaced, starting to pace again. "They were due to ride out this morning. But yes, he arrived after they fought the Comyns." All of which happened over five hundred years ago, she reminded herself. The impossibility of the entire thing made her want to scream.

"And he was sure it was the Comyns?" Jeff pressed.

"Yes." She stopped again, frowning at him. "Frazier recognized them at Dunbrae. So there's no question. But that isn't reason enough to abandon me. If Bram truly cared, he'd have taken me with him."

"Maybe Jeff's right. Maybe his not taking you is the important bit." Elaine reached out to touch her hand, and Lily stilled, her emotions rioting.

"That doesn't make any sense."

"Of course it does," Mrs. Abernathy soothed. "If the man loves you, he's not going to risk putting you in harm's way."

"It might seem a bit harsh by today's standards, but we're talking about a different time," Jeff said. "Violence and vengeance ruled the clans in those days. It wasn't safe for women."

"But you let your sister go there." She knew she was foundering. That her logic wasn't making sense. But he'd left her, damn it. And no matter his reasons, she was the one left to pick up the pieces.

"I didn't let my sister do anything." Jeff's eyes flashed in warning. "She makes her own decisions. And nothing I could have done would have stopped her. She loved Iain and that was the end of it."

"My point exactly. It should have been my decision. And the fact that he didn't let me make it means that he can't possibly care about me in any meaningful way."

"With the risk of being throttled for the sins of all my sex, I think you are missing some important points," Jeff offered, holding his hands up to signal peace. All three women looked at him and he grimaced. "I'm just trying to help."

"The points?" Elaine prompted.

"Love, honor and commitment."

"Which means what? That Bram owes more to his dead father than to me?" The minute the words were out, Lily regretted them. One couldn't choose between the people one cared about. But then again, maybe he didn't really care about her. Maybe he hadn't meant all that he'd said.

"It means, as Elaine and Mrs. Abernathy said, that he cared enough to let you go. He knew that dragging you into his fight could very well mean your death. I've been there, Lily. I've seen what it can be like. Katherine was almost killed. Then when push came to shove and we thought she was going to die, Iain let her go. He sent her home with me. Where she could have the help she needed to recover."

"After which she went right back to Iain," Elaine inserted, clearly taking Lily's side.

"Yes, but that doesn't change the fact that when it was important, Iain loved Katherine enough to let her go."

"But even if you're right," Lily said, dropping down on a bench next to the hearth, "Bram still chose his father over me." That was the crux of it really.

"That's where honor comes in." Jeff shrugged. "It was never a choice. He wouldn't be able to live with himself if he didn't fight to avenge his father. And more importantly to clear his own name. What can he possibly offer you if he doesn't do that?"

"Himself. Alive and well. And in the same damn century as me." She closed her hand over her chest, daring him to argue. "He promised he'd take me with him." She paused, closing her eyes. The truth was that he'd only promised she had a right to her opinion. Suddenly she saw the previous night's triumph for what it had really been. "Oh God, he never meant to take me at all."

"But he didn't want to leave you either," Jeff said, his voice full of conviction. "When did he give you the brooch?"

Lily glanced down at the silver cat winking up from the bust of her dress. "It was there when I woke up this morning."

"Do you ken the significance of it?" Mrs. Abernathy asked, her gaze fixed on the pin.

"It's beautiful, but I don't know that it has any meaning."

"It's a clan crest," Elaine stated. "Macgillivray, if I had to guess." She looked across at Mrs. Abernathy, who nodded.

"Every clan has their own crest, you see," Mrs. Abernathy explained. "And each holding adapts it to be their own. I canna say for certain, but I'm guessing the pin belonged to Bram's father. And for him to have left it for you…" She shrugged, her meaning clear.

"I'd rather have him."

"But at least you know that he wanted you to have the brooch," Elaine said.

"Commitment," Jeff seconded. "If he didn't care about you, Lily, he'd never given you something so precious to him."

"Cold comfort," she said, stubbornly clinging to her anger, even as her fingers circled the brooch, the metal cool between her fingers.

"Well, I, for one, think that rather than sitting around here rehashing what happened and what it did or didn't mean, we'd be better off seeking more information. Knowledge, after all, is power."

Lily frowned at Mrs. Abernathy, still battling her raging emotions. "And how do you suggest we do that?"

"Simple. We go straight to the source. At least as much as we can, given the difference in time." She smiled, pushing out of her chair with a firm nod. "I say we pay a visit to Ridge Manor."

"Because?" Jeff asked, also pushing to his feet.

Mrs. Abernathy smiled. "Because that's where Bram's gone. To *Tigh an Droma*, Alec Comyn's holding."

CHAPTER 16

✦

"I THOUGHT I might find you here," Katherine said as she walked out onto the battlements. "Iain and Ranald are almost ready to go."

Bram turned back toward the valley below, his eyes drawn to the spot of white that marked the cottage.

Katherine took a step forward, stopping a few paces back from the low battlement wall, shooting a wary look down before lifting her head defiantly. "I'm not all that fond of heights," she said by way of explanation.

"Then why come up here?" he asked, his eyes still trained on the stone structure across the river.

"To find you." She smiled with a shrug. "And because I figure if I do this often enough, it'll become less of a bother." She moved forward, resting one hand on the wall.

"Iain's a lucky man." Bram clenched his fist, trying not to let his rioting feelings get the best of him.

"Yes, well, we're both lucky. And tenacious. What we have is a gift. But it didn't come easily. And it has to be maintained. Which sometimes means fighting to protect it."

"That's what I thought I was doing," Bram whispered, his mind conjuring the image of Lily as she lay sleeping in their bed. "I know it had to be done, and yet I feel as if I betrayed her."

"I take it she didn't know you were going to leave her?"

He didn't question how she knew what had happened. Katherine had a way of seeing the truth without any need for words. "Nay. She wanted to come with me. To fight the Comyns." He struggled against a wash of pride and fear, the juxtaposition of the two emotions threatening to unman him. "I couldna let her do it. Surely you can see that?"

"I can see that you believed it was the right thing to do."

"But you do not agree."

"It isn't my place to agree or disagree. You did what you thought was right. That's all that matters."

"Mayhap. But what if I was wrong? Or even if I was right, what if in leaving her, I've lost her forever?"

Beside him, Katherine sighed. "I wish I had answers for you. Something that would make it all okay."

He frowned at the last bit, not recognizing the word.

"Make it all right," she amended with a smile. "It isn't easy trying to live in one century when you're from another. And the decision to come here to stay isn't one to be made in haste."

"So you thought about it long and hard, did you?" Bram asked, fairly certain he already knew the answer.

Katherine laughed. "Well, yes and no. I mean, it did take me a while to realize I needed to come back to Scotland."

"Eight years," Bram said with a huff of impatience.

"Yes. But I didn't know that Iain was real. It's different with you and your Lily."

He started to correct her, to say that she wasn't 'his', but the words died in his throat. They belonged to each other as surely as he was breathing. The only difficulty was that they didn't occupy the same space and time. "But after you knew. That he was real, I mean. Did you do the logical thing then?"

"No." She shook her head, wrapping her arms around her waist as she remembered. "All I could think about was how much I loved him. And nothing could be allowed to stand in the way of that."

"But that's exactly what I've done, isn't it? Let my father's death and the situation with the Comyns come between us. I left her behind, Katherine. After a night like I've never known."

"Why did you walk out the door, Bram?" she asked, her voice gentle, full of understanding.

"Because I was afraid the daft woman would truly follow me into battle. And if anything were to happen to her, I'd...I'd..." He trailed off, his gaze still locked on the distant cottage.

"You wanted to protect her. There's nothing wrong in that."

"Except that she'll no' understand. She'll see it as a betrayal. And I canna help but think she willna want to come back here again."

"I think you're judging her too harshly. She'll be angry, I'm certain. And perhaps at first she'll see what you did as a betrayal. But I'm also sure that once she has a chance to think on it, she'll understand that you did what you did because you love her."

"I do," he said, the thought making him ache inside. "Love her, I mean. Ach, Katherine, what have I done?"

"You've made a choice. And now you just have to have faith that it will all come out right in the end."

"Like it did for you and Iain."

She laid her hand on his arm. "It wasn't easy for us either, Bram. There was far more than just the eight years of separation. We had enemies to fight as well. One of them almost destroyed me in the process. Which meant that when it mattered most, Iain had to let me go. He had to send me back to my own time."

"Aye, and it was the hardest decision I've ever had to make." Iain's deep voice echoed over the battlements as he came to stand behind his wife. His arms circled her waist and Katherine leaned back against him. "But even though I thought I'd lost her forever, I knew I'd chosen true."

"And he moped around here like there was no tomorrow despite all his blustering." Ranald laughed as he joined the group at the wall.

"Well, what did you expect, man? I'd lost my own true love." Iain wagged his eyebrows at his cousin, and Katherine's eyes sparkled with laughter.

Bram felt a wave of jealousy. He'd held his love in his arms and now he'd lost her. Possibly forever.

"Faith, Bram," Katherine repeated. "No one said it would be easy. But believe me, it's worth the effort."

He nodded, staring off into the distance, then with a sharp exhale of breath turned to his kin, forcing himself to face his greatest fear. "I went back."

The others waited in silence.

"In the end I couldna do it. I couldna walk away. So I went back." He closed his eyes, fists clenched as he remembered. "But I was too late. The cottage was empty. Lily was gone."

"Perhaps for the best?" Ranald queried. "We do have a battle to fight."

Katherine tensed in Iain's arms.

"No worries, my love," he said, his arms tightening around her. "We've fought in worse battles and won."

"I know." Katherine sighed, then squared her shoulders and lifted her head to kiss her husband's cheek. "And the sooner we get the lot of you on your way, the sooner you'll all come back to me." Her words included Ranald and Bram, but her eyes were only for Iain.

He bent to kiss her. "All will be well, I promise."

"See that it is," she admonished, pushing away the fear that had surfaced momentarily in her eyes. "And you," she added, turning to Bram, "as I said, have a little faith. What's to be is meant to be. But as a dear friend of mine used to say, everything happens in its own time. If your Lily truly loves you, she'll understand why you left her behind. And somehow the two of you will find a way back to each other. You just have to believe it's possible."

Which was the crux of the matter, really.

With a nod, Bram squeezed Katherine's hand, then turned to follow Ranald as he made his way down to the forecourt and the waiting men.

The battle was at hand.

After Duncreag and Dunbrae, the Comyn manor house was a disappointment. Not that it wasn't amazing in its own right, but it lacked the ancient appeal of the two holdings, the one nothing but ruins, the other surviving almost intact.

Like most homes in this part of the world, it spoke to the generations, the harsh Georgian façade giving way to Elizabethan wings running both to the east and the west. Although Lily doubted the Scottish forbears would have described their homes based on English monarchs and their inspired architecture.

Ivy and small pink roses curled around the pillars set on both sides of the entrance, the ivy having jumped from column to wall, its fan of dark green plumage climbing upward, spreading until it covered a large part of the right side of the manor. It should have softened the sharp lines of the stone edifice, but somehow it only managed to add to the house's grandeur.

"There's nothing left of the original tower?" Lily asked as they walked up the steps to the massive front door. "I'd hoped..." She trailed off, not sure really what it was she wanted. Another flash of the past perhaps. Something to let her know with certainty that Bram was all right.

Despite her anger, she couldn't stand the thought that he could be hurt. Or worse. She shook her head, the illogic of her thoughts threatening to swamp her emotions. Bram was dead. Alec was dead. All of them were dead.

She shivered, and Mrs. Abernathy laid a warm hand on her shoulder. "It's going to be all right, lamb. You just have to keep going. One step at a time. We need to find the truth of what happened and once that's accomplished, you'll know what to do."

Lily nodded, squeezing the older woman's hand as Mrs. Abernathy pounded on the door. Lily fingered her father's ring nervously. She'd left Bram's brooch at Duncreag, fearful that even after all this time something so blatantly Macgillivray would hinder any connection she might establish with these modern day Comyns.

The ancient door swung open on surprisingly silent hinges. A small woman with graying hair and a cheerful smile ushered them both inside. "Good afternoon. I'm the housekeeper. Mrs. Potter. The mistress is expecting you," she told Mrs. Abernathy, pausing to look back as Lily stepped across the threshold.

For a moment the woman stood, stunned, eyes wide as her gaze locked on Lily. She swallowed once, her hand clutching her throat, and then with a shake of her head, she looked away, motioning them forward. "I'm sorry. I just didn't expect..." She trailed off on a sigh. "It's just down the hallway. Second door on the right."

"What in heaven's name do you think that was all about?" Mrs. Abernathy asked.

"Maybe she's seen pictures of me in the tabloids." Lily shook her head. "My parents' death and the subsequent discovery that they were insolvent has been fodder for weeks."

"I suppose it's possible." Mrs. Abernathy nodded, her frown indicating that she wasn't convinced. "Perhaps Mrs. Comyn will shed some light on the matter."

The parlor was both elegant and comfortable, a combination not always easy to achieve. A graceful marble fireplace was centered on the far wall, a cheerful blaze in the grate. Ceramic figurines, Wedgewood and Limoges, were displayed at either end of the mantel, and a large oil painting that looked very much to be an original Gainsborough hung above it. Two wingbacks sat to one side of the fire with a graceful sofa across from them.

It was from the sofa that the lady of the manor, Mrs. Comyn, rose, her welcoming smile fading as Lily and Mrs. Abernathy stepped into the light.

"Oh my," she whispered, her hand rising to her throat in the same manner as her housekeeper's. "I had no idea. I mean…dear God." For a moment she too seemed to be held in thrall, and then on the quick release of a breath, she forced a smile. "Please forgive my manners. I didn't mean to stare." She moved her gaze to Mrs. Abernathy. "It's just that when you called, you didn't say that your friend was…well, I wasn't expecting her to be…well, to be…family."

"I don't understand," Lily said, frowning at the woman and her obvious distress. "We're not related."

"Well, no of course not. At least not by blood. But you're most definitely related to my husband." She nodded, her smile more genuine now. "Come, I'd thought to visit with you on my own. I know a fair bit about the family lore. But under the circumstances, you'll want to meet Reginald. And I've no doubt that he'll want to meet you."

Lily turned to Mrs. Abernathy, tilting her head in silent question as Mrs. Comyn led the way from the room.

"I've no idea," Mrs. Abernathy said with a shrug. "But I've a feeling we're about to find out."

Mrs. Comyn led them farther down the hallway, pausing to rap on a door to the left of the staircase. After a murmured "Come," she ushered the two of them through the doors.

This room was larger than the parlor, more elegant and slightly more daunting. Like the parlor, there was an ornate fireplace with a fire burning in the grate. But unlike the smaller, more intimate room, this one boasted a mural on the high ceiling and portraits displayed in clusters on almost every inch of wall space.

Settees and chairs were arranged artfully throughout. And to Lily's eye, the room held an essence of time gone by, of elegance and artfulness that were often missing from today's more relaxed existence.

In the far corner, a large gentleman strode around the end of a desk that had been placed to take advantage of both the grandeur of the room and the beauty of the gardens on the other side of the windows that lined the far wall.

The light held him in silhouette for a moment, and then he stepped forward, brows raised in obvious question.

It was Lily's turn to gasp. Although his dark hair was peppered with gray, he walked with an assured grace that belied his age. And his eyes glittered green as his gaze slowly raked her from head to toe.

"Good God," he said, his shock echoing both his wife and his housekeeper's. "You look just like her."

"Her who?" Lily managed, her gaze still captured by Mr. Comyn's. "I look just like you."

"Aye, that you do." The man smiled, his eyes crinkling at the corners. "But then I suppose that comes as no surprise. With us both being Comyns."

"But I'm not..." Lily began.

"Oh, but you most assuredly are," the man informed her, taking her arm and leading her across the room to one of the groupings of portraits. "See for yourself." He gestured at a small painting in the center of the group. "If that's not the spitting image of you, then Bonnie Prince Charlie won his war and his kin are now sitting on the throne of England."

"Merciful heaven," Mrs. Abernathy croaked as she moved to study the painting. "Except for the difference in your dress, the thing could be a mirror."

The woman in the painting smiled at them from her canvas. From across time. Her green eyes were glittering and bright—her gaze strong and direct. Her dark hair was woven into an intricate braid, but even with the attempt to tame it, her curls had escaped confinement, twining around her neck and shoulders.

Lily touched her own rioting curls, her gaze riveted on the woman in the gilded frame. This was a strong woman. A true lady. And Mrs. Abernathy was right; the portrait *was* like a mirror. The lines of her nose, the curve of her lips, even the tilt of her eyes was the same. And even if all of that could have been ignored, there was the finely wrought chain around the woman's neck, the filigreed links dropping to reveal the intricate silver of the ring strung upon it.

A wedding ring. The same as Lily's father's.

The same as the one that she too wore around her neck.

CHAPTER 17

⚜

"WHO IS SHE?" Lily asked as she whirled around to face the Comyns.

"We don't know actually," Reginald Comyn said, gesturing toward a group of chairs and a small sofa.

"But we think we do," Mrs. Comyn put in helpfully. "At least the painting has been dated to the right time."

"Aye," Reginald acknowledged. "But we canna be certain. It isn't much more than a legend, really. And for me at least, I think the more pertinent question is who are you?"

The silver of the ring seemed to burn the skin between her breasts, but Lily wasn't ready to share her treasure with the Comyns. At least not yet. There were too many other questions. Questions she hoped they could answer. "My name is Lily Chastain. My father was an entrepreneur. A quite infamous one, actually. You might have heard of him."

She waited for a moment, watching the Comyns as they settled in the chairs across from the sofa she and Mrs. Abernathy were seated upon.

"American?" Mr. Comyn frowned.

Lily nodded.

"And he died recently," his wife added. "Oh dear, your mother, too." She was a statuesque woman, elegant and refined. Not, Lily suspected, one given to emotional outbursts. Yet there was a quick flash of sympathy. "I read about it in the magazines."

Mrs. Abernathy harrumphed, but didn't say anything more.

"I'm so sorry, my dear," Mr. Comyn said. "But you must understand that your arrival here, looking as you do, is a bit of a shock for us. And we can't help but wonder how you fit into our family tree, so to speak. I mean, your friend is right. The portrait is like a bloody mirror." He smiled then, his gaze softening. "I'm afraid we've most likely given you a fright."

"But you did request the interview with us," Mrs. Comyn said. "So you must have suspected something."

Oh God, faced with the two of them, clearly dying of curiosity, Lily suddenly found herself at a loss for words. How in the hell was she supposed to explain to these people what had happened to her? And worst of all, if the woman in the portrait was indeed a Comyn then that meant she, too, carried Comyn blood. Which meant that she and Bram...it was beyond belief. His mortal enemies were her kin.

In modern day terms it might mean nothing, but in his day—in his time—family was everything. And if the worst were true, her family was responsible for his father's death. And at this very moment, in some other plane of time, Bram was about to attack her ancestor.

She closed her eyes, cold sweat breaking across her brow.

"Lily, are you all right?" Mrs. Abernathy's hand closed over hers. "Breathe, lamb. Just breathe."

She nodded, concentrating on the simple act of inhaling and exhaling. Then opened her eyes slowly, the room swaying a little and then coming clear. "I'm fine. It's just that all of this—" She waved a hand towards the portrait. "—is a bit much."

"So you'd no notion that you were our kin?" Mr. Comyn asked.

"No, sir. I had no idea. In fact, I'm still not certain how we're connected."

"Call me Reginald," the man insisted, leaning forward earnestly in his chair. "We are family after all."

"And I'm Tildy." Mrs. Comyn smiled, the gesture lighting her blue eyes. "Short for Matilda. I always thought it was an overpowering name."

They were trying to set her at ease, which made her heart swell. Good lord, if they were right, she had family. Living family. On the wrong side of a blood feud. She sucked in another breath.

"Best to start at the beginning, I always say." Mrs. Abernathy smiled at all of them. "Your last name is Chastain. Clearly not a Scottish name."

"No. My father's family was originally from Provence. His grand-father was French."

"He could have married someone Scottish," Tildy suggested.

"It's possible, but my great-grandmother's given name was Lily. Like mine. Only she spelled it with an 'i'."

"What about your mother?" Mrs. Abernathy queried.

Lily forced herself to focus on the conversation, ignoring her riot-ing thoughts. "She was a Mandel. German, I think. But her father was like fifth generation American. Made his money in steel." She closed her eyes, thinking back on her mother's stories. "I don't know much about my grandmother, Lydia. She died before I was born. But I re-member my mother saying she was originally from South Africa..." She scrunched up her nose. "I remember my mother showing me a letter. And then going to look the address up on a map once to see if I could find it."

"Well, that would seem a dead end," Tildy said on a sigh.

"Not necessarily," her husband interjected. "A lot of Scottish people immigrated to South Africa. Where did she live?"

Again Lily had to rake her memory. "It was outside the city of Constantia. A place called Airlie."

"But Airlie is a Gaelic name," Mrs. Abernathy protested.

"Aye, and as with most immigrants, people named their new homes after their old ones." Reginald frowned, tapping a finger against his chin as he thought. "There's an Airlie in Aberdeenshire. Near to Cuminstown."

"Named for your family?" Lily asked.

"Aye, that it is." Reginald was smiling now. "Can you remember your great-grandmother's name perchance?"

"That I do know. Her name was Niven. Like the actor. David. Only her first name was Jeanne." Lily smiled triumphantly at the assembled company. "Jeanne Niven. I remember because we had an old quilt her Sunday School class embroidered one year when she was sick. It had all of their names and hers as well. Now that I think on it, it would have had to have been before she was married. My great-grandfather's last name was Balog. But it doesn't matter. Niven is an English name, surely."

"It is," Reginald said, exchanging a glance with his wife. "But it's an Anglicized version of a Scottish name. Macniven."

"And," Tildy added, "Macniven is a sept of the Comyns."

Lily shook her head, not familiar with the term.

"A related clan. Often by blood," Mrs. Abernathy explained. "Which means your great-grandmother's family was most likely from Scotland. Perhaps near Ailie. And given the resemblance you and Reginald share, not to mention the lady—" She tipped her head toward the portrait. "—I'd say you most definitely carry Comyn blood."

"But this is awful," Lily gasped without thinking.

"I beg your pardon?" Reginald's gaze hardened.

"Oh God, I didn't mean it like that. In fact, it's marvelous to have found family just after I've lost all of mine. It's just that it complicates things a great deal."

"Such is life, I'm afraid." Tildy shrugged with a smile. "I'd never thought to see the lady come to life in such a way. I'll admit you gave me a turn when you walked into the parlor."

"Mrs. Potter too if I had to call it," Mrs. Abernathy said. "The puir wee woman was as white as a banshee."

"I think we can all agree that this, err, development, took us all by surprise."

Lily's gaze was drawn again to the portrait. "Tell me what you know of the lady. You said something about a legend."

"It's just a story. There's nothing to substantiate it. Not even the portrait."

"But the timing is right. The art historian said it was probably painted sometime between the twelfth and fifteenth centuries. Which means she could be Tyra."

"Or any other of a thousand Comyn women long dead and gone."

Lily shivered, her gut tightening as she stared up at the woman.

"But surely there's no harm in sharing the legend," Mrs. Abernathy said. "I mean, in light of the fact that Lily is clearly the lady's descendent."

Reginald shrugged, and nodded to his wife. "Tildy tells the tale far better than I."

"How much do you know about the Comyns?" Tildy asked.

"Not much." Nothing except what a five-hundred-year-old Macgillivray had told her. "Just that they were a powerful clan. And that there was some kind of blood feud between the Comyns and a rival clan. The Macgillivrays."

"Well, that's the heart of it really." Tildy nodded her approval. "And the legend is the source, I'm sad to say, of that very feud. Many years ago, when David was king of all Scotland, the Comyn clan was already very old and powerful. And because of that, they'd made their share of enemies along the way, the most virulent of those, the Macgillivrays. The initial cause of the two clans' dislike is lost in time, but doubtless it stemmed from their rivalry for positions of power.

"But their animosity toward one another was no more or less than that between any powerful opposing clans. Until Graeme Macgillivray fell in love with Tyra Comyn."

"And the portrait?" Lily interrupted. "You think she's Tyra Comyn?"

"There's no proof, lass," Reginald said. "But family lore has it as true. The portrait has been handed down through the centuries. And no matter what befalls the family, the portrait always manages to survive."

"The woman was known as the light of the valley. And as such, was supposed to have been uncommonly lovely." Tildy smiled, shooting a glance in Lily's direction. "As are you, my dear."

Lily blushed and shivered, her feelings at odds with each other, something almost approaching memory teasing at the corners of her mind. She shook her head, forcing herself to focus on Mrs. Comyn and her story.

"Anyway, as you can imagine, a love between the two clans would have been forbidden. And so our lovers, Graeme and Tyra, hid their burgeoning relationship from their respective families until the day that Tyra told Graeme that she was with child.

"Overjoyed at the news, Graeme pledged his love, and begged her to marry him. And they did so, in secret, fearing for the wee bairn's life. But Graeme also believed that he could convince his father to accept his bride. His father, a great laird, 'twas no' happy with the news, but could see that his son would ne'er be convinced to leave the lass. So he agreed to accept the union and invited all of Tyra's clan to a great feast to celebrate the nuptials."

"The Red Wedding," Lily whispered, her stomaching quaking with the image.

"I'm sorry?" Tildy responded, her brows furrowing in question.

"It's from a book. By George R.R. Martin. It's not important." She waved a hand for Tildy to continue.

Mrs. Comyn nodded. "The Comyns had doubts of course about the sincerity of the Macgillivray laird. Kendrick was his name. But they went nevertheless, willing to put aside their distrust for the sake of Tyra and her happiness. And so the two clans gathered at the Macgillivray holding. Then sometime during the celebration, the Macgillivrays rose up against the Comyns. The party was a trap, meant to lure the Comyns to their deaths."

"Oh God," Lily said, her breath coming in short bursts. It felt as if the story were happening to her. A Comyn in love with a Macgillivray. "So Graeme turned on her?"

"Ach, no," Reginald said, taking up the tale. "He remained true to his love, jumping in front of Tyra to save her from his father's blow, if the story is to be believed. And his own father struck him down."

"And Tyra?" Lily managed to choke out, tears filling her eyes for these long dead people.

"She lived," Tildy responded. "Somehow in the melee, her kinsmen helped her to escape. But men were killed on both sides. For the Comyns it was a slaughter. And when it was over, very few were left standing. But Kendrick, the mastermind of the entire ordeal, managed to escape unscathed. He was quick to point fingers at the Comyns. At Tyra in particular. Claiming the Comyns attacked the Macgillivrays. He blamed her for his son's death. Even claimed that she had been the one to kill him."

"How horrible," Lily cried. "But the story doesn't end like that, surely."

"Well, it wasn't a truly happy ending," Mrs. Comyn admitted. "Tyra had lost her one true love. But she still carried his bairn. And swore to love Graeme's child until the end of her days, knowing that through the babe, a part of Graeme would live on. So in the end, love found a way. Even in the wake of tragedy, Tyra held on to her love.

"But both clans were destroyed. The Macgillivrays more so even than the Comyns. With so many dead, they were scattered to the far corners of Scotland, their power lost. And of course they blamed the Comyns. Although fate was no kinder to them. They too were eventually scattered and fated to a lesser history. But that's not truly the end. The legend has it that when the circle is again complete— Macgillivray and Comyn joined by love, then both clans will rise to power again.

"As I said, however, there's only sparse evidence to support the truth of what really happened. We know that Tyra truly existed. And that Kendrick was laird of the Macgillivrays at the time. We also know there was a battle between the two clans. And that the Macgillivrays were decimated by the outcome."

"But you have nothing to prove that the lady in the portrait was Tyra. Beyond the fact that it's old, I mean."

"Just the ring," Tildy said.

"The ring?" Lily answered, her voice catching as she struggled for words.

"Yes. The ring." Tildy waved off her husband, who was clearly about to protest. "I'm afraid I left the best part of the story out. You see, supposedly when Graeme and Tyra first married, she had a ring made specially for him. And he wore the ring from the moment they were wed until that fated day." Tildy paused, her gaze shooting to the portrait.

"After he was struck down, Graeme apparently held on to life for short while. And Tyra held him close as he breathed his last. And then before her kinsmen spirited her away, she took the ring, and according to the story, wore it on a chain around her neck until the day she died. There are some who say the circle in the legend refers to the ring. That when a Macgillivray again wears the Comyn ring all with be right with the clans."

"Which is a lovely story, except that the ring doesn't exist." Reginald crossed his arms over his chest on a cynical sigh. Clearly the man wasn't a romantic.

"But there is proof. Right there in the painting. The lady is wearing the ring," Tildy insisted.

"Ah, but even though it is clear she's a Comyn, it's more than possible that someone romanticized her painting by adding the ring. Or maybe it's some other ring altogether."

"But there's writing on the ring," his wife argued. "You can't read it, but you can see it. In Gaelic. It says—"

"*Mo chridhe gu bràth*. My heart forever." Lily spoke softly, her hand to her chest, her heart pounding so loudly she feared they could hear it.

"How in the world could you possibly know that?" Tildy asked, her expression puzzled. Reginald and Mrs. Abernathy also turned to her in question.

"Because—" She licked her lips nervously and pulled the chain from beneath her shirt. "—because I have the ring."

CHAPTER 18

"THIS IS ALL rather hard to believe," Reginald Comyn said, his eyes still riveted on the ring.

Of course the Comyns didn't know the half of it. Although Lily had shared information with regard to the ring, she had no intention of mentioning her slips through time. Especially when said slips had led her to a Macgillivray. It didn't seem likely that her newly discovered cousins were still holding to the feud, but it didn't seem worth the risk of opening herself up to what were essentially strangers.

Although that's exactly what she'd done with Elaine, Jeff and the Abernathys. And if she were being totally honest, with Bram. Still, she'd shocked the Comyns enough for one day. Better to leave them trusting her sanity.

They'd retired back to the parlor, the smaller room much more comfortable. And frankly, Lily wasn't certain she wanted to be within range of the portrait. Something in it called to her. Tugged at her memory. She shook her head, forcing herself to concentrate on the conversation at hand.

"I know it's a lot to take in," she said, her gaze encompassing both Tildy and Reginald. "But there's certainly no denying that I have the ring."

"Or that your family has been in possession of it for centuries," Mrs. Abernathy added.

"I think it's a marvelous find," Tildy exclaimed. "And it's wonderful to find you as well, my dear. There are other Comyns about of course, but none that we can directly link to the legend." She smiled and poured Lily a second cup of tea.

"So since you obviously had no idea what you were walking into, what with the portrait and the legend and all, I presume you had some other reason for wanting to see us?" Reginald sat back in his wingchair, balancing a teacup and saucer on his knee.

"Yes." Lily returned Tildy's smile and accepted the replenished tea. "I've been doing some research. More relevant to me than I'd supposed." She exchanged a glance with Mrs. Abernathy, who nodded, urging her onward. "Anyway, I'm looking for information on a fight that may have taken place here at the manor. Sometime in the fifteenth century. When the tower house still stood. Alec Comyn would have been the laird."

Reginald set his teacup down and reached for a stack of files he'd brought from his office.

"Reginald is bit of an historian himself," Tildy said, while her husband sorted through the papers in the files.

"Ah, yes. I have it here. Alec Connal Nivan Comyn. Fourth laird of *Tigh an Droma*. He inherited from his father."

"Is there anything about his life? Particularly a battle or skirmish with the Macgillivrays?"

"In those days I'm afraid such fighting was rather common. Especially with a Macgillivray holding nearby."

"Dunbrae. Yes, we've been there," Lily said, trying to keep her emotions in check.

"I don't see anything specific." Reginald frowned as he thumbed through the contents of one folder. "No, wait. Here it is. There was a fight. In early May of 1468. Apparently a band of Macgillivrays, led by the son of the neighboring clan, along with a group from Clan Chattan attacked the tower. There aren't any specifics unfortunately. The only reason it's recorded at all is that the tower was damaged. But there are records of Alec beyond 1468, so you can rest easy knowing he survived the attack."

"And the Macgillivrays? Is there anything about them?"

Reginald studied the paper in his hand again. "No details. Other than that the Comyns held strong. Apparently the Macgillivray's leader was killed in the fray, and with him gone, the rest of his forces withdrew."

Lily's heart sank.

"My dear, you've gone quite white," Tildy said, her voice filled with concern. "Is everything okay?"

Lily opened her mouth, but words refused to follow, tears filling her eyes. Bram. Dear God. Bram.

"She's just a bit overwhelmed." Mrs. Abernathy was quick to fill the silence, her arm coming around Lily as she pulled her to her feet. "I think after everything that's happened, it might be best if I get her home. There's just too much to process."

"Yes. Yes, of course," Reginald, too, rose to his feet. "I wasn't thinking. I confess I'd never even considered the possibility that there was any truth to the old stories. And to find out that somehow there might be a link through my line—well, as you said, it is overwhelming. And I'm not the one who is a ringer for a dead woman."

"Reggie," Tildy chided as they all walked toward the door.

"It was lovely to meet you both," Mrs. Abernathy was saying, her arm still around Lily.

"Yes," Lily echoed, her heart still twisting at the news of Bram's defeat, and what appeared to be his death. If she'd been with him, maybe he'd…She shook her head. If she'd been there most likely she would be dead as well. But then it hadn't happened yet—had it? Her heart stuttered, hope blooming. Reginald had said May. The battle was in early May. But it was still the end of April.

Maybe there was something she could do. She squared her shoulders, determination replacing her anguish, her fingers closing around the ring. All she had to do was find her way back.

"I canna see a blasted thing in this mist," Ranald groused, his face scrunched in disgust as they made their way across the rocky ground. "We might as well be blind."

"Aye," Iain agreed as they pulled their mounts to a stop at the crest of a hill. "'Tis only getting thicker. And the path here is treacherous." He nodded toward the rocky edge of the cliff, barely visible through the swirling fog.

"Best to stop here for the night, I'm thinking," Ranald offered.

Bram fought against frustration. "You sure we canna push a wee bit further?"

"Not with night falling." Iain shook his head. "There's a copse of trees just over there." He lifted a hand to indicate the shadowy outline of branches waving in the wind. "We can make camp just beyond it, at the base of the rocks." Granite thrust out of the earth like giants' fingers, the formation offering protection from the night.

"Aye, 'twould seem best," Ranald agreed.

Bram bit off an objection as he dismounted. There was no point in blaming Iain for the weather. Still, it rankled that they'd made little progress and now, thanks to the mist, were being forced to stop early for the night.

"Save your ire," Ranald said, slapping a beefy hand against Bram's shoulder, obviously recognizing his frame of mind. "There's naught to do but wait it out. And you know that's the truth of it."

"Besides," Iain added, "if we can't see then neither can our enemies. Which means that even if they're about, we should be safe enough here for now."

"You think they've sent more men, then?" Bram asked.

"Ye canna predict what a Comyn will do," Frazier said, pulling his horse to a halt next to Bram's. "Especially when angered."

"You canna predict at all to my way o' thinking." Ranald's grin loomed out of through the mist. "The only Comyn you can truly count on is a dead one."

"So we stay alert," Iain agreed. "But we still stop for the night. We dare not risk the horses. 'Tis too easy to stumble off the cliff in this mist."

Bram saw the truth in what Iain was saying, but that didn't make it any easier to stomach. He wanted it over with—the Comyns vanquished and Dunbrae restored to its rightful owner. His uncle be damned. There'd never been any love lost between Malcolm and Seamus. And clearly his uncle was not interested in reconciliation with his nephew. Otherwise he'd have quashed the rumors and called for Bram to come home.

Instead, the lies were still circulating, Bram's honor sullied by the innuendo. Anger forced his fingers into fists. He'd never felt so impotent. And leaving Lily had only made it all that much more unpalatable.

Although, in truth, had his father not been betrayed, he would never have been at the cottage and so never met her at all. Fate, it seemed, had a wicked sense of irony, the loss of his father leading to the love of his life. And now, it was possible that he'd lost her as well.

For even if he did manage to vanquish Alec Comyn, there was no telling if he'd be able to find her again. And perchance that miracle were to occur, there was nothing to say that she'd forgive him for what she no doubt saw as a betrayal.

For the first time he wondered if the price of honor might not be too high.

He shook his head, banishing the thought. There was nothing more important. Were he here, his father would demand vengeance against both the Comyns and the brother who had so deftly put his son aside. And even if Bram could overlook all of that, there was the matter of his clansmen, slaughtered by the Comyns, many of them in an effort to let him slip away.

He owed them all his life, and that was a debt he intended to pay. Lily would simply have to understand. He'd make her see.

After he'd defeated Alec Comyn.

But first they had to wait out this damned weather.

With a start, Bram realized the hillside had gone quiet. While he'd stood there ruminating, his cousins and the rest of the men had disappeared into the mist. He strained into the silence, relieved when he could just make out the distant whinny of a horse. His own mount shuffled nervously, hoofs echoing against the loose rocks littering the hillside.

"Ho there," he soothed, reaching out to stroke the horse's flank. "'Tis nothing to be afraid of. Only a wee bit o' mist. Come now, and I'll find you some nice oats for your dinner."

He led the horse in the direction of the copse of trees. They moved slowly and carefully. As predicted, the mist had thickened. It would be easy to become disoriented. To the right he knew the cliff dropped away sharply. A wrong step and he'd surely fall to his death.

He squinted into the gloom, the movement of the shadowy branches in the distance barely visible. He hoped Iain was right and that there weren't enemies about. Fighting in the mist was a dangerous endeavor. One to be avoided if at all possible.

Bram stopped, frowning into the night. Even the shadows of the trees had disappeared. Silence surrounded him, only the soft hiss of the horse's breathing filling the air. He strained for some sign of the camp ahead. But there was nothing. No firelight. No neighing from the horses. Just the heavy weight of the mist as it swirled around them.

He led the horse forward again, their movements louder now as their footsteps rang against the stones, the sound still smothered by the mist. Each step was taken slowly, Bram's eyes locked on the ground in front of him. He trusted his sense of direction, but even so, knew it was easy to lose one's way in this heavy a fog.

Behind him stones rattled, and his horse reared in fright. Bram whirled around, pulling his claymore from the sheath against his back. The mist entombed them, the clearing gone quiet again. His horse skittered nervously, but held its ground. Bram waited, listening, and then chided himself for being so jumpy.

He slid the claymore back into its sheath and then picked up the horse's reins. Best to get on with it, before Ranald and Iain came looking for him. He'd never hear the end of it if they believed he'd managed to lose himself in the mist.

He took a step forward. And then another.

Then something hit him hard from behind. He stumbled forward as the horse screamed in fear and reared again, hooves flying through the air. He tried to turn to face his attacker, but instead he felt himself teetering at the edge of the cliff. Still reeling in fear, the horse pivoted and ran, the motion sending Bram backwards, arms flailing as he tried to find purchase, something—anything—to stop him from falling.

For a moment there was nothing but air, and then he felt the solid strength of an arm, fingers closing around his wrist as he was yanked from the precipice back onto firm ground.

Iain's face swam out of the mist. "Steady on. I've got you, now."

Bram released a breath he hadn't realized he'd been holding. "Holy Mary, mother of God, I thought I was done for. You always did have excellent timing."

Iain grinned. "I aim to please."

"How did you find me?" Bram asked. "You can barely see your hand in front of your face."

"You've the mare to thank for that. We heard her all the way from the encampment. She sounded like a banshee. Which had to mean trouble."

"I'm afraid she ran off." Bram grimaced, turning slowly to search for the horse.

"Dinna fash yourself. Ranald and Frazier have gone to find her. And if they miss her for the mist, she'll no doubt find her way to the other horses." Iain frowned. "So what happened to spook the beast?"

"I canna say for sure. We heard rocks fall and then I'm fairly certain someone pushed me. Although it could have been the horse. You're right. She was a wee bit crazed. In truth, I had no idea we'd gotten so close to the edge."

"'Tis easy enough to lose your bearings in a fog like this." He waved at the swirling mist.

"I'm just happy that you found me in time. I dinna think I could have saved myself." His heart had settled back to its normal rhythm, but that didn't mean he wasn't aware of how close he'd come to losing it all.

"I don't know." Iain shrugged. "I've seen you pull yourself from worse predicaments."

"Aye, but no' where I had to sprout wings."

Iain sobered, squatting down to inspect something in the muddy turf.

"What do you see?" Bram asked.

Iain shifted back, pointing at the ground. "It looks like it wasn't the horse."

Bram knelt beside his cousin, his breath hitching as he recognized the shape of a footprint. One that most definitely wasn't his.

Behind them something scraped against a stone.

Both men sprang to their feet, weapons drawn.

"Hold," Ranald called as he and Frazier emerged from the mist. "We come bearing gifts."

Bram sheathed his claymore, his pulse pounding again as he examined the man struggling between Ranald and Frazier.

"And who have we here?" Iain queried as he too sheathed his weapon.

"Canna say. The man willna talk to us," Ranald said, his eyes glittering with anger. "But I'm willing to bet he's no' here to make friends."

As if to prove the point, the man made a concerted effort to break free. But he was no match for Ranald and Frazier.

"To be sure, laddie," Frazier spat out, his grip tightening on the man's arm. "He's wearing Comyn colors."

Bram studied the man for a moment, noting the worn plaid. "Aye, but his eyes are dark and his hair a reddish brown."

"Not all of them are black haired and green eyed," Frazier grumbled.

"True enough," Iain nodded, his eyes too locked on the prisoner. "But whoever he may be, I'd be willing to bet he's the one who tried to push Bram o'er the cliff."

CHAPTER 19

✦

"ARE YOU SURE this is what you want to do?" Mrs. Abernathy asked, her forehead wrinkled in question.

"No." Lily shook her head, unwilling to be anything but honest. The older woman had been her rock for the past few days, and Lily suspected that before this was all over she'd be glad to have a dose of Mrs. Abernathy's wisdom. "I'm not sure of anything. But if there's even the remotest possibility that I can do something to save him, I don't see how I have any choice." She paused, sucking in a breath.

"I canna argue with you there, but I feel compelled to remind you that Bram himself wanted you to stay on this side of time."

They were sitting in Mrs. Abernathy's office, sipping scotch-laced tea, the Scottish answer to everything that ailed one, while Lily tried to make sense of everything she'd learned at Ridge Manor. *Tigh an Droma*. Her mind whispered the Gaelic almost as if it were familiar. Then again, maybe it had been. In another life.

She shivered and took a gulp of her tea. "Bram doesn't know the significance of this," she said, holding up the ring on its chain. "He doesn't know who I really am."

And of course that was the really relevent fact. Lily was a Comyn. The great great to infinity cousin or some such of the very man who'd killed Bram's father. And to the Macgillivray way of thinking, most likely the great odd granddaughter of the murderer of his somewhat fewer but still many greats grandfather Graeme.

It was slightly insane on the face of it, but when one added in the fact that they were separated by over five hundred years, it made her head spin and her stomach roil. Or maybe the latter was the scotch. Hard to say for certain. But either way she felt sick.

And afraid. For Bram. For herself. Hell, even for Alec Comyn. He was kin, after all.

"What if I go there and Bram rejects me?"

"What if he doesn't?" Mrs. Abernathy queried, her gaze accurately reading the gist of Lily's thoughts. "After all, he loves you."

"You can't know that for certain. I mean, all you've got to go on are my crazy ramblings. For all we know I dreamed the whole thing."

"Well, then there's still no need to worry because everyone knows you canna truly be hurt in a dream." Mrs. Abernathy calmly refilled Lily's cup.

Lily sighed on a frown. "But I don't want it to be a dream."

"I know, child. I know." Mrs. Abernathy's eyes were full of understanding. "And I also know how very difficult this all is. 'Tis no' easy to trust in love even when it's standing right in front of you. And you and Bram are separated by over five hundred years."

"But he needs me," she pleaded, not sure if she was arguing with Mrs. Abernathy or herself. "If I don't go, he'll die."

"In truth, he's already dead, lamb."

Lily jerked as if Mrs. Abernathy's words were bullets. "But Jeff said that it was all parallel. Happening at the same time, so to speak. So don't you see? If I can get back, it might not be too late. There's still time."

Mrs. Abernathy's face broke into a smile, her eyes shining as if Lily was a star pupil. "As I've said before, true love takes a leap of faith.

The only question here is whether you're willing to take the risk. And I think you just answered that in the affirmative."

"I suppose you're right, but what if I can't get there?" Lily reached for her teacup, her stomach still in knots. It was amazing her throat allowed her to swallow at all. "I mean, he's always been in the same place that I've been. And I can't very well camp out at the Comyns' manor on the off chance that we might manage to inhabit the same space at the same time. Reginald and Tildy were lovely, but somehow I don't think they're going to open their arms for a relative whose time traveling could put their entire existence in jeopardy. What if by saving Bram, that means that Alec must die? Doesn't that change everything?"

"It doesn't seem to work like that," Jeff said, stepping into the office, Elaine trailing on his heels. "We didn't mean to eavesdrop but—"

"I couldn't stand not knowing what had happened," Elaine finished for him. "I hope you don't mind."

"Of course not," Lily said, gesturing for them to have seats. "I'd have told you myself, but you weren't in when we got back."

"So you're really a Comyn?" Elaine asked, her eyes falling to the ring.

"It's seems so." Lilly shrugged and then filled them in on everything they'd learned at Ridge Manor. The painting, the ring, the legend.

"And I thought Katherine's story was crazy." Jeff shook his head and settled back into the sofa cushions with a cup of tea. "This is truly one for the books."

"Or legends," Elaine added. "So you're going to go back."

"If I can." Lily nodded, realizing her decision had truly been made when she heard the outcome of the battle. "But as I was saying, I'm not sure how to achieve it. And even if I can, I'm a little concerned about what kind of damage I'll do if I...if I change things." She paused, chewing her bottom lip as she watched her friends. "You said that it didn't work like that. But I thought that things did shift when Katherine went back. Both there in her time and here in yours as well."

"Things did change. But only for the better—if that makes any sense at all," Jeff replied. "I alluded to it earlier when I first told you about Katherine and Iain. We believe that the way it all came out was in fact the right order of things."

"As if time had been stuck in the wrong loop. I remember. But still, it seems such a dangerous thing to do. I'm hoping to change the outcome of a battle. And in so doing, what if I inadvertently hurt other people? People I care about?"

Her thoughts turned to the Comyns. They were family. She might not know them well, but she certainly didn't wish them any harm.

"I think things will work out the way they're supposed to," Elaine explained. "I mean, if Katherine hadn't gone back to Iain, then Jeff and I might never have gotten together." She shot a look in Jeff's direction—her eyes full of love. "And my niece, Anna, would never have been born."

"Not to mention the fact that Jeffrey and Elaine wouldn't own Duncreag."

"But that meant you lost it, Mrs. Abernathy," Lily prompted.

"Aye, but as I said before, I gained a family." She smiled at the assembled company. "The point here is that maybe there are forces at work beyond what you can ken. And if that's so, then you've got to find it in your heart to believe that what will be will be."

Lily smiled. It might be a lot of purple prose, but damned if it didn't make her feel better somehow. She swallowed. "Even if I accept all of that, there's still the matter of getting back at all. And then once I'm there, how in the world am I supposed to find Bram? I mean, I know where *Tigh an Droma* is, but it's not like I can catch a bus or rent a car. You and Bram both, Jeff, warned that it's a far more dangerous time."

"It is. But I know that Katherine will help you. And I——" He broke off and turned to look at Elaine. For a moment it was as if the world shrank, containing only the two of them, and Lily felt like the worst voyeur, but then Elaine squeezed her husband's hand and nodded.

"Jeff will go with you."

"But you can't," Lily protested, her heart rising to her throat. "You have your life here. You have each other."

"I'm not going to stay. I'm just going to help get you there. I've done it before. For Katherine. And I know I can do it for you." He smiled. "Or at least with you. And I'll stay to help you find Bram."

"But what if…" She trailed off, looking at her new friends with what she knew was complete incredulity.

"That's the beauty of having someone you love," Elaine soothed. "It's how I'll get him back. Our love is like a beacon. A way for him to find his way home. He's linked to the past through his sister, but he's tied to the present because of me."

"But still, what if something goes wrong? I can't let you do this. You don't even know me."

"Well, first off," Jeff said, his tone brooking no argument, "I'm not going just for you. If Bram loses this battle—if he dies—then it's quite possible that Iain will be in peril as well. And if there's something I can do to save my sister's husband, then you can be damned sure I'm going to try."

"And second off," Elaine continued, her hand on Jeff's knee, "you are family now, Lily. If for no other reason than because Duncreag holds the same magic for you that it did for Katherine. But you know that it's more than that. You belong here. You can feel it. And so do we."

Tears sprang to Lily's eyes. She'd lost so much. And somehow managed to gain even more. "I can't...I don't...it's just that..."

"We're all in this together," Mrs. Abernathy finished for her. "And unless we get a move on, it will all be for naught."

"So we're going now?" Lily hadn't expected it to happen so quickly. And she surely hadn't expected to have a partner in crime.

"No time like the present," Jeff said.

"I assume you'll be wanting the wee *sgian dubh?*" Mrs. Abernathy queried, already pushing to her feet.

Lily raised a brow in question. "*Sgian dubh?*"

Elaine nodded. "'Tis a wee knife. It belonged to Iain once upon a time. Jeff used it to go back before. And you've got the ring, but more importantly, you've got Bram's brooch."

Lily reached into her pocket, the metal cat cold against her touch. "So we go to the cottage?"

Jeff shook his head. "I think we'll have better luck here at Duncreag. In Katherine's old room." His gaze met hers, his eyes flickering with determination. "It's your room now. That's where I crossed over before. And where you saw Bram the night of the attack at Iain's Duncreag."

"So we just go there, hold our talismans and we're transported?" she asked, certain it couldn't possibly be that easy.

"Well, it takes concentration. And I suspect as Mrs. Abernathy said, it'll only happen if that's the way it's supposed to be. But it's our best chance, I think."

"So this is it." She turned to face Elaine and Mrs. Abernathy. "I'm really leaving."

"Going home, is more like." Mrs. Abernathy beamed, pulling her into her arms for a warm hug.

Across from them, Jeff looped an arm around Elaine, the two of them walking from the room, gazes locked on each other. As if in so doing they'd forever be bound. But then again maybe they already were.

"Is there anything you want me to say to Valerie?" Mrs. Abernathy asked.

The words pulled Lily away from thinking of her friends, her mind drifting to the past, and the woman who'd somehow known that this was her destiny. "Tell her what's happened. And that I love her. And that I'm happy. Or at least that I'm trying to be. I think she'll understand."

Mrs. Abernathy nodded. "Of course she will. She only wants what's best for you. And she'd be the first to tell you to grab it with both hands while you've still got the chance."

Tears filled Lily's eyes. "And tell the Comyns…well, tell them…" She trailed off.

"I think they already know. People forget that we Highlanders aren't afraid to believe in a little magic. They've seen the portrait, after all."

Lily blinked, understanding slamming home with a powerful thrust. "You don't think the painting was of Tyra. You think it was of me."

Mrs. Abernathy shrugged, her own eyes suspiciously bright. "I think anything is possible. Especially when love is involved. Now go on with you. Jeffrey will be waiting."

~

"I canna get the man to talk," Ranald said, walking into the clearing where their men were making camp. "I tried most everything I know. But he'll say naught but his name. Murdoc Macniven."

"Macnivens have pledged themselves to the Comyns, no?" Iain asked. Frazier and Bram both nodded in assent. "And do you know the name?"

"Nay," Bram said. "But then I've no' had interaction with Alec Comyn or his clan until that night at Dunbrae. Frazier? What say you? Have you heard of the man?"

All eyes turned to the old warrior, who was sitting on a log, absently twirling a stalk of thistle. He frowned for a moment, then lifted his gaze to encompass the others. "I'm fairly certain he's the son of Dougan Macniven. Dougan was Alec's father's man. His captain, if I'm remembering true."

"And did you see either of them during the fighting at Dunbrae?" Iain asked, his eyes narrowed in thought.

Frazier shook his head, his eyes full of regret. "No' that I remember. 'Twas nigh impossible to see anything o'er much. The fighting was fierce." The older man looked to Bram for confirmation.

"Aye, that it was," Bram agreed, images of the carnage echoing through his mind. "I dinna see faces, only swords and shields. And honestly, I dinna know that I'd recognize Alec Comyn himself if he'd stopped for me to take a look."

"It was worth asking," Iain replied with a shrug.

"Do you have reason to doubt Macniven?" Frazier asked, tossing the thistle aside.

Iain considered the idea on a frown. "I canna say that the man has a reason to lie. But none of this feels quite right to me."

"Aye." Bram nodded, considering the thought. "Why take a chance on his own? If Alec knows we're on the march then why wouldn't he just attack us in force?"

"'Tis possible this Murdoc was merely a scout," Ranald replied. "But when faced with the opportunity to throw your scrawny arse off a cliff it presented an opportunity too tempting to resist."

"Scrawny, eh?" Bram eyed his cousin with disdain. "That's not what you were thinking the night I saved your hide from the Macsween brothers after you bedded their sister."

"Ach, a comely lass she was, too." Ranald smiled at the memory. "And I canna fault your timing, cousin. But there's still some question as to whether I truly needed rescuing. I was holding my own, after all."

"Aye, from the bottom of a pile o' Macsweens," Bram responded.

Ranald eyed him ruefully then, after a moment's bluster, threw back his head and laughed. "They were rather a lot of them," he admitted with a shrug.

"Five, if I remember right." Bram waggled his eyebrows as Iain and Frazier joined in the laughter. There was something comforting about remembering their past. As if the bond he shared with his cousins could help to ease the pain of all that he'd lost.

"Well, as far as I see it, the world might have been a better place if you'd just let the Macsweens teach him a lesson or two. Might have humbled the man a wee bit." Iain shot Ranald a benevolent smile, but his eyes still glittered with mirth.

"Humble or no', there's nothing like knowing your friends have your back," Frazier said. "'Twas the way of it with your father and me, Bram. But times change. And now Seamus is gone." Something dark passed across the old warrior's eyes, but then he shook his head as if banishing the memories. "And now…it seems I'm at the mercy of nature's call." The man shrugged, his grizzled face breaking into a grin.

"Where is Macniven now?" Iain asked as Bram watched his father's friend disappear into the mist. No doubt in search of the perfect tree.

"I've left Collum Macilbra to guard him," Ranald answered.

Bram nodded with satisfaction. Macilbra was a giant of a man. Not one to easily be taken advantage of. It seemed Murdoc Macniven was well and truly captured. Which served the bastard right.

"Perhaps we should take him to your uncle," Iain suggested. "His attack on you would go a long way to proving your innocence."

"Would that it were that easy," Bram said on a long sigh. "All he has to do is accuse me of being the traitor and say that Murdoc was sent to tie up loose ends. The only way I'll truly have any peace is to take my vengeance on Alec Comyn. And then when we're finished with him, I'll be ready to face my uncle."

"And in the meantime, maybe we can coax the truth out of Murdoc Macniven." The hard glint in Ranald's eye gave a sinister twist to the word 'coax.'

From behind them out of the mist came the sound of raised voices. Bram reached for his claymore, his cousins doing the same, the three of them moving to stand back to back, weapons at the ready.

Frazier and two of Iain's men burst from the clearing. Blood dripped down Frazier's face, his sword clasped in his hand. He stopped in front of them, his breath coming in gasps. "Macniven has escaped."

One of the men with him nodded in agreement. "And Collum is dead."

CHAPTER 20

"WELL, THIS IS getting us nowhere." Lily dropped down on the bed with an audible sigh. She'd been clutching the damn brooch for what felt like hours, Jeff pressing the *sgian dubh* as if it was some kind of magic talisman. Which of course was exactly what it was supposed to be.

Only somehow it hadn't gotten the message.

"It takes patience, Lily. The last time I did this, it took hours. And a lot of concentration."

The room was cloaked in shadow, the moon having yet to rise. Mrs. Abernathy and Elaine had started out just beyond the bedroom door. But when nothing happened, they'd all decided that it was best if Jeff and Lily were alone. So after more hugging and reassurances, they'd left. Presumably for scotch-laden tea and comfort.

"So you said." Lily sighed. "But when you did it before you didn't do it with a stranger." Jeff opened his mouth to object, but she waved him silent. "A friend then. But both times you traveled, Katherine needed your help."

"Well, Bram needs yours. And even if she doesn't know it, Katherine needs mine. That has to count for something. We just have to focus our energy. Try and picture Bram. Think about how much he means to you. Concentrate."

Lily tightened her hold on the brooch with one hand, her fingers closing around the ring with the other, and obediently closed her eyes. If things weren't so dire, it would almost be funny. The two of them in here, clutching ancient relics and trying to slip back in time.

She shook her head and blew out a breath. Then she focused on picturing Bram. His chiseled face and arctic eyes. Slowly, as though through a mist, her mind conjured an image of him sitting in firelight. His face was tight with anger and something else. Something like regret. He clenched a fist and then relaxed it, but she could see the tension in his shoulders, the pain etched across his handsome face. She watched as he ran a hand through his hair, and her fingers tingled as if she'd been the one to touch him.

He tossed a twig into the fire and it crackled, the light expanding to a ring around what she could see now was clearly a campfire. Her heart cried for him, and she reached out a hand, but in so doing, released the brooch and as quickly as the image had appeared it vanished. Gone before she could protest the loss.

"What is it?" Jeff asked, jerking her firmly into the present. "Lily, tell me what happened."

She struggled to clear her thoughts, to find words, but instead she felt like she was drowning. As though she'd already failed Bram, lost him to a battle she was helpless to prevent.

"Lily," Jeff urged, his hands enclosing hers, pulling her from her terrified thoughts.

"I saw him," she whispered. "He was sitting by a campfire. And he looked so angry. And I...I don't know...so...so sad. It made my heart hurt just to look at him." She clutched at her chest as if the pain were physical. "Oh God, Jeff, I was there. But I wasn't. I could see him. But I couldn't move or talk. All I could do was look at him. Want him."

"Were there others?" Jeff asked, still holding her hands.

Lily nodded, forcing herself to push aside her roiling emotions and recall the scene. "He was alone at first. And then the light got brighter and I could see others moving in the shadows. I tried to reach out for him, Jeff, to comfort him. But in so doing, I...I let go of the pin. And he was gone." She looked up, anguish twisting at her gut. "Oh God, Jeff, I've lost him."

"No," Jeff asserted. "You just lost contact. But at least you know that you're still connected. And if you can do it once, you can do it again." His fingers tightened on hers. "But this time, we'll do it together."

Bram stared into the fire, willing the image back. He'd seen her. For one brief moment she'd materialized in the fire. Reaching for him, her green eyes glistening in the dancing light. There for a moment and then gone. He fisted his hand, calling on everything inside him, needing her now in this moment more than he could put into words.

Damn honor. Damn her safety. Damn everything but the two them, here together. His mind knew it was a selfish demand, but his heart didn't care. He stared into the fire, willing her to reappear. And suddenly she was there again. Only this time she wasn't alone. His heart stuttered, anger washing through him as he watched her clasp hands with another man. A tall, handsome one.

His eyes glittered blue as he stared into Lily's. His long fingers linked with hers. She nodded once, then smiled, tightening her grip.

Bloody hell. Bram swallowed the curse. He'd lost her. In walking away, he'd driven her into another man's arms. Reflexively he reached out, gut churning, mind spinning. She'd been his everything and now...now...all he wanted to do was rip her from the stranger's arms.

"Mother of God, Bram, are you trying to get burned? What the hell do you think you're doing?"

The vision vanished, the fire popping and hissing as Ranald hauled Bram back from the flames.

"I saw her." He gestured toward the fire, his breathing still ragged, the anger inside him easing a bit as he realized how foolish he must look. "Lily. She was right there. And then...and then she wasn't."

Ranald's frown echoed both resignation and incredulity. "Did she have another warning for us?"

Bram shook his head. "No. She said nothing. Only reached out for what I thought was me, and then—" He dropped back down to sit by the fire, burying his face in his hands.

"Then what, cousin?" Ranald asked, his big hand settling on Bram's shoulder. "Tell me. It's no' like I haven't heard this kind o' thing before."

"I thought it was me she wanted, but I was wrong. She was reaching for another man. I saw him. I saw them." The words came out on a whisper, the pain biting so deeply he thought he might be sick. He closed his fingers around a small stone, clenching it as though it were a lifeline.

"There are other men in the world, you know. And being with one is no' the same as, well, *being* with one, if you take my meaning."

"They were holding hands, Ranald. And looking into each other's eyes. And they were standing in a bed chamber. Lily's chamber. The damned scene is burned into my eyes." He looked back into the flames, avoiding his cousin's gaze. He was disgusted with himself for his weakness and could only imagine what his cousin thought of him.

As if to underscore his mortification, Iain joined them by the fire.

"Bram saw Lily," Ranald said without provocation.

"Here?" Iain asked, his gaze moving from Ranald to Bram.

"In the fire," Bram mumbled, nodding to the flames as if they would substantiate his story.

"With another man," Ranald added, shrugging once in apology. "In her bed chamber."

Iain was quiet for a moment, no doubt fighting his disdain for Bram's weakness. "Everything isn't always as it seems," his cousin said finally, his voice full of empathy. "And sometimes you have to trust your heart over your head."

"Well, just at the moment, they're both of an accord." Bram's hand tightened on the rock he was still holding. "They'd like nothing better than to have a go at the bloody fair-headed bastard that had his hands on my woman. And believe me when it's over, I'd be the only one left standing."

Not that he had any rights in the matter. He'd sent Lily back, after all. Abandoned her without even bothering to say goodbye. He'd done it to keep her safe, but he'd known she'd see it as a betrayal. And perhaps, in truth, it was.

"Fair-headed did you say?" Iain asked, breaking into Bram's thoughts.

"Aye, the color of straw," Bram acknowledged grudgingly.

"And was he tall?" Iain questioned.

"Yes. Tall and brawny and handsome, if you must know." His nails dug into the stone as he fought his emotions.

"And you said they were in Lily's chamber. At Duncreag."

"Come now, Iain," Ranald groused. "You don't have to rub it in. Canna you see that the man is hurting?"

Iain waved a hand absently in Ranald's direction, his focus still on Bram. "And the vision, it was in Lily's time, not ours."

Bram closed his eyes and forced himself to see her again—standing with the stranger, their hands linked. "Aye. Her time. His clothes were as strange looking as hers."

"Surely in this situation clothes are a good thing," Ranald quipped, lifting an eyebrow.

Bram scowled at him.

"And could you see the man's face clearly?" Iain asked, ignoring Ranald's attempt at levity.

Bram shifted his attention to Iain, uncertain where his cousin was leading, but then nodded once, humoring him anyway. "The damned thing is burned in my brain. All blue eyes and floppy hair—and he was smiling down at Lily as if he had every right to put his hands on her." Anger washed through him again, and he tossed the stone into the fire.

"You said he was only holding her hands. That's hardly all over her, now, is it?" Ranald was trying to help. Bram understood it intellectually, but emotionally it still wasn't working.

"Did he perchance look like my wife?" Iain asked, patently ignoring Ranald's nattering.

Bram lifted his head in surprise, his mind obligingly presenting an image of Katherine. Her bright hair and laughing blue eyes. He sucked in a breath. "Now that you mention it, he did seem to favor her." He waved at his own face, still concentrating on the images in his head. "The color o' his eyes and his hair, but also the tilt o' his mouth and the turn of his chin."

"You think it was Jeff making eyes at Lily?" Ranald asked, then immediately clapped a hand over his mouth. "I dinna mean…" He trailed off, his gaze dropping to his feet.

"Jeff?" Bram barked out the name. "Katherine's brother?"

"The man who came here to help us rescue her," Iain confirmed.

"But I…he…"

"Is married to someone else. Or at least I assume they married. He was most definitely in love with her when he was here."

"Her name was Elaine," Ranald offered helpfully. "She was Katherine's best friend before, well, before Iain."

"Aye, Lily mentioned them both."

"Then you've no need to worry," Ranald replied.

"You dinna see them…" Bram was having trouble finding words. "They were…"

"Anything is possible, I'll grant you that." Iain, as usual, spoke without gilding the truth. "But the Jeff we knew was an honorable man. And he certainly had no interest in any lass except Elaine."

"Then why was he—" Bram started, only to be interrupted by Ranald.

"You said they were holding hands. Looking in to each other's eyes." His cousin waited for Bram to nod and then continued. "Well, if I remember correctly, Jeff traveled both here and back on sheer determination. It's possible he was trying to help Lily."

"To do what?" Bram asked, anger, regret and frustration still clogging his mind.

"Get back to you, you great oaf," Ranald said with a frown. "I know from personal experience that telling a woman to wait for you is like waving a red flag and daring her to come after you. Especially if she fancies she's in love."

"Ranald's right. When a woman believes the man she loves is in danger—" Iain's gaze encompassed them both. "—there's naught anything anyone can do or say to stop her. The only thing left then is to offer to help in whatever way possible."

"And Jeff," Bram asked, a small glimmer of hope dispelling the darkness. "He's the kind of man who'd offer his aid?"

"Aye," Ranald nodded. "That he is."

Lily fought against the hopeless despair that washed through her. She wanted Bram so badly she could almost feel his arms around her. Feel his lips pressed against hers. But these were memories and no matter how dear, they weren't helping her at all.

Instead she forced herself to concentrate on the feel of Jeff's hands. The warmth of the room, the shadows and light that were the heart of Duncreag. She focused on the image of Katherine and Iain. Katherine laughing up at her husband. She'd made it back to him, not once, but twice. Her love had led the way. Just as Jeff's love for his sister had brought him to her. And in turn Elaine's love had brought him safely home again.

Love.

Love was the key. And in an instant Lily saw the truth of it. Katherine loved Iain. Jeff loved Katherine. And she…she loved Bram Macgillivray. It might be insane. It might even be impossible, but it was true nevertheless. She loved him. And as long as there was breath in her body, she wasn't going to let him die.

She tightened her fingers on Jeff's, her mind reaching out— reaching back. For a moment it seemed she teetered on a brink and then the world went black, an icy wind cutting into her from every side, shrieking through the darkness, frigid fingers squeezing her heart and her lungs. Panic threatened. It hadn't been like this with Bram, but then they'd always been together.

This time she was alone.

And then as if in answer, she felt the strength of Jeff's grasp. And she clung to it even as the cold wind clawed at her, trying to tear her away. It tugged at her, pulled her...and then, as quickly as it had begun, it stopped, the only sound the pounding of her heart and the soft hiss of her breath.

She opened her eyes to the sight of tapestry adorned walls and a huge canopied bed curtained in dark velvet. The floor was covered with straw. And...

"Jeff?" a soft voice cried, the sound filled with wonder. "Oh my God, is that you?"

Lily turned toward the source of the voice. A slender woman in a pale gown with embroidered sleeves and a silver cord tied at her waist stood at the entrance to the room. Her golden hair fell in waves over her shoulders, her blue eyes flashing with delight.

"Kitty," Jeff breathed, pulling his hands from Lily's as he moved to embrace his sister.

Lily struggled for breath, her vision swimming, even as her mind presented all that she was seeing. They'd done it. They'd beaten the darkness. They'd traveled through time. Her heart rejoiced even as her head spun with the enormity of it all.

She tried to say something, but her mouth refused to work, her body tingling as the darkness encroached again. She tried to fight, but the pull was too strong and with a slow sigh, she slid bonelessly to the floor, her last thought that she'd been too quick to celebrate. That perhaps the darkness had won after all.

CHAPTER 21

✦

"YOU'RE AWAKE." KATHERINE'S face swam into view as Lily forced herself to sit up. She way lying on a bed, velvet coverings soft beneath her fingers. There were candles flickering in standing candelabras and tapestries on the walls and quite clearly she was no longer in her own century.

"What happened?" she asked, her voice coming out on a croak.

"You fainted." Katherine's tone was kind. "Not surprisingly. It's no picnic being jerked through time. Especially when you're doing it on your own."

"But I had Jeff." Lily frowned, still trying to shake the cobwebs from her head. She glanced around the room, but Katherine's brother was nowhere in sight.

"True enough. But you didn't have Bram." Katherine held out a pewter tankard. "Have a sip of this. It'll help clear your mind."

Lily took the cup and sipped, then screwed up her face in protest. "What is this?"

"A mixture of herbs and a little bit of scotch. I'm afraid this part of Scotland doesn't run to the best in tea. And the herbs will help restore your strength. I've actually become quite good at mixing potions." She laughed. "Which makes me sound like either a witch or a tottering old fool. Welcome to the fifteenth century."

Lily shuddered as she swallowed, but forced herself to take another sip. At least one thing hadn't changed. Scottish restoratives were still laced with whisky. And despite the horrible taste and the strangeness of her situation, Lily found herself smiling. "I'm actually feeling a lot better."

She shifted, the pounding in her head reminding her that she was improved but not completely back to normal. "Is it always like this? Travelling alone, I mean? The first time I was with Bram I was injured and out of it. So I can't really say how I felt." She felt herself blush. "Well, at least about the travelling. And the next time was more like a dream."

"When you warned him about the riders in the canyon?"

Lily nodded. "And then the last time, at the cottage, he wasn't there—and then he was." She felt herself go hot again at the memory and Katherine's smile was knowing.

"I understand. It was never hard for me until the very last time. Iain thought I was gone for good. He'd sent me back to my time, you see. I was injured and he was afraid I'd never be whole again if I stayed. But once I was better and worked it all out, all I wanted to do was get back to him."

"Which you did." The answer was obvious, but Lily needed to say it out loud. "Despite what he wanted, you still came back."

"Yes. Nothing was going to keep me away from him."

Lily nodded with satisfaction, but her heart dropped. "Still, with Iain, his sending you away was for the best. I mean, you were hurt. And Elaine told me that you wouldn't have recovered if you'd stayed here."

"Well, we'll never know that for certain, now will we? But I do believe that Iain did what he thought was best at the time. And I know what that choice cost him."

There was silence for a moment, and Lily sipped the bitter brew, turning Katherine's words over in her mind.

"Bram didn't want to leave you, you know," she said.

Lily lifted her gaze to meet Katherine's. "What do you mean?"

"He told me, himself. He was full of regret. He only did what he did to protect you. It's not that different from what Iain did for me."

"But Iain was trying to save you. Bram pushed me away."

"He wanted to keep you safe."

Lily opened her mouth to argue, but Katherine waved her quiet.

"I'm not saying that I agree with Bram. I'm just saying that he thought he was protecting you. And making that decision cost him, Lily. He even told me that he went back for you."

"He did?" Some of the fear that had been hounding her slipped away.

"Yes. But it was already too late. You were gone." She smiled, her eyes kind. "He loves you, you know."

"I suppose I do." Lily sighed with a weak smile. "And I must love him. I mean, here I am in the middle of what could only be described as a fractured fairy tale. Who's to say that I haven't lost my mind completely? I mean, for all I know this is all some kind of demented fantasy."

"Except that it's not. And I'm proof. Me and Jeff—and Elaine. We've been through it before. And so we're your touchstone. You're not going crazy. At least no more than anyone would when they'd just traveled back in time." Her smile was contagious and Lily felt better.

"Did Jeff tell you why we're here?" she asked. "It's about more than just my feelings for Bram."

Katherine's smile faded, worry creasing her forehead. "Yes. He explained everything. The battle. The outcome. All of it."

"And my being a Comyn. Did he tell you that part, too?"

"He did. And you still have the ring?"

Lily lifted the silver chain. "Yes. It's partly what helped me to get here, I think. That and the brooch Bram left for me." With her other hand she produced the little cat from her pocket. "Do you think he'll forgive me?" She hadn't meant to say that. But the words had just come tumbling out. And now they seemed to hang there in the air, taunting her. "I mean, the Comyns are his worst enemy. And now it turns out I am one."

"But you didn't know. So there was no deception. And if he really loves you—it won't matter. Besides, for all you know that's the point of all of this."

"Jeff told you about the legend?"

"He did. Of course Bram's version is a little bit different, not surprisingly. But maybe that's the point. Maybe fate is trying to right a wrong. Comyns and Macgillivrays reunited. Or at least a new bond forged."

Lily blew out a long breath. "That makes it all sound so overwhelming. Less than a month ago I was living in Connecticut wondering how I was going to cope with the loss of my parents and now I'm planning to march off to try and stop a medieval battle. God, I am insane."

Katherine laughed. "No. Just in love. And you won't be the first woman to try and stop needless bloodshed. But first we have to be certain you're ready for the journey. Drink." She motioned to the cup in Lily's hand, and she dutifully swallowed some more of the bitter brew, the ensuing warmth welcome.

"Where is Jeff?" Lily glanced again around the bedroom but there was still no sign of Katherine's brother.

"He's with Fergus, Iain's captain. The two of them are getting together the things you'll need. I'm afraid most of our men left with Iain, Ranald and Bram. But I'll send Fergus to guide you. He only stayed here to protect me."

"Then we can't take him away with us," Lily protested.

"Nonsense. He's the best tracker I know. And you'll need someone who is more familiar with the way of things than you or Jeff. I'd go myself, but I can't leave Anna."

"Your daughter." Lily nodded. "Elaine told me about her. Although I don't really understand how she knew."

"It's a long story, but let's just say it was foretold."

"Well, no matter, I'm truly happy for you."

"Thank you—she's the light of our lives. And so, understandably, I cannot leave her. And seriously, you don't have to worry about us. You have far bigger concerns. Even without Fergus, there are people here to protect us. And honestly he's been chomping at the bit ever since Iain left. He's not one to be left out of a fight."

"Well, if we're lucky, maybe there won't be one."

"So you have a plan?" Katherine's skepticism belied the question.

Lily shook her head. "No. I wasn't even sure I'd get this far. But I know I have to try. If I can find Bram and tell him what happens then maybe I can convince him to step down."

Katherine laughed. "I wish I could be there to see you try."

"I know it won't easy. But it has to be done. Surely you see that." Lily felt her throat tighten at the thought of what failure might mean.

"Of course I do." Katherine was quick to console. "I just have first-hand experience dealing with pig-headed men. And despite the fact that you come knowing the truth of things, I fear that Bram and my husband will still want to proceed. They're not foolish, but they are proud."

Lily tilted her head defiantly. "If they won't listen, I'll just have to find another way."

"And Fergus will be there to help you." Katherine nodded, reaching into a trunk at the end of the bed. "I'm sending William as well.

He's loyal to me and will do what I ask of him. So you can count on him no matter what." She handed Lily a piece of folded linen. "This is an old shirt of Iain's. From when he was younger. I wear it sometimes when I want to travel more easily.

"You're smaller than me so it'll be big, but you can use the belt to make it work over your leggings. And this," she said, handing over a folded length of soft wool, "is a Mackintosh plaid. Drape it like a shawl over the shirt and secure it with the belt. It'll keep you warm. And hopefully help you pass as someone from this century."

"I don't know how to thank you."

"It's simple." Katherine's smile didn't quite carry to her eyes. "Watch out for my husband and brother."

"I promise that I will."

Katherine nodded, and handed her the belt as Lily struggled into the billowy shirt. "You can ride, I take it?"

"Yes. Actually, quite well. When I was younger I had my own horse. One of the privileges of wealth, I suppose."

"I'm sorry about your parents," Katherine said, reaching over to help Lily arrange the plaid.

"Thank you. With everything that's happened, it feels so long ago. I know that you lost your parents when you were really young. That must have been awfully hard. At least I had mine as long as I did."

"Well, I know it's not the same, but now you've found a new family." Katherine helped her fasten Bram's pin into place as tears filled Lily's eyes. "And I promise you that together we'll see everything come out right."

"Lily, are you ready?" Jeff stood in the doorway, looking very much a man for the ages. He, too was wearing a linen shirt and plaid over his jeans. But unlike her, his made him look fiercer somehow. Especially with the broad sword swung across his back.

"If the situation weren't so serious, I'd say you were enjoying yourself," Katherine quipped, smiling at her brother.

"I'm not relishing what we're off to do, if that's what you mean." Jeff frowned. "But I will admit to being more comfortable with a sword than I was the first time I was here. I've been practicing."

Katherine's smile widened, love reflected in her eyes. "I don't know what I'd do without you."

Lily suddenly felt very alone, but it wasn't a new feeling. And she most certainly wouldn't have anyone if she gave into her own insecurities. Squaring her shoulders, she broke the moment. "I can't very well carry a sword like that." She nodded at Jeff's weapon. "But surely I'll need something to defend myself."

"Can you use a bow and arrow?" Katherine asked.

"I can actually." It was Lily's turn to smile. "Best in my class back in the day."

"Great," Jeff said, his grin infectious. "Nice to know you'll have my back."

Lily smiled, grateful again to have found such good friends. "And you'll have mine."

~

Bram pulled his plaid close around him as Iain's men came to a halt in a small clearing in the woods. The mist had lifted, and a soft wash of orange above the craggy cliffs indicated dawn was well on its way. The bubbling burn they'd been following veered sharply to the left, taking the narrow valley with it. Straight ahead loomed the sharp rocks that led up into the mountains. Bram's mare pulled against the reins, her eagerness to keep going echoing his own driving need.

"Why are we stopping?" he asked as Iain came up beside him. Ranald and Frazier reined in their horses as well, the three of them all looking to Iain who, as always, assumed the role of leader.

"We've a decision to make," Iain said, nodding toward the burn. "To the west lies *Tigh an Droma* and Alec Comyn. And to the north the pass that Frazier indicated."

"I thought we'd decided to take the pass." Ranald frowned. "Use the element of surprise."

"We had," Iain agreed. "But things have changed with Macniven escaping. There's always the possibility that he overheard our plans and has shared them with Alec Comyn. While there can be no argument that using the pass is a good way for us to spring a surprise, 'twould be just as easy for the Comyns to use it as a trap."

"I dinna think Macniven had the chance to hear much of anything," Frazier growled, his hand tightening around the hilt of his claymore. "We isolated him as soon as he was captured. And ye canna think that Collum would have told him anything."

"Collum is no' what I'm worried about," Iain said. "But we dinna ken how long Macniven was following us. And we've no' been shy about talking amongst ourselves. So there's no way to know what he may or may not have heard."

"I still say Frazier's way is the best," Bram urged. "Even if he did overhear us, he's only just escaped and there's no' much chance he'll reach Alec before we can get through the pass."

"Which means it's still our best hope," Frazier agreed, his ruddy face flushed with anger. "If we attack head on, then Alec and his men will have more of a chance to best us. Particularly if he's been warned. I say we stick to the plan. Surprise or no."

"Ranald?" Iain asked, his gaze meeting his cousin's.

"I dinna ken that there's a difference in which way we go. If Macniven has the way of our plan, then Alec will be watching for us either way. He'll know that we know that Macniven might have gleaned our strategy. So there is every chance he'll believe we'll change course because of it."

"Which means the odds are in favor of our keeping to the mountain pass," Bram said, reining in his prancing mare. "If Macniven knows nothing, then we will take Alec by surprise. And, as Frazier said, even if the man has news to impart, Alec shouldn't have time to respond quickly enough to intercept us before we're through the pass. So although we might lose the element of surprise, we'll still be in place for the battle. I say we follow the mountains."

Iain paused for a moment, his gaze drifting up to the harsh peaks. Then he nodded his acceptance. "The mountains it is then."

Frazier grunted his approval, and then, with a grin, spurred his horse into the woods. The other men followed, Iain, Ranald and Bram bringing up the rear.

"We're putting our faith in your man, you know." Iain's expression was grave.

"That I do," Bram acknowledged. "But there's naught to fear. Frazier saved my life at Dunbrae. He and Robby Corley. And he would have done anything for my father. Which means he has as much to avenge as I do. So, if nothing else, I believe in that."

CHAPTER 22

DESPITE THE BLUE sky and bright sun, a cold wind swept up the narrow valley as they rode higher into the mountains. Lily pulled her borrowed plaid closer. They had been riding since sunup, moving as quickly as possible. The mist had evaporated, sliding back to wherever it had come from, but the placid countryside was deceiving.

The rushing stream, whispering leaves and plaintive calls of the birds might be heard in any century. What sent chills racing through Lily was the underlying quiet. It echoed across the forest and meadows—no cars, no airplanes, no machinery of any kind. In the entire time since they'd left Duncreag, they'd only passed one person—a crofter driving sheep across the narrow track they followed.

Above her a hawk screamed and her horse shied. Lily tightened her hold on the reins. Jeff and Fergus rode in front of her, the two of them deep in discussion. The older man's face was ruddy and grizzled, a warrior through and through. By comparison, Jeff looked less seasoned, although he sat well in the saddle.

Reflexively, Lily reached back to touch the quiver of arrows slung over her shoulder. There hadn't been time for practice, but bows and arrows hadn't changed much over the centuries, and she felt certain if called upon she could do the weapon justice. She shivered, thinking about the potential battle to come. If they didn't reach Bram and his cousins in time, there'd be hell to pay. Still, she was here, and that alone had to change the balance somehow.

Unless this was the way it always happened. And she was already too late.

She shook her head, banishing the thought. Behind her, bringing up the rear, Lily could hear the soft jingle of William Macgowen's horse's bridle. The young man hadn't been all that eager to join their party at first. Apparently, he considered himself Katherine's personal bodyguard, and it had taken both Fergus and Katherine's considerable influence to convince William that he was needed as an escort.

Since leaving Duncreag, however, he'd thrown himself whole-heartedly into their quest. Actually spoiling for a fight, if Lily had to call it, with all the accompanying enthusiasm that only a young man could pull forth. And most surprising of all, he seemed to have trans-ferred his allegiance from Katherine to Lily, staying close, determined to protect her from whatever might come. She allowed herself a small smile. Just a few weeks ago she'd felt all but rejected by men in general and now here she was with not one but two champions. More, she sup-posed, if one counted Fergus and Jeff.

Of course in truth, the jury was out when it came to Bram. He'd left her behind for a reason. And even if Katherine was right and he regretted leaving things as he had, it didn't mean that he'd welcome her presence now. At least not here on the cusp of potential fighting. He'd made it perfectly clear that a battle was no place for a woman. And he wasn't all that wrong. But this was an exceptional situation in every possible way, and Lily would be damned before she'd abandon him when he needed her most.

Squaring her shoulders, she spurred her horse onward as William rode up beside her. "Ye look as if you're right at home on yer horse. Have you many then on yer holding?"

Lily smiled at William's earnest expression. He understood that she, like Katherine, had come from the future. And like the others at Duncreag who'd been told the truth, he accepted her fantastical tale without question. But that didn't mean he truly understood the vast differences between his world and hers.

"I don't actually have a holding. I live—well, lived—in an apartment in a large city called Manhattan. There isn't room for horses."

"Then how do people get around?" he asked, frowning. Then, quickly, his face cleared. "I remember now. Katherine told me there are carriages that don't need horses. A magical thing, that."

"Indeed." Lily smiled at his enthusiasm. "And in Manhattan even those carriages are difficult to deal with, so people do a lot of walking. And…" She trailed off, not sure how to explain subways. "…and whatever it takes."

"And are there many people in this Man-Hat-Tan?"

"Yes. More than you can imagine."

"More than at the Clan gatherings?" His expression mirrored his disbelief.

Lily had no idea how many people came to such an event, but she doubted it would put a dent in the population of Manhattan. "Many more. And they're all crowded together—practically living on top of one another."

"Then you must be glad to be here." He waved at the surrounding woodlands. "'Tis much nicer than what you describe. Here, there's room to breathe. And space to grow. There's no more wondrous place in all the wide world than this part of the Highlands."

Lily's smile widened. "And have you been many other places then?"

William's cheeks reddened. "Nay. I havena'. But I canna imagine any place more bonny."

"It is beautiful." As if to echo the thought, they rounded a corner and the small stream they'd been following dropped down into a series of pools, the water splashing merrily as it moved over the rocks. Overhead, the trees formed an arching canopy that shaded the grassy banks dotted with colorful wildflowers. She recognized bluebells and anemones.

Ahead of them, Fergus and Jeff had pulled to a stop, the former swinging down from his horse.

"Why are we stopping?" she asked, trying to curtail her frustration. These men had agreed to help her almost without argument, Jeff risking the journey across time. She hadn't the right to be angry. But in her heart she knew that time was of the essence. Every second mattered.

"We willna' be o' use to Bram and Iain if we ride our horses into the ground. Best to let them have a rest and a drink. It wouldna hurt us either, I reckon." Fergus released the reins and his horse made for the stream, drinking deeply.

Lily felt a wash of guilt. She owed these men more consideration. Swinging down from the saddle, she felt weak at the knees. It had been too long since she'd been riding.

"So how close to them do you think we are?" she asked.

"Hard to say, lass," Fergus said, his bushy white brows drawing together as he looked towards the mountains towering on the horizon. "If they sat out the mist, which makes the most sense, then we shouldn't be too far behind. But I canna say for sure what they've done, ye ken?"

"I know. I'm just so worried."

Jeff came up to give her a comfortable squeeze. "We're here. That's the best we can do for now. You just have to believe we'll be in time."

Lily sighed and knelt beside the stream, cupping the cool water in her hands before lifting it to her lips. In her mind's eye she could see Bram sitting by the fire. But that had been last night. Today there'd been no contact. No matter how many times she'd reached out to him. Perhaps their clairvoyance, if that was the right name for it, was of no value when they occupied the same time.

"I want to believe. But all of this is just so extraordinary." She drank deeply then sat back on her heels, watching Jeff and the others.

"If you think this is hard for you, then imagine how we feel," Fergus said. "William and I. 'Tis not our first time, mind, but I ne'er expected to meet another lass from the future."

"But you know Jeff. He was here before. Surely that makes it less of an anomaly."

"I dinna know the word yer using. But if you mean odd, then nay, 'tis no more a part o' our world than it was the first time it happened." Fergus's frown would have been off-putting except for the soft understanding deep in his eyes.

"But you've seen Katherine and Iain," Jeff said. "You know how important it is. Destiny and all that."

"Aye, that I do. And even if I didn't, I would still have come, for Iain. And for Katherine."

Lily struggled not to show her jealousy. She'd never inspired that kind of devotion in anyone. Her parents had loved her, but they'd loved each other more. And Justin. Well…he'd showed his true feelings when it had mattered most.

But there was Bram, her heart whispered.

And her mind was quick to remind that he'd left her. Walked away when there'd been everything between them.

"I canna speak for Fergus, mind you," William was saying, "but I for one am happy to have an excuse for a bit of adventure."

"Ach, lad, yer enthusiasm is guided only by yer love fer a pretty face. First Katherine and now Lily." Fergus slammed William on the shoulders with a beefy hand and the boy flushed bright red and coughed.

"I ride for Iain. And for Bram. And I ride for their ladies, as should you, ye ald coot."

Fergus laughed, his merriment including them all. "I find I canna fault with the lad, more's the pity."

"And I would never admit it to Elaine, but I'm glad to be back in the thick of things," Jeff said.

Lily hid another smile. Lord, they were all little boys when it came to battle. But then that's what got them killed. She sobered, wishing suddenly for the safe harbor of the cottage. There she and Bram had been sheltered from the fears that haunted them both. Bram, his father's death. And Lily, her parents' deaths and Justin's betrayal. In the cottage everything had seemed possible.

But now...

She blew out a long breath and met Jeff's gaze. "I need to find a private place. And then we can be on our way."

He nodded, and turned back to Fergus and William, the three of them still engaged in the neverending game of male one-upmanship.

Lily turned and walked back the way they'd come, watching the dappled light dance against the water as it streamed through the trees. Quiet descended, and she made her way upstream until she reached a copse of small trees. Weaving her way among the saplings, she found shelter behind an outcropping of rock and relieved herself.

Score one for the future. Flush toilets couldn't be discounted. But there was more to life than modern conveniences. Laughing at her musings, she stood up again, tugging the linen shirt and plaid back into place.

The quiet seemed to have deepened. As if the animals who lived in the woods had all paused—listening. Lily shivered. She was letting her imagination run wild. Fergus and William and Jeff were only a few yards downstream. There was nothing to fear. Yet somewhere, deep inside her, something called for her attention.

She stopped, listening, waiting for some sound to validate her hesitation. Her fear. For a moment there was only silence. And then she heard it.

A keening wail. The hair on the back of her neck rose and she strained to hear more as the sound died away. For a moment there was nothing but the wind and the trees and the rushing water. And then... and then the sound repeated itself. A hollow, echoing cry. Soft and yet penetrating. An animal—no, a human—in pain.

Senses on alert now, Lily stood, heart pounding, waiting for the sound to come again, knowing with every fiber of her being that someone needed her help.

Silence. One beat. Two. And then again the cry.

She ran forward, heedless of the noise she was making, intent only on finding the source of the sound, of helping whomever might be in need. From behind her she heard footsteps crashing through the undergrowth. Fergus, Jeff and William, no doubt. They, too, must have heard the cries.

But despite the knowledge that they were coming, she didn't stop. Her need to help superseded every other instinct—including caution. Someone was in trouble and she was the closest. Crashing through the undergrowth, she leapt across a fallen tree, marveling at her own agility. Adrenaline spurred her onward as a groan of pain filtered through the forest.

Ahead, the stream curved into a horseshoe creating a small clearing filled with sunlight, the trees forming a ring of silent guardians on its edges.

"Wait," Fergus gasped as he reached Lily, grabbing her elbow and pulling her to a jarring halt. "Ye canna ken if 'tis friend or foe."

"Whoever it is, Fergus, he needs our help." Lily jerked her arm free, despite knowing that the older man was speaking the truth. All she could think was that someone was in need and that she was in a position to help. God knows she'd had her own pain of late and she'd been grateful for the people that had offered their support. Strangers all of them—Bram included. She knew she was being a fool, and yet the cry resonated deep inside her. Someone needed her. And she was damn well going to be there.

"Lily." Jeff's voice reached her as she started creeping forward again. "Caution."

She hesitated, her gaze sweeping across the clearing. Fergus and Jeff moved to flank her on either side, William just behind. All of them waited—listening.

The wind rose, and then the keening began again. Rising and then dying as the breeze rushed across the waving grass.

"Over here," Lily called as she moved forward.

A large rock rose out of the ground on the far side of the little meadow. Lichen covered one side, silvery-gray stretching up like long fingers across the face of the boulder. At its foot, a dark shadow moved, then was still.

"He's here." Lily dropped to her knees, her eyes assessing the man who lay at her feet. A thatch of chestnut hair matted with sweat and blood. Dark brown eyes staring up into hers. Pain dimming everything but the barest hint of humanity.

"It's all right," she whispered as she searched his body for injury. "We've found you now."

The man—not much older than she was—sighed, the exhale colored with pain and relief. Besides the blood on his head, his shirt was also stained with blood, the sheer size of the spot taking Lily's breath away.

"Oh God," she whispered as she reached for the hem of his shirt, ripping away the bottom. Folding the linen, she made a bandage of sorts and pressed it to the wound, feeling the pulse of his heart beneath her hands.

"What've ye found, lass?" Fergus asked as he joined her on his knees before the fallen man.

"I don't know."

The injured man's eyes met hers, his fear palpable. "We're here to help," she soothed, wishing for better words. "Can you tell me your name?"

The man opened his mouth, a gurgle of God knows what escaped, and then he swallowed, his eyes taking on a glint of determination. "Robby."

She could barely make out the sound. "Robby?" she asked, her heart pounding.

The man nodded. "Corley."

"Can ye tell us what happened then, lad?" Fergus asked as William and Jeff joined them.

He opened his mouth but no words came, his gaze still locked with Lily's.

"It's okay. It doesn't matter, Robby. What matters is that we're here. And we're going to help you."

His name seemed familiar somehow, but remembering was nothing in the face of making sure that he lived. Obviously, he'd been there for some time. The crust of blood on his head and chest gave credence to her thoughts, but even so, the pulsing new blood was her main concern. If it could not be stopped then Robby could not be saved.

Gritting her teeth, she tore the linen shirt, exposing the wound. It was a long gash, a sword wound, clearly. And while the edges were trying to heal, the center still oozed. "We need to clean this and maybe cauterize it." She wasn't sure where the knowledge was coming from. Girl Scouts or maybe some biology classes, but she knew she was right. "We've got to stop the bleeding."

Fergus leaned over her shoulder. "She's right. And I think burning it is the only way. Although it will hurt beyond reckoning."

Jeff nodded and motioned to William and the two of them set about starting a fire.

Lily pressed the folded linen to Robby's chest. "I know this is frightening," she crooned, "but I'm not going to leave you. And in the end this will save your life. I'm certain of it." She wasn't certain of anything, but she needed him to believe her. Living was part believing, after all.

Robby nodded, squinting his eyes as he bit his lip, trying to not to give in to the pain.

"I'm here, Robby." She struggled to maintain her composure. Now wasn't the time to lose it. She concentrated instead on the young man's face. Somehow she couldn't shake the fact that she recognized his name.

"Who are you?" he asked.

"Lily." She smiled at him, then lifted her concerned gaze to Fergus. "Try to tell us what happened," she said, returning her attention to her patient.

"Betrayed," he breathed.

Lily nodded, not wanting him to stress himself further. "It's going to be okay."

He frowned at her words.

She focused and smiled. "All right. Robby, it's going to be all right."

Behind her, Jeff was holding his sword, the tip red hot.

She leaned down toward the injured man, shifting so that her arms encircled him. "I'm sorry, Robby, but this is going to hurt. It's the only way to stop the bleeding."

He tightened his jaw and nodded, his eyes locked on hers. "Do it, then."

Lily nodded to Jeff, while Fergus and William moved into place to secure Robby's arms and legs. Lily stroked his face, tears filling her eyes. Jeff crouched beside the injured man, the heated sword in his hand.

"Ready?" he asked.

Robby nodded, and Lily cupped his chin. "Think of something lovely." It wasn't enough, but it was all she had.

Jeff dipped the tip of the sword against the wound. Robby bucked and screamed and then was quiet.

"Jesus," Jeff whispered. "Bloody brave bastard."

"Aye, a rare hero, that," Fergus added.

"Shite" was all William had to say.

Lily felt her stomach heave, but she fought against the wave. If Robby could stomach what had happened, so could she.

"Will he be okay?" she asked, her voice barely more than a whisper.

"I canna say." Fergus shook his head. "Puir wee bastard. He shouldna have lasted as long as he did."

"I feel like I should know him," Lily said, still trying to sort through her memories.

"Well, considering that you've only been here a couple of times, I'd say that isn't likely." Jeff stared down at the still man, sympathy etched on his face. "But regardless, I'd say he's a man we should all take our hat off to. I mean, hell, who knows how long he's been out here like this? The fact that he survived is nothing short of a miracle."

"And if he lives to see the morrow it will be yet another miracle," Fergus added.

"So it's that bad?" Lily knew the answer, but somehow she needed to hear it put into words.

"Aye, lass, that it is. I wish that it were different, but it's no'. That said, we've given the lad his best chance. We'll know on the morrow."

"But we canna stay here," William protested. "If we do, we might not catch up to Iain and Bram in time."

"We can't leave him." Even as Lily said the words she realized the conundrum they faced. If they stayed to help Robby, then Bram might be at risk, but if they left Robby, then Lily wouldn't be able to live with herself.

A rock and a hard place if ever there was one—except that there wasn't a choice.

"We have to stay," she declared, her eyes meeting Jeff's and Fergus's, daring them to argue.

"I don't see that there's a choice," Jeff agreed, echoing her thoughts.

Fergus gave a gruff nod. "William, we'll need to build up the fire. We've got to keep the lad warm. And we'll need water." For this he looked to Jeff. "And the rest we'll have to leave to God." His gaze met Lily's and, despite the pain in her heart, she relished his approval. Sometimes the difficult choices were the right ones.

If only Bram could wait. Please God, let it not be too late.

CHAPTER 23

"THE CUT-THROUGH TO the pass is just beyond those rocks," Frazier said. "'Tis very narrow, ye ken."

"And you say it follows a burn?" Bram asked as they all pulled to a halt at the foot of the outcropping of rock.

"Aye, a wee wash o' water. Although with the spring thaw it'll be running higher than usual, I suppose."

"Any reason that would be a problem?" Ranald asked Frazier.

"Nay. 'Tis too small a stream to bother the horses. And toward the bottom, where the burn falls from the rocks to form pools, the pathway widens so that we willna have to cross the water. The pass dumps us right in to Alec Comyn's backyard."

"Is there anywhere to camp along the way?" asked Iain, his eyes moving from the rocky slope to the sky. "If not, then we'd best make camp here. We've only got a few hours of daylight left."

Frazier scratched his beard. "There's a copse of birch about half-way along. 'Twould be as good a place as any to camp for the night."

"And it would mean being closer to Comyn's holding at sunup." Bram couldn't keep the impatience out of his voice.

"Well, as much as I want to make the man pay for what he did to your father, I've got to be equally sure that we're not rushing into this like angry fools," Iain said.

Bram bit off his reply, clenching a fist as he tried to contain his frustration. He'd always been a man of action, and so was aching for a fight. Something to take the edge off his own guilt. About Lily, about his father, about everything. He felt as if he had no control, his life spiraling away from him without so much as a by your leave. It wasn't as if he couldn't handle the challenges, but to do so, he had to meet them head on. And all this prattle wasn't getting him any closer to his enemy.

"You're sure about this passage?" Ranald was asking, his cousin eyeing Frazier speculatively. "When was the last time you were up here?"

The older man shrugged. "'Twas last fall. Seamus and I went hunting."

"For Comyn cattle?" Ranald asked, raising his brows.

"Ach, no." Frazier shook his grizzled head. "No' to say that it wasn't tempting. But these old bones canna handle reiving. So we made do with smaller game. Pheasant and rabbits and such. Anyway, the point is the pass was clear then. As was the stand o' birch."

Bram looked to Iain and his cousin nodded.

"Best get to it then," Ranald said, urging his horse forward. "Time's a wastin'."

An hour or so later they were climbing full out, single file, following the path of the rushing burn. Water from the spring thaw sprang through gaps in the rocks, creating tiny waterfalls cascading down the craggy cliffs and swelling the stream with the runoff. Clumps of gorse clung to the rocky scree. In another few weeks, the mountains would be abloom, but for now everything was on the cusp, the predominate colors grey and green, leafy boughs of alder and birch blending in with the darker needles of the pines.

DEE DAVIS

"We can make camp just around this bend," Frazier called out, swinging around to face Bram, who had been riding just behind him. And true to the old man's word, the trail widened, then disappeared as it was claimed by a grassy meadow ringed by a stand of birch.

"The trail continues o'er there." Frazier pointed to the far side of the clearing as Ranald and Iain pulled abreast of the two of them.

Bram turned his attention to the opening just beyond the trees, then urged his mare forward, crossing the meadow and pulling to a stop again just at the head of the narrowing canyon.

"Bollocks," Ranald grumbled as he reined in his horse. "We'll no' be going through that."

It looked as if half the mountain had come crashing down, the great piles of stones that now blocked the pass seeming to mock them with their impenetrability.

Bram blew out a slow, frustrated breath. "I canna see any way around it either." Both sides of the rock slide were flanked with rocky cliffs. The one on the right was covered with scree and stunted pines. The one to the left sheared off sharply, as if a mighty blacksmith had cleaved it in two.

"Looks as if it's been that way a while," Iain said as he and Frazier rode up beside them. "Look at the gorse growing amidst the rocks. And there's more growing on the cliff face."

"Must have happened this winter." Frazier frowned. "'Twas clear when I was last here. I swear it."

"No one doubts you, man," Ranald said, his tone affable.

"And whether it was here or no' doesn't change the fact that we canna go this way now." Iain and Ranald exchanged a telling look, and Bram wondered for the first time if they'd been wise to put their faith in Frazier. He was older even than Bram's father. And though he seemed spry enough, there was always the possibility that his mind wasn't as good as it had been.

A faded memory tugged at his brain. Something about Frazier. But that part of the conversation had been lost. It had been his father's next words that had stuck with Bram. The guardsman had suggested that Seamus consult with his son.

"The day I need my son's advice is the day I go to my grave," his father had scoffed. And Bram had stalked away in anger, his father's words echoing in his ears. Nothing he did was good enough for the old man. Seamus refused to accept the fact that Bram was a man grown. And a worthy one at that. Bram had more than proven it in service to both Moy and to his great uncle, Ian Ciar. But Seamus had never acknowledged any of it. And now...he never would.

"I think the best thing is to make camp," Iain was saying, the words pulling Bram's thoughts back to the present. "And rethink our strategy."

"From where I sit, we have only one option now," Bram replied. "We hit the Comyns head on. Attack them at *Tigh an Droma*."

"Aye, but by the time we manage to get there, Macniven will have surely made it back," Ranald cautioned. "Which means they'll know we're coming."

"And be more than ready for us," Iain added.

"Then we should go now," Bram said, scowling at his cousins. "Take them unaware. They'll never expect an attack at night."

"Ach, laddie, I'm afraid yer cousin is right." Frazier shook his head, his expression apologetic. "The horses are tired. We canna push them further. Best we rest and make our move with first light."

Bram opened his mouth to argue, then shut it again. Frazier was right. To attack now would be foolhardy. They needed a plan. And for that they needed time. With a curt nod to Frazier and his cousins, Bram wheeled his horse around and rode back across the clearing. It wasn't their fault. They hadn't caused the rock slide. But it seemed as if even the mountains themselves were on the Comyns' side.

Bram leapt down from his horse, handing the reins to one of Iain's men, then strode off for the solitude of the woods that ringed the clearing. They had to make plans, but first he needed time on his own. Time to fight his demons. Bram had spent the bulk of his childhood alone, a motherless child, roaming wild over the countryside, he and Robby getting into all kinds of mischief. He supposed they were lucky to have escaped without reckoning. But in truth, his father hadn't cared enough even to take him in hand.

It had only been when he'd gone to Moy and formed a friendship with his cousins that Bram had begun to believe he might have worth. Like Bram, Iain's father had never shown any feelings for his son. And Ranald, a third son, had always felt the odd man out. So the three of them had found common ground easily enough. But even then, Bram had never felt as if he truly belonged. Some part of him hungered for something more. Something that was only his.

Lily.

His heart clenched at the thought.

Lily, too, was alone in the world. And she belonged to him. Or she could have, if he hadn't walked away. Pain and guilt combined with his frustration over the rock slide, the resulting anger sending him thrashing through the trees. Why must everything be so difficult?

He pushed aside a low hanging branch and moved deeper into the woods. Quiet descended, all the noise from the men setting up camp behind him dying away. Above him he could hear the twitter of birds, but beyond that there was only the rushing of the stream and the whisper of the wind through the leaves.

He knelt beside the burn, his mind tumbling with unanswered questions. What if his uncle refused to accept that Bram wasn't a traitor?

What if his father was never avenged? What if Ranald was right? What if, thanks to Macniven, the attack on Alec Comyn's holding proved to be a trap? And most importantly of all, what if he never saw Lily again?

He dipped his hand into the water, remembering the vision by the fire. Lily in the arms of another man. In his head, be believed Iain. Katherine's brother was not a threat. But in his heart? If he were honest, he'd admit to a shred of doubt. A smidgeon of fear. He'd thrown her away for the sake of his father. What if she could never forgive him for that? Or worse still, what if they were forever separated because of it? He'd chosen vengeance over love. Surely that must be a mortal sin? And yet, what choice did he have? He had nothing to offer Lily without clearing his name, and to do that he must face the Comyns.

'Twas a paradox of the very worst kind. Damned if he did—damned if he did not.

And what if his cousins were right? What if she had defied him? Come here on her own? How was he to protect her when he was here and she was God knows where? He slapped the burn with the flat of his hand, the water rippling in protest.

She was just a woman. It wasn't as if he'd never had another. Most lasses seemed to find him fair of face. Leastwise they offered themselves often enough. And he'd been more than happy to return the favor. But not a one of them had ever made him feel the way he felt about Lily. As if she'd become a part of him. In truth, without Lily his life would mean nothing. She was his heart. His soul.

She was everything.

He stared into the water, trying to conjure her image. See her face. Surely if she were here somewhere, he'd feel it. Know it.

Behind him the silence was broken. Harsh cries and the clank of metal against metal. Bram frowned, scrambling to make sense of the sounds as the reflection of something over his shoulder shifted, took form.

Not Lily.

A Comyn—claymore held high.

It seemed the choice was made, the battle at hand.

—~—

"How's he doing?" Jeff asked, dropping down beside where Lily had resumed her position holding Robby's head in her lap.

"He's still breathing, which I'm going to take as a positive sign, but he hasn't regained consciousness."

It had been several hours since they'd cauterized the wound. The bleeding had stopped, although the injury was still fiery red, and from the feel of things Robby was running a fever. His head thrashed and he mumbled something too low for her to be able to make out the words.

Across the way, Fergus was tending the fire while William turned a spit holding roasting rabbit. William had snared the animal, and although a small part of Lily rejected the notion of eating Thumper, hunger and the need to survive held sway. Besides, the rabbit could be used to infuse a nice broth for Robby when he came to.

If he came to, a voice deep inside her goaded.

As if answering her thought, Robby moaned again, but his eyes remained closed.

"Do ye think you can get him to take a sip, lass?"

Lily looked up to find Fergus standing next to Jeff. "I can try," she offered. "He's still out, but he seems to be at least peripherally aware of what's going on around him."

Fergus nodded and handed Jeff a pewter tankard. "'Tis tea steeped from yarrow and some other herbs. Katherine always uses it when someone is in pain. And it's also supposed to suppress bleeding and help prevent putrification. Although I canna say that I believe wee plants can do all of that."

"Katherine did her dissertation on the use of Medieval plants. Funny how it's always the oddest pieces of information that turn out to be the most useful." Jeff shrugged. "I'm told she's turned into something of a healer."

"'Tis true," William said from across the fire. "She saved my leg and my life." His green eyes glittered with devotion. "I owe her everything."

"Well, now, lad, I think Iain might have something to say about that," Fergus said, his voice stern but kind.

William's face flushed a deep red—the color at odds with the fiery orange of his hair. "Well, I'd give my life for her, that's for sure."

"As would we," Jeff agreed as he gave the tankard to Lily.

Again she was surprised at the pang of jealousy their words brought. But then, that kind of dedication had to be earned. And Katherine had clearly surpassed the mark. Maybe someday she'd prove herself to these people as well. The thought brought her up short. It implied long term relationships, and to do that she'd have to stay. But if Bram didn't want her...

She blew out a breath and shook her head, forcing herself to concentrate on Robby. Sliding an arm beneath his shoulders, she lifted him up and pressed the rim of the tankard against his lips.

"Robby?" she crooned. "Can you hear me? I've got some tea for you. It's meant to make you better. Fergus made it." Robby was still, his eyes closed, his mouth shut.

"Come on then, lad," Fergus urged. "It's meant to help with the pain. Just one sip."

But again nothing happened.

Lily's eyes met Jeff's, telegraphing her worry. "He's got to take it. He's burning up."

Jeff leaned over Robby and cleared his throat. "Drink the tea, damn it."

Robby moaned once and obediently took a sip.

"Clearly you have the touch," Lily laughed, urging Robby to take another sip and then another. "Hopefully this will do some good." Robby groaned and she stroked his hair, trying to soothe him. "I feel so helpless."

"Naught left to do but wait," Fergus said, pushing to his feet and taking the tankard. "Might as well leave him be, and come have something to eat. Ye canna help him if ye make yourself sick."

"Fergus is right." Jeff nodded in agreement. "Robby needs to sleep and you need to eat. So settle him in and come have a bite." He too pushed to his feet, then after a last firm look, followed Fergus over to the fire and the roasting rabbit.

Lily watched as the three men talked in obvious camaraderie. The sun was almost gone, shadows lengthening with the advent of evening. The wind was cold, and she pulled her plaid closer around her, then carefully shifted Robby's head so that it rested on the makeshift pallet they'd constructed of piled leaves covered with a blanket. It wasn't much, but it was a far sight better than before they'd found him.

Robby moaned then mumbled something. Lily leaned closer to try and hear. He thrashed to the right and then seemed to settle, but his eyebrows drew together as he fought against something only he could see. "I'm sorry," he whispered.

"Shush," Lily soothed, laying her hand over his. "There's nothing to be sorry for."

"Nay," Robby shook his head again, obviously lost in a dream. "Nay. 'Tis a sorry friend I turned out to be."

"I don't believe that," Lily said, unable to stop herself.

"Traitor," he whispered, his words dying away and Lily shivered, her mind suddenly presenting her with a memory. Bram telling her about his father's death, and his friend's. Robby. Surely then this was Bram's oldest friend. And the man wasn't dead at all. But what did he mean 'traitor'? Bram had said that there must have been a traitor. Someone who helped Alec Comyn. Did Robby know who it was? Or worse still, was Robby the traitor?

She looked down at the man, discarding the thought even as she had it. When they'd first found him he'd mentioned being betrayed. Someone else was the traitor. And she'd lay odds he was responsible for Robby's injury. Anger flashed through her. Bram had lost so much. And now the fate of his oldest friend lay in her hands. And honest to God, she had no earthly idea what she was supposed to do.

But one thing was certain; she sure as hell wasn't going to give up.

The brush beneath the trees around the clearing rattled ominously. Shifting to protect Robby, she rose to her knees, watching as Fergus, William and Jeff reached for their weapons. Then suddenly, the clearing was full of men, all of them brandishing weapons. She reached for an arrow from her quiver, instinct alone helping her to lift and arm her bow. Pulling back, she centered her sights on a towering man holding a claymore.

For a moment the world narrowed to just the two of them. His green-eyed gaze met hers, his wild blue-black hair framing a face that was the masculine equivalent of her own. Air whooshed out of her lungs, but she held her position and stared defiantly into his eyes.

CHAPTER 24

✦

MOVING ON INSTINCT alone, Bram pulled his claymore and sprang to his feet, dodging to the side as his enemy's broadsword cut through the space he'd just vacated. The man, enraged at his failure, turned and swung again. But this time Bram was ready, countering his opponent's parry with his own weapon, the jarring impact sending them both backward.

Circling each other now, Bram tuned out the sounds of battle coming from the campsite, concentrating on the man in front of him. He couldn't help his cousins until he managed to rid himself of his attacker.

The man was taller than Bram and broad as a tree, but Bram was quicker, and he knew how to press his advantage. "Come on then, let's see what you've got," he taunted, breaking to the right. The man snarled and lunged. Bram danced to the left, out of reach of his attacker's blade. Pivoting on his right foot, Bram swung the claymore, satisfied when it glanced off his opponent's arm.

With a cry of rage, blood dripping, the man lunged again, his sword nicking Bram's side. Looking down, he saw a fine line of blood seeping through the linen of his shirt. Pain sliced through him, but it only served to increase his determination.

"You have the luck of the devil, but you bleed like a man," his opponent taunted.

"No more than you." Bram moved out of range as the man swung again. "Tell me who you are and I might just let you go."

"Yer assuming you have the advantage." The man thrust again and their swords hit hard, the sound ringing through the forest. "But 'twill be a cold day in hell afore a Macgillivray takes a Comyn."

There it was then. By the man's own mouth. "So yer Alec's kinsman?"

"Aye, son o' Macniven." He moved as he spoke, rocking back and forth on the balls of his feet.

"I believe I've met yer brother."

The big man's lips curled in a feral grin. "Ach, that you have. Canna say I'm sorry that he didn't kill you, though. Seeing as how it left the task to me."

Ignoring the pain in his side, Bram lifted his sword and feinted to the left, tricking the other man into following suit, and leaping forward. Bram lowered into a crouch and swung his sword, just catching the edge of Macniven's shoulder.

The man howled in pain, his eyes narrowing as he lunged forward again, slicing his claymore through the air. Bram danced back, managing to miss the blow. Once more they circled, changing places, and then moving back again, eyes locked as each waited for the other to act.

Blood stained Macniven's shirt and he was breathing hard, but Bram knew better than to assume an advantage. Macniven's eyes narrowed and Bram swung, parrying the other man's thrust. They circled once more and then a shout from the clearing behind Bram caught Macniven's attention. Taking advantage of the mistake, Bram moved back and to the right, his weapon arcing over his head in a full-blown attack.

The claymore cut through muscle and bone, and with a satisfied grunt, Bram pulled the weapon free. Macniven's eyes rolled back as he fell to the ground, his last breath hissing from his lips.

"Take that, you bloody bastard."

Again there was a shout from the clearing. Bram pulled his bloody sword free of Macniven's body and sprinted toward the fighting, his thoughts turning to his cousins and the battle they were obviously waging. God willing, they too were winning the day.

Suddenly, off to his left, a second man came charging through the undergrowth, broadsword at the ready. Bram swung his claymore using both hands, the force knocking the other man's blade free. With a second thrust the man was down, and Bram was running again.

He burst into the clearing, blood pumping, heart pounding.

Iain fought off to his left, and Ranald off to his right. There was no sign of Frazier, and Bram's gut twisted with worry, but there was no time for further thought. Iain struck a death blow, then both he and Bram ran for Ranald, who was still engaged in the fighting. He deftly fended off one man, only to have another rush him from behind. But Iain reached Ranald in time, drawing off the new attacker.

Iain and Ranald were back to back now, their opponents circling around them, crouched and ready. Behind them, a man on horseback urged his mount closer, clearly intending to push the odds into Comyn territory. Bram jumped onto a large boulder, lifting his claymore and swinging as the man rode by. The blow glanced off his thigh, but had the intended result. He swerved away from the two circling men just as Iain made his move, lunging forward to take out the man on the right.

Almost simultaneously, Ranald rushed the other man, their swords clanging as they jockeyed for position. The first man was down, most likely dead. And the horseman—apparently the leader—seemed to realize that the battle had swung in favor of Iain's men.

Wheeling his horse around, he let loose a cry that resounded off the rocks.

Men scrambled to horses and melted into the trees. Retreat.

One minute the clearing was ringing with swordplay and the next it was resoundingly quiet. Bodies littered the ground. Mostly the enemy, praise God. But Bram could see that at least some of Iain's men had been injured or killed. He walked quickly through the carnage, searching for Frazier.

"Bram," a voice from the trees called. "I'm here, lad."

He hastened into the cover of the trees, following the sound of Frazier's voice. "I'm coming."

The woods were gloomy after the faded light from the meadow and he stopped a moment to get his bearings. "Frazier, can you hear me? Are you hurt?"

"Not mortally," came the reply. "But I need your help."

Bram pushed through the undergrowth, whacking at saplings and bushes with his sword. "Hang on. I'm almost there."

Ahead of him, in the distance, a shadow loomed against a large tree. It shifted, and then he caught the glint of a sword. "Frazier, have a care," he called. "You're not alone."

Running now, mindless of the undergrowth, he hurried to aid his father's man. He burst into a small clearing by the burn. Frazier was standing by the tree, his weapon in hand, blood dripping from his leg. Frantically, he looked for signs of an attacker. Frazier took a step closer, his face pinched in pain and anger.

"Where's the other man?" Bram asked.

Frazier took another step. "I dinna ken. He was here and then gone. Mayhap you scared him."

Bram nodded, still on alert as he moved over to his father's captain. "Can you walk?"

"With yer help," he said.

Bram lowered his sword and moved closer to Frazier.

"'Tis how it must be, ye ken," he whispered as Bram reached out to give him support.

"Iain, they're over here," Ranald called as he came into the clearing.

Frazier's eyes narrowed, and then he sighed, squaring his shoulders, knuckles white around the hilt of his sword.

"Are either of you hurt?" Ranald asked. Iain followed on his heels.

"I've got a cut on my side, but I dinna think it's anything to worry o'er." Bram's gaze moved to Frazier. "But Frazier's been sliced at the knee. He needs help to walk."

"Nay, lad." Frazier shook his head, pride flashing in his eyes. "I think I can manage well enough."

"No point in suffering," Ranald said, coming to Frazier's other side. "Hand me your sword."

For a moment there was silence, and then Frazier nodded, handing the claymore to Ranald. Then Iain and Bram propped up the older man, and slowly the four of them walked back toward the camp.

"Truly it isna as bad as it looks," Frazier said. "Just a flesh wound, I've no doubt."

"Still, it can't hurt to take the weight off it until we've had the chance to look and be sure."

Frazier grumbled his acquiescence. And Iain grinned at Bram over the old man's head.

"Seems odd they'd retreat the way they did." Ranald frowned. "Not that I'm sad to see the backs of their sorry hides. Still, I'd have expected them to make a better show."

"We had them outnumbered," Iain said. "Their leader could see the way of it, and made the only call he could."

"To run away?" Ranald asked. "That doesna seem like the Comyns to me."

"I'll grant you that," Bram acknowledged. "Did you recognize the man on the horse? It canna have been Alec. The man had red hair. And Alec's is black as pitch, or so I've been told."

"Aye, I've seen him." Iain nodded. "Black hair and green eyes. Definitely no' the man on the horse. Or any other I saw, for that matter."

They'd reached the clearing. Iain's men were cleaning their wounds and gathering their belongings. Together Bram and Iain lowered Frazier down onto a large rock.

"But why would Alec Comyn have bothered to set a trap, for that is surely what this was, and then not have seen to the fighting himself? It certainly doesna track with what I've heard about the man." Ranald knelt at Frazier's feet and began inspecting the gash on his knee.

"Nor I." Iain frowned. "None of this feels right. It's as if we're missing something."

"I think it's just as it appears," Frazier argued. "Alec Comyn hasn't the bollocks to take us on himself. He'd rather sacrifice his underlings." He bit out an oath as Ranald cleaned his wound.

"You were right about the knee," Ranald said, tying a bit of linen around Frazier's leg. "'Tis no' much more than a scratch."

Frazier nodded and pushed to his feet. "What next?"

"We tend to my men's wounds." Iain's gaze moved over the meadow. "Bury our own and then we ride out."

"Now?" Frazier asked.

"Aye. There's still about an hour of light. We'll go back the way we came. I don't know about you, but I dinna relish making camp here amidst the carnage."

"And besides," Ranald said, moving to have a look at the gash on Bram's side, "staying here would be tantamount to waving a flag asking to be attacked. Between the landslide and the mountains, there's only one way out. And I dinna want to make it any easier for the Comyns to take another swipe at us."

"Aye, we'll find a safer place to make camp," Iain said. "And then tomorrow we'll ride on *Tigh an Droma*."

Bram clenched a fist as Ranald poured whisky on his wound. "If Alec Comyn willna come to us, then we'll just have to take the fight to him."

"Holy Mary, mother o' God," a second dark-haired man swore, crossing himself. "She could be yer sister."

"Aye, that she could." The green-eyed man nodded, his gaze still locked on Lily's. "I'll thank you to drop the weapon, lass."

"Only if you drop yours," Lily said, lifting her chin and holding tight to the bow.

For a moment silence stretched through the clearing. Then the big man lowered his claymore. Slowly, Lily lowered the bow and dared to glance around. The rest of his men still held their weapons, as did Fergus, William and Jeff. All were staring at Lily and the green-eyed man. Their looks would be comical if the situation wasn't quite so dire.

Lily swallowed the bitter taste of fear. "You're Alec Comyn."

For a second the man's eyes widened in surprise, but just as quickly the expression was gone. "Aye. Have we met, then?"

"No." Lily shook her head. "But I've heard of you."

"And from the look on your face, I'd say 'twas nothing good." His face twitched in a sort of half smile and then he shifted his attention shifted to Fergus. "I take it you're the leader?" he asked, for the moment dismissing Lily. She fought a wave of resentment. It wasn't as if she wanted his attention, after all.

The older man's shoulders straightened, his gaze steady. "Fergus Mackintosh. I stand as captain to Iain Mackintosh of Duncreag."

"And your companions—are they Mackintoshes, too?" Alec eyed William and Jeff.

"Aye, that they are." Fergus' nod was curt but respectful.

"And what are you doing on my land?"

"We're standing escort for the lady." Fergus' heavy white brows drew together as he watched the younger man.

"I see." Alec shifted his attention back to Lily, his green eyes sparkling with some unnamed emotion. "And who exactly are you that they would be escorting you across my land?" Everyone's attention turned back to her, and she lifted her chin, her posture unconsciously regal.

"My name is Lily Chastain."

"A French name," Alec said, eyes narrowing.

"My father's, yes."

"And your mother's?"

"If you're asking if we share blood as well as a face, then yes—we do. My great-grandmother was a Macniven."

"It explains much." It seems Alec Comyn was a man of few words.

Behind her Robby shifted, trying to say something, but the words were garbled, distorted with his pain.

Alec's eyes narrowed again as he focused on the injured man. "And the man behind you? Is he why you're here, then?"

"No." Lily shook her head, lowering her guard to reach over to touch Robby's shoulder. "We found him here. He's been injured. We've tried to help him the best that we can. But the wound is bad and there's no telling how long he's been on his own out here."

"And do you know his name?"

"Yes." Lily's gaze locked with Alec's. "Robby Corley." She waited, watching for his reaction.

"From Dunbrae? And how exactly did he wind up here?"

Lily struggled to answer, wondering how much she should admit to knowing. She flickered a glance at Fergus, who lifted an eyebrow and then at Jeff, who shrugged. Great, no help from that corner. She looked back at her cousin—a hundred times removed or whatever. The man was family after all. Murderous, barbarous family—but still. Honesty it was.

"One of your men injured him. When you massacred the Macgillivrays." She sucked in a breath, watching her cousin for signs that she'd spoken rashly.

"I've massacred no one. In fact, I've no' set foot on Macgillivray lands in years." His eyes glinted with unspoken anger.

"Maybe you weren't there in person, but I was told that it was you who gave the order." Their green-eyed gazes collided, each of them sparking anger. It was like looking into some kind of fun-house mirror.

"As I said, I've ordered no one killed and my men have been with me," he insisted. "But I've a healer with me. If you like, I can have him see to the man."

"And finish what you started?" She pulled to her feet, blocking Alec's access to Robby, raising her bow again. "I hardly think so."

"You're no' one for believin' a man, now are you?"

Lily glanced over at her friends again. Fergus tipped his head, signaling her to answer. "No. I'm not." A lifetime of being the rich man's kid had taught her to be careful.

"I canna say I fault you." Alec smiled, and the transformation was almost shocking. To say that he'd looked fierce was an understatement, and now he seemed almost to be laughing at her. Or, just maybe, laughing with her. "One thing canna be doubted," he said. "You're most definitely a Comyn. Stubborn to the core. I swear to you, lass, I mean the man no harm."

Indecision washed through her. She didn't trust her cousin as far as she could throw him, but Robby needed help.

"Have your men discard their weapons," she ordered. Alec's warriors—for there was no doubt that's what they were—had moved closer. Her pronouncement caused a ripple of amusement. Clearly they were surprised that a woman had the audacity to stand up to their laird.

Alec's lips twitched, but he held her gaze. "You first." He nodded toward Fergus, William and Jeff.

"How about we do it at the same time?" Lily fought against a grin. Who the hell would have thought she'd be orchestrating a cease fire in the middle of the fifteenth century? She was from Fairfield county, for God's sake.

Alec nodded, sheathing his weapon.

Lily laid down her bow, praying she was making the right decision, but something about Alec made her believe him. Although the idea of that left so many unanswered questions she didn't even know where to begin.

Fergus released a gusty sigh and sheathed his claymore. The huge man beside Alec did the same. And the rest of the men, including William and Jeff, followed suit.

Alec motioned to a smaller man at the back of the crowd. "Come, see to him."

Lily stepped aside, but stood close as the man knelt beside Robby.

"I've promised you I'll no' let him come to harm. And I'm a man o' my word." Alec's voice came from close to her ear and she jumped. "Now tell, me, Lily, why are you truly here?"

Again she wondered at how much truth she should share. So much of it was overwhelming. Still she'd already admitted that she thought he was a killer—and he'd done no more than deny it. Maybe it was best to stick with as much truth as she could manage.

"I'm here for Bram Macgillivray."

This time the ripple in the crowd was anger, but Alec held up a hand, quieting his men. "And why would you be looking for him?"

Lily's chin lifted again. "Because I love him." Her gaze collided with Alec's. "And because the two of you are on a path of destruction that has to be stopped before one or both of you wind up dead."

"But I told you I dinna kill the man's father."

"Ah, but you're aware of the fact. I certainly didn't mention it." She was glaring at him now, feeling heat wash across her face.

"Blast it, woman, everyone knows about it. 'Tis no' a secret. And admitting that I know is no' the same as admitting my guilt." They squared off. "And while we're talking o' guilt, what does your mother think of her daughter conspiring with the enemy?"

"My mother is dead." The words fell into the clearing with the power of a broadsword, silence holding as the big man next to Alec crossed himself again.

"I'm sorry." Alec's voice was gruff with emotion. "And your father?"

"Dead as well. But don't go getting ideas that I'm suddenly under your wardship or something."

This last brought a smile. "I can see you're a woman with her own mind. But still—a Macgillivray?"

There was no reasoning with a Scot, clearly. They all seemed to come with the same thick head. "You and Bram are not as different as you might think. And besides, you can't help who you love. It just happens." Even when said person is from another century.

"And Bram Macgillivray—he loves you, too?"

The flush across her cheeks burned brighter. "I believe so."

"I'm not saying I doubt you. But you ken the last time a Macgillivray and a Comyn were together it dinna end so well."

Lily pulled the silver chain from beneath her shirt and plaid, lifting the ring for everyone to see. "Yes, Alec, I *ken* it well."

CHAPTER 25

✦

"I CANNA SAY 'tis an easy tale to swallow," Alec Comyn said, frowning at her. They'd withdrawn to sit upon a fallen log. Fergus sat across from her on a large boulder with William glowering over at Alec from just behind Fergus. Alec's man Dougan Macniven stood just opposite William, his hand never leaving the hilt of his claymore.

Across the way, she could see Jeff keeping watch as the healer ministered to Robby. If the situation had been less serious, Lily would have smiled. But instead she moved her gaze back to her cousin's. Convinced that Alec was telling the truth about not attacking Dunbrae, they'd told him everything, including the bit about her and Jeff coming from the future. And Lily, had it not happened to her, doubted she'd have believed the story either.

"Nevertheless," she said, opening her hands in supplication, "what we're telling you is true."

"I said it isna easy to accept." Alec shrugged. "I dinna say that I doubted you. If for no other reason than the ring you wear. In all honesty, I find it harder to believe that you love a Macgillivray than that you traveled through time."

"Which just shows you how ridiculous this blood feud really is."

"I canna argue with you there. I have no trouble defending my honor or my clan when the moment calls for it, but I dinna hold with ancient grudges. Whatever truly happened all those years ago, it should no' affect what's happening now."

"But clearly it is having an effect," Fergus answered. "And if it's no' you, then someone else must be using the feud to their own advantage."

The conversation was interrupted as a rider galloped into the camp. Alec started to rise, but Dougan waved him down again. "I'll handle it." The big man strode off toward the rider just as Jeff walked up to the group.

"One of my scouts," Alec said, as he waved Jeff to a seat on another stone. "How fairs Corley?"

"Geordie believes that he's turned a corner," Jeff replied. "He credits Lily's intervention with having saved him. Especially cauterizing the wound."

"Thank God," Lily said, relief flooding through her. Although in reality he was little more than a stranger, once she'd realized Robby's connection to Bram, her heart had become involved. If Bram cared about this man, then so did she. And she'd been so afraid he'd die on her watch. One more thing for Bram to have to forgive.

"Did he say anything more?" Alec asked.

"No. He's still really out of it," Jeff replied. "Keeps talking about traitors. And then cries out for Bram and someone named Frazier?"

"That would be Bram's father's captain," William said.

"Aye." Fergus nodded. "The man managed to escape the attack and make his way to Duncreag. Bram was much relieved to see him alive. Although, if I remember correctly, he believed that Robby was dead."

"Bram told me that as well." Lily blew out a long breath. "That's how I knew who Robby was. At least that will be good news. Assuming I can figure out a way to circumvent all the misunderstanding."

"If anyone can do it, you can." Jeff's smile was comforting.

"Aye, but in the meantime, we'll no' be going anywhere until the morning, so I say we pool our knowledge and try to get to the bottom of what's happening." Fergus looked to Alec, his expression masked. "There was another attack, ye ken. On Duncreag."

"Right." Lily nodded. "With everything happening, I'd forgotten that bit."

Fergus's grizzled gaze held Alec's. "The attackers were wearing Comyn colors."

Alec frowned. "'Twas no' my men."

"I believe you, lad. But someone clearly wanted us to believe that it was you."

"And perpetuate the idea that your clan attacked Dunbrae," Jeff said. "The whole thing seems really hinky to me."

Alec lifted his eyebrows in question.

"I know that one." William grinned, clearly catching Alec's confusion over Jeff's choice of word. "He's saying something feels off."

"Aye, well, I canna deny the right of that. Heen-key. As you say." Alex's lips twisted into a crooked smile.

Fergus frowned. "But if it wasn't you? Then who?"

"That I canna even guess. Like Bram, I've only just returned to the area. When my father died, I had no other choice but to become laird of *Tigh an Droma*. I'm responsible for its people."

"Your clan," Lily offered.

"Yours, too." His green eyes sparkled.

"Of that there can be no doubt," Fergus said, his eyes moving from Lily to Alec and back again. "Even without the ring."

"And in your time, you say that *Tigh an Droma* is gone?" Alec pulled the attention back to their story.

"The tower, yes. But not the family. Or the holding. Your people—my people—carry on. But Scotland is much changed."

"And no' for the better..." snorted Fergus.

"Aye, I suppose that is the way of things," Alec mused, ignoring the other man. "And the Macgillivrays?"

"The family exists, of course. But they're scattered. And Dunbrae is long gone. If Reginald—the present owner of *Tigh an Droma*—" She paused, struggling with words. She supposed she really meant the future owner, since she was sitting here and this was her now, but it was all really too confusing "—was right, then you and Bram will fight and Dunbrae and the Macgillivrays will suffer as a result. Or at least that's what I believe."

"And what of Bram?"

Lily felt tears threaten. "I can't say for certain. But Reginald seemed to believe he was killed in the battle. And that his death is what saved you. By ending things, I mean."

"And the prophecy remained unfulfilled."

Like Reginald, Alec had been aware of the legend of the ring. The story of Graeme and Tyra. Their love and Kendrick Macgillivray's vicious betrayal. And the resulting belief that when a Macgillivray again wore the Comyn ring, both clans would rise to power again.

"'Twould seem so," William said, all eyes swinging to him. "But you must also understand that the Macgillivrays—indeed Bram and his kin—believe Kendrick's version of the story. That the attack was planned by the Comyns. And that is was Tyra herself who killed Graeme. So the truth, as they know it, allows for no prophecy."

Lily's heart twisted. Bram had no idea who she really was. But once he saw her with Alec there could be no room for doubt. And if he believed her ancestor killed his, and that the result was the destruction of his clan, how could he ever find it in his heart to love her? It was too much to ask. Justin couldn't handle her loss of status and money. How could she expect Bram to love his sworn enemy? Even if he was wrong in his beliefs.

"What am I going to do?" she asked Jeff, forgetting for a moment the other people present.

"You tell him the truth. All of it. And if he truly loves you, he'll understand." Easy for Jeff to say. Lily blew out a breath, running a hand through her hair.

"But first," Alec added, "you're going to have to convince him that I'm no' the enemy. If you're right, he's coming for me even as we speak. And while I dinna wish you or yours any harm, if I'm forced to do so, I will defend what is mine."

Looking at the hardened warrior sitting beside her, Lily had no doubt that he meant every word he said. Maybe Bram was right. Maybe she had no place in this world. And yet even as she had the thought, she rejected it. Bram wasn't Justin. And she wasn't going to give up. Some things were worth fighting for.

"All I ask is that you give me a chance," she said. "Let me try to reason with him."

"I've no taste for battle with the Macgillivrays. So you need have no fear of my initiating hostilities against your Bram. But if he attacks *Tigh an Droma*, I'll have no choice but to join the fight."

"I understand." And she did. It wasn't as if Alec could allow Bram to destroy him—especially for something he didn't do. But her heart railed against the possibility that fate would win out and Bram would die.

"Remember that nothing is set in stone," Jeff said, clearly reading the expression on her face. "There's still time to change things. To explain to Bram."

"Yes, but we have to find him first."

"I don't think you have to worry about that," Dougan said, returning to the group. "I've just talked to a scout. Bram Macgillivray and his men are almost here."

Long shadows stretched across the meadow, the trees ringing the clearing already blending together as the sunlight continued to fade. Beneath his thighs, Bram felt his horse shift, muscles tensed, waiting for his command. Iain and Ranald flanked him on either side, Frazier and the rest of Iain's men arrayed behind them. Across the way, Alec Comyn's men too sat at the ready, weapons drawn, horses prancing. But although he was aware of the warriors, it was the center group that held his attention. By some fluke of placement a last golden ray of sun fell over the three people gathered there.

Alec Comyn rode with the command of a king. His dark hair curled wildly around his head, his green eyes piercing even at this distance. Beside him rode a tall man with blonde hair. The man from Bram's vision. His clothes were an odd mixture of familiar and strange, and although he seemed comfortable on his mount, it was clear that he was not as comfortable with the claymore he held in his hands. If Iain was to be believed, this man was Katherine's brother.

But why then was he riding with the Comyns?

And more importantly, what manner of lie had Lily perpetuated?

For there was no doubt in Bram's mind that the woman beside Alec was his kin. There was no mistaking the blue-black curls and the glittering green eyes. Fool that he was, he hadn't seen it until now. Hadn't recognized that he'd been duped by his worst enemy. It was as if the curse of the Comyns had been visited upon the Macgillivrays all over again, and he had been stupid enough to fall right into their hands.

Although at least he'd left her behind.

His gaze traveled from her tousled head to her boot-clad feet. She rode astride, a quiver of arrows at her back. But unlike the others, she had not armed herself. Instead, her eyes never left his, her chin quivering even as she held it aloft. Always the brave one, his Lily.

His horse moved forward, and Alec shifted his, protecting his own. God, how had Bram been such an addlepated ninny? He'd allowed his heart to rule his head and now it was breaking in light of her betrayal. Everything that had passed between them was a lie. She'd tricked him into believing she was his savior when, in point of fact, she was his worst enemy.

As if privy to his thoughts, Lily swallowed, her hand at her throat, her mouth forming a soft 'o' of surprise. And despite his anger and frustration, he felt his body react. Damn the woman. She was a temptress of the worst kind. A Comyn. And just like her ancestor, she'd stop at nothing to destroy him and his kind.

Anger turned to rage, and he spurred his horse forward, intent on finding satisfaction at the end of a sword. Alec answered in kind, further blocking access to Lily, his claymore held high—at the ready. The movement to protect only served to goad Bram further, some part of him still believing that Lily belonged to him and that no one had the right to protect her save himself.

But even as he had the thought, he banished it. His Lily had never truly existed. This woman was a Comyn. An enemy. First, last and always. He rode forward, ready to engage, aware that Iain and Ranald called to him from behind. Ignoring them, he closed the distance, Alec's men rumbling as they too prepared for battle.

He was close enough to see the determination in the Comyn's eyes. And then suddenly Lily spurred her mount around Alec, coming straight at him, her shoulders set in defiance. He fingered the hilt of his sword, his arm raising to take the blow. And then he met her eyes, crystal clear, like a slow moving burn. And for a moment, he forgot his anger, his heart reaching out for hers.

Frozen, he sat atop his horse, the sounds around him fading until there was only the two of them. "Why?" he managed to choke out, his sword arm falling to his side.

"It's not what you think," she said, shaking her head, tears filling her eyes.

"Then say you're no' a Comyn." He already knew the answer. It was literally as plain as the nose on her face, but some part of him longed for her to deny it.

Instead she dipped her head, sucking in a fortifying breath, then lifted her face back to his. "I can't do that."

His heart shriveled, actual pain ripping through his chest. "Then there's nothing more to say."

"But that's where you're wrong. There's so much to say. Nothing is as it seems. But you'll have to take that on faith. You'll have to believe me. Because to understand you have to trust enough to hear what Alec has to say."

"I'll never trust the man who killed my father. I canna believe you'd ask that of me. And besides, now that I know who you really are, I've no reason to put any faith in your words."

"She's telling the truth," Alec Comyn said, pulling his mount up beside hers. "And I'll no' see you calling her a liar."

"Ah, but then what would you know of honesty?"

The two men raised their weapons.

"Stop it. Both of you." Again, heedless of her own safety, Lily pushed her horse between them.

"If you won't listen to her," the blond man said, "perhaps you'll listen to me."

"I dinna know you from Adam," Bram growled. "Why would I care what you have to say?"

"Because I have no horse in this race."

Bram frowned, shaking his head. "I dinna ken what you're speaking of."

"Right." He lowered his voice so that it wouldn't carry. "Because I'm not of your world. And neither is Lily. And there's no plot against you. At least not from this quarter."

"Jeff," Iain hailed as he and Ranald rode up beside Bram. "What in God's name are you doing here? With him?"

"Happenstance. Well, at least winding up with Comyn. We started out looking for you. At Lily's behest. Fergus and William are over there." The man called Jeff turned his attention to Bram. "You don't know me, but Iain does. And Ranald." He nodded toward his cousins, who pulled their horses up on either side. "And I'm telling you that there's more to the story than you know."

"You cannot believe any of them," Frazier said, his horse sidling as he jerked on the reins to pull the animal to a stop. "I don't care who this man is. He's riding with the Comyn. There is nothing he can say that will negate the fact." Clutching his claymore, he made to move forward.

"Hold," Iain ordered. And with a furious frown, Frazier stopped. "I'd trust Jeff with my life. And if he says there's more to hear, then I believe him."

"Aye," Ranald agreed. "He's no' going to betray us."

"No' going to betray *you*—you mean. Why should I believe he gives a damn about me and mine?" Bram's gaze met his cousin's.

"Because you are my kin and for Jeff family is everything. He would never betray you."

"And neither would Lily," Jeff added, his gaze shooting in her direction. "She came here for you, man. After you deserted her, I might add. And to be totally honest, at the moment I'm not sure that I understand why she came."

"Nor I," Alec spat. "A Macgillivray. I canna even stomach the idea." He moved again, his stance threatening.

Bram responded in kind, fingers tightening on his claymore. "'Tis a far sight better than being a bloody, thievin' Comyn, I'll wager."

Ranald and Iain drew their weapons again as well.

"Stop it. All of you." Lily held up a hand, and despite the fact that she was only a woman, everyone froze, their attention shifting to her. "This is getting us nowhere. Bram, if you won't believe me or Jeff, then perhaps you'll believe your own kinsman. We found him in the woods. Near to death. But, thanks to Alec's man, he lives and when he's conscious asks for you."

"What trick is this?" His gut clenched at the thought of his slaughtered clan. "You know my kinsman are all dead. All but Frazier. He saw the rest of them die."

She shot a speculative look at the older man. "Then he must have made a mistake, because your man lives as surely as I do."

"How could you possibly know who he is?"

"Because he keeps asking for you." Her green eyes were flashing with anger now. "And because you told me about him. Robby. Robby Corley."

"Is dead," Frazier said. "I saw it myself. The bitch lies."

"Mind your tongue," Bram barked, surprising himself with the depth of his ire. His instinct to protect Lily had apparently not died with her betrayal. "Is this true?" He turned his attention to Jeff St. Claire and to Fergus, who had ridden over to join them.

"Aye, that it is," Fergus said, his grizzled gaze on Iain. "I dinna know what games any o' these folk are playing, but I can tell you with certainty that the lad is who he says he is. He's too far gone to be capable o' a lie. As it is, he can barely talk."

"Did he tell you what happened to him?" Frazier asked. And again Bram waved a hand to silence him.

"No." Lily shook her head. "Like Fergus said, he can barely talk. For the most part all he's done is ask for Bram."

"Will he live?" Bram asked Alec, the words coming despite himself.

"I canna say. My healer is good. But the man was far gone when Lily found him."

Bram exchanged a look with both Ranald and Iain. There seemed to be no choice in the matter. For the moment they had to trust Alec Comyn. At least long enough to find out the truth about Robby.

CHAPTER 26

BRAM HADN'T LOOKED at her, not once since the confrontation in the clearing. Nor had he spoken to her or to Alec. She tried to give him the benefit of the doubt. It had been a shock to find out who she really was. But it wasn't as if she'd lied to him or done anything to truly earn his wrath. Except perhaps disobey his implicit demand for her to stay behind.

To stay safe.

The word whispered through her mind as she watched Bram question Alec's man Geordie. They were huddled around the makeshift tent covering Robby. Not much more than a plaid stretched over a wooden frame, it at least provided a modicum of protection against the encroaching weather.

The last of the sun was sinking beneath the horizon, the beginnings of a mist twirling wraithlike across the ground.

She'd had no way of knowing her true heritage when she'd first encountered Bram. And, even if she had, it wasn't as if they'd taken time to ask a lot of questions. Surely if he truly loved her, he'd have to accept her for who she was. But then again, he obviously believed she'd betrayed him. Intellectually, she knew that should make a difference. That she should cut him slack. But her heart wasn't having any of it. Either he loved her or he didn't. It was as simple as that. Some things had to be taken on faith.

So maybe he didn't love her at all. Maybe in truth he wasn't any better than Justin. But even as she had the thought, she knew that it wasn't true. Sucking in a breath, she looked to Jeff for reinforcement. Elaine's husband smiled at her reassuringly and immediately she felt better, containing a smile at Bram's immediate scowl in Jeff's direction.

Maybe he did care—at least a little.

Jeff stood with Iain and Alec just at the boundary to the make-shift tent, giving Geordie and Bram room. Bram squatted down by his friend, his eyes on the healer. Lily sat near Robby's head, feeling protective even in the face of Bram's concern.

"How long has he had the fever?" Bram asked the healer, his voice harsh with emotion.

For his friend, Lily reminded herself, containing a shiver. Even angry, the sound of his voice curled deep inside of her, sending heat washing across every inch of her skin.

"Since before I was summoned," Geordie was saying. "But he's resting easier now than he was. And in truth, your friend needs sleep to help him recover."

Robby moaned and twisted, and Lily reached out to stroke his brow. He calmed but Bram's scowl deepened and she noticed his fingers clenching and unclenching.

"He doesn't feel as hot as he did," Lily said, lifting her gaze, praying that he'd meet it. But instead he returned his attention to the healer.

"Is he still in danger?"

The older man shrugged. "I canna pretend that it doesna worry me. Although 'tis to be expected after all that he's been through. The injury itself was grievous enough, but being out here exposed to the elements hasna helped things at all. As I'm sure Alec has already told you, your friend owes his life to Mistress Lily."

A muscle ticked in Bram's jaw. "And to you, I'm told. I'm grate-ful." Again he refused to meet Lily's eyes. Behind him, Jeff blew out a disgusted breath. At least she had someone on her side. "When can I expect him to wake?" Bram asked.

"'Tis no' something I can predict. Mayhap the sound of your voice will call to him. I've seen it work before when a man is lost to this deep o' sleep."

Bram shifted so that he was leaning over his friend, his body so close Lily could feel his warmth. Her breathing stuttered and she forced herself to focus on the injured man.

"Robby?" Bram called softly. "Can you hear me, man?"

Robby moved slightly, but there was no answer.

"'Tis I, Bram. I've come to bring you home." The skin around his mouth tightened and Lily squelched the urge to reach for him. He wouldn't appreciate her touch. Not here. Not now. But she could feel his pain. "You canna tell me you'd rather lie here in this nest of vipers. Comyns aren't known for extending hospitality to Macgillivrays. No matter how comely the man's face might be."

He waited, his fingers clenching again, his eyes fixed on his friend. "Robby. Please. Open your bloody eyes. I need to see that you're all right. That these bastards haven't been feeding you poison."

Geordie tensed, his hand moving toward the knife at the waist of his plaid. Apparently even healers were warriors in these times.

"Hold." Alec's deep voice filled the little space, brooking no argu-ment. "He's grieving. Let him be."

Geordie settled back. "I'm no' poisoning him. If he dies it'll no' be on my head."

Bram's gaze shifted to Lily. She could feel the heat of it. Feel his anger.

"Nor will it be hers," the healer said, his voice taking umbrage with Bram's obvious conclusion. "Whatever befalls yer friend, 'tis the fault o' those who attacked him. So save yer retribution for them."

"Believe me, that's exactly what I intend to do," Bram said, pushing to his feet, fingering the hilt of his claymore as he turned to face Alec. "I believe you and I have things to discuss. Iain?" His cousin nodded, and the three men strode a short distance away to the shelter of a small stand of trees. Alec's second, Dougan, followed close behind.

Lily resisted the urge to run after Bram. Better to let him deal with Alec on his own. Still, it pained her that he'd walked away without so much as a backward glance. Pained her that he could dismiss her so easily.

"He's just angry and confused," Jeff said, dropping to his knees beside her.

"He thinks I betrayed him," Lily said, emotion clogging her throat. "That I'm working with his enemy."

"But Alec isn't his enemy. And you didn't even know you were a Comyn when you met Bram. None of this is your fault."

Lily felt tears threaten and brushed angrily at her eyes.

"Give him time to think. To assimilate all that's happened. Then you can talk to him. Explain about your family. About the legend and the ring."

"We already know what he thinks about the legend. He thinks my family killed his. And now he believes I've been trying to do the same."

"But you haven't." Jeff reached over to squeeze her hand. "And he'll see that. He cares about you. A lot. Otherwise he wouldn't be so angry."

"He wouldn't even look me in the eyes."

"True, but he also couldn't take his eyes off of you. Let him sort it out. It'll be okay, you'll see."

Robby moaned, and Geordie lifted his head to meet Lily's gaze, a smile spreading across his weathered face. "His fever is breaking."

"Thank God." Lily answered his smile just as an older man ducked beneath the woolen tarp.

Lily frowned up at the man. Frazier. "You work for Bram," she said, taking in his stocky, well-muscled build. The graying hair and bushy beard were indicators of the man's age, and yet it was clear he was a warrior still. His faded blue eyes were wary.

"I was his father's captain," Frazier agreed, his voice holding a warning. "But I am my own man. I work for no one."

"I'm sorry." Lily held up a hand in apology. "I meant no offense." Something about Frazier bothered her. Maybe it was the fact that his eyes glittered with dislike. Although considering the circumstances, she wasn't certain she blamed him.

"Bram allowed you to stay with Robby, then?" Frazier asked, his gaze falling to the injured man.

"I'm not sure he really had a choice," Jeff said, his tone congenial, but Lily could hear the undernote of caution. So she wasn't the only one with misgivings.

"Bram was right; you've betrayed Iain and allied yourself with *her*." Frazier sent a contemptuous nod in Lily's direction. "And the rest of the Comyns."

"I've betrayed no one," Jeff said, his hand moving to the hilt of his sword. "And neither has Lily."

"Aye," Geordie said, fingering the little knife again. "She's been nothing but steadfast when it comes to yer man."

"I meant no disrespect." Frazier waved a hand, his lips lifting in the semblance of a smile. "Only to say that I canna understand why Bram would leave Robby here with the en—" He stopped, frowned, then amended his words. "—with people he distrusts."

"And I told you," Jeff said, "he didn't have a choice. Besides, even if he did, he'd find no one better than Geordie and Lily. Geordie is a healer. And as Geordie alluded to, Lily has been with Robby continuously since he was found. She refused to leave him. Even when Fergus wanted to move on to try and find Iain."

"There's no need to defend me, Jeff." Lily sent her friend a smile and then lifted her head to meet Frazier's gaze. "Robby will come to no harm in my care. Of that I can assure you."

As if to underscore her words, Robby moaned and automatically Lily smoothed back his hair, her gentle motion quieting the thrashing man.

"Is he waking, then?" Frazier stepped forward, his focus now on the injured man.

Geordie touched his cheek. "Nay, only fighting off the last of the fever. With the crisis past, he should settle in and sleep until morning at least."

"Mayhap I should be the one sitting with him," Frazier offered. "After all, he's my kin."

"That he is," Geordie said, his narrowed eyes making him seem more dangerous. "But what the lad needs now is peace and quiet. So I'll thank you to take your leave. If he wakes I'll call for the Macgillivray."

Frazier's frown deepened and he seemed about to say more, but then abruptly he turned on his heel and left the lean-to.

"Not a man to trifle with," Jeff observed.

"Nor a man to trust," Lily noted, watching as the older man strode away.

~

"Ach, you're a stubborn man." Alec threw a rock across the clearing, shaking his head. "You'll believe Lily's story about where she came from, but you willna believe it when I tell you it wasna my men at Dunbrae."

"I don't know what to think anymore." Bram pushed to his feet and ran a hand through his hair. Dougan followed suit, although the big man's hand was on his claymore. Alec waved him down again and he sat with a dissatisfied grunt. "From the way it looks, I'd say that Lily was lying, too."

"Except that you know that isn't the case." This from Iain, who'd remained uncharacteristically quiet as Alec had continued to deny the allegations against him and his clan.

"Yes, I suppose I do. At least about some things," Bram grudgingly admitted, dropping back down to sit on a fallen log. "But even so it doesn't mean she's not conspiring with Alec against me."

"Are you crazy, man? She didn't come here for me. She came for you. And believe me, she's made that more than apparent to all of us." Alec's voice echoed across the open expanse beyond the trees, and Bram could see Lily's head turn, her dark hair swirling around her shoulders.

He didn't want to feel anything at all, damn it, but just seeing her, even from a distance, made his blood stir. Bram jerked his attention back to the conversation. "She's a Comyn."

"Who loves a Macgillivray," Alec countered. "It doesn't appeal to me either. But it is what it is."

"A hell of a mess," Fergus summarized as he joined the four of them.

"What of the men?" Iain asked.

"Ranald is watching o'er them. And for the most part they're settled. Although I canna say they're pleased with the situation. I suspect everyone will be sleeping with their hand on a weapon and one eye open tonight. But for the moment at least, there's peace." He sat down on the log beside Bram, first eyeing Dougan and then turning to Iain. "I take it you've decided to believe Alec?"

"We're agreed to try and keep an open mind," Iain said. "Partially because you believe him."

The older man sighed, stroking his beard. "That I do. Or at least I have to admit there's a ring of authenticity."

"But then how do you explain Dougan's sons trying to kill me?" Bram asked, still not trusting the other man. They'd told Alec of the attack at Duncreag but hadn't gone as far as to mention the other attacks.

It was Dougan's turn to look astounded. "What rubbish are ye spouting now?" His eyes narrowed as his gaze met Alec's and his hand moved to his weapon. "I told ye we couldna trust the whoresons."

Alec frowned, but waved his hand to still his second. "What makes you believe the men you're speaking of were Dougan's sons?"

"They told me themselves," Bram said, frustration cresting. "First Murdoc Macniven when he attacked me in the mist and then his brother today in the mountains."

Dougan sputtered and Alec's amused gaze met Bram's. "Ach, but you see there's a wee problem with that notion."

"And that would be?" Bram challenged.

"Dougan has no sons." Alec shrugged and looked to his captain.

"Only three braw lassies," the big man said with a shrug. "No' fer lack of tryin', mind ye. And even if I did, I'd no' name one o' them Murdoc." He almost smiled, then seemed to remember the serious nature of the situation and his countenance darkened again. "I tell you true. I have no sons."

And suddenly Bram felt his anger deflating. As barmy as it seemed, he believed everything Alec as saying. Which didn't mean he'd start calling Alec Comyn friend. But it did seem that someone else had betrayed him. Betrayed his clan. Someone who wanted him to believe that his most hated enemy was behind it.

Alec's green-eyed gaze seemed to pierce right through him. "I ken this is hard on you. And I accept that you dinna trust me. I canna say I trust you either. But for the moment, at least, it seems we share common interests."

Without thinking, Bram's head turned, his gaze moving to the lean-to and the shadowy image of Lily tending to Robby. Common interests indeed. His body tightened and he fought a wave of pure desire.

Bollocks.

She might not have been in league with Alec against him, but she was still a Comyn and common interests aside, Macgillivrays and Comyns were not meant to fall in love with each other. The last time that had happened his clan had practically been destroyed.

"I dinna see what we could possibly have in common," he snapped, forcing himself back to the matter at hand.

"Alec's right, Bram." Iain laid a hand on his shoulder, and Bram jerked free.

"How can you say that? He's a Comyn." He knew he was letting his emotions hold sway, but somehow the idea that this man had a claim—albeit a familial one—on Lily made his blood boil. Not that he had a claim anymore. Even if he could get beyond the fact that she was a Comyn, how could she ever forgive him? He'd let her down in so many ways. It was all such a bloody nightmare.

"We're no' talking about Lily," Alec said, cutting right to the heart of the matter. "We're talking about someone trying their damnedest to play us off against one another. Someone who orchestrated the murder of your clansmen and tried to pin it on me."

"And that same bastard is behind the rumors of your involvement as well," Iain interjected. "They want your kin to believe that you betrayed your own clan."

"But I didn't." Bram felt as if the world were spinning out of control. Again he looked toward Lily, this time with longing. But it was too late for comfort. "I'm no' a traitor."

"And I did no' betray you either," Alec said. "Which means that, at least for the moment, we're fighting on the same side."

There was no arguing the fact. It was time to put their differences aside. Alec might never be his ally. But the man was right—he was not an enemy. And truth be told, at the moment, Bram could use all the help he could get.

"So how do we go about identifying the traitor?" he asked, feeling as if he'd fallen into a deep, dark hole.

"I dinna ken," Fergus said, "but I reckon the best place to find answers is to start at the beginning."

"Dunbrae." Just saying the name brought Bram's resolve to bear.

"Bram?" He jumped at the soft sound of Lily's voice, his skin prickling at her nearness. He'd been so engrossed in his mutinous thoughts he hadn't even noticed her approaching. "Robby's awake. And he's asking for you."

CHAPTER 27

✦

"IS HE ALL right?" Bram asked as he followed Lily back across the clearing, Iain and Alec close on his heels. He refused to meet her eyes. In truth, he had no idea what to say. He was still angry. Maybe irrationally. Maybe with cause. Who the hell was to say? He was just so confused, and the feeling didn't sit well at all.

"He was well enough to drink some broth," she replied, shooting a glance his direction, clearly aware that things were not right between them. They might never be right again. "And Geordie thinks that's a good sign," she continued. "But he needs rest, only it seems he won't be still until he's talked to you."

"'Tis to be expected, considering everything that's happened," he shot back, his tone harsher than intended.

"I know." She nodded, eyes on the ground as they walked. "But he's not the only one who needs to talk to you."

His breath caught in his throat at the pain that echoed through her words, but he waved a hand in frustration. God's blood, he wasn't handling this well at all. He opened his mouth to tell her that he needed time, but for better or worse, Frazier chose that moment to stride across the clearing calling for attention. "Bram, a moment, if ye will."

Relief spread through him. Relief and chagrin. He'd never thought himself a coward. But this woman had a power over him like no other.

"What do you want?" he snapped at his father's man, stopping abruptly, Lily almost falling when she tried to follow suit. Automatically his hand closed around her elbow, sparks of unfettered desire chasing up his arm. He jerked his hand away, his eyes on Frazier.

"Tell me it isna true. That yer no' throwin' yer lot in with Comyn and his men."

"I'm no' throwing my lot in with anyone, Frazier. Least of all a Comyn. But I canna dismiss what I've learned here today."

"They're lies. All of them. I saw them at Dunbrae. They slaughtered yer father. And tried more of the same with you."

"I think maybe we're the ones who have the wrong of it. And until I can find the answers I seek, I'm giving Alec Comyn the benefit of the doubt."

"Well, then I expect you'd best be explaining that to Iain's men."

Bram frowned. "It's my understanding that they already know much of the situation."

"Aye, from Ranald and from me. They need to hear it from you."

"But I'm on my way to see Robby."

"He's awake?" Frazier frowned. "But the healer told me it would be tomorrow at least."

"Apparently he was wrong." Bram started forward again, but the man pulled on his arm.

"Let me go to him then. He knows me. That should settle him until you've talked to the men."

Bram blew out a breath of frustration. "Frazier, Iain's men haven't a care what I have to say. If anyone should speak to them it should be Iain."

Iain nodded. "I'm happy to do so. Although I canna believe they're doubting Ranald."

"Are you satisfied?" Bram asked Frazier, not actually caring what the man thought. At the moment, he was simply in the way. "Now if you'll excuse me, I'm off to see Robby."

"Fine." Frazier nodded. "But I'm coming, too."

For a moment Bram considered refusing the man, but then thought better of it. No matter what else might be true or false, Frazier and Robby were kin. And the two of them had saved his life. He owed Frazier that much at least. "'Tis glad I am of your company."

He started forward again, but stopped when Frazier didn't follow. "Is there something more?"

"Aye," the man said, his eyes narrowing. "I ken yer hurry to talk to the man, but surely you dinna wish to do so with an audience?" He nodded toward Alec and Lily. Then toward Jeff and Geordie still tending Robby. "Seems to me that whatever Robby might have to say is best kept among ourselves. At least fer now."

There was truth in the old man's words. And if Bram hadn't been so muddle-headed about Lily he'd have thought of it himself. He raised his brows in question as his gaze met Alec's.

"I've no need to pry. You'll tell me what I need to know when you've talked to your man." He lifted a hand and waved Geordie to him. Jeff rose as well, and the two men closed the distance between them. "Geordie, we'll give Macgillivray time alone with his man."

"But, he still needs a healer." Geordie started to protest.

"Mayhap, but right now they need privacy."

"I'll stay," Lily offered, her voice so low it was almost a whisper. Almost as one, the assembled company turned to look at her. "I'm not interested in eavesdropping. Only in making sure Robby is all right. I can stay out of hearing range, but that way I'll be close in case I'm needed."

"'Tis a compromise," Alec offered with a shrug. "Find me when you're finished." He walked away, Geordie following.

"You won't let anything happen to her?" Jeff asked, his frown a warning.

Bram's hand curled into a fist, and he resisted the urge to plant one between the man's eyes. After all, he'd seen them together in his vision—or whatever the hell it was. And despite Iain's reassurances, the man seemed too bloody protective when it came to Lily.

"Have no fear. I'd ne're let anyone hurt her."

"Does that include you?"

Bram took a step forward, but Lily moved between them. "I'll be fine, Jeff." The two of them exchanged a long glance and then with a sharp nod, Jeff walked away.

Frazier shifted his gaze between Bram and Lily. "Surely ye canna mean to tell me that ye trust her. To hear ye tell it she's betrayed ye at every turn."

Lily started to protest, but Bram cut her off. "I dinna know what I believe and what I don't. But right now we canna take a risk with Robby's life. Let's just say that she's the lesser of two evils." Beside him, he felt her tense as his words sank in.

"Bram, please…" Lily began but Frazier cut her off with a wave of his hand.

"Yer makin' a mistake, lad. Best that you send her back where'er she came from."

Bram closed his eyes for a moment, wishing that they would both just disappear, but since that wasn't likely, he'd better get on with it. With a sigh, he opened his eyes again and lifted a finger to stop Frazier from further comment.

"She stays. But she'll stay back." His gaze met Lily's and she nodded, green eyes banked with something he couldn't quite identify. "All right, then, we go."

The lean-to was silent, Robby still and unmoving. Bram ducked beneath the canvas, followed closely by Frazier and then Lily, who moved to the far side of the enclosure, where she dropped down onto a large rock near the pouches that held the healer's herbs and poultices. If he hadn't known her as intimately as he did, he'd have assumed she had no cares at all, but the tension around her mouth and her tightly interlaced fingers sent a far different message.

Purposely ignoring her, he turned to Frazier. "I want to talk to him first. You can wait over there. I'll motion when it's time for you to join us."

Again the man looked as if he wanted to object, but with a sharp sigh he moved to the edge of the lean-to across from where Lily sat.

Bram knelt beside his friend.

"Robby, can you hear me?"

His friend moaned and moved restlessly. From his periphery vision, he saw Lily start to rise, but he waved her back.

"Robby?"

"Bram?" The name came on a guttural whisper. Robby swallowed and then his eyes flickered open. The ghost of a smile chased across his face. "Ach, yer a sight fer sore eyes."

"I could say the same for you." Bram felt the back of his eyes prick. Bloody hell, he'd not expected to ever see the man again. And yet here he was smiling up at him. *All of that thanks to Lily*, a small voice whispered in the back of his mind, but he ruthlessly pushed the thought aside. "How are you feeling?"

"As if I've been gutted like a pig and then roasted on a spit for all to see."

"Well, 'tis my understanding that between the attack and the healers you're no' far wrong. But the important thing is that they're saying you'll get better."

"The lass?" Robby asked, struggling to sit up. "Lily?"

"Be still," Bram soothed. "You're far too weak to be trying to rise. Lily is here. Just over there." He nodded in her direction and his friend calmed.

"She saved my life."

"That she did," Bram agreed. At least of that much he was certain.

Behind him, he felt Frazier creeping closer, the man clearly needing to feel a part of things. But Bram wanted time alone with his friend, so he turned and waved Frazier back again. With a grimace, the man obeyed.

Turning back to Robby, Bram was surprised to find his friend's face gone white, his eyes wide with concern. "You've brought Frazier?" he asked, his breathing harsher now.

"Aye, he managed to escape as well."

Robby shook his head slightly and whispered something Bram couldn't hear.

"Hold on," Bram said, bending closer. "I can barely hear you."

Robby's face had gone from white to red, his mouth moving, his eyes, if possible, even wider. "Traitor," he whispered. "Traitor."

Bram struggled for understanding. Was he still talking about Lily? Bram's blood ran cold at the thought, but surely he'd missed something.

"Robby, I know——" he began, but was cut off by Lily's scream.

"Bram, watch out, he's got a knife."

Almost simultaneously, Robby surged up, his face twisted in anger. "Traitor," he said again.

And for half a second, Bram believed Robby was coming for him. But then in an instant his mind cleared, the truth sinking in, and he grabbed his dagger, swinging around to face Frazier as the other man snarled and leapt at him, showing no favor at all to his supposedly injured knee.

Off to his left, he could see Lily edging toward Robby, who was trying valiantly to push to his feet. But it was Frazier who held his attention, the other man swinging his blade, managing a cut across Bram's shoulder.

Behind him, he heard Lily's sharp intake of breath, and then Robby speaking. "'Twas Frazier. He's the one who tried to kill me. He's in league with the men who attacked Dunbrae."

Bram dodged another of Frazier's thrusts, his mind scrambling to make sense of what had just been revealed. "But you helped to save me." The words came out of their own volition as he circled the older man.

"No' by choice," Frazier snarled, brandishing the knife. "I had no weapon, so there was no way I could take both you and Robby. I had to let you go."

"And then followed me to Iain's."

"After making sure your own people believed it was you who'd betrayed yer clan." His smile was twisted, almost feral, his eyes glittering with hatred. "If the attack on Duncreag had worked, I'd no' have had to come at all. But someone had to make sure you were taken care of."

"Murdered, you mean." Bram shifted, looking for an opening as he realized it must have been Frazier who let Murdoc go and that the old man had most likely pretended to be injured earlier in an attempt to lure Bram into a trap. Only his cousins' timely arrival had spared his life.

"Aye," Frazier was saying. "With you dead, everything will finally be as it should be."

Frazier lunged again, but Bram managed to dodge the blade, this time answering with a thrust of his own. He felt the knife slice through the man's plaid but knew he hadn't managed to draw blood.

Frazier danced back, his agility belying his age. With a quick twist, he freed a second blade from his boot and advanced slowly, his eyes dark with rage.

Bram reached for his claymore, cursing himself when he felt the empty scabbard. In the heat of his desire to see Robby, he'd left it in the copse of trees where he'd been talking with Alec. Still, he was younger and stronger than Frazier.

Frazier attacked again, using both knives to advantage, forcing Bram to retreat slightly, the two of them still circling. As Frazier moved toward Robby, Lily stepped closer, clearly wanting to protect the injured man, but in so doing she'd also put herself in range of Frazier's knife.

With an angry roar, Bram lunged forward, intent upon saving her from harm, but it was too late. With a snarl, Frazier kicked out at the injured man, who fell to his knees and then grabbed Lily by the hair— yanking her in front of him. It took every bit of control Bram had to force his hand to stop the forward motion, to keep from stabbing Lily.

Her eyes widened as Frazier moved one of the knives to her throat, the other still waving in Bram's direction. "Put away yer knife, or I'll kill her," Frazier growled.

Bram's gut churned as he tried to find a way out. He couldn't let Frazier hurt Lily, but as soon as he put the knife down, they were all as good as dead. If Robby still lived, that was. Bram could see his friend collapsed on the ground beside and slightly behind Frazier and Lily.

"Let her go," he asked. "It's me you want, not her. I promise I'll drop the knife when you release her."

"Ye always were a man to think with your cock," Frazier taunted. "And a Comyn bitch at that. Yer father is no doubt spinning in his grave."

"My father is dead because of you." He slowly inched forward, knife still in hand.

"Yer father deserved what he got." Frazier tightened his hold on Lily, a thin trail of blood forming across her neck where he held the blade. "Tried to turn me out to pasture. Said I was past my prime. Told me he had no more use for me. As if I were no better than an aging plow horse."

"And so you betrayed him." Bram's attention was still locked on Lily as he tried to keep the old man talking.

"Nay. He betrayed me. I chose to follow someone who recognized my worth."

The true meaning of the conversation he'd once overheard regarding Frazier became clear. His father had rejected Frazier. Turned him away. And the old man sought revenge. But in so doing he'd taken so much more. "It wasn't just my father, Frazier; it was your clan. Your people. You disgust me."

The man snarled again, his grip on Lily tightening. "I'd remind you that I'm the one holding yer lady."

"She's no' mine." He hated the flash of pain in Lily's eyes, but if his denial could save her life then he would not regret the words.

"Dinna lie to yerself, lad," Frazier growled. "I can see it in yer eyes. Ye want her still."

"You said it yourself. She's a Comyn." He inched forward, praying for an opening to strike.

"Aye, that she is. And once I dispose of you, a bonny prize for Malcolm."

"Malcolm?" Surprise flittered through him, but then was quickly replaced with brutal realization. "My uncle? This is all his doing?" It made sense in a twisted sort of way.

"He's only taking what is rightfully his. And I'll be at his side. But first I need you dead." The blade cut further into Lily's skin. "Drop the knife or I slit her throat."

Bram's gut tightened, his heart thudding in his ears. It was an impossible choice. And either way the odds were that Lily would die. Then from just beyond Frazier, Robby pushed to his knees, his face twisted with pain, but his eyes determined. The older man failed to notice, his attention still focused solely on Bram.

With a quiet gesture, Robby signaled his intent. He'd startle Frazier and hopefully in so doing draw the man's attention and give Bram a chance. It was a risk. But when his gaze darted to Lily, she seemed to understand—giving him a nod as she shot a glance in Robby's direction.

For a moment, it seemed the world held only the two of them, and then Robby moaned, simultaneously rising to his feet, holding a large stone as a weapon. Frazier swung around, knife at the ready, his grip on Lily loosening enough that she managed to bring a sharp elbow to his ribs.

Frazier grunted and threw her forcibly into the rock on which she'd been sitting. Fighting against the panic that shot through him at the sight of her slamming to the ground, Bram focused on Frazier, charging as the man made a move on Robby. Robby threw the stone and it glanced off Frazier's shoulder with enough force to cause him to stumble. But the effort had cost his friend, and Robby collapsed back onto his pallet.

Blood lust surged as Bram leapt on the older man, driving him to the ground. One of Frazier's knives skittered away, beyond the lean-to. But he still held the bigger of the two. They grappled with each other, rolling on the ground, each trying to avoid the other's blade.

Bram managed to slice across Frazier's face, but it was no more than a surface wound. He twisted, trying to find a better angle as both men continued to struggle. Then Frazier managed to grab Robby's stone, slamming it into Bram's knife hand. Pain lanced through him, and reflexively his hand opened, his knife falling to the ground.

Frazier managed to roll on top of him, his knife descending for the kill. Bram grabbed his opponent's hand, trying to push it back, to fight against what suddenly felt inevitable. He should have died that night at Dunbrae. But for the fluke of Robby's finding him, no doubt he would have. And now, everything had been for naught.

He kept his grip, but felt Frazier's knife slipping lower. And then lower still.

"Let him go." Lily's voice was harsh with emotion—anger and something else he couldn't quite put a name to.

Above him, he could see her standing with his knife held against the side of Frazier's throat.

"I'll kill him afore ye can kill me, I reckon," the older man said.

"Maybe so," she replied. "But you'll still be dead."

It was a stand-off. One that very well might end with his death, but even so he had to admire her fortitude. The woman had bollocks.

Frazier held his position for a moment, and then loosened his grip. In less than a moment, Bram had seized the advantage, rolling the man beneath him, his own weapon now pressed to Frazier's throat. Lily sprang back, lifting her hand to her mouth as she watched him with wide, terrified eyes.

"Give me one reason why I shouldn't slit your throat here and now?" The idea was more than appealing. Rage swelled through him. Anger for his father. His clan. For Robby and for Lily. Damn the bastard all to hell.

He clenched the knife, moving in for the kill.

"Hold," Iain said, appearing off to Bram's right, the barked word a command.

"Why?" Bram snarled, looking up as Alec, Ranald and Jeff rushed up beside Iain, their expressions fierce, their claymores at the ready.

"Because, as much as you want him dead," Iain continued, "it's better off for us if you let him live. At least for now." He shot a contemptuous glance at Frazier. "There's much he can tell us."

For a moment, Bram's blood lust was stronger than even his cousin's logic. But then reason reasserted itself. He needed to know the truth. All of it. With a sigh, he removed the knife and pushed to his feet.

Ranald and Alec moved to contain Frazier and haul him away. Iain knelt to see to Robby. Without thinking, Bram turned to find Lily, only to see Jeff leading her away, his arm around her shoulder. He shouldn't be jealous. He shouldn't have feelings for her at all. But he did, damn it. He did. Comyn or no'.

Bram sucked in a breath, and forced himself to turn back to Iain and Robby. "How is he?"

"Breathing. Which for the moment is a good sign." Iain pushed to his feet, signaling for Geordie, who was hovering nearby. "Did he say who is behind all of this?"

"Aye," Bram said, struggling with the weight of Frazier's pronouncement. "'Tis my uncle."

CHAPTER 28

✦

LILY PUSHED THROUGH the brush with only moonlight to steer her. In the distance she could hear the sound of laughter. Either Comyns or the Mackintosh men, neither of whom seemed willing to talk with the other, regardless of the fact that Alec had satisfied both Iain and Bram that there had been no attacks from his people on either Bram or Dunbrae.

If Frazier Macbean was to be believed, the fault lay with Bram's uncle Malcolm. Lily ducked beneath the low-hanging branch of a rowan tree. Not that that knowledge had seemed to resolve anything. In point of fact, it had only seemed to make Bram angrier and more determined to exact revenge.

Not that he'd shared any of his feelings with her.

For a moment, before Frazier attacked Bram, when he had questioned Bram's allowing Lily to stay, she'd believed Bram might actually stand up for her. But then he'd issued those hateful words. "Lesser of two evils." Lesser of two evils, her ass.

She shoved a length of overgrown ivy out of the way, mumbling beneath her breath. But then when Frazier had held her captive, she'd seen something in his eyes. And felt a spark of hope. Until he'd declared for all to hear that she wasn't his lady. Not that she wanted to be anymore. If he wanted to be ruled by some centuries old blood feud, so be it.

Of course, none of that explained why she was out here in the dark looking for the stupid man. It's just that she couldn't help herself. She wanted—no, needed—to be certain he was all right. It had all been rather a lot today. For all of them. But for Bram most of all. His trusted advisor had turned out to be a traitor. And his best friend, though seemingly returned from the dead, still had a long road to recovery. Add to that the fact that his uncle had apparently orchestrated his father's death and well, it was more than most men could handle. Even Bram.

Not that she was excusing him for remaining angry about her heritage. For God's sake, it wasn't as if she'd known she was related to Alec. And now it turned out the man wasn't even the enemy Bram had believed him to be. Although based on the conversation around the campfire earlier, she wouldn't exactly call them bosom buddies either.

She sighed and skirted a large lichen-covered boulder, the fungus shining silver in the moonlight. At least the blasted mist had dissipated. She paused for a moment, trying to get her bearings. According to Iain, Bram had gone to the river, and if she stood perfectly still she could hear the rushing waters in the distance.

Damn the man. Why couldn't he have just confronted her head on? Instead of glaring at Jeff and avoiding her altogether. It would have been funny—except that it wasn't. His rejection hurt. It was like Justin all over again. Except this time she wasn't willing to let it go without a fight. Maybe it was too late. But as far as she could see, she hadn't come all this way just to give up at the first little hurdle.

She blew out a breath, admitting that it was more than a small obstacle. But it wasn't something that couldn't be overcome. Not if they truly loved each other. She had his freakin' pin, after all. Her hand covered the brooch on her borrowed plaid. The fact that he'd left it behind had to mean something. Right? And it wasn't as if she didn't have a bone to pick with the man. He'd left her behind. After promising that he wouldn't. Sort of. If she could get past that, surely he could deal with the fact that she happened to carry Comyn blood.

If the prophecy had any reality at all, surely he'd see that her having the ring meant everything. If nothing else, it proved poor Tyra's innocence in the blood bath that had occurred so long ago. She'd kept Graeme's ring. Cherished it so much that she'd passed it down to their child, who'd passed it on to his or hers, like the freakin' shampoo commercial, until it wound up in Lily's hands. So that she could travel through time, fall in love with Bram and make things right again.

If she wasn't living this, she'd laugh at the complete absurdity of the idea. She stepped over a fallen log, grateful to hear that the sound of the water was much closer now. Her body still ached from the stupid journey to get here, not to mention riding the damned horse across rocky terrain. And then there was the major cut across her throat thanks to some crazy-ass Highlander with a revenge fantasy against Bram's father.

At least he was under lock and key—or at least burly Comyn and Mackintosh guards. Her heart stuttered at the memory of Bram grappling with Frazier on the ground, the damn knife descending as Frazier tried to ram it home. Thank God they'd managed to stop him before anything had happened to Bram.

If she lost him…

And that then was the crux of the matter. When Justin had dropped her like a hot potato, she'd accepted it as fact. And if she were honest, she'd had absolutely no desire to chase after him, despite the injury to her pride. But with Bram it was completely different. She was willing to follow him anywhere.

Even through a medieval woods in the middle of the freakin' night with nothing to guide her but the sound of falling water and a wash of moonlight.

Double damn the man.

She burst through a stand of pine trees to find herself in the middle of a small clearing, the river curving as it rushed on its merry way. And there, sitting on a large boulder near the bank, was the man of the hour. She froze, her anger vanishing in the wake of stronger emotion. Need and desire. She wanted this man like she'd wanted no other. And the idea scared her to death.

He lifted his head, the shadows of the night keeping his expression hidden, but she could see the light in his eyes. And for a moment, she imagined that he had been wishing for her as much as she had been wishing for him.

"Go away. I dinna want company."

So much for fantasy. But his response was enough to banish her fear. He wasn't going to get away that easily. At least not without the two of them attempting to talk things over.

"I don't care what you want," she said, her voice ringing out across the little clearing as she closed the distance between them. "We have things to say to each other."

"Yes. I'm a Macgillivray and you're a Comyn." He pushed to his feet, anger sparking in his eyes, and she had to force herself not to take a step back. He towered over her.

She let out an inelegant snort, and took another step closer. "Big freakin' deal. It's not like we have any control over who our relatives are. The only thing that matters here is us. And if you're still angry because I didn't tell you, I would have if you'd given me the chance."

"With thirty-odd Comyns looking on."

"Again, not in my control. Besides, it's not exactly like you've been Mr. Honesty. You swore you wouldn't leave me. Twice, in fact. And yet at the first opportunity that's exactly what you did."

"I did that to keep you safe."

"And look how well that worked out." Even as she said it, she knew that the point was actually his. But damned if she'd admit it. "At least I never lied to you. When we were first together I didn't know I was related to your Alec."

"He bloody well isn't my Alec. He's yours."

"I've known the man less than forty-eight hours. I'd hardly say that makes him mine."

"Then what about Jeffrey St. Claire? The two of you certainly seem to be close." They were standing toe to toe now.

"He's a friend. A *married* friend, I might add. And for a man who doesn't care about me you certainly sound jealous." The idea sent a warm shiver racing through her. That and the fact that his breath was fanning her face.

"I'm no' jealous. You can flirt with whomever you please."

"Then it pleases me to flirt with *you*." Not that she was exactly doing that at the moment—more yelling at him like a fishwife.

"I'll no' have a woman I dinna trust in my bed." He poked her in the chest with his finger, his ice-blue eyes narrowed in anger.

"I'll not have you in my bed period until you apologize for the way you've been acting. I came through time for you, damn it." The minute the words were out she felt a rising bubble of hysteria. God, she was living a freakin' movie. And unfortunately if she was playing the part of Kyle Reece, it didn't bode well for happily ever after.

His frown deepened. "So now you're laughing at me?"

"No." She shook her head, sobering in an instant. "I was reduced to quoting movies."

"Quoting what?" He was bellowing now.

"Nothing. Just something from my time. It doesn't matter. Or maybe it does. Maybe the whole point here is that I came through time for you. Just a few weeks ago I lost my entire family. I was completely alone in the world. And then something wonderful happened. I met all these amazing people. Mrs. Abernathy and her husband, Jamie. Elaine and her husband, *Jeff.* My cousins Reggie and Tildy. Not to mention Katherine and Iain. And Robby and Alec. Suddenly I have more family than I can count. But most miraculously of all, I found you. And nothing, not even your biases and fears about my relatives, is worth standing in the way of that."

He growled deep in his throat, then opened his mouth in protest, but she laid her fingers over his lips. "I don't want to have to choose between you and Alec. But if you make me choose, then I choose you. And I'll choose you every single time. I came through time for you, Bram Macgillivray, and I'll be damned if I'm going to let you push me away because of some stupid blood feud between your family and mine. Just because you think you understand what happened all those years ago doesn't mean you have the right of it." She reached beneath her plaid to pull the ring free.

"I have the damn ring. The one that changes everything. The one meant to unite the Macgillivray and Comyns. The one meant to unite *us.*" She waved the ring at him, her voice echoing off the cliffs across the river. "*Mo chridhe gu bràth*—my heart forever. That's what it says. All those years ago Tyra had it made for Graeme. And my mother gave it to my father. And now I've got it—and I met you. I don't know what else I can say…"

"That I'm a great stubborn oaf." He framed her face with his hands, his gaze colliding with hers.

"Well, that goes without saying," she snapped.

"Then since we're agreed, why don't you close your beautiful mouth so that I can kiss you?"

Said mouth gaped open like a fish as she stared up at him, his fingers warm against her skin, his breath stirring the tendrils of her hair around her face. Her heart stuttered, and her stomach clenched as he lowered his head, his lips covering hers.

All rational thought was swept away by the intensity of his touch. His tongue traced the seam of her lips and with a sigh, she opened for him, feeling as if finally, finally she'd come home. He tasted of whisky and smelled of smoke and peat, the heady combination sending sparks of heat dancing across her skin.

No matter how foreign, no matter how far from her world, this was where she belonged. Here. With Bram. His arms tightened around her as the kiss deepened, the two of them locked in a timeless dance of giving and taking—melding together until it became impossible to tell where one ended and the other began.

His hands ran down the length of her arms, his fingers feathering against her skin until they settled on the curve of her hips. He pulled her closer still, and she could feel the hard length of him as he pressed against her. With a soft sigh, she relished the proof that she wasn't alone in her desire. Her hands skimmed across the breadth of his chest, and then dropped lower to his taut stomach and then lower still to trace the hard line of his burgeoning heat. He shuddered at her caress, groaning against her lips.

"Ach, lass, I canna breathe when you touch me like that."

"Then let me touch you skin to skin," she whispered, her body trembling now with need. "Please, Bram. Love me, now."

He groaned again, and with a flick of his hand removed his plaid, laying it down upon the ground at their feet. Then he pulled her until they knelt face to face upon the soft woolen blanket, his crystalline blue gaze meeting hers. "Are you sure this is what you want? I'm afraid I've naught to offer you but the man you see before you."

"What I see is more than I ever could have wished for."

He reached for her hands, their fingers lacing together by their sides. "And you meant what you said? That you'll always choose me?"

She nodded, emotion clogging her throat. "Always."

"And there will ne'er be anyone for me but you. This I swear."

"Bram?" She swallowed, tears filling her eyes. "Are you...are we..." A vague memory of the notion of handfasting flitted through her brain.

"Aye." He nodded, uncertainty chasing across his face. "If you're willing. I know 'tis no' the perfect time. But I canna—"

She reached up and covered his lips again with her fingers. "Yes. Yes, Bram, I will marry you. Here. Now. I promise you my life and my loyalty. I am yours, for all time, if that is what you wish."

"I've never wanted anything more."

She nodded, pulling the fine silver chain from around her neck and releasing the clasp to free the ring. "I've no idea how this is done, but it seems this is a good place to start." She waited, her heart in her throat, her gaze still locked with his.

He covered her hand with his, the silver ring warm between their palms. It seemed to Lily that the world had shrunk to include only the two of them and the soft sound of the river flowing by.

"From this day on it shall be only your name I cry out in the night and into your eyes that I smile each morning. I will cherish and honor you through this life and into the next," Bram said, his voice hoarse with emotion.

"I too give you my body and my heart. Forever and a day. I love you."

"And I you, *mo ghràidh*."

The words seemed to wrap around them like a warm cocoon, protecting them from all that threatened their happiness. Or maybe it was their love. Lily wasn't sure of anything more than the fact that this was where she was meant to be. In this time. With this man.

With shaking fingers, she slid the ring onto Bram's finger, the silver gleaming in the moonlight. "It's done then."

"Aye, you belong to me."

She smiled then. "And you belong to me."

"But I have no ring for you."

"It doesn't matter. I don't need a reminder. Not when you're right here in front of me."

A shadow passed across his face, and she knew he was thinking about the looming confrontation with his uncle. But this wasn't the time. This moment belonged only to the two of them.

She stroked his cheek, the warmth of his skin sending heat spiraling through her. "And when you're not with me, I'll have you here." She touched her chest. "In my heart. See? Your father's pin guards the way." The little silver cat winked up at them.

Their gazes held for another moment, as the power of their pledge flowed through them both, and then Bram leaned forward to kiss her, his touch gentle and reverent. For a moment, Lily savored the feel of his lips against hers, and then with a shiver of anticipation she opened her mouth and with a groan, she felt his control shatter.

His hands cradled her face as his mouth slanted over hers, their tongues dancing together—thrusting and parrying, advancing and retreating. And she wondered if she could ever possibly get enough of him.

As if he read her thoughts, his mouth lifted in a slow crooked grin and he bent his head, leaving hot, open-mouthed kisses along the soft line of her throat, pausing to kiss the angry mark Frazier's blade had left.

"I'll no' let anyone else hurt you, Lily," he growled softly, nipping at her earlobe. "You belong to me now. You're mine."

And then his fingers found her breast through the thin material of her borrowed shirt, first caressing and then teasing her nipple between his thumb and forefinger, the resulting sensation sending heat pooling between her legs. With an economy of motion, he removed her plaid and her shirt, cupping both breasts with his hands.

She tilted back her head, eyes closing as she offered herself to him. His mouth closed over one breast, the wet warmth sending her arching upward to press her body even closer. He sucked harder, pulling her deeper into his mouth, his fingers teasing the other nipple. She ground her pelvis against his, needing more. Wanting more.

His hand circled lower, and then lower still, slipping into the waistband of her leggings, beneath the elastic of her panties. Slowly, so slowly, his fingers stroked through the curls between her legs, circling just above the place she longed for him to touch. Moaning, she arched upward trying to force his play, but instead she felt his smile as he lifted his head.

"Patience, *mo ghràidh*."

He kissed her on the lips—hard, and then helped her remove the rest of her clothes. Then with trembling hands, she pulled the long linen shirt over his head.

"You're hurt." She reached out to run her finger across the skin adjacent to the angry slash on his chest.

"'Tis no' but a scratch, I swear to you."

"Well, I'll not let anyone hurt you again either."

His smile was crooked and slow, stealing her breath away. He helped her remove the rest of his clothes, and naked, they lay down against the soft wool of his plaid, the stars twinkling through the trees above them.

Bracing himself on his elbows, he lowered his big body to cover hers, the hair on his chest brushing seductively against her breasts. His mouth found hers, his tongue taking control as he circled her wrists and lifted them above her head. He kissed her eyes, her nose and the corners of her lips. Then he sucked her earlobe into his mouth, his hot breath torturing her with the promise of what was to come.

He kissed his way down the valley between her breasts and across the taut plane of her stomach. And then he freed her hands, pushing her legs apart, her thighs braced on his shoulders. She shuddered again with need as his fingers held her open and his tongue dipped unerringly into her core, stroking, sucking, laving. She bucked against him, feeling the sweet tension begin to rise. Her hands braced against his shoulders as he took her higher and then higher still, his tongue driving her toward the precipice.

And then just as she reached the pinnacle, he withdrew, and she bit off her protest as he slid up her body, his mouth finding hers as the head of his erection pressed against her opening. Wrapping her legs around his hips, she lifted as he thrust deeply, filling her with his heat. For a moment they held still, the fragrant night air surrounding them, the soft sounds of the river providing a private symphony.

Then he began to move. Slowly at first then with more urgency and power. She found his rhythm and rose to meet each thrust, their bodies moving in tandem, pleasure intensifying until it was just this side of pain. Together they moved. Higher and harder. Faster and deeper. And Lily felt her world began to break apart, the power of her climax sending her crashing over the edge.

Flying on pure sensation, she cried out his name and felt her body contracting around his as he thrust into her, his breathing guttural as he too found his release. Her heart pounded against his, her body singing in pure delight—as if she were an instrument that had been well-played. His mouth found hers, his kiss deep and thorough.

Then, with a sigh of contentment that echoed her own, he rolled off of her, pulling her into his arms, her head cradled on his chest. They lay together quietly, hearts beating in tandem. He stroked her hair and tugged her plaid across them both to keep them warm. She felt cherished. Loved.

And as she drifted off to sleep, it occurred to Lily that if she were to die now, in this moment, she would die happy. Truly, blissfully, honestly happy.

CHAPTER 29

✦

BRAM WOKE TO the sounds of the river. Stars still studded the black velvet sky. The air was cold, but it was warm in the cocoon they'd made of their plaids. Lily's leg was draped across his thighs, her hair tickling him as it curled beneath his chin. She was beautiful in sleep. Almost as beautiful as she was in the throes of passion. He felt his body respond to the images in his brain. And he indulged in a satisfied smile as he pulled her closer, the soft whoosh of her breath warm against his skin.

She murmured something in her sleep, and then stretched, her breasts pressing into his chest. "Did I fall asleep?" she asked, her voice not much more than a whisper.

"Aye. As did I." He felt her smile.

"Well, if you're going to wear a girl out like that, it's to be expected, I suppose."

She rose up on one elbow, pushing her rioting hair out of her face, green eyes glittering with laughter and something more. Something that made him swallow with anticipation, desire stirring to life again. He wondered if he'd ever get enough of her. And just as quickly let the notion go. They belonged to each other now. And nothing would separate them.

He blew out a harsh breath. Would that it were that simple. But there was so much uncertainty. For a moment, he felt a wash of guilt.

He shouldn't have brought her into this. Shouldn't have asked her to give him her life. Not when so much was at stake. Not when tomorrow might mean his death.

"What is it?" She was still watching him, but frowning now. "You're not regretting this, are you? You're not regretting us?"

"Nay, lass, never." He reached over to kiss her, trying to ignore his fears. Tonight belonged to them. And he'd not let his uncle take this too.

"Good." She settled next to him, her fingers softly tracing patterns through the hair on his chest. "Because I have no regrets either. But that doesn't mean that I'm not worried about what tomorrow will bring."

"Dinna think on it now," he said, wishing it were that easy.

"I can't help myself. I came back to stop you from fighting Alec. To keep you alive. But now I fear I've just thrown you from the frying pan into the fire."

"An interesting turn of phrase," he said, twining a lock of hair around his finger. "But you canna fash yourself o'er something you canna control."

"I might not have control. But you do. You don't have to challenge your uncle."

"I dinna have to, no, but to honor my father, I must. Surely you can see that?"

She sighed. "I suppose I do. But that doesn't mean I have to like it. I guess you and Iain have a plan?"

"Aye. We're to ride on Dunbrae on the morrow."

"I see." Her voice had gone quiet, barely more than a whisper. "And what about me?"

"You'll stay here with Alec. And with Robby."

"And Frazier?" She was back on her elbow, looking down on him. He tried but couldn't read her expression in the shadows.

"He'll stay here too. I canna risk his coming with us. Alec has agreed to keep watch o'er him. And you."

"And if I don't want to be watched over?"

"Lily, you canna come with me. 'Tis no place for a lady."

"Maybe I'm not a lady. After all, I wasn't afraid to take a knife to Frazier earlier today." She sounded so fierce, he smiled.

"Ach, but you were magnificent indeed. But you also were in grave peril. And I canna risk being distracted with worry o'er you. As much as I'd prefer to have you with me, I need you to stay."

Her gaze was mutinous. "I'll not let you ride off into God knows what without me. I'm your wife. My place is with you. I can stay back. Out of the fray. That way I won't be a bother. But I'll not stay behind. If you insist on it, I'll only follow."

It was his turn to sigh. He'd married a strong-willed woman. And while he'd have it no other way, it meant that she was telling the truth. She wouldn't stay behind. Not unless he tied her to a bloody tree. And although the idea held some appeal, he was not stupid enough to believe she'd easily forgive something like that.

"All right then, you can come with us, but you'll not engage in combat and you'll stay out of sight until I come for you. Agreed?"

She paused, considering his offer. Then with a frown, she nodded in acceptance. "It's a compromise, I suppose. Do you think your uncle is expecting you?"

"He's no' a fool and he has to know that his other attempts have failed. That said, he doesn't know that I've made peace with Alec."

"And have you?" She was still frowning. "Made peace with him, I mean?"

"Of a sort. I canna get rid of a lifetime of believing him an enemy as easily as that. But I no longer believe he was involved in the attack on my father. Or the attacks on me. Frazier damned himself and my uncle when he slipped and mentioned Malcolm's name."

"But why would your uncle want to take Dunbrae from your father? I mean, they were brothers."

"Because it rightly should have gone to him."

"I don't understand."

"My grandfather wasna a kind man." He pulled her back down to his chest again, his arm circling her and holding her close. "He took great pleasure in playing people off against each other. Most particularly his sons. My father was the second son. Born from a second marriage. As was his younger sister, Ealasaid. Malcolm's mother, Bradana, was my grandfather's first wife."

"Ealasaid is Ranald's mother, right?" Lily queried.

"Aye, that she is," Bram smiled and then sobered. "Anyway, by all accounts the marriage between Bradana and my grandfather wasna a happy one. It was an arranged marriage, and there was no love lost between the two of them."

"But that wasn't the case with your father's mother?" Again she had cut to the heart of the matter. He stroked her hair, his mind thinking back to the stories his father had told.

"According to my father it was a passionate match. And one that happened well before Bradana died, I'm afraid. My grandmother, Deirdre, was a beautiful woman."

"She was his lover?"

"Aye, 'twould seem so."

"And your father?"

"Born safely on the right side of the blanket, but you can ken how well his father's infidelity sat with Malcolm. He believed himself to be the heir after all."

"I'm sorry, you've lost me again. As the oldest wouldn't that be an absolute?"

"In England surely, but no' in the Highlands. A laird names his own successor and, while it is common for it to be a son, nothing says it must be the eldest." He smiled down at the woman who was now his wife. "Or for that matter, even a son."

"A woman can inheirit?" Her eyes widened at the thought.

"Aye, if 'tis believed to be best for the clan."

"Imagine that." She nestled closer with a smile, then tipped her face to meet his gaze. "So Malcolm believed he was your grandfather's heir."

"That he did. And being close to his mother, he resented my grandmother from the beginning. And once his mother was dead and Deirdre became the new wife, his anger grew. It festered and found a worthy source once my father was born."

"What about Ealasaid?" She was chewing on her bottom lip as she contemplated his story. "Did Malcolm hate her too?"

"Nay. I dinna believe he saw her as a threat. And I think for a while she acted as a shield of sorts. Protecting my father from Malcolm's ire. But then, when Deirdre died, my grandfather sent her away. To the Macqueens, which is where she ultimately met Ranald's father."

"But that meant there was no longer anyone to stand between the two boys. How terrible for them both."

"True enough. And mayhap it would have passed as Malcolm grew to manhood, except as I said, my grandfather liked to play the boys against each other. And for better or worse, my father often came out on top. So Malcolm's ill feelings grew. And my grandfather's games only fanned the flames."

"Which in turn fed Malcolm's anger and jealousy." She snuggled closer, her warmth keeping Bram's emotions safely at bay.

He sighed, then nodded. "Then fate stepped in to make it worse. When my father came of age he fell in love with my mother. Aileen Mackintosh was a beauty and a wealthy woman in her own right. And there were many men who sought her hand. But she never had eyes for anyone but my father."

"And I'm guessing Malcolm was one of the other men."

"That he was. And when my mother agreed to marry my father, he was incensed. Demanded that his father grant him Aileen's hand. He was older than my father, after all. But my grandfather refused. So Malcolm appealed to his uncle."

"The head of your clan?"

"Aye, and because my grandfather had always gone his own way, my great uncle was only too happy to countermand his orders."

"He gave Aileen to Malcolm?"

"He tried, but my father would have none of it. He and Aileen sought the approval of the head of her clan."

"Chattan," Lily prompted.

"And the Mackintosh gave the couple his blessing. They were married at Moy. Of course this dinna sit well at all with my great uncle or with Malcolm. But it was too late and Ian Ciar couldna risk angering the head of Chattan. Although he ne'er forgave my grandfather or my father. Anyway, Malcolm turned his mind to other things. My grandfather was getting old, and my uncle pushed him to let him take over Dunbrae. But my grandfather was still angry over what he viewed as Malcolm's betrayal."

"Going over his head to his brother."

"Aye. And so in a fit of anger, he gave the lairdship to my father. Malcolm swore revenge and began gathering men to the cause. But Iain's grandfather stepped in and with the might of Chattan behind him, forced a truce."

"I bet that went over well."

"My great uncle never forgave my grandfather or father for bringing the wrath of Chattan down on him and the clan. When my grandfather died, my great uncle was forced to let my father take over Dunbrae, but he cut off any kind of support from Dunmaglass. And he showered favors upon Malcolm. He gave him a prosperous tract of Macgillivray land and helped him make a strategic marriage. He was, for all purposes, the favored son of the clan."

"But it wasn't enough for Malcolm," Lily said. "He still wanted Dunbrae. And he wanted your father dead."

"If what Frazier says is true, then that would seem the way of it."

"Oh, God, Bram, I'm so sorry. What a horrible situation."

He shrugged, the twist in his gut belying his dismissal of her words. "I've never had any love for my uncle. And I know he has none for me. But I ne'er believed he would do something like this. When my mother died, it seemed that his vengeance had at long last been served, for my father was never the same again. I truly believed that was the end of it."

"But instead, now you have to face him. To take back what rightfully belongs to your family."

He rolled over to face her, grasping her hands in his. "Yours now, too. And one day our wee bairns."

A soft smile tipped her lips. "You want children?"

"I do. And you?"

"Of course." Her smile widened. "Lots and lots of them. I was an only child."

"As was I."

"And I wouldn't wish that on anyone." A shadow chased across her face. "At least you had your cousins. I had no one."

He squeezed her hands, then flipped her beneath him, relishing the press of his body against hers. "Well, now you have me. And if I have my way, we'll be swimming in bairns before you know it."

He bent his head and pressed his lips to hers, desire usurping thought. As their tongues swirled together, tasting, tempting, teasing, Lily parted her legs, and Bram drove himself into her welcoming heat. Together they established a rhythm and started to move in tandem, meeting each other thrust for thrust as together they climbed higher and higher. Sensation winning out over thought. Emotion leaving little room for logic or fear.

There was nothing but the two of them, and the pleasure building between them. He felt Lily reach the peak, her body spasming around him, her passage hot and tight. He drove deep into her, losing himself in the sweet smell of her skin and her hair. And then his mind exploded in white light. He called her name, his body pumping life into hers, his ecstasy beyond anything he'd ever felt before.

Later, much later, he held her in his arms, her soft breathing signaling that she slept. The silver of Lily's ring was cool against his finger. And in that moment, he felt as if anything was possible. Magic—old magic—had brought them together. Against all odds. God's blood, against time itself. And now that they were together, he'd not let anyone or anything tear them apart.

Lily opened her eyes to the sound of the rushing river. Overhead a green canopy of trees danced amidst a patchwork of dappled sunlight.

She blinked, for a moment forgetting where she was, her mind struggling to make sense of her woodland bed. And then memory returned.

She was in Scotland and last night...

The enormity of the promises she'd made last night took her breath as she realized she was alone in the clearing, wrapped in nothing but her Mackintosh plaid. Had she dreamed it then? Bram. The handfasting. Had none of it happened? Automatically her hand rose to the silver chain around her neck, her fingers following the links to the hollow between her breasts. No ring.

It had been real then. But where was her husband? Surely after last night he wouldn't have left her. She pushed aside the plaid, shivering in the cool morning air, realizing only belatedly that she was still naked.

"I see you're awake." William Macgowen stepped out from behind a tree and it was hard to tell who was more startled. Lily shrieked and grabbed for the plaid. William, red as a beet, ducked back behind the tree. "Ach, my lady, I beg yer pardon. I dinna realize...I mean...I never..."

"It's all right William," Lily said, her voice emerging in a croak as she hurriedly pulled on her leggings and shirt. "You can come out. I'm dressed now."

The young man emerged, his cheeks still red, his eyes glued to the ground. "Bram went to meet with Iain and Alec. He was afeart to leave you alone and so asked me to watch o'er ye. But I dinna think he meant for me to take that so literally."

"It's okay, I promise." She held up a placating hand. "We'll just pretend it didn't happen."

"I thank you for that." William almost bowed in his enthusiasm to put the episode behind them. "'Tis a great kindness. For I'm quite certain that Bram would no' be pleased to think I'd been ogling his new wife."

She smiled. So Bram had already shared their news. That certainly seemed to negate the notion that she'd imagined the whole thing. "He'd understand, but as it is there's nothing to tell him."

"Aye. So be it then. And may I be the first to congratulate you." This time he swept into a full and courtly bow. "'Tis no' every day that we have a wedding while in route to a battle."

She shivered at the mention of fighting. "They haven't left, have they?" She didn't really believe Bram would leave her again, but still she couldn't stop herself from asking.

"Nay." The young man shook his head. "They wouldna go without me. And Bram said he'd be back here directly with something to break yer fast."

She nodded, relief making her giddy and slightly guilty. If she and Bram were to make a go of it, she had to trust him. Just as he had to trust her. Her head spun with the knowledge of how very far she'd come from that moment in Greenwich when she'd first heard of her parents' deaths. She hoped they'd approve.

"But now that yer awake," William was saying, his words pulling her from her tumbling thoughts, "I can take you to him if you like."

"Yes, thank you. I'd like that. Just let me put on my boots." She sat down on a log, her back to William as she adjusted her belt and pulled on her boots. Tendrils of mist still curled close to the banks of the stream, although the growing sunlight would soon disperse them as it continued to warm the ground.

She reached for her hair, quickly braiding the curly mass, securing it with a length of ribbon Katherine had given her at Duncreag. Behind her the bushes rustled. "There's no need to keep hiding, William. I meant it when I said everything was fine. I'm completely decent now."

"More's the pity."

She swung around, her stomach clenching as she recognized the voice.

Frazier Macbean stood only a foot or so away, a vicious looking knife in his hand. And flanking him on his left was an enormous man holding a claymore. A second man stood farther to the left, his eyes trained on the woods that separated them from the encampment.

Lily pushed to her feet, muscles tensing to run.

"There's nowhere to go, my sweet," Frazier crooned, the sound sending a shudder racing through her. "The river is too deep to try and cross it here. Ye'll drown if you try."

Visions of her parents filled her mind, bile rising in her throat as she held her ground. "How did you…" She trailed off, her mind spinning as she tried to find a way out.

"I had a little help. Ye dinna think I was in this alone, did you?"

She shook her head and then opened her mouth to scream, but Frazier was faster, one hand bringing the knife to her throat as the other covered her lips to prevent her crying out. "If ye dinna want to die here and now then I suggest ye hold yer tongue. Do ye ken what I'm saying?"

She nodded. And he released her, but kept one hand circled about her wrist. "There's a good lass."

"Where's William?" she asked, her stomach churning with worry.

"My man has him." Frazier's smile held no humor. "And unless you want something more to happen to him, you'll give me what I've come for."

She shook her head, fear holding her tongue captive.

"The ring." He held out an impatient hand. "Give me the ring."

"I can't," she croaked. "I don't have it."

"Of course ye do." He snarled and reached between her breasts to grab the chain, his eyes flashing when it yielded nothing but silver links. "What have ye done with it then?"

She lifted her chin, determined not to let this man get the better of her. "I gave it to my husband. Last night when we pledged ourselves to each other."

The man with the claymore cursed. "We've the need to move, Frazier. We canna be sure they havena discovered that yer gone."

"Only a moment more," Frazier replied, stroking the edge of his knife as he watched her, his fingers still clamped about her wrist. "I'm afraid I dinna see that one coming. I'd assumed the boy would reject you because of your kin."

"Well, he hasn't. And if he finds you here, he'll kill you. And then he'll kill your master." Again she lifted her chin, feigning a bravado she was far from feeling.

"I'd thought to bring Malcolm the ring. A token of my devotion. But perhaps this new turn of events is even better." He took a step closer and she backed up, her heels at the edge of the river bank. "I'll bring him his nephew's bride." With a swiftness that belied his age, Frazier jerked her into his arms and called to his friends, "Kill the boy and help me with her."

Lily fought like a wildcat, striking out with her free arms and her legs. A knee landed squarely in Frazier's groin and with satisfaction she heard the man grunt in pain. But if she'd thought to stop him, she was wrong. Frazier cursed and then brought the full force of his fist against her cheek and temple. Red hot pain exploded through her head, white light obliterating the scene before her.

She fought to hold onto consciousness but the pain was too great, the light fading quickly as blackness invaded, flowing through her brain, obliterating her thoughts until it swallowed her whole.

CHAPTER 30

✦

"SO I HEAR congratulations are in order." Alec Comyn walked up to the campfire where Bram, Iain and Ranald were talking.

"Aye, my cousin has seen fit to take himself a bride." Ranald slapped Bram on the back with a beefy hand, his face split with a grin. "I assumed he'd tup the wench; I had no idea he'd up and marry her."

"Watch your tongue," Bram cautioned, boxing his cousin's ear. "I'll no' have you talking like that about my wife."

"Come now," Alec said. "Seems to me like this calls for a wee dram. Or maybe two."

Bram grinned as Alec produced a bottle and poured a measure in each of the cups they held.

"To Bram," Iain offered, holding his cup aloft. "May your marriage bring you the same degree of happiness as mine."

For a moment the two men's gazes met and held—a world of meaning passing between them. Ranald and Alec might be aware of the story behind both Katherine's and Lily's strange appearances, but neither of them could truly understand the sheer magic of it. Nor the accompanying fear that at any moment it might be snatched away.

Alec waited until they'd all drained their cups and then filled them again, lifting his high. "To Lily."

"To Lily," the others echoed as Jeff emerged from the edge of the woods.

"Why are we toasting Lily?" he asked, pushing his hair back from his face.

"Bram has wedded and bedded her," Ranald said, the crooked smile still fixed on his face.

"I beg your pardon?" Jeff asked with a frown. "I thought the two of you weren't speaking."

Bram felt some of his elation vanish as he recognized the concern in the other man's face. Lily had said that they were just friends. That Jeff was in love with his wife. God's blood, the man had said as much himself. But suddenly Bram wasn't as certain. "We had a long talk. Among other things. And all is well between us. Better than that, in truth. Last night we pledged our lives to each other."

Jeff studied him carefully for another moment or so, and then his lips turned up into a smile. "Then I can understand the cause for celebration." He took the cup that Alec offered and lifted it toward Bram. "To you and your Lily. She loves you more than you know."

"Ach, I think I've an idea of it now. And more importantly, I realize just how much I love her."

"Then what are you doing lollygagging around here with us?" Ranald asked. "Go to your woman, man."

Bram shot a questioning glance at Iain.

His cousin smiled. "Go on with you, then. We've an hour or more until we're ready to go. Time enough for fighting. Take a moment and savor what it is you're fighting for."

Bram handed Ranald his cup and turned toward the woods just as Dougan Macniven burst into the clearing. "Frazier's escaped," he bellowed without pretense.

In an instant, anger replaced jubilation and Bram swung to face the man. "What do you mean he's escaped? I thought you had men guarding him."

"We did," the big man replied, a great gash gaping above his left eye. "But they took us by surprise."

"They?" Alec asked, as he and Iain moved to flank Bram on either side. "How many were there?"

"Three," Dougan said. "Two of them caused a distraction and I'm sorry to say we fell for it. While we fought them off, the other man snuck in behind and managed to free Frazier. By the time we realized the ploy it was too late; they had us by the bollocks. Killed Timothy and knocked me out cold."

"How long ago?"

"I dinna ken." The man blew out a long breath, swiping at the blood dripping into his eye. "Long enough to get away, I'm afraid."

"Bloody hell." Bram's eyes moved toward the woods and the river. *Lily.* He started forward, then froze as his worst nightmare materialized in the form of William. He was limping, and even from here, Bram could see the sorrow on the young man's face.

"She's gone," William gasped as he stopped in front of Bram, bent at the waist as he struggled to breathe. His plaid was stained with blood, and he held a hand to his side.

"Are you injured, lad?" Alec asked, coming forward to offer an arm.

"I'll live," William said. "All that matters now is Lily."

"Is she...is she..." Bram couldn't bring himself to say the words, and he felt Iain's hand on his shoulder.

"Nay," William was shaking his head. "She lives. But they've taken her."

"By God, I swear I'll cut my uncle's heart from his body if he hurts a hair on her head." He jerked free of Iain's grasp and turned toward the horses.

"Hold." Iain's voice held him in place, if only because he knew his cousin would never do anything that would endanger Lily. "We need to understand what's happened before we take action."

"It's clear enough to me," he barked, agony searing through him like a brand. "The bloody Comyns let Frazier get away and now, no thanks to William, he has my wife." From the haze of his rage he saw William flinch and, despite his despair, knew a moment of regret. "I'm sorry. I'm angry. I dinna mean to lash out at you, lad. I know you wouldn't have let them take her if there was anything else to be done."

William still looked miserable, but Bram knew there was nothing else he could say that would ease the lad's remorse. Still he had to try. Had to at least be honest.

"If this is anyone's fault, 'tis mine. I should never have left her."

"You couldn't have known that any of this would happen," Alec said, his expression as grim as Bram's no doubt was. "I would ne'er have expected them to have the bollocks to come right into our camp."

"We were vigilant, Alec, I swear it." Dougan looked to Bram. "And we fought with valor. 'Twas just too much of a surprise."

Bram nodded, unwilling to totally absolve the man, yet certain even so that none of it had been intentional. "It still remains that they have Lily and we have to go after them."

"Agreed," Iain said. "But we cannot go off without knowing the whole truth." He turned to William, who was being patched up by Geordie. "Tell us exactly what happened."

William swallowed as the healer tied off the bandage, then turned his attention to the assembled men. "I was standing at the edge of the trees. Lily was dressing and I dinna want to see...I mean, she needed her privacy."

"And then?" Ranald asked, his frustration clearly matching Bram's.

"She was putting on her boots—her back to me, and then someone grabbed me. I tried to fight back, but there were three more of them and I knew I dinna stand a chance."

"And Lily?" Bram asked, pacing in front of the fire.

"She's a brave one, yer wife. First she argued with the man."

"Frazier?" Alec interjected.

"Aye. He wanted the ring. But Lily said she'd given it to Bram." He cut his gaze to Bram's hand and the silver ring he wore. "Frazier was none too happy. But he said that Malcolm would have to do with her instead." William blanched. "I tried again to fight my way free. I was still in the bushes; Lily couldna see me. And before I could do anything to get away, the man who held me stabbed me. I managed to twist away, but in so doing, I fell and hit my head. The last thing I remember is Frazier saying he would make use of having Bram's bride."

"And how long ago was that?"

William glanced up at the sun. "Too long, I'm afraid. They'll have made good time. I heard horses. I'm sorry, Bram. I've failed you. And worse, I failed Lily."

"What's done is done," Iain said. "What matters now is that we take action to get her back."

"Unless I miss my guess, they'll be headed for Malcolm and Dunbrae," Ranald interjected.

"That's only about an hour's ride from here," Alec confirmed.

"Then what the hell are we waiting for?" Bram asked, already signaling for his horse. "The bastards have my wife. We haven't a moment to spare."

"You realize we'll be riding into a trap," Iain said. "Malcolm will be expecting you to try and rescue her."

"Aye, that I do." Bram clenched his fists. "I can't ask you to risk your lives for me and mine. Not like this. But you have to understand I canna sit back and let my uncle threaten my wife. Even if it means my death."

"We ride with you." Ranald's tone brooked no argument. Behind him, Bram could see the Mackintoshes already beginning to ready themselves for battle. "Iain just wants you to be aware of the facts."

"Even if your uncle knows for certain that you'll come," Alec added, "he canna be sure that Iain's men will follow you. And he definitely willna believe that mine will ride with you as well." At that, he too signaled his men to ready themselves.

Bram's heart threatened to leave his chest and despite his anguish and fear, he felt humbled. These men—his family and Lily's—were willing to risk everything on their behalf. Lily was right; despite all that they'd lost between them, they'd found not only new family but friends as well.

Bram took the reins of the horse Dougan brought him, swinging up into the saddle as the others mounted around him. He turned his mare to the northeast. Toward Dunbrae. To his wife—to Lily. And as he rode from the clearing, Bram prayed that he wasn't too late.

～

Lily awoke to the pungent smell of sweat and urine. Combined with the wracking pain in her head, the odor had her stomach churning. Her eyes flickered open and she gingerly touched her head, her fingers coming away sticky with blood. For a moment, memory failed and then she remembered.

Frazier.

She jerked upright, her stomach revolting with the sharp motion, but fear was a stronger motivator and she scooted across what appeared to be a straw-covered floor until her back was firmly against the room's stone wall. A fire flickered in the grate on the opposite wall, pale sunlight streaming in through two narrow oblong windows. Lit torches sat in bronze sconces at equal distances around the room, the fire doing little to alleviate the chamber's gloom.

A large wooden door stood partially open. She shifted slightly so that she could better see the room beyond. A great room possibly. She could see tables. And what looked to be a large group of men. There were platters of meat and pitchers of ale. Conversation rang out, punctuated with bursts of laughter.

At least someone was having a good time.

Gritting her teeth against the pain in her head and using the stone wall for leverage, she managed to push to her feet, the room spinning with the effort. She stood for a moment breathing in and out until the whirling subsided. Inching along the wall, using it to maintain her balance, she made her way over to the door and cautiously peered outside.

She'd been right; it was a great hall. The floor was littered with reeds and rushes and other things she'd just as soon not identify. Torchlight barely illuminated the giant room. The small windows were all shuttered for warmth or protection—or both. A great fireplace dominated the room, half of a tree trunk burning inside the yawning cavity. And like the room she'd awakened in, this one smelled of dirty bodies. The sights and smells served as a rude reminder that she was far from the world of modern conveniences. Seemed people here couldn't even be bothered to find a bathroom.

Unless she missed her guess, this had to be Dunbrae. She shivered, forgetting about creature comforts. Frazier had said he'd take her to Malcolm. And it appeared he'd succeeded. Fortunately, they'd not bothered with a guard. But then again, maybe they hadn't needed to. The room she was standing in held only the one door. And the only escape from the great hall appeared to be a large door in the opposite wall, that and an adjacent staircase going up.

Still, she couldn't just stand here waiting to be discovered. If the only way out was across the great hall, then she'd just have to figure out a way to get there. She scanned the men in the room. They were sitting in clusters. Most of them armed. And all of them eating and drinking. Twenty, maybe thirty altogether. Not exactly great odds.

Moving amongst the men were several women. Like the men, they seemed to be in a jovial mood, refilling a glass here or a platter there. She watched as a man pulled a woman holding a platter down for a bawdy kiss and a pinch on the rear. The woman offered no resistance, but she soon pulled free and moved on to serve another, a smile on her lips.

Lily fought a wave of dizziness, pressing her hands against the cool stone wall until the vertigo passed. Her head was pounding, but she knew she hadn't the luxury of waiting until she felt more stable. Frazier would come for her sooner rather than later. She scanned the room for her captor, relieved to see no sign of him. Nor was there anyone sitting at the main dais. Surely if Malcolm Macgillivray were present he'd be holding court at the table befitting his position as laird.

Which meant that just maybe, if she was lucky, she could make her way around the edge of the room to the doorway. It was a long shot, but it beat the heck out of staying here and meekly awaiting her fate. Removing her plaid from her shoulders, she wrapped it around her waist, fashioning it into a long skirt, using the broach to secure it in place. Then she reached up and pulled the ribbon from her hair, shaking it free of its braid. With her dark curls hanging around her face and shoulders, her hair would effectively screen her face as long as she kept her head down.

Sucking in a fortifying breath, she stepped into the great room, grabbing a pitcher from the nearest table. Hopefully they'd mistake her for a serving girl. At least long enough to get her through the door and out of the room.

She strode forward, head tipped toward the floor, heart hammering. She'd made it about halfway when suddenly a thick arm snaked around her waist. "Ach, and what have we here?" a deep voice asked, pulling her to an abrupt halt.

She risked a glance from beneath the veil of her hair. Whoever he was, he was huge. With a crooked scar that bisected his face, his hair was oily and he smelled so rank her stomach recoiled in rebellion again.

His lips parted in a feral smile, yellowed teeth bright against his dark beard. "Aren't ye a bonny lass? I've no' seen you afore. I'm thinking the laird has been hiding you away."

He had no idea.

She gave him what she hoped was a careless shrug, and lifted her pitcher as she tried to pull herself free. But the man was having none of it. "Ah, come on then, lassie, give us a kiss." He pulled her closer and she fought the urge to gag. It was hard to stay under the radar when one threw up all over a man.

"Please, sir, I've others to serve." She sounded ridiculous, but it was that or bean the bastard with her pitcher, which most likely would only raise his ire and draw unwanted attention. She be damned if she'd let him touch her any more than he already had.

"Dinna be coy with me," he growled. "Yer only purpose for being here is to please us. I heard it from the laird himself."

For a moment, she thought he knew who she was, and then with horror she realized he thought she was a whore.

His big hands tightened on her waist, jerking her to him. If she wanted to be free, she'd have to give the man a kiss. Holding her breath, she gave him a peck and then tried to pull away again, but he was having none of it, his beady eyes filling with undisguised lust. "I'll wager ye can do a wee bit better than that." His hand slid lower, his fingers kneading her bottom, pressing her against his erection.

She struggled, lifting the pitcher, thinking only of making him stop. But as if he'd read her mind, he reached up and plucked it away, tossing it onto the table. Then he pushed her against the wall beneath an alcove, shadows swallowing them from view.

She fought him openly now, but he was twice as big as she was and every bit as determined. His putrid breath assaulted her as he leaned closer, holding her captive with his body, his hands pushing up her makeshift skirt. His fingers reached the brooch holding it closed and he froze, looking down at the small salient cat.

"Mother o' God," the man growled. "Yer no' one of the laird's women. Yer the Comyn. The one that Frazier brought."

She thought for a moment that he was going to push her aside, and even though she didn't relish the idea of losing her freedom, captivity seemed better than what this man was offering. But she'd misinterpreted his reaction. Instead of pushing her away, he grabbed her more forcefully.

"I've a mind to show ye what we think of yer kind. But first I'll bury myself so deep, I'll tear you apart." He shoved her over onto a table, ripping at her plaid.

Bile filled her throat, fear turning to panic. He was going to rape her. Right here in front of all these people. And no one was going to do anything to stop him. Enraged, she struck out at him, kicking and biting and struggling for all she was worth. But he was a big man, and he straddled her, holding her firmly in place.

"Now then, I'll show you what a real man feels like."

Tears gathered and she closed her eyes.

"What in God's name do you think you're doing, Tormond? Get your hands off the wench. She's no' for you."

The man released her with a curse. "Mayhap when you've finished with her I'll have a go." With a last lascivious glance at her, he turned his back and walked away.

Lily sat up, pushing her hair out of her eyes as her gaze collided with the man who'd rescued her. Not exactly a savior—more likely a trade of one devil for another. Although not as big as the man who'd attacked her, he was tall, and relatively clean. But it was his eyes that gave away his identity, their cool icy blue currently devoid of any emotion as he assessed her.

Despite her disheveled state, she stuck out her chin. "Malcolm Macgillivray, I assume." Behind him Frazier stood, eyes bulging, looking very much like the toad he truly was.

Malcolm dipped his head. "At your service, my lady. I understand felicitations are in order."

She frowned, certain that she'd heard his voice before, but unable to place where or how.

"Your marriage," he prompted, a flash of anger lighting his eyes. "My nephew is a lucky man."

"Right. Lucky," she responded, her own anger coming to the fore. "I find that rich coming from you. First you kill his father, then you take his home. And now his wife. What, may I ask, has my husband ever done to you to deserve all of this?"

His lips curled into a sneer. "He had the misfortune to be born to the wrong father."

"But the right mother?" She knew she should watch her mouth, but she couldn't seem to help herself. If possible, Frazier's eyes had gone even wider. She pulled her focus back to Malcolm. "The one who had the audacity to choose your brother over you?"

His hand flashed out, striking her before she had time to realize what he was about. She lurched backward, the edge of the table saving her from a fall. "You've the tongue of a shrew."

"And you've the manners of a swine," she retorted, wiping away the blood that trickled from her mouth.

His gaze slid slowly from her head to her toes, lingering on her hips and breasts. "Believe me when I say that it will be a pleasure to bring you to heel," Malcolm said, his sneer bordering on lechery now. "But first I need to deal with your husband. And what better bait than his lady love?"

CHAPTER 31

✦

"SO HOW DO you want to handle this?" Iain asked as he and Bram knelt with Ranald, Fergus and Jeff in the woods near the back wall at Dunbrae. Clouds had obscured the sun, leaving the day cold and gray. Tree branches arched over their heads, rattling in the wind. Just ahead of them, Dunbrae's stone tower gleamed eerily silver in the faded light.

Bram forced himself to focus on the task at hand, but his heart remained centered on the tower and the woman conceivably locked inside. Alec's man Dougan had found tracks indicating that the men who'd taken Lily had indeed come this way. He prayed that whatever his uncle's plans, Lily was still alive.

Knowing they couldn't be more than an hour behind, they'd pushed their horses to the limits. But now faced with the enormity of all that had happened here—his father's death, his clan's demise and his wife's kidnapping—Bram's rage knew no boundaries. He'd make his uncle pay if it was the last thing he did.

"If you're going to help Lily," Ranald said, "you canna give in to your anger."

"Ranald's right," Iain agreed, laying a hand on Bram's shoulder. "You'll need a clear head if we're to make this work."

They'd agreed that Alec and the bulk of their forces would attack the tower head on, pulling Malcolm's men into the battle and giving

Bram and company the opportunity to sneak through the back gate. It was a risk, since Frazier knew about the entrance, but Bram was betting that he hadn't had time to secure it properly. Now they were simply waiting for a signal that Alec and the rest of the men had engaged.

"My head is clear." Bram closed his fingers around the hilt of his claymore as he answered his cousin. "All I ask is that you leave my uncle to me."

Ranald exchanged a glance with Iain.

"What?" Bram snapped, his gaze moving between the two of them, his patience wearing thin.

Iain sighed. "Only that your attention is better spent on rescuing your wife. 'Tis a far better thing than obsessing about vengeance."

"But Malcolm has to pay for what he's done to me and mine," Bram growled.

"Aye, that he does," Ranald agreed. "But Iain's right, Lily's safety is far more important."

"Don't you think I know that?" His words were spoken through clenched teeth. "I would ne'er do anything that would put her in danger. But that doesn't mean I canna be the one to take my uncle down."

Iain held up a hand. "I'm just saying you need to be sure you don't let your anger get in the way."

"And how was it with you and Davidson when he had *your* wife?" Bram asked, his anger now directed at his cousin. "Did you just ask him to let her go all nice and polite like?"

"Nay. I strung him up and killed him. And if I could have done it a dozen times more, I would have, believe me. So I know what you're feeling. But I also know what could be happening in there." A dark shadow of memory crossed his face. "And if in an effort to hurt you, Malcolm has hurt Lily, then she's going to need you more than you need revenge."

Fear threatened his resolution and he shook his head to banish it. "I'll deal with what we find when we find it. But unless I say otherwise, Malcolm is mine."

"Fine," Iain said. "Have it your way. I'm only here to help."

As quickly as it came Bram's anger at his cousin vanished. This wasn't Iain's fault. Any of it. "I know. I dinna mean to snap."

"Under the circumstances, 'tis to be expected," Iain replied.

"Listen," Jeff called, cocking his head toward the front of the tower.

Above the rustling of leaves, the blood curdling cries of battle sounded. Horses screaming. Men charging. Metal clanging against metal.

"Alec has begun the attack," Fergus noted. "Best we get on with it then. Use his sacrifice to good end."

Bram nodded and motioned their little band forward. He led the way across the uneven ground between the edge of the forest and the tower's wall. As with the other side, the gate here was also obscured by vegetation. Using both hands, he pulled it out of the way and then pulled on the rusted handle of the iron gate.

It refused to budge, and for a moment he feared Frazier had remembered the entrance and locked the gate. But then Ranald added his strength to Bram's and the gate screeched wildly and swung open. They stood for a moment at the opening in the wall, waiting to see if the noise had alarmed Malcolm's men, but it seemed that the din of battle had obscured the sound.

Bram rushed through the gate and came to an abrupt stop. The great front portcullis hung drunkenly from one chain, the wood splintered and broken. Alec had made good on his promise to breach the walls, but even as Bram felt a surge of triumph he was stabbed with pain. Dunbrae was his home—had been his home.

But unless they won the day it would be true no longer.

The inner bailey was full of fighting men, the smell of blood and battle filling the yard. Light flickered amongst them, almost as if it were following in their wake. Bram moved forward, claymore raised, dodging a thrust here, a parry there. Ranald and Iain had spread out to flank him, Jeff and Fergus taking up the rear. They moved like a wedge, cutting through the fighting men as they edged around to the front of the tower.

It was only when they had gained the front courtyard that Bram realized what the flickering was. Fire. The tower was on fire. It raced up the wooden steps that led to the door. And he could see more flames thrusting out of the windows, black smoke spiraling into the windswept sky. To his left he could see Alec and Dougan, the two men fighting together, handily taking out all who dared to challenge them.

With a nod to his cousins, Bram ran up the steps, but was stopped by one of the tower's guards. The man raised his claymore, his eyes narrowed as the deadly blade began its descent. Bram pivoted, and then swung his own weapon. The man fell, only to be replaced by another. Bram lunged, cutting the man across the arm that held his weapon. Behind Bram, on the stairs, Ranald fought a second man. Iain, still in the courtyard, fought alongside Jeff and Fergus as they held off others.

With a twist and a parry, Bram drew the man off and then made quick work of him, stepping over his body as he and Ranald, with the others on their heels, took the last of the stairs, dashing through the opening of the tower, through the hallway and into the great hall. A place meant for comfort, it offered only danger now. It too was full of flame, and lined with enemies.

Bram's heart screamed at him to hurry. If he did not then that which was most precious to him would be lost. For a moment it felt as if he'd lived this moment before, but he pushed the thought aside as he surged into the fray, moving toward the stairway at the far end of the room, fear urging him onward. He had to get to Lily.

He quickly dispatched one man and then turned to find Ranald at his back, two men circling them both as they twisted together, trying to keep their enemies in sight. Behind the attackers, Iain and Jeff emerged from the din, killing the men with swift blows. With a jaunty grin, Ranald tipped his head to his cousin and turned back to the battle at hand.

Bram, grinning despite the severity of the situation, made for the staircase, Fergus fighting ahead of him to clear the way. Suddenly the battling warriors parted, and Bram could see a man standing guard at the foot of the stairs.

Frazier.

With a bellow of rage, he charged forward. This was the man who had killed his father. The man who had betrayed him and taken Lily. And for that he deserved to die.

His sword reverberated with the first strike, the older man's mouth open in a snarl. The two of them circled each other as if in a dance, the steps intricate and deadly. Frazier swung, but Bram blocked the blow with his claymore, then pivoted and returned the strike, catching Frazier on his thigh.

Blood oozed from the wound and the man stumbled, but quickly regained his balance. "I'll see you in hell," he cried as he lifted his claymore above his head, but in his zealous need to answer Bram's blow, he left his body unguarded, and with a swift thrust, Bram drove the blade home. Blood gurgled from the man's mouth as he dropped to his knees and then fell to the floor.

Bram stepped across the body and then ran up the steps, taking them two at a time, knowing that Lily's life depended on speed.

Ranald and Iain were close behind him, leaving Jeff and Fergus to keep the rest of the warriors at bay.

———

Lily struggled against her bonds. She was surrounded by shadows, the windows boarded shut, the torches here unlit. Malcolm had tied her to the bedpost. Her arms were stretched around it, rope binding her wrists. The post rose up at least eight feet, probably more, ending with a flourish that connected to the bed's canopy. She blew out an exasperated breath. There would be no sliding out of this one.

The smell of smoke was thick here. Oppressive. Frightening. Her eyes watered, and somewhere below her she could hear the clanking of metal against metal. Swords, her mind whispered. Which could only mean one thing. Bram was here.

Joy and fear warred for a place in her heart.

A candle flamed in the darkness.

"He comes." The voice was low, grating, the words an eerie echo of her thoughts. A shiver ran up her spine. She turned toward the light and the sound; nothing was visible except the flame, and the shadowy shape of a hand and an arm.

Malcolm.

"Who?" she asked, the words a whisper, her heart already sure of the answer. "Who comes?"

Malcolm didn't reply, but he stepped close enough for her to see his face. See the demented gleam in his eyes. She looked down between the gaps in the plank floors to see flames flickering below. She jerked her head up, recognizing now that flames also wreathed the doorway and licked at the floorboards and walls.

More men—warriors—stepped from the shadows, their weapons raised. It was a trap. She opened her mouth and screamed.

At the top of the stairs Bram froze, the thick smoke disorienting him. The fire was much worse here. Pushing forward, he breathed through the heavy wool of his plaid, keeping sword at the ready, Ranald and Iain still behind him. The first chamber was empty. As was the solar and the chamber beyond it. But then from down the narrow hallway he heard a scream.

Heart thundering in his ears, he ran through the flames and smoke. A timber fell, glancing off his shoulder, and he hardly felt it, the need to find Lily overriding everything else.

He called for her, his voice swallowed by the raging fire. Another timber fell, and a wall collapsed. He jumped across a gaping hole in the floor, landing hard but still moving. The doorway loomed ahead edged in flames, the smoke and fire roiling like some kind of evil spirit. Iain reached out a hand to hold him back, but he shook it off. Lily was in there. She needed him. Nothing was going to stop him. Nothing.

Ignoring the danger, he sprinted forward, bursting through the opening, again calling her name. And then, through the shimmering heat, he saw her, tied to the bedframe, her long hair unbound, her green eyes wide with fear.

A shadow moved behind her. Rage threatened to engulf Bram. "God's blood, what have you done?"

"Naught but what you deserve," came the answer as his uncle stepped into view.

"Go back," Lily screamed. "It's a trap."

But he pushed onward, stumbling as still more of the burning tower fell. "I'll no' leave you." His words were whipped away by the inferno surrounding them. But he knew that she had heard him.

Other shadows moved into view. He was surrounded. Ranald and Iain surged forward, moving to stand between Bram and his challengers, their backs to him, swords facing out. As they moved to defend their position, Bram turned to see his uncle edging away. His body wanted to follow, to fight. To finally have vengeance on the man who had killed his father. But the fire was taking hold, moving across the floorboards toward the bedpost where Lily was tied.

He turned from his uncle, his entire being focused on Lily. She was his life. His blood. Without her, he would be nothing. There were only a few feet separating the two of them now. There was bruising on her face and a trickle of blood at the corner of her beautiful mouth, and he swore if given a second chance there would be hell to pay.

But right now, he had to get her free.

He reached out a hand, but as he did so the floor in front him collapsed, crashing to the ground below. One moment he was looking into her eyes and the next, she was gone.

~

Bram reached for her and then there was a cracking noise, the fire whooshing across the bed linens. For a minute Lily felt as if she were suspended above hell itself. Then the bed tipped and she lurched with it, the bedpost careening like a broken mast in the face of a hurricane. The hole in the floor yawned beneath her and then she was falling, fiery debris raining down on her as the burning rushes below signaled the looming stone floor of the great room.

She opened her mouth to scream, but was jerked suddenly so hard her arms felt as if they'd been pulled from the sockets, her wrists slamming into the bedpost as it jammed across the open hole. Below her, flames swallowed tapestries and tables, men still fighting, the clamor of swords filling the smoky air. She hung above the melee like some macabre chandelier, her heart threatening to break free of her chest as she twirled slowly back and forth.

"Lily. *Mo ghràidh*, can you hear me?"

She tipped her head up to meet Bram's ice-blue gaze. "I'm here." Her voice came out barely more than a whisper.

"Hang on now, love, I'm coming." He leaned down through the hole, flames licking through one side. But before he could do anything, another face appeared—along with a hand holding a knife.

Malcolm.

"Wouldn't it be a shame if all your heroics were for nothing, nephew?" He leaned through the hole, the knife just above the ropes that held her hands, binding her to the bedpost.

Bram roared into action, his anger a palpable living thing. Both faces disappeared and then the floor above her split further, and Malcolm came hurtling through the hole, his face contorted with fear. Lily screamed, closing her eyes at the thwack of Malcolm's body as it crashed to the stone floor below. The sound was punctuated by the crack of the bedpost as it slipped in its mooring, sending her spinning around at a dizzying angle.

"Lily, are you all right?" Bram's head reappeared, although he too seemed to be spinning.

Lily fought to pull herself together. "I'm okay." Fire shot in earnest out of the left side of the hole above. And she felt panic rising. "The fire, Bram. It's going to burn the floor holding the bedpost."

"Dinna fash yourself, I'll handle the wee fire."

She swallowed a bubble of hysteria, shooting a glance at the raging flames. "Wee fire?"

His grin shot straight to her heart, and she struggled for courage. "Ach, to be sure I've seen worse." He withdrew his head, and she heard the sound of something thumping and then the flames disappeared. Her arms screamed in agony, but she fought for composure. She needed to remain calm.

"All right then, that's the fire." His head appeared again in the gaping hole. And after an awful crash, Ranald's face appeared as well.

"Looks like you've managed to deal with your uncle," he quipped, his smile not quite reaching his eyes. Lily swallowed and risked a look downward at the mangled body on the floor beneath her. There were still men fighting, unaware that she dangled over their heads, and clearly without care for the dead man on the floor.

"'Twill be all right, *mo ghràidh*. I promise you." His words reached into her heart, giving her courage, and she smiled up at him. "Right, then," he said. "Here is what we're going to do." He leaned down until his shoulders and arms were free of the hole. Then Ranald moved until his arms too were extended, Malcolm's knife in his hand. "On my count you're going to swing yourself up toward me. I'm going to catch you and pull you up while Ranald cuts the rope. It'll probably hurt like bloody hell, but if I untie you first, you'll fall."

Great, she was going to have to pull off a move worthy of freakin' Cirque du Soleil. She shot a glance again at the scene below and sighed. She supposed it beat the alternative. She lifted her gaze back to Bram's.

"Can you manage, do you think?"

She nodded and shot him another smile, already beginning to rock her body back and forth, building momentum.

"That's my girl. On three." He nodded at Ranald, his gaze still locked with hers, arms extended. "One. Two. Three…"

She swung harder, arms screaming in agony as she let her body's own momentum carry her higher and then higher still. Just a few more inches. Splinters from the bedpost stabbed into her wrists, the ropes cutting deep into her skin.

"Aye that's it, Lily. Just a little bit more."

Gritting her teeth and using her knees to propel herself higher, she felt his fingers close around her thighs. For a moment, she felt weightless as the pressure from her wrists eased, and then Bram yanked her toward him as Ranald cut the rope free from her wrist. Her skin scraped against the jagged edges of bedpost and then she was in Bram's arms, tumbling backward against unbroken floor.

Pain stabbed through her arms and shoulders again, but the only thing she could truly feel was the driving beat of his heart beneath hers. "I've got you now, *mo ghràidh*. I've got you."

His hands stroked her hair as he held her close, his breath soothing as he pressed a kiss against her brow.

"Bram." Ranald's voice cut into the moment, his urgency unmistakable. "The fire up here, 'tis out of control. We've got to get out of here. Now."

Bram was on his feet in an instant, pulling her up into his arms. As he lifted her higher against his chest, she saw a burst of flame and more of the floor disintegrated into ash, falling into the great room below. The walls themselves were on fire now, or at least the tapestries that had covered them. Flames and smoke curled everywhere, choking them. Bram pulled his plaid around them, cradling her close. "Turn your face into my chest. Keep your breathing shallow."

He turned to follow Ranald as they pushed their way from the room, jumping over more falling timbers and gaping holes. The hall beyond was also on fire. Lily buried her nose against the linen of Bram's shirt, coughing as the acrid smoke seeped into her lungs. The heat had become almost unbearable. At the opening to the stairs, Iain beckoned them.

"Alec and Jeff?" Bram called out.

"Outside. Alive and well," came the satisfied answer. "Fergus, too. The fighting is almost done. All that's left is to get the three of you out of here."

She felt Bram's sigh of relief and nestled closer. The stairs themselves were burning, but thankfully still intact, and with Iain and Ranald's help Bram was able to negotiate them without putting her down. At the bottom, she realized the room had grown silent except for the flames that fed upon everything, turning the room a ghastly shade of flickering red.

"Cover your face," Bram urged as he strode forward, following Iain and Ranald as they made their way across the great hall. At the doorway, Bram paused. Lily lifted her head to see that the wooden stairs had been burned clean away.

Iain jumped down, landing on a roll. Ranald followed. Seeing what was happening, several men helped to push a wagon underneath the doorway. Iain hopped up into it and reached up. Cradling her as tenderly as a baby, Bram lowered her into his cousin's arms. Then he too jumped free of the burning tower.

Pulling her back into his arms, Bram carried her away from the flames to a stone bench sitting in front of what looked like a well. Together they watched what was left of Dunbrae burn.

"I'm sorry," she whispered, watching as part of an upper wall fell away.

"'Tis nothing but wood and stone," he replied, his arms tightening around her, the silver of his wedding ring winking in the half-light.

"All that truly matters is here, in my arms. As long as you're with me, Lily, then all is right with my world." She nestled closer, reveling in the slow steady cadence of his breathing. "Wherever you are, *mo ghràidh,* I am home."

EPILOGUE

ONE YEAR LATER...

"IT'S AN AMAZING likeness," Katherine said as she came up to stand beside Lily in the long hallway that served as Alec's gallery. Behind them, she could hear Bram and Robby laughing at something Iain was saying, Alec's arguing a counterpoint to the sound. Ranald and his wife Ailis were talking with Fergus and Dougan, the two men improbably having become the closest of friends.

"It is, I suppose, although it still feels strange to see myself like that," she replied, her eyes still on the portrait that had recently been hung in a place of honor among the room full of Comyns—past and present.

Alec had insisted on it, claiming that history would want a record of her time here in the fifteenth century. She'd wanted Bram to pose with her, but he and Alec had agreed that, despite their newfound friendship and the peace between their clans, the hallowed halls of *Tigh an Droma* weren't ready to be graced with a portrait of a Macgillivray.

But as a nod to their new alliance, she'd worn the ring, the feel of it against her breast reminding her of all that she'd lost—and gained.

It wasn't until the painting was done that she realized what it was. She turned to smile at Katherine. "I guess what continues to throw me is that I've seen it before—in our time, I mean. I kind of feel sorry for

Reginald and Tildy. They believe it's a portrait of Tyra. I suspect they'd be disappointed to discover that it's only their distant American cousin."

"Who traveled through time, averted catastrophe and brought success and well-being to both Clan Comyn and Clan Macgillivray."

"Well, when you put it like that…" Lily grinned, linking her arm with the other woman's.

So much had happened since the battle at Dunbrae. Not only had Alec and Bram allied themselves, but Ranald and Iain had also joined their pact. And in so doing, there had been a subtle but powerful shift within the workings of Clan Chattan. Bram's great uncle had been forced to recognize him as the legitimate heir to Dunbrae.

Robby's wound had healed, and he'd agreed to stand as Bram's captain, the two men determined to rebuild what Malcolm had destroyed.

"When will the new tower be finished?" Katherine asked, as if following Lily's thoughts.

"Bram says within the month. Two at the most. Which is just as well." She ran a hand across her softly swelling belly. "As much as I love my cousin, I'd much rather my baby be born in my own home."

"I totally understand that. I feel the same way about Duncreag. It is Anna's home. As it will be her brothers' and sisters' when that day comes. And hopefully, my brother's children as well."

"Do you miss him terribly?" Lily asked. After the battle, Jeff had returned with Iain and Ranald to Duncreag, and after a short visit with his sister, returned to Elaine and his own century. He'd proven, along with Elaine, to be the dearest of friends, and she hoped that somehow they'd find a way to meet again. Certainly stranger things had happened.

"Every day," Katherine was saying. "But we're both where we belong. And that makes it easier. Besides, I carry him here." She touched her heart. "Always." She sighed and then smiled, patting Lily's hand. "Now, as to babies being born here at *Tigh an Droma,* I'd have to say that even were you to desire it, it wouldn't be the best of ideas. Alec's home doesn't exactly lend itself to creature comforts."

"It's true. He's created that rare combination of chaos and austerity that only a dedicated bachelor can achieve. What he needs is a wife."

"What he needs," Bram's deep voice replied, "is a less meddlesome cousin. Just because we've found our happiness doesn't mean we should try and force it upon everyone we meet." He slid his arm around her, the smile in his eyes removing the sting from his words.

"Alec isn't everyone," Lily admonished, "he's family." And that said it all really. She leaned back into her husband's embrace, her eyes moving back to the portrait. It might not be Tyra looking back at her, but Lily liked to think that if she were here, the woman would approve.

She'd loved Graeme beyond everything else. Of that there could be no doubt. But she'd loved her family as well. Enough to pass the ring down through time until it had reached Lily and the circle had been completed. And now, here Lily stood in a room full of people who loved her. Family. Every one of them.

But none more so than the man who held her in his arms.

"So, *mo ghràidh*," he whispered, his breath warm against her ear, "what's a man have to do to get a kiss around here?"

"Simply ask." She smiled, turning in his arms to lift her lips for his kiss.

"Aye, that I will." His blue eyes twinkled down at her. "Or mayhap, I'll just take what I want."

"Not much of a battle, when you consider that it's something I gladly give," she teased as he slanted his mouth over hers. She closed her eyes, reveling in the feel of his lips against hers. And, as she let herself sink into the warmth of her husband's love, she sent a glance heavenward, knowing that somewhere up there her parents were smiling.

SNEAK PEEK AT WILD HIGHLAND ROSE

And Now A Sneak Peek at Wild Highland Rose,
the third novel in Dee Davis'
Time After Time Series!

SCOTLAND, 1468

MARJORY WALKED THROUGH the gorse damning Ewen Cameron. The man had been the devil himself or at least the spawn of the same, and if she'd had her way she'd not be trekking through the mountains trying to find his body.

The sky threatened rain, the clouds so close to the ground now she could almost touch them. The weather in the mountains was always fluid, calm one moment, stormy the next, without so much as a by-your-leave in between. Pulling her plaid close around her, she stopped for a moment on an outcropping of rock, letting her eyes drink in the valley.

The lands of Crannag Mhór stretched below. The tower itself, situated on its islet in the loch, glistened white against the blue-black of the lake, the turrets already disappearing into the gathering mist. She breathed deeply, letting the cool mountain air fill her lungs.

This was her home, and she'd not let a Cameron take it away from her. Living in hell had always been a small price to pay for preserving her heritage.

Fingal stopped beside her, his large hand heavy on her shoulder. "We'll find a way, Marjory. We always do."

She nodded, comfortable with the fact that he could read her mind. Since her father's death it was Fingal to whom she turned. Fingal in whom she confided. At least about most things.

She forced a smile, looking up, comforted by the fierceness in his eyes. Fingal would protect her with his life, and she'd return the favor without pause. But, even so, there were things she could not share with him. Things she kept locked away tight in a dark corner of her heart.

"It's no' far now." He moved back, his gruffness meant to hide his emotion, but she knew him too well. "Just 'round the bend."

As if to underscore the point, Allen appeared from behind a jutting spray of rocks, his face twisted in anger. "He's no' there."

Fingal frowned, his hand automatically reaching back for his claymore. Marjory laid a hand on his arm, leaving it there until she felt him relax. "Maybe this is no' the place." They moved forward, flanked by two more Macpherson men. "Sometimes the mountain plays tricks." Crannag Mhór was an isolated place, many of its crannies and crags inaccessible to those who didn't know it well.

Fingal shook his head as they came to the foot of the cliff, rocks and debris clearly indicating a recent landslide. "This is where he fell."

Allen growled low in his throat, eyeing the older man. "What have ye done with him, then?"

"I've done naught." Fingal roared. "I left him here same as you."

Again Marjory stepped between the two men. She glared at Allen. "You know as well as I that there are wolves in these mountains.

Anything could have happened to him." She narrowed her eyes, daring Allen to argue with her.

He glowered at her, holding her gaze for one beat and then another, and then with a snort, he turned away, walking over to his men, the division between the two groups, Cameron and Macpherson, symbolic of the everwidening gulf between the clans.

Ignoring both, she headed toward the burn. Solitude was always the best for thinking, let the men deal with the disappearance of Ewen's body. Fingal was always saying she lacked the sensibilities of a lady. So she'd use the fact to her advantage.

The flowers of summer were in fierce bloom, their color vibrant even against the mist. If it weren't for the fact that her dead husband had gone missing, she'd have stopped to revel in the beauty of the mountains. *Her* mountains. But there was no time for idling. She had to come up with a plan, and without a body it was going to be that much more difficult.

Coming out of a small stand of birch she walked toward the stream, and a large rock. A favorite thinking place since she was a child, it afforded the perfect view across the valley. Except of course when the mist hugged the ground. Then it was more like a cloister. Silent and safe.

As if in answer to her thoughts, a breeze rose, its gentle touch lifting the fog, revealing something lying across the rock. Something bulky. With baited breath, she crept forward, using the undergrowth to quiet her steps and shield her from view.

The mound began to take shape, and she recognized it for what it was. A body. She'd been right about the wolves. Steeling herself, she crept forward, torn between a desire to run back to Fingal and the macabre need to know for certain that it was him.

With a trembling hand, she pulled back a tree branch for a clearer view. It was indeed Ewen. Relieved, she released the branch and stepped into the clearing.

Suddenly, the body shifted. Marjory stopped mid-step, her heart jumping into her throat. She screamed as the body rose, the face all but obliterated by crusted blood. Flinching, she held out a hand, and shut her eyes tightly, certain that she was in the presence of the dead.

"What the hell?"

The voice was garbled, but definitely human. Alive. Marjory braced herself and opened her eyes. He stood there, staring at her as if she were the ghost, his left hand fumbling to open his sporran.

Involuntarily, she took a step backward, her head spinning, her hand still out as if to ward him off. It seemed the devil had alluded death yet again.

Cameron closed his eyes and then opened them again, stupidly staring down at the young woman who had collapsed at his feet, out like a light. She was a tiny thing, her features as delicate as her frame. Ethereal was the word that came to mind.

He knelt beside her, trying not to jar his aching head, and lifted her wrist, automatically feeling for her pulse. It was rapid, but strong. Releasing her hand, he pushed the hair back from her face, surprised at how soft it was.

"Unhand her, or I'll slit your throat." The voice came from off to his left, and Cameron was certain that the owner meant every word.

He rose quickly, his head spinning with the action, hands raised in what he hoped was still the universal gesture of surrender. Pivoting slowly, he turned to face the voice, and immediately felt a shudder of alarm. The man before him was roughly the size of an oak, built every bit as solid, and he held the largest sword Cameron had ever seen.

Their eyes met, and the man blanched, the sword wavering for a moment. "Ye're a dead mon." His tone held a mixture of fear and awe, and with his free hand he managed the sign of the cross.

Cameron, hands still held high, took a step forward, and the man swallowed, but to his credit held his ground, the sword steady now.

"Be gone, spirit." The man waved his weapon threateningly.

Cameron, more than aware of his mortality, stepped back. "Your friend needs help." He spoke slowly, as if to a child. The man's English was garbled at best, and although Cameron understood him, it was obviously not his native language.

The sound of his own voice startled him, the tone deeper than he remembered, more guttural. Almost as if he, too, were speaking something other than English.

Ridiculous thought.

"Move away from her, Cameron."

The man knew his name. The thought was somewhat less than comforting, and Cameron searched his memory for some hint as to who he might be. He lowered his gaze to the sword. Obviously not a friend.

"I said move." The giant barked again, edging forward slowly, his narrow-eyed gaze fierce.

Cameron did as suggested, watching as the man inched toward his friend. "She's only fainted," he volunteered. "I checked her pulse and she's fine."

"Ye've no right to touch her." This last was hissed between gritted teeth. The big man bent down to touch the woman, who was beginning to stir.

"Holy Mary, Mother of God." Another giant rounded the corner, crossing himself in the same way as the first. The tangle of red hair, both on his head and face, left only a white swatch of face visible.

Again, Cameron searched for recognition, but there was nothing. Enemy or friend, these people were strangers to him, the idea far more frightening then the monstrous swords they held.

The woman was sitting up now, her gaze locked on him, her expression guarded. Pushing aside the first giant's offer of help, she scrambled to her feet, and moved toward Cameron, tipping her head first to one side and then the other, as she studied him.

"You're supposed to be dead." Her voice was low, the timbre velvety. It raked across him like a warm breeze, sending his senses reeling.

"That seems to be the consensus." Cameron glanced toward the two men, noticing they'd been joined by others, all sporting swords and kilts. Apparently he'd fallen down the rabbit hole and landed in the middle of *Braveheart*. The only thing missing was the blue war paint.

Not a comforting thought, and not something he wanted to examine right now. The situation was puzzling at best, downright frightening at worst. And the truth was this wasn't the time for a melt down. As if in contradiction to his thoughts, his head spun, black spots swimming across his line of vision.

"I saw you fall." Giant number one had moved closer. "There's no way you could have survived." He looked toward giant two for confirmation, and though it looked as if agreement was not in his nature, the man gave a brief nod, his gaze still locked on Cameron.

"Fingal, 'tis obvious that he has survived," the woman said. "And nothing we wish to the contrary will make it less than so."

Another vote of confidence. It was pretty obvious he wasn't going to be voted Mr. Popularity in this crowd. Cameron opened his mouth to tell them he wasn't who they thought he was. That in fact as far as he could tell, he wasn't anyone at all, but another look at the still drawn swords changed his mind. Best to find out the lay of the land before committing to anything.

Maybe there was a way out of this Scottish version of *Deliverance*, a hospital around the corner, or a nice cold beer. Something that fit into his concept of reality.

"We'd best get you back to the holding. It'll be dark soon." The first giant, the one they called Fingal, took a step toward him, and involuntarily Cameron stepped back. "Allen, he's your brother, perhaps you should help him."

Brother.

The word washed over him and he waited for emotion, some connection to the big man striding toward him. But he felt no sense of belonging or recognition. The man was a stranger. Again he moved backward, this time following his instincts. The other man's expression changed, his eyes narrowing in confusion and something else. Wariness possibly. It seemed there was intelligence under all that hair.

"Marjory," Fingal said. "Perhaps you should be the one to help your husband."

Her eyebrows shot up in surprise, a look of loathing crossing her face. "I'm sure he has no need of me." Despite her words, she moved to take Cameron's arm.

Her skin against his started pheromones firing. *Husband?* Yet another revelation. He should have been put off. After all he had no memory of the woman, and she certainly hadn't bothered to hide her disdain for him. But his body wasn't listening to reason, and an absurd sense of elation swirled through his head.

He turned to say something, to explain that he had no brother, and certainly no wife, but before he could open his mouth, the ground rushed up to meet him, the world going suddenly black.

ABOUT DEE DAVIS

 Bestselling Author **Dee Davis** worked in association management before turning her hand to writing. Her highly acclaimed first novel, *Everything In Its Time*, was published in July 2000. Since then, among others, she's won the Booksellers Best, Golden Leaf, Texas Gold and Prism awards, and been nominated for the National Readers Choice Award, the Holt and three RT Reviewers Choice Awards. To date, she is the author of over thirty books and novellas. When not sitting at the computer, Dee spends time in her 1802 farmhouse with her husband and cardigan welsh corgis.

Visit Dee at http://www.deedavis.com or catch up with her on Facebook at http://www.facebook.com/deedavisbooks or follow her on Twitter at http://twitter.com/deesdavis

Sign up for her newsletter at http://www.deedavis.com/newsletter/index.php

Photo: Marti Corn

CPSIA information can be obtained
at www.ICGtesting.com
Printed in the USA
LVOW01s2124170516
488747LV00012B/113/P